P9-CMT-312

ALSO BY JILL McGOWN

Record of Sin
An Evil Hour
The Stalking Horse
Murder Movie

THE LLOYD AND HILL MYSTERIES

A Perfect Match
Murder at the Old Vicarage
Gone to Her Death
The Murders of Mrs. Austin and Mrs. Beale
The Other Woman
Murder . . . Now and Then
A Shred of Evidence
Verdict Unsafe
Picture of Innocence
Plots and Errors
Scene of Crime
Death in the Family

UNLUCKY FOR SOME

UNLUCKY FOR SOME

A NOVEL OF SUSPENSE

JILL MCGOWN

BALLANTINE BOOKS · NEW YORK

3 0231 2275

Copyright © 2004 by Jill McGown

Published in the United States by Ballantine Books, an imprint of The Random House Publishing Group, a division of Random House, Inc., New York.

Ballantine and colophon are registered trademarks of Random House, Inc.

Originally published in Great Britain by Macmillan, an imprint of Pan Macmillan Ltd., London, in 2004.

Library of Congress Cataloging-in-Publication Data

McGown, Jill.
    Unlucky for some : a novel of suspense / Jill McGown.— 1st Ballantine ed.
      p. cm.
    ISBN 0-345-47655-7 — ISBN 0-345-47656-5 — ISBN 0-345-47657-3
    1. Lloyd, Inspector (Fictitious character)—Fiction. 2. Hill, Judy (Fictitious character)—Fiction. 3. Police—England—Fiction. 4. Serial murders—Fiction. 5. Policewomen—Fiction. 6. England—Fiction. I. Title.

    PR6063.C477U55 2005
    823'.914—dc22

                                                        2004058565

Printed in the United States of America

www.ballantinebooks.com

9 8 7 6 5 4 3 2 1

First American Edition: February 2005

Text design by Susan Turner

Unlucky for Some

I N THE COLD, GRAY LIGHT OF A MID-FEBRUARY AFTERNOON, Michael Waterman watched Detective Chief Superintendent Raymond Yardley's putt roll gently over the manicured green heading toward the thirteenth hole, and walked over, hand outstretched, conceding the putt before the ball had stopped moving. "Too good," he said, taking out his wallet, and extracting five twenties. "I believe we said a hundred?"

"We did." Ray grinned, sliding the notes into his back pocket. "Which means a lot more to me than it does to you."

Michael picked up both balls and put his redundant putter back in the bag, hoisting it to his shoulder as the two men walked together toward the clubhouse. He'd lost at the thirteenth hole on the thirteenth of the month—maybe there was something in the superstition after all.

But Ray's burly figure dwarfed the slight, wiry Michael, and that was much more likely to be where Michael's problems lay. Admittedly, Michael was looking closely at fifty and Ray had just turned forty, but they were both fit, they were both competitive. Age wasn't a factor. Ray could drive the ball farther, it was as simple as that; he gave himself a better chance of a simple approach shot to the green. Maybe, Michael thought, he should go to one of these coaches to help him get more power into his shot.

"I'd have thought you'd know better than to gamble," said Ray. "At least when you know you don't stand a chance of winning."

"I make my living from people who gamble when they've no

chance of winning. And I would remind you that some of my best customers are coppers."

Ray grinned. "Oh—policemen gamble on anything. I think our unofficial bookies sometimes take more than you do in a day's trading." He pulled open the clubhouse door, and stood aside to let Michael go ahead. "The current book is on who's going to head the major crime unit—the betting's been very heavy."

"Oh?" Michael frowned. "I thought that had been shelved."

"The serious crime squad's been shelved—it was felt that the specialist units already in place covered the causes of most serious crime. Drugs, fraud, terrorism—that sort of thing. The major crime unit will have a different brief," he said, as they reached the bar. "What'll you have?"

"A whisky, thanks." It was a rare treat; Michael never drank when he was driving, and he was usually driving. "So what would this major crime unit do?"

"It would deal with the serious crimes non-criminals commit. The thinking is that detectives used to dealing with known offenders and hardened criminals aren't so hot when it comes to honest citizens turned murderers? Crimes like that need a different approach. It would be a small, hand-picked unit."

"Is there enough of that sort of crime to keep a specialist unit going?"

"I think so, because of the length of time they can take to investigate. But they'll also reopen cold cases, see what someone with a bit more imagination than the average copper can do with them."

Michael smiled. "I'm tempted to say that *everyone* has—"

"I know, I know," said Ray, before Michael could finish. "But some of us can see past the ends of our noses."

Present company excepted, thought Michael. Ray might have fast-tracked his way to his current job of heading Malworth CID, but he had no imagination whatsoever. "So who's the frontrunner?" he asked.

"Detective Chief Inspector Hill, assuming she applies for it. I told you we gambled on anything—she might not come under starter's orders. She's based at Malworth—she's done a good job there." He smiled. "She's very attractive, too."

"Well—maybe I can get an introduction."

"Sorry, Mike, she's taken. She's married to DCI Lloyd over at Stansfield."

Even better, thought Michael. Married women didn't expect anything from you. "She kept her own name?"

"Only to avoid confusion. They are happily married, with a two-year-old daughter."

"More fast-track coppers?"

"No. This is second time around for both of them—she's ten years younger than him, though. I think you've met DCI Lloyd—he's Welsh, not particularly tall. Very dark hair, what there is of it."

"Oh, yes. I remember him." Michael smiled. "A two-year-old daughter will keep him on his toes."

"They've been together for years, but they only got married about eighteen months ago." Ray asked for the menu, and once they had ordered, he settled in for a gossip. "Apparently, it all started twenty-odd years ago when they were both in London, at the Met. He was married, but she wasn't. Then next thing, she goes and marries some man and goes to live in Nottingham, while he gets a divorce, but she doesn't know that. Anyway, she manages to persuade her husband to move to Stansfield . . ."

Michael stopped listening, as he often did with Ray. He liked his brother-in-law, but he seriously suspected that he never actually stopped talking. Having a conversation with him was almost impossible, once he'd got going. Michael wondered if he was like that at work.

Being related by marriage to casino owners was not something the constabulary recommended to its senior officers, but it hadn't held Ray back, because in his line of work Michael heard the odd whisper of use to the police, and it sometimes worked to their advantage. And Michael played it straight, for the most part. His business dealings were squeaky clean and always had been, but if Ray really believed that he just resigned himself to writing off large gambling debts that he couldn't recover in court, that just showed how little imagination he had.

During the meal, Michael was given a minute assessment of everyone's chances in the Bartonshire Constabulary promotion stakes, and by the time he was being deposited at his front door, he could have opened a book on the outcome himself. He re-trieved his golf bag from the boot, slammed it shut and tapped the roof of the car, watching as the X-type Jaguar swept back down his graveled driveway. He raised a hand in salute as its taillights dis-appeared from view, and smiled. He had never bought a Jag—he drove a modest Ford Focus, and it got him from A to B in comfort, so he was quite happy with that.

All his adult life he had consciously veered away from the overt trappings of self-made wealth; no camel-hair coats and gold identity bracelets for him, no flashy sports cars or Havana cigars. He wasn't about to play the part of the East End boy made good, even if he was one. His family had moved to Bartonshire from London when he was fifteen, so the accent had been ironed out, but he was an East End boy at heart.

The Grange was the only ostentation he had ever allowed himself, and it was different, because Josephine had grown up in Stoke Weston village, and her dream had been to live in the Grange, so when it came on the market twenty years ago, Michael had bought it. It sat in several picturesque acres of Stoke Weston, and had once been someone's country house. Whoever that was had probably only used it part of the year, and that *was* ostenta-tion in Michael's book. At least he lived there all year round. But he did employ a full-time housekeeper and gardener, not to men-tion part-time cleaners and groundsmen, and it was a hell of a size for just him and Ben.

Come to that, Ben was hardly here now that he was at university—perhaps he should think about selling. But then, Ben loved it, too; it had been a great place for a boy to grow up. He and his friends had played for hours in the woods, and the old summerhouse by the lake had in its time been everything from a prehistoric cave to a spaceship. They had camped out in it—though Michael would hardly call it camping, in something as sturdy and weatherproof as that—and it had been a self-important clubhouse for some secret society at one time. It was kept in good order, but no one used it at all now Ben's friends were all grown up.

They had held barbecues, played cricket and croquet on the lawns, messed about in boats on the lake, and everyone had had great fun. Ben might want to live here when he got married and had kids, which he would do sooner or later. No, he'd hang on to the Grange for the moment.

Anyway, he liked being able to host parties and business gatherings here—he was very fond of Stoke Weston, and enjoyed showing it off. And he took not a little pride in the fact that he was a one-man job provider; wherever possible, he employed people from the village in his various enterprises. He knew who he could trust, and what capabilities they had to offer, so it suited him, and the resentment that might have been felt at this upstart in the villagers' midst was totally absent.

Fine snow began to fall, shaking Michael from his reverie. As he went into the house, he could hear Ben on the phone to someone. He had come home for the weekend for a friend's twenty-first birthday party, and was going back tonight. Michael leaned the golf bag silently against the wall, and listened.

". . . but I'll be gone by then, I don't want to go without seeing you at all. I've missed you. I always miss you—you know that. Can't you get the time off? Ask to leave early? Good. So you'll meet me there? You know where they are, don't you? No—not them. The ones on Waring Road. They're only about five minutes from the bingo club. They're empty—he's just had them done up, but they're not on the market yet. Yes—that's the ones. It's quicker to come on foot through the alleyway from Murchison Place— the one-way system takes you miles off the route. I'll be in number three. OK, Stephen, see you at half past eight or so."

Michael frowned, then let the door close with a bang, and went along the hallway to the sitting room. Perhaps he'd misheard. He'd thought Ben had finished with that sort of nonsense years ago.

Ben rose from the sofa with the easy grace that he had inherited from Josephine, along with her dark hair. Michael's was sandy and, these days, sparse.

As he thought of her, Michael looked quickly down at the thickly piled carpet. It had been seventeen years since she'd died, and he still felt tears prick the back of his eyes when she came into his mind. She had married him when he was twenty years old, and hadn't enough money even to take her out for a meal, and she had given him the capital he needed to open his first betting shop. She had been ten years older than him, and everyone had thought she was mad, that he'd married her for the money, but that wasn't how it was at all.

And she had been right to believe in him: the betting shop had turned into shops in the plural, and he had expanded into bingo clubs, nightclubs, and the Lucky Seven casino, making himself a millionaire several times over. That was when he'd bought the Grange. Now, as Ben had just mentioned on the phone, he was moving into property development. He had repaid Josephine's investment with handsome interest, despite her protests that she was his wife, and didn't want the money back. She had put it all into a trust for Ben, then just a baby, to be paid out on his twenty-first, and that, unbelievably, was just three months away. Time moved on at an alarming rate.

"Good game?"

He looked up with a determined smile, not wanting to embarrass Ben with his show of emotion. "Not really. Ray sees me as some sort of income supplement."

"Oh." Ben smiled. "I can never see the attraction of golf myself—something I daren't say in St. Andrews, of course."

"I should think not."

He might have been blessed with his mother's looks, but the brains that had allowed Ben to go to university in the home of golf were acquired from Michael himself, and the mature confidence and expensively educated accent—whether Ben liked it or not— from his cash. Ben had always been a little uncomfortable with the source of his privileged upbringing, Michael thought. Bingo clubs and betting shops were a little too down-market for him.

"And why you should want to play on a freezing cold day in the middle of February is beyond me. It's snowing, for God's sake!"

Michael sat down, and picked up the newspaper. "It wasn't snowing when we were playing. It was a bit fresh, I grant you. But it's character-building." He turned the page of his newspaper. "Will I have the pleasure of your company this evening?" he asked, with studied would-be indifference to the answer.

Ben glanced at his watch, reminding Michael irresistibly of a clothing catalogue model. Tall, slim . . . whatever he chose to wear looked like what everyone else should be wearing. What with that and his rosy financial prospects, the girls should be queuing up. But he still hadn't got over that foolish notion.

"Sorry—no. My train leaves at ten past ten, and I've promised to meet some people for a drink before I go."

"Have you eaten?"

"No—I'll grab something on the train. I'm off to have a quick shower—I'll pop my head round the door before I go."

Michael nodded acknowledgment, and waited until he could no longer hear his son's footsteps in the hallway before picking up the phone and hitting the redial button.

IN MALWORTH, KEITH SCOPES WAS GLOOMILY EYEING THE SAFE IN the security office of the Stars and Bars nightclub, thinking that if he could just borrow two hundred quid to buy some stuff, he'd be able to pay it back in no time. Long before Mr. Waterman missed it—he wouldn't be emptying it until tomorrow morning. If he could just get hold of some Es and some coke, he could sell it tonight and put the money back before anyone knew it had gone.

Being security personnel was the perfect cover—he was there to prevent drug abuse or any other sort of trouble on Mr. Waterman's various premises, and that's what he did. He didn't know where the street-dealers he sold the stuff to plied their trade, but the deals were made on the understanding that they steered clear of anywhere he was working. And he didn't deal very often, which was why the police didn't know that he did it at all. Just now and then, when he needed to boost his income with something more certain than gambling. The problem tonight was that he had no income left to boost.

The safe was sitting there with over two thousand pounds in it, Keith knew. Just a couple of hundred, that was all he needed. Then a quick trip to Barton, and he'd be laughing. It would be so easy, but he had no access to the safe, so it was wishful thinking. Mr. Waterman might call him a security officer on his wage slip, but in his case that was code for hired muscle. Keith had plenty of that; plenty of muscle, plenty of hair—Michelle said he looked a bit like Elvis in his prime. That was why she went out with him in the first place, apparently, even though he was a bit on the short side for her.

Funny that, he thought. A bloke that's been dead for a quarter of a century still turns them on. But whether or not he had Elvis's looks, he didn't have his money. And he didn't have a key to the safe, or anything else, come to that. No one with his record was ever going to be given the key to someone else's safe. Mr. Waterman wasn't stupid.

"You couldn't lend me twenty until payday, could you?" he asked Jerry.

"Jesus, Keith—it's only Sunday!"

"Yeah, well—my hot tip is still running."

"Sorry, mate." Jerry fished a fiver out of his back pocket. "That any good to you?"

Not really, but Keith took it, nodding his thanks.

"Why don't you tell Waterman not to bother paying you at all? You just give it all back to him."

"I don't bet in his shops," said Keith. "I don't want him knowing all my business."

"Oh, right—you've certainly got one over on him there, Keith." Jerry clipped on his tie, and checked himself in the mirror.

Mr. Waterman was very particular about how his staff looked. Jerry said he was worse than his sergeant-major in the army had been. Nightclub doormen wore dark suits, white shirts and clip-on ties. Casino staff wore black-tie. Keith, who worked where he was needed, even had a security guard's uniform, because he sometimes looked after the security at Mr. Waterman's house parties, and the security men at the Grange had to look official.

"You want to marry Michelle and have some kids," said Jerry. "Then you'd have to stop throwing your money away."

"Why would I want to do that? I'm twenty-one, not forty-one. We're all right as we are."

"That Tony Baker bloke should be interviewing you for his book."

"Who?"

"Tony Baker. You know—the guy off the telly who was at the casino on Saturday night. Sharp dresser—light brown wavy hair, tall, permanent tan. Thinks he's it."

"Oh, him. I didn't know he was on TV. Why should he interview me?"

Jerry shook his head. "He's researching gambling, isn't he? He might want to find out what makes a born loser give his pay-packet away every week. It's time you settled down—you can't duck and dive all your life."

"Why not?" Keith's mobile phone's ring vied with the music that was suddenly booming out from the club as the DJ tested the sound system, and he kicked the door shut as he fished it out of his pocket. "It's my life." He still had to hold a finger in his ear when he spoke. "Hello?"

"Got a job for you," Waterman said. "Tonight."

It was his fairy godmother. Keith listened to what he had to do, already spending the money. Mr. Waterman was pretty generous when he wanted something done that he couldn't do himself.

"I'll text your mobile when it's time. Come to the bingo club for your money when you've done. Any questions?"

"No," said Keith. You did what Mr. Waterman wanted you to do, or you didn't. All you needed to know was where and when it had to be done; why it had to be done was Mr. Waterman's business, not yours. If you needed anything repeated, you hadn't been listening in the first place. If you had a problem with it, you turned it down, simple as that. Keith never turned anything down, and never asked questions.

Besides, with Jerry in the room, all he could do was say yes and no, because Jerry didn't know just how much ducking and diving he really did, and he never would.

"WHY?"

Charlotte's brown eyes looked into Lloyd's with the same frankness that characterized her mother's interview technique. Even the silence following the question seemed to have been passed on through the genes.

And it had long been a source of wonder to Lloyd that the two-year-old mind, unable to grasp as basic a concept as left and right, only capable of stringing two or three words together, not up to the task of simple arithmetic, was entirely happy to encompass something as fundamentally challenging and abstract as "why."

He glanced up at Judy. "Why?" he repeated.

Judy looked from him to Charlotte. "Because your daddy says so," she said.

"You're not supposed to *do* that!" Lloyd protested. "The child is asking for a logical explanation as to why she should go to bed when we're the ones who are complaining about being tired, and she's wide awake."

"That *is* why."

Charlotte was looking solemnly at each of them as they spoke. There was no way she could follow what they were saying, but she gave every indication of doing so, and it captivated Lloyd every time she did it. He looked back at her.

"Because you need a lot more sleep than we do," he said, knowing he was laying himself wide open.

"Why?"

"Because everything about you is growing very fast. And that takes a lot of energy. So does learning to walk, and run and jump. So you use up a lot of calories, and that means you have to rest to get more energy to use up even more calories tomorrow."

She liked long, complicated answers that she didn't understand, but this time she frowned. "Carlies," she said, quietly, to herself.

Lloyd put his forehead close to hers, looking into her eyes. "Calories are units of heat energy, though you'll find that one calorie is more usually expressed as 4.1868 joules."

She giggled.

"How on earth do you know that?" asked Judy. "Or are you making it up as you go along?"

"Of course not! Would I lie to Charlotte? A calorie is 4.1868 joules." He grinned. "I don't know what I'd do with one joule, never mind 4.1868 of them, but it's a fact, isn't it, Chaz?"

Charlotte and Judy both smiled, and Lloyd shook his head slightly, looking from one to the other. The same soft dark hair, the same nose, the same smile. He might have had nothing to do with Charlotte—he had searched in vain for some aspect of his appearance or personality—because from day one, she had been just like Judy. He gathered Charlotte up in his arms. "Who's daddy's gorgeous girl?"

"Chaz!" she squealed, as he tickled her.

"You wouldn't have thought she was daddy's gorgeous girl if you'd been shopping with her this afternoon. I've never been so embarrassed in my life."

"Again!" shouted Charlotte.

Lloyd tickled her again. "She's two. They're supposed to have tantrums when they're two. What did she want, anyway?"

"If I'd known that, I'd have given it to her—believe me, I'm quite prepared to give in to blackmail. But I hadn't the faintest idea what she wanted."

"Sometimes it's just that they can't express themselves," said Lloyd, as Judy joined them on the floor. "It must be a bit frustrating, knowing what you want to communicate and not being able to."

"Especially for a Lloyd. Come on, you two—it's bedtime. Who do you want to give you a bath, Charlotte?"

"Tickle me!"

Judy tickled her. "Who do you want to give you a bath?"

"Again!"

"No. Bath. Who?"

Charlotte gave that some thought. "Nana."

"Nana's watching television. You can have Daddy or me."

Judy's mother lived with them now, in their pleasantly elderly detached house. It was in the old village of Stansfield, where life still moved at a slightly slower pace than it did in the town itself, a new town built in the fifties, after the war. No one had been too sure how well the setup would work, but so far, Gina had been a godsend, and there had been no more difficulties than you would expect in any family, once they had got over being too polite to one another.

"Daddy."

"All right," said Lloyd. "Come on, Droopy Drawers." He stood up with Charlotte hanging round his neck, and some difficulty. As he turned to leave the room, she squirmed round.

"Mummy bath!" she shouted, her arm reaching back imploringly to Judy.

"Oh, no, you don't," Lloyd said. "Make up your mind."

She thought again for a moment. "Daddy bath. And Mummy bath."

Lloyd felt himself swell with pride as his daughter hurdled another linguistic barrier. "Both of us?" He raised his eyebrows at Judy. "Is that all right with you, Mummy?"

Judy gave him The Look. "It's perfectly all right by me. But," she added sweetly, "if you ever again address me as 'Mummy,' I'll divorce you."

TONY BAKER HADN'T BEEN PREPARED FOR THE EXCITEMENT THAT he was feeling. He could see why the Malworth regulars might find it passed the time pleasantly enough, but his life was not like theirs. He didn't need artificially created excitement.

Eighteen years ago, he had had the tabloids clamoring for his story, the one that landed it paying him an enormous sum of money. When they had discovered that he was an ex-journalist and could write it himself, they had paid him even more, and had given him a weekly column on crime, which he still wrote.

But the real turning point had been when he had made a TV documentary about the whole business. Then someone else had made a TV movie about it. One thing had led to another, and since then he had appeared on countless chat shows, been invited to premieres, and had been honored by the Queen. He had fronted a very successful television series that was still being shown on satellite and cable channels around the world, and in that series he had traveled to wherever serial killers had followed their inclination, especially if there was any doubt as to the perpetrators of the acts. He had interviewed people on death row; some that he was quite certain had killed repeatedly, and some that he felt just as certain had been victims of miscarriages of justice. He had witnessed three executions. So his forty-seven years of life had been, to say the least, interesting.

So what was it that had his pulse racing, was causing his breathing to be shallow and nervous, was making his hand shake with excitement, for God's sake? He smiled, laughing at himself for being so susceptible to something so simple and mindless. He was waiting for just one number on his bingo card.

Tony Baker was working, contrary to appearances, bingo not being his recreation of choice. But he had been playing it every night for a week, and for the first time each of the numbers on his card was neatly marked with a bright pink splodge of ink from his bingo marker pen, except one. His objective research had become personal. It was the last house of the first half of the main session, and it was the Link game, when all of Waterman's bingo clubs played the same game together. Eight hundred and sixty pounds was up for grabs.

He didn't need the money—the pile he had made from his story had been invested carefully. Since then his life had settled down into a routine of producing and presenting a TV series every two years on the connection between crime and leisure, each time concentrating on a different leisure activity. The accompanying book routinely made the bestseller lists; he understood how to catch the public's interest.

His first love, however, was murder. It fascinated him, and, if the viewing figures were anything to go by, it fascinated a lot of people. The networks just said that he'd already done that when he suggested it, but he might try thinking of attacking the subject from a new angle, make a determined try for another murder series. Even Jack the Ripper still had legs if you thought of a new perspective.

But for the moment, his bread and butter was gambling. During his research into the gambling habits of the human being, he had won a few times; he'd made money now and again on horse races, slot machines, the gaming tables. He'd even won a quite sizeable amount on a football pool. It had been better than losing, that was all. It hadn't given him a thrill. But this . . .

This was different. And it was a valuable addition to his research, because what had seemed to him a particularly boring and unproductive way to spend one's leisure time, with no input at all from the gambler, had suddenly become very appealing, and he had to try to analyze why.

He looked round the big, bright hall, with its bar running

along the length of one wall, fruit machines along the length of the other, and in between them rows of plastic-topped tables strewn with bingo tickets, drinks, snacks, their occupants listening intently for the numbers. It wasn't at all like the image he had of bingo. These days it was high-tech, with the numbers flashing up on a screen as they were called. There were no balls dancing about in a drum to produce the numbers—random number selectors were used now. And gone were the old-fashioned nicknames for the numbers. Now, it was all very slick and clinical.

The average age was probably not much above his, at a guess. The customers weren't young, but they weren't in their dotage either. It was mostly women, of course, still. What men were there were all years older than him; they hadn't yet tempted young men into bingo halls. But the youths who frequented Waterman's nightclubs might be surprised if they did venture into his bingo clubs, because they didn't look all that different, and the drinks were a lot less expensive. There was music, and a restaurant, and the chance of coming out richer than when you went in. No wonder the place was packed.

The bingo caller intoned the numbers—it was all jokes and double entendres between games, but during games, he was Mr. Efficiency, with a straight face. This was serious.

Tony heard his number, saw the confirmation on the screen, felt his blood pressure go off the scale, like the weight hitting the bell on a test-your-strength sideshow, and heard his own voice shout "House!" at the same time as another, female voice. He felt elated and irritated both at once, as she doubtless also did.

Her card was checked first. She sat a couple of tables away from him, and he realized that it was Wilma, one of his interviewees, who had won. She was a faithful member whose biggest win until now had been forty pounds, two years ago. Wilma was in her fifties, maybe sixties, her graying hair cut short, and her face was flushed as her numbers were checked off with the caller.

Like him, she was alone at the table. Mostly people came in pairs or groups, but there was the odd solo player.

His turn now, and he too was confirmed as a winner, after producing his club card.

"Just stay there, Mr. Baker," said the checker. "A steward will bring your winnings to the table."

The steward was young Stephen Halliday, his landlady's son, whose fair hair was gelled into spiky obedience, and whose white shirt was dazzling against the red jacket and tie that Waterman's stewards wore. Stephen was very particular about his shirts, but it was of course his mother who washed and ironed them. Tony had been brought up to look after himself, and felt that Grace should acquaint Stephen with the intricacies of the washing machine before he got much older.

It was through Stephen that Tony had discovered the delights of the Tulliver Inn in Stoke Weston, a travelers' inn since the seventeenth century, which nowadays still did a very good bed-and-breakfast and evening meal. He hated provincial hotels; a village inn was much more to his liking. The only drawback was Grace Halliday herself, a blonde, forty-something divorcee, who was itching to get her hooks into him. Tony nodded to Stephen as he went to the woman's table first.

"Here you are, Wilma—not bad for ten minutes' work."

Wilma, still slightly pink, smiled at him as he counted out the money. "You're looking very handsome tonight," she said.

". . . two hundred and fifty—thank you, Wilma. You're looking good too, especially now you're rich—three hundred, three hundred and fifty, four hundred, four hundred and ten, twenty, thirty. There you go," he said, tucking in the flap of the envelope. "Your place or mine?"

"Oh, I should be so lucky!"

Stephen came toward him with the satisfactorily thick envelope, and took out the notes. "Fifty, one hundred, one-fifty . . ."

Waterman paid out in cash up to a thousand pounds; he

thought that the thrill of being given a bundle of banknotes was all part of the fun, and he was right, thought Tony. It was much more satisfying to see the money being counted than to be handed a check.

Tony had come to Bartonshire a month ago, purely to try the Waterman experience. He could have stayed with Mike Waterman at his enormous house, but he had felt that accepting his hospitality might prejudice his findings, and had turned him down. Having had to endure Grace Halliday's inane chatter and fluttering eyelashes, he wished he hadn't. But he would only be here for another two weeks; he would survive.

". . . three-ninety, four hundred and ten, four hundred and thirty. Spend it on something you don't need."

"I will," said Tony, picking it up. The envelope's edges were decorated with a repeat design of two champagne glasses and a champagne bottle having just popped its cork, with the words "Bull's Eye Bingo Winner" printed on it. Underneath, in the same print, were the words "Congratulations, Tony!" He smiled. Waterman added finishing touches that cost him virtually nothing, but it worked.

"That's me finished," said Stephen. "I'm getting off early tonight."

"Do you want a lift home?"

"No, it's all right, thanks," said Stephen. "I've got the bike out back."

"Oh, you got it fixed, did you?"

"Fingers crossed. It got me here, so it seems to be okay."

Stephen left, walking quickly toward the staff area, and Tony stood up, taking his jacket from the back of the seat, and made for the exit. As he pushed open the big glass door, he literally bumped into Michael Waterman.

"You're not leaving, Tony? It's only the interval."

"I've just taken some money off you, Mike, and I think I'll quit while I'm ahead."

"Oh—but it's the national game in the second half," said Waterman. "You could win two hundred thousand quid if your luck's in."

"I'll pass," said Tony, with a grin. "I think I've had my share of luck for tonight." He put his jacket on. Mike Waterman might want to stand out here all night chatting, but he didn't.

"Do you have any children, Tony?"

"No."

Waterman sighed. "Ben's been home for the weekend, and if I saw him for five minutes at a time I was lucky. He's off out somewhere, and . . . well, the house seemed a bit empty. That's why I'm here—I thought the bingo club atmosphere might cheer me up."

Tony wanted to get off, but it seemed a bit impolite just to go, if the man needed cheering up. He could surely spare him five minutes. He took a surreptitious glance at his watch. Five minutes—no more than that, because Grace would have his meal ready for him. This new insulin program that he was trying out was supposed to mean that a delayed meal was no longer such a problem, but Tony was used to eating when he'd arranged to eat, and besides, he wasn't cut out to be a counselor. And apart from anything else, he was cold.

STEPHEN SPENT SOME TIME GETTING READY BEFORE HE LEFT THE club; finally, he used his fingers to brush a touch of gel through his fair hair, tweaking it into the peaks that he currently favored, then rinsed his hands, straightened his tie, and stood back a little from the mirror to see the effect.

"You're beautiful, Steve—don't worry."

The voice belonged to Jim, one of the other stewards, as he emerged from a cubicle, the only place that any of them could have a cigarette without getting caught. The customers could smoke, but the staff couldn't, and the smokers among them found that quite hard to take.

Stephen flashed Jim's reflection a mock toothpaste-ad grin—

one that was free of the pollutants of cigarette smoke—and he knew that the comment had been only half in fun. He was vain; he knew that. Everyone made fun of the care he took with his appearance. But his public loved him for it.

That was how he thought of them, the bingo regulars whose cars were parked nose-to-tail outside. They had to get here early if they wanted to park on the road outside; most people had to use the big car park on Waring Road, a five-minute walk away. But Stephen could always leave his bike at the back of the club, so he didn't have that problem.

One last check, then he pulled on his leather biking jacket, picked up his helmet, went out into the club and pushed open the door to the street just as another of his colleagues passed.

"Oh, you're bound to pull tonight, Steve," she said.

"He doesn't need to," came Jim's voice from behind him. "He's getting plenty already, aren't you, Steve?"

Stephen practically walked into Michael Waterman, who was standing right outside the club with Tony Baker. He felt himself flush as he walked quickly away, hoping Mr. Waterman hadn't heard. But he had been using his mobile phone, not taking any apparent notice. Stephen smiled. Mr. Waterman was always on the phone; if he wasn't ringing people he was texting them. Stephen wondered what he would have done if he had been born a century earlier. He would probably have had a flock of carrier pigeons at the ready.

Stephen had been a steward at the Bull's Eye bingo clubs for almost three years now, ever since he'd left school, and he enjoyed it. He liked the women—they were mostly women—who played bingo; they were unpretentious, always ready to have a laugh. And they loved him, for some reason. He was always getting joke propositions. He liked Mr. Waterman, but if he ever found out about him and Ben, there would be trouble. Of course, Jim had only been making a joke—he knew nothing about it, and no one at all knew that he was going to meet Ben. But Stephen hoped Mr. Waterman hadn't heard, all the same.

He felt fine snow hit his face, and stopped to button up his jacket. Some way ahead of him, he could see Wilma, who never stayed for the second half—she had to get home to walk her dog, and she didn't like doing that late at night.

Wilma, disorganized as ever, had a large shoulder bag gaping open, and Stephen saw what looked very much like the envelope he had given her slide to the ground. He ran to pick it up, then carried on after her, calling her name, but she was too far away to hear him. She was crossing the road, heading toward one of Malworth's many alleyways, halfway along which was the entrance to the flats where she lived.

Stephen ran as fast as he could, and caught up with her as she turned into the Victorian covered alleyway, long and dank, its roof supported by thick pillars. Cobbled, dimly lit, covered with fly-posters and graffiti, it was an uninviting place at night.

"Are you so rich you can throw it away, or what?" he asked, his voice echoing in the damp, cave-like passage.

"What's that?" Her mouth fell open when she saw what he was holding. "Oh, my God—I thought I'd put that in my purse. I was in a state. I've never won that much."

"Well, put it in your purse now."

She fumbled about in the bag, finally fishing out the purse, handing it to him. It was the kind that fastened with two twists of metal that snapped together. "Here," she said. "You do it. My hands are too cold."

Stephen took it from her, then shook his head. "It's a coin purse," he said. "It won't take all those notes. They'd fall out when you opened it. I'll just leave them in the envelope, and put it in here. All right?" He slid the envelope into her shoulder bag, dropping the purse in after it, and zipped it up. "I'll walk along with you," he said. "I'm going that way anyway."

JACK SHAW WAS ALREADY WALKING IN THE GLOOM OF THAT ALLEY-way on his way to the nightclub, his virtually undetectable limp slightly more apparent than usual, as it always was in very cold weather.

He was still puzzled as to why Michael Waterman had suddenly wanted to be driven to Malworth. He had turned up at his cottage, asking if he was doing anything this evening, and when Jack had said that he was doing nothing in particular, had asked him to be his chauffeur for the evening.

"I want to go to the Malworth bingo club," he'd said. "But I was out this afternoon, and I've been drinking. So if you can take me and bring me back, I'll make it worth your while. I'll be leaving again about ten, I think."

Jack was never averse to making a few extra quid, and had happily driven his boss to Malworth, parking behind the bingo club in the space reserved for him. His staff certainly wouldn't be expecting to see him; Waterman usually had Sunday off.

"Are you not coming in?" Waterman had asked, as he had got out of the car.

"No," Jack had said. "I've got something I want to do."

"Right—see you later."

Waterman Entertainment employed Jack as a fruit machine technician, and he knew most of the people who worked for Michael Waterman. He couldn't warn the bingo club staff of their boss' arrival, but he could at least tell Jerry Wheelan over at the Stars and Bars that he might be going to get a spot check.

He could hear the voices of the people behind him in the narrow passage, their words carrying on the still, cold air. Stephen's voice he'd recognized; the other evidently belonged to someone who had had a win at bingo.

"I still can't believe I won all that money. Four hundred and thirty pounds—it's a fortune."

"It was a shame you had to share."

"Oh, no. It's quite enough as it is. Why shouldn't someone else be lucky too?"

Stephen gave a snort. "Oh, like he needs the money," he said.

"Do you know him, then?"

"He's staying with us. But you know who he is, don't you?"

"Sort of. I know he's on telly. He interviewed me—wanted to know why I play bingo all the time when I never win anything."

"Trust him to get half of it when you finally did get a decent win."

"Don't you like him then?"

"Not much. But you should see my mum—she can't get over him staying in her pub. She's all over him."

Jack slowed to a stop, not wanting to get out of earshot, and stood in the shadow of a pillar. He didn't want them to see him, but he wanted very much to hear what Stephen had to say. Tony Baker thought he was God's gift, and Grace Halliday was waiting on him hand and foot, which made matters worse. Jack hadn't been too sure how Stephen felt about him, and he wanted to know.

"Ah—is that why you don't like him? Are you jealous?"

"No! No. If she found someone she liked, I'd be happy for her. I just think he's a bit full of himself, that's all."

"Is it serious? Do you think you'll be getting a stepdad?"

"I don't think so. He's not a bit interested in her. But if you knew my mum—she doesn't give up, so you never know. I hope not."

Jack didn't listen to the rest of the conversation.

"KELLY'S EYE TO CHARLEY SIERRA."

"Charley Sierra receiving."

"We're in position at the Candy Store."

The Candy Store was the code name for the premises they were watching, and Trainee Detective Constable Gary Sims watched as Detective Sergeant Kelly checked that the cameras, both video and still, were pointing directly at the front door of the block of flats across from the room that the observation team was currently occupying.

Gary, on detachment to Force Drugs Squad, knew from pre-vious observations just how mind-numbingly boring CID work could be, but there was something unusual about the sergeant's manner on the radio, his almost obsessive checking that all the equipment was in working order, and that Gary and the others knew exactly what they had to do. Something was in the air.

This one was going to be an all-nighter, but at least they were in a room in someone's house—the last one had seen them all crammed into a van, which became less and less habitable as the night wore on. At least here they could stretch their legs from time to time, and use a regular toilet when required to do so. There had been a strange funnel arrangement rigged up in the van in order that no one had to leave it.

And now that they were there, Kelly informed them that Op-eration Sweet Sixteen—so called because that was the average age of the people to whom the merchandise would ultimately be peddled—was about to achieve its objective. There were eight teams carrying out similar observations all over the city, and when they had recorded enough to prove that dealing was taking place, the raiding parties would go in and take out one of the biggest drug-dealing rings in the city.

Gary fancied he heard a hint of pride in the sergeant's voice as he used the word "city," for Barton had only recently achieved city status, and the status of its police had thus been enhanced.

The guys on the raids would get all the fun, all the action, Gary thought disconsolately. His job consisted of pointing a cam-era and noting descriptions and times for someone else to write down. He said as much to the sergeant.

"We're going to take these bastards right out," said Kelly. "We'll have video and photographs and a log detailing every deal that goes down. And when we move in we'll have them, their equipment, the drugs and the money. No smart-ass lawyer's going to get any of them off." He smiled. "And with any luck, their whole operation in this city will fall apart."

"Fair enough, sarge," said one of the others. "But we still haven't got the big boys. So we take out eight middlemen—so what? They'll recruit another eight."

"I know." Kelly sat back. "But they've got to find people they can trust. And premises. And new equipment, and bring in another shipment of stuff before schedule. It's all risky, and it means the National Crime Squad or Customs and Excise have all the more chance to catch them at it. And meanwhile, their Barton lieutenants are banged up, and they can't be sure one of them won't talk. This is major, major disruption."

"I think we're about to get some action," murmured the man at the window.

Gary focused the camera on the door of the flat opposite.

JUDY AND LLOYD WERE PLAYING THE BATH GAME WITH CHARlotte, which involved everything that floated being in the bath with their daughter, and then being solemnly handed back to them when they asked for them. Then it all had to start again. It had begun as an educational game so that Charlotte knew which was a duck and which was a frog, but she had known that for some time now; they just couldn't make her move on to a new game. When this activity began to pall, Judy left Lloyd to it and went back down to the living room, where her mother was reading the paper.

"Is your program finished?" she asked, looking at her watch. "I had no idea it was that late. Charlotte should have been in bed two hours ago." She flopped down on the sofa, and yawned. "She's just like Lloyd. She'd stay up all night if we let her."

Her mother smiled. "Lloyd will be pleased to hear that," she said. "He keeps saying that she's a clone of you."

"I know," said Judy, yawning again as she spoke. "I don't think she's like me at all. And if you'd seen her this afternoon—that was Lloyd to a tee. Suddenly flying into a rage about goodness knows what, and blaming me."

"You're the one who looks as if she should have been in bed two hours ago."

Judy nodded. She always found the weekends much more exhausting than the working week, no matter how busy she had been. Charlotte at two was great fun, just as Lloyd had promised she would be—learning new words every day, becoming her own person—but her energy was boundless, and her curiosity about the world meant that she had to be watched every minute.

"We've got to get a garden gate," she said. "It'll be spring soon."

She would have been looking forward to that had it not been for the loft conversion, currently scheduled for April. It should have been done last April, and it kept being put off for one reason or another. But the contractor would be coming any day now to talk to her mother about what exactly she wanted done, and give them his estimate.

"Have you thought yet what you want?" she asked. "In the loft?"

Her mother put down the paper. "Well," she began, "I was going to talk to you about that. Do you think it's really necessary?"

It would save them a lot of time, trouble and expense if they abandoned the idea, thought Judy, and she wondered if that was what had prompted her mother's change of mind. Having her own space had been a precondition of her coming to look after Charlotte for them. "Not as far as I'm concerned," she said. "But are you sure you wouldn't rather have your flat?"

"I don't think I'd use it."

No. Judy couldn't really imagine them behaving as though her mother lived somewhere else altogether. She had her own TV in her bedroom if she got fed up with Lloyd's choice of viewing, and that was all she wanted, really. It was much friendlier if they all shared the whole house.

*   *   *

BY THE TIME DETECTIVE INSPECTOR TOM FINCH ARRIVED ON THE scene, the alleyway had been sealed off, and a route to the body had been marked out for essential personnel that cut the already narrow alley almost in half, and made negotiating the pillars far from easy.

Detective Sergeant John Hitchin, young and keen, was standing talking to a man whose face Tom knew, but couldn't place. He excused himself when he saw Tom, and walked down to meet him.

Tom blew out his cheeks as he arrived. "Were you actually born in Antigua, Hitch?" he asked.

"No, I was born in Malworth. So was my dad. It was my granddad that came over from the West Indies in the fifties."

"I'll bet he wishes he was back there with this weather."

"Probably wishes he was anywhere, sir. He died five years ago."

"Oh. Sorry."

Hitchin smiled. "That's Mr. Baker, the man who found the body. I've suggested that he wait in one of the cars until you get the chance to talk to him. He saw it happen, and the assailant ran off along there in the direction of Murchison Place. No one else used the alley before we got here, so that's why I cordoned off that side of the alley in the hope that he might have dropped something that could identify him."

It was a long shot, thought Tom, but they might get something useful. It was amazing how often those given to violent crime did lose their possessions in the course of the assault.

"No description, though," Hitchin went on. "He said he just caught a glimpse of the assailant. It was probably a man, and he was wearing dark clothes. It happened at nine o'clock."

"Do we know who the victim is?" Tom asked.

"Mr. Baker knows her. Her name's Wilma Fenton, and she lives here, in the ground-floor flat. One of the lads is talking to her neighbor now, to find out who we should notify. She'd won money at bingo—it looks like she was mugged for her winnings, but he just dropped the money and ran when he saw Mr. Baker."

Tom was still trying to place the informant. Baker, Baker. He mentally snapped his fingers. Baker—of course, it was Tony Baker. No wonder he couldn't place him—he'd only ever seen him on TV. That explained Hitch's scrupulous attention to detail, because Tony Baker would be watching their every move.

"Were there any other witnesses?"

"No. Mr. Baker says the street was deserted, and so was the alleyway, but I've got a house-to-house organized for the flats, in case anyone saw or heard anything."

"Right, thanks, Hitch. I'll go and talk to Mr. Baker. You know who he is, don't you?"

"Yes—he makes these TV programs about popular pastimes that attract crime," said Hitchin. "He's doing one on gambling— that's how come he knows the victim. He was at the bingo club himself." He glanced over to where the body lay. "Her pastime attracted a crime, all right."

Tom realized with a jolt that at twenty-six, John Hitchin would have been too young at the time to care how Tony Baker's TV career had come about. And Hitch hadn't known that he was under the microscope when he cordoned off half the alley; he really was that conscientious by nature. He turned to go, then turned back again. "Has this alley got a name?" he asked.

"Innes Passage," said Hitchin. "But unless they're from round here, no one'll know what you're talking about if you call it that."

All the old alleyways in Malworth had names, but the signs on most of them had long since perished. Tom had come to live in Bartonshire from Liverpool, and had noticed over the years that the locals thought if they knew something, everyone did; Malworth natives knew the names of the alleyways, and they had never seen any need to put up new signs.

There was nothing lying around that looked like a murder weapon; in fact, the only plus that this alley had was that it was litter-free, as if it had just been swept. Tom hoped it hadn't just been swept, because if it had then the waste-bins and Dumpsters might have been emptied already. Searching them was never a very popular duty, but finding the murder weapon was probably going to be their only chance of resolving this one.

But there was a nightclub at the other end of the alley; someone there might have seen something. Tom would have a word with the doormen in due course.

The Forensic Medical Examiner arrived then, puffing and blowing, edged past Tom, and crouched down by the body, muttering about people being so inconsiderate as to get themselves murdered out of doors in such inclement weather, just as a detective constable came out of the flats and almost fell over him.

Reinforcements had now arrived, and Hitchin and a couple of others went off to talk to the people in the bingo club, to see if anyone saw someone follow Mrs. Fenton out after her win.

"Life extinct," the FME said, his breath streaming out as he spoke, and glanced at his watch. "21.40 hours. From the body temperature, I'd say she died within the last couple of hours."

"We think it happened at about nine o'clock," said Tom.

The FME stood up. "That would fit." He handed Tom a sheet of paper. "The temperature reading for the pathologist. She's a lot warmer than I am, I can tell you that. Goodnight."

The cordon made a narrow passage even narrower, and would make bringing equipment to the scene a bit difficult. It was barely wide enough, Tom realized, with a smile, for one fairly rotund FME to pass a video and photography unit coming in the opposite direction.

Tom had called in all the usual back-up services, but it might be a waste of time. The SOCOs were arriving now, setting up powerful lights to help them find whatever was there to be found. Perhaps Hitch's scene-preservation would save the day. Perhaps, and perhaps not. A fatal mugging was possibly the most difficult crime of all to clear up, and with no description of the attacker and no murder weapon, it could prove impossible.

But once he had looked at the body properly, and once he had heard Tony Baker's story, Tom began to revise his thoughts on that, because it didn't after all seem to be a straightforward mugging. And in view of their star witness being known to be more than a little critical of the police, he thought his boss would want to see the scene for herself.

CHAPTER TWO

S TEPPING OUT OF THE TAXI, STEPHEN SAID GOODBYE AND ran through the thickly falling snow to where his bike was parked behind the bingo club. He screwed his eyes up against the flakes to try and see the church clock, but he couldn't. He thought it must be about twenty to ten.

He wished he could have seen Ben properly this weekend, but they had to be so careful, and it just hadn't been possible. But Ben usually thought of a way round things, and the flat had been an inspired last-minute thought. The flats were just about to go on the market, so the show flat had everything you could want. It had been sheer luxury, but they had only had an hour together, and that wasn't enough.

At first, he thought the bike wasn't going to start, and cursed the motor mechanic who had promised him that everything was in good working order. But at the third attempt it started, so maybe he had really fixed it. He put on his lights, got his helmet on with the visor up, kicked the stand away, and roared off into the snow.

"WHERE THE HELL HAVE YOU BEEN?" DEMANDED JERRY. "A SMOKE, you said. It didn't take you an hour and twenty minutes to smoke a bloody cigarette!"

Keith held up his hands in apology. "Sorry, Jez. Something came up."

"You're lucky Waterman didn't find out you'd gone AWOL.

Jack Shaw was here earlier—he says Waterman was at the bingo club tonight, and I couldn't have covered for you if he'd come here. So if you're going to make a habit of this, you'd better understand that. If anyone asks me about you, I'll tell them. I'm not going to lose my job because of you."

Keith grinned. "You could worry for England, you know that? What do you do for fun, Jerry?"

Jerry grunted. "I don't have time for fun," he said. "And I'm frozen to the spot. You're on the door from now till we close, mate."

"What's going on in the alleyway?" Keith asked.

"How should I know? I can't see the alleyway, can I? I've been here, doing my job, not swanning off like some."

Oops. He really had pissed Jerry off.

THE ROOM WAS LIT ONLY BY THE SOFT LIGHT FROM THE LANDING, the idea being that the half-light would be soporific.

"Nuther one."

She couldn't still be awake. It was five to ten, for God's sake. Lloyd was having trouble keeping his eyes open, but Charlotte was as bright as she was first thing in the morning. He sighed. "All right. Taffy was a great big, beautiful tabby cat, and he lived in a big house with a big garden and . . ."

His stories were always about Taffy the tabby, and he always began them the same way with absolutely no idea of where they were going, but Charlotte's critical faculties weren't too highly developed. And he had a sneaking suspicion that in this she was 'once again just like her mother, who professed to like the sound of his voice, but admitted that she rarely actually listened to what he was saying. At least Charlotte wasn't yet at the stage where she wanted the same story over and over again, so he amused himself, if no one else, with his impromptu tales of Taffy the tabby.

He had heard Gina's ideas concerning the loft conversion, and had at least steered her in the direction of waiting to see what the designer came up with before making up her mind. He usually found life much easier if he made the concessions, but this time he didn't think he could. The discussion had ended when Judy had put Charlotte to bed, then summoned him to tell her a story. In the middle of the second story, Judy had come in to say that she had been called out to the scene of a fatal mugging. It was, Tom Finch had said, "a funny one," so Lloyd had no idea when she would be back, and neither had she.

Charlotte's eyes at last began to droop just as Taffy had plucked up the courage to leap down from the big tree in the big garden so that he could end up in front of the big fireplace in his big house, where he always finished his adventures. Lloyd left the story—and Taffy—in mid-air, waited to see if there was a protest, and when none came, he tiptoed to the door.

"Want one."

Lloyd turned. "You want one what?"

"One Taffy." Her eyes were closing again.

This time Lloyd waited until he was absolutely sure that she was asleep before moving. Downstairs, Gina was making a cup of tea, and brought one in for Lloyd, for which he was grateful. Marathon storytelling was thirsty work.

"Do you still put Chaz down for an afternoon nap?" he asked.

She shook her head, smiling. "No. You can't blame me. Judy says Charlotte's just like you as far as that's concerned."

"True. Staying awake until all hours definitely isn't one of Judy's traits. She's always ready for bed by eleven."

"You could do worse than follow her example," said Gina. "What do you find to do until two in the morning, anyway?"

It's none of your business what I find to do, he thought, but his face wasn't giving away his irritation at her question. No one could lie more smoothly or more convincingly than Lloyd. "Oh, this and that," he said, smiling. "I potter about. It's relaxing."

"So is a good night's sleep."

The sooner this granny-flat was in existence, the better, as far as Lloyd was concerned. He had always liked Gina, and he didn't know what they would have done without her, but he wanted his own space, even if she didn't. Judy's university lecturer father had died shortly after Charlotte was born, and Gina had had trouble adjusting to solitary life in London. They had needed someone to look after Charlotte, and she had needed family around her—the solution to both their problems had been obvious, and it had worked. He didn't want to rock the boat by getting irritated with her, so it was time, Lloyd decided, for a change of subject.

"Do you like cats, Gina?" he asked.

She looked a little surprised. "Yes, I love them. We always had cats when I was growing up. But John and I lived in a flat almost all our married life, so . . ." She shrugged. "Well, that was John's excuse. He was never too keen on them. I think they scared him a little, but he'd never admit it."

"Does Judy like them?"

Gina looked at him, her eyebrows raised. "You've known her for over twenty years," she said. "And you don't know if she likes cats?"

Lloyd shrugged. "There's a lot I still don't know about her. You know what she's like—if you don't ask the direct question, you don't get told. Sometimes even if you do."

"Oh, I know. I had no idea how she felt about you until she'd been married to Michael for about five years. And then it was John who told me—she didn't say a word to me."

"If it makes you feel any better, it was years before I could get her to admit to me how she felt about me." Lloyd smiled. "And, for the record, she didn't tell her father about us—I did."

"You know, that's just how John's mother was. Kept everything to herself, like Judy does. I always feel as though I don't know her as well as John did. Maybe it's because his mother was like that. He grew up with it—knew how to get past it."

Lloyd nodded. "Well, let's hope Chaz has got a few more of my genes than she seems to at the moment," he said. "I don't think I could take two enigmatic women in my life."

Enigmatic was the wrong word, but he had never been able to

hit on the right word to describe Judy's self-contained way of living her life. Sometimes, just sometimes, the control slipped, and he was allowed to glimpse what was really going on in her head. Not often.

"I couldn't even get her a Valentine for tomorrow," he grumbled. "The only time I did she looked at me as though I had two heads."

Gina laughed. "She's never been one for hearts and flowers."

"Don't I know it. She doesn't even like breakfast in bed. And she says she prefers roses growing in the earth. So the best thing I can do for her tomorrow is ignore her."

"But in answer to your question, she does like cats. She pestered us for one when she was a little girl—that was when John came up with the excuse about a flat not being a proper place to have a cat. That's probably why she's never had one—she's always lived in flats too, until now. And she probably wouldn't have wanted one when Charlotte was really little."

A tabby cat would be a pleasant addition to the household, Lloyd thought. He'd talk to Judy about it. He looked at the gas fire, its imitation coal being licked by reasonably convincing flames, and wondered if they should get the big fireplace that Taffy had in his house in order to complete the picture.

But no. Though he had grown up with a real fire, he supposed that introducing one to a house with a two-year-old in it would be a foolish move, however well guarded it was. But maybe one day, when she was older . . .

"TONY BAKER?" SAID JUDY. "SHOULD THAT MEAN SOMETHING TO me?"

"You remember, guv—the guy that caught the serial killer. The South Coast murders? About eighteen years ago? These days he does all these TV programs about people's social habits affecting the crime statistics. The last one was about drinking."

"Oh, *him!*" Yes, Judy knew him, and remembered only too

well his reason for shooting to fame. Every police officer in the country remembered. Tony Baker had been a crime correspondent for a broadsheet newspaper, and had covered the South Coast murders and the arrest and trial of the man the police had charged. He had been convinced that they had convicted an innocent man, so he had left his job and spent the next twelve months physically tracking down the real murderer, preventing what would certainly have been a fifth murder.

"The cops were made to look like idiots," Tom said. "And maybe they were, because he was right, and they were wrong. This one—well, I'm having problems with it. There's the way the notes have fallen, for a start. If they fell. Come and see."

The scene-of-crime officers were erecting a tent to preserve the scene, a less easy job than it might be because the other occupants of the flats had to be able to get in and out of the door outside which the victim lay.

Wilma Fenton had left the Bull's Eye bingo club at approximately half past eight, having just won four hundred and thirty pounds. She always left at the interval of the main session in order to go home and walk her dog, because she didn't like doing that late at night. Half an hour later, she had been found outside the street door to the flats in which she lived. Baker had seen the incident, and her assailant had run off as he approached. He had apparently dropped the money in his haste, and in the still, cold night, the banknotes were still lying there, on Mrs. Fenton's body.

And it was indeed difficult to see how the money could have landed in that fashion if it had merely been dropped. The notes were separate, spread out, and not one had fluttered to the ground round the body; they were all neatly contained on it.

"According to her neighbor, Mrs. Fenton was a widow with no children. She thinks there's a brother in Cumbria—we're trying to trace him, but the neighbor has officially identified her. She also says she'll take care of Heinz the dog until the RSPCA can come and get it." He smiled. "Heinz is a mongrel, as you might have guessed."

Judy crouched down beside the body. "What's that?" she asked, pointing to a torn piece of paper partially covered by Mrs. Fenton's arm.

"That," said Tom, "is another of the problems I'm having with this. According to Tony Baker, that's the envelope her bingo winnings came in. He recognized it because he shared the prize with her, and the winners' envelopes have that decoration on the border. They've got Bull's Eye bingo club and the winner's name printed on them, but you can't see that because of how she's lying."

"So if the money was in a recognizable envelope, why would a mugger take the time to open it at the scene? Come to that— why wouldn't he just grab her bag? And how come she's lying on the envelope, instead of the other way round?"

"Quite."

They were clearly getting in the way of the tent-erectors, and they made their way down the route marked through the alley-way, out into the snow, heading for Tom's car, parked farther down Murchison Place.

Judy had a problem of her own. "Did you say Tony Baker had shared the prize with her?" she asked, as they got into the car. "Why on earth was he playing bingo in Malworth?"

"Research. He's doing a TV program about gambling."

"Oh, I see." She didn't really. Malworth seemed a funny place to choose to do research into something that you could do any-where. Why not somewhere more interesting? More flamboyant, like Blackpool, or more sophisticated, like London or Manches-ter?

"Baker left the bingo club a couple of minutes after half past eight—that's two minutes or so after Wilma left, and he went through the alleyway to the car park. He didn't see anyone at all on that trip, in the street or the alleyway. He went to his car and wrote up his notes, and had been doing that for about twenty min-utes when he remembered something he wanted to ask Michael Waterman—he's the guy who owns the bingo club."

Judy nodded.

"So he was going back there to talk to him, and when he got to the alleyway, he could see what looked like a scuffle between a man and a woman ahead of him. He thought they were probably drunk. Then he saw the woman fall to the ground. The man knelt beside her."

"He didn't see what he hit her with?"

"No. Baker didn't exactly hurry, not being that anxious to get involved, but as soon as the man heard him approach, he ran off. He may or may not have dropped the money in his desire to get away."

"Would he have had time to arrange the notes like that on Mrs. Fenton's body?" asked Judy.

"Just about," said Tom. "It's mostly fifties, isn't it? Eleven notes altogether—that wouldn't take too long. Anyway, we've got no description, and no other witnesses, but I've still got to talk to the nightclub bouncers—they might have seen someone hanging about."

"What are your other problems?"

"Mrs. Fenton obviously didn't go straight home. And since her whole reason for not staying for the second half is to walk her dog—*why* didn't she go straight home? Where was she for that half hour?"

"Did any of the people at the bingo club see anyone with her, or following her when she left?"

"No, guv. We're drawing blanks everywhere."

There was a knock on the passenger window, and Judy turned to see the long, thin face of Freddie, their tame pathologist.

"Good evening, Mrs. Lloyd," he said, as they got out of the car. "How is Miss Lloyd?"

"Very lively." Judy walked through the snow back toward the alley, the two men behind her.

"And Mr. Lloyd and your mama?"

"Probably worn out."

"Not come to blows yet?"

Judy shook her head good-humoredly. "Oh, you'd love it if they had, wouldn't you? Sorry to disappoint you, Freddie, but they get along very well."

"And how are Master and Miss Finch?" he asked Tom.

"They're blooming, thanks. They've not come to blows yet either."

"Good, good. Tell me, was it something they put in the tea? Or were you all just suddenly seized with an urge to reproduce in order to make sure that there are little coppers and copperettes for the future?"

Freddie was always cheerful when he had a murder victim to poke around in, something Judy found inexplicable. He was clearly eager to get started on his grisly task, because the sooner he got this bit over, the sooner he could get the body to the mortuary and really have fun.

The light from inside the tent shone eerily in the gloom of the narrow alleyway, and Judy shivered as they walked toward it. She told herself the cold weather had produced the shiver, but it hadn't. To the eyes of any normal mortal, murder scenes were uniformly dismal and bleak.

But to Freddie they were positively uplifting, and he beamed as they went into the tent. "Gangway," he said, crouching down and conducting the careful, eyes-only examination with which he always began. This one didn't take very long; after just a few moments, he sat back on his heels. "One blow to the back of the head which fractured the skull. Not a great deal of external bleeding, so the assailant isn't likely to have blood on his clothing." He looked up. "The usual blunt instrument," he said. "I suspect it might just have been an accident."

"Hitting people with blunt instruments isn't accidental, Freddie."

He smiled. "You're getting as bad as your husband. You know what I mean. I think her *death* might have been accidental, because I don't think this blow was intended to kill her—he probably meant just to knock her out. Some people have abnormally thin skulls—I think that's what we've got here. One blow wouldn't normally do this amount of damage."

"There's nothing to suggest that it might be more than just a spur-of-the-moment mugging?"

"Ah, now, that's where you differ from your husband. He groans if I suggest that a murder has deeper implications than are apparent at first, whereas you clearly want me to say that." He grinned. "Well, sorry, but so far it looks to me like a mugging with an unintentionally tragic outcome."

"We've got a missing half hour. It's possible the assailant was with the victim for thirty minutes or so before she died."

"Yes?" Freddie looked interested. "Well, leave me to it, and I'll see what I can come up with. There's no apparent reason to suspect sexual assault, but obviously I'll take swabs. And there are no other obvious injuries, but once I've got her clothes off I might find more." He got to his feet. "That's it," he told the attendants. "You can take the body to the mortuary now."

As the body was being put in the body bag, all three left the tent, and Freddie headed back down the alleyway to his car. "I'll be doing the postmortem examination at nine o'clock tomorrow morning," he said wickedly, as he walked away. "I don't know which of you wants the pleasure of my company just after you've had your breakfast." He raised his hand as a farewell, and didn't wait for a reply.

Judy smiled at Tom. "Didn't you say you were taking me to a nightclub?"

IN THE LITTLE LOUNGE BAR—THE ONLY BAR—OF THE TULLIVER Inn, Jack Shaw listened as Tony Baker recounted his story for the third time. Everyone who came in had to hear it, though that wasn't Baker's fault, Jack had to concede. Grace insisted.

She had brought a meal for him as soon as he came in, and now he was holding court while he ate, and she was hanging on his every word, even though she'd heard the story three times herself. Suddenly, he wasn't just handsome and suntanned and rich and famous—he was a bloody hero as well. And for what? Stumbling over a dead body.

In his capacity as editor, reporter, printer, publisher and distributor of the *Stoke Weston Clarion*, Jack had interviewed him. He had wondered what was going on in the alley, when he had left the nightclub to go back for Mr. Waterman. He had had to go the long way round, because the police had cordoned it off. So Baker's story was, Jack had to admit, interesting. The first time.

"I wish I'd chased the bastard now, because there was nothing I could do for her," Baker was saying.

Oh, yes, that would have been good, wouldn't it? Yes, Baker must be kicking himself for stopping to help a dead woman instead of getting himself all over the papers again. Jack got up and went to the bar before it closed. He didn't really want another drink, but Rosie the barmaid wasn't in tonight, so Grace would have to serve him.

Grace detached herself from the knot of people at Baker's table. "Yes, Jack, what can I get you?" she asked, lifting the flap and going behind the bar, smiling at him professionally.

"I'll have another one in there, please." He pushed his empty pint glass over to her.

Grace pulled his pint. The Tulliver still had old-fashioned beer-pumps, and it had been a while before Grace had got the hang of them. She was the consummate professional now. She put the replenished glass on the towel on the bar. "There you are, my love."

My love. Funny how people used expressions like that every day, to anyone and everyone. To complete strangers, sometimes. They weren't declarations of love—they didn't even suggest affection. My love, darling, pet, sweetheart . . . they were meaningless forms of address, and she wouldn't even know that she'd said it.

Jack paid for his beer, wishing he could think of something to say that would keep her from going back to Baker. Other people

had small talk, but he didn't. He spoke when he had something to
say, and he couldn't think of anything he wanted to say except
things that he couldn't say. Like how much he admired her, going
on a course and taking on this pub on her own when her husband
ran out on her before they'd been in the pub six months. Like how
much he enjoyed her company, or at least had enjoyed it before
Baker came here and she suddenly had eyes for no one else. Not
that she'd ever had eyes for him, not really. They were friendly—
he had hit it off with Stephen when he was a boy, and was as close
to the Hallidays as anyone was. But not the way he wanted to be.
He wanted to say all that, and he wanted to tell her how much
he would give to have her call him my love and mean it. But he
couldn't.

She was back with Baker now, as he had known she would be
as soon as her bar duties had been discharged. Stephen had confirmed that she fancied him. He hadn't really needed to hear
Stephen say it, but he had hoped that it was just jealousy that was
making him imagine that she looked at Baker the way she did.
Evidently not.

He supposed it really was jealousy that made him dislike
Baker as much as he did, but he couldn't be sure of that. Everyone
else seemed to get on with him, but Jack didn't like him and he
didn't trust him, and it seemed that Stephen felt the same way. If
Grace got involved with him, she'd regret it, he was sure of that.
A man like Baker would take whatever was on offer, and then
he'd be off, without a qualm. He and his wife had split up over the
South Coast murders business, because it was much more important to him than she was. Grace would do well to remember that.

Jack sipped his drink at the bar, and tried to ignore the ani-
mated chat from their table. Stephen had said that Baker wasn't
interested in her, and he certainly didn't seem to be making any
sort of a play for her. In fact, he barely included her in what he
was saying, to the point of ill manners, it seemed to Jack. So he
probably didn't have designs on her.

But the way she had reacted to Baker underlined just how little chance Jack stood with her. He wondered whether or not to do what he had come to do, and decided that he would. From his inside pocket, he pulled out the long, thin envelope, and left it on the shelf under the bar for Grace to find when she cleared up in the morning.

INNES PASSAGE RAN FROM MURCHISON PLACE TO WARING ROAD, which formed a T-junction with Stansfield Road, dead ahead of the alley. The last twenty yards or so of the alleyway formed the side wall of the nightclub, and Tom and Judy became aware of the dull beat of the disco as they walked toward the snow-filled night. As they exited the alley, they stopped for a moment to get the lay of the land. Across Waring Road, to the right, was the car park, with exits onto Stansfield Road, which stretched straight ahead of them, and Waring Road itself.

"Did Tony Baker have a view of the alleyway when he was in his car?" asked Judy.

"No, he didn't. He was parked right over there." Tom pointed to the far corner. "I had a quick look in his car in case the murder weapon was in there," he said, with a smile. "You can't be too careful."

"Did you think it might be?"

Tom wasn't entirely sure. He had no reason to suspect Tony Baker, but there was something about his story that he didn't like. He couldn't put his finger on it. So he had walked him to his car, and, on the pretext of being interested in buying one like it, had even got him to open the boot.

"No," he said. "Not really. But he knew her. And we've only his word for it that he was in his car on his own during that time, so we can't rule him out, can we?"

"But you didn't hang on to him," she said.

"No—well, he's diabetic, and he had to get back for his evening meal. I didn't want him passing out on me."

"What did you make of him?"

Tom scratched his head. "I don't know, to be honest. He's my other problem. I think you should talk to him yourself, guv. See what you think. He's coming in first thing to give us a formal statement."

"All right," said Judy. "I'll talk to him."

They turned left, and walked toward the door of the nightclub, the music growing ever louder. "Waterman owns the nightclub, too," said Tom. "I don't know if that's significant."

"It might be, but I doubt it. Michael Waterman owns a nightclub and a bingo hall in just about every sizeable town in Bartonshire. Not to mention betting shops." Judy stopped, and pointed up Waring Road, past the nightclub, and on the opposite side of the street, to what had once been three police houses. "He owns them, too," she said. "He's turning them into six luxury furnished flats. He heard about them through his brother-in-law, who is none other than DCS Yardley."

Tom objected to their recently appointed head of Bartonshire CID on principle; Yardley was only a couple of years older than him, and it had taken Tom all his time to make it to inspector, never mind chief superintendent. "I hope the flats have got good soundproofing," he muttered.

A man dressed in a dark suit, white shirt and tie was leaning against the wall just inside the door of the club, looking cold and very fed up, and detached himself from the wall at their approach. "It's members only," he said.

Tom explained who they were, and Jerry Wheelan allowed them to join him in the comparative shelter of the doorway. He said that he had seen a few people during the evening, but as he had no view of the alleyway, he didn't know if any of them had used it. Tom turned to check what view of the car park he had, and the answer was that he had no view of the car park either, so he wasn't going to be able to corroborate Baker's story. The most likely-sounding sighting that Wheelan had had was a youth with fair spiky hair, wearing a black leather jacket and dark trousers, and carrying a crash helmet.

"He ran along here, and crossed the road toward the old police houses," he said. "He disappeared round the back."

"What time was this?"

"About 8.35 or so."

No good, then, unless he came back, but Jerry hadn't seen him coming back.

"Of course, I'm not out here all the time," he said. "Well—not quite. Keith could have seen someone."

"Keith?"

"Keith Scopes. He's the other doorman. He's inside just now."

Tom glanced at Judy, and could see that she knew the name as well as he did. Keith Scopes had a fairly impressive record of street theft; nothing since the youth court as far as Tom could remember, but he had been very active in his early teens. And one of the times that he had tried to grab a woman's handbag he had hit her when she wouldn't let go, and she had to have stitches over her eye. He had been sent to a youth detention center for that, and that seemed, for once, to have done the trick, because he hadn't been in trouble since.

"And have you both been here all evening?"

Wheelan nodded, then backtracked. "Well—no. I've been here all evening, but Keith went off somewhere for a bit. He's supposed to be out here now to make up for it, but I got talked into letting him go in for a warm."

"When did he go off?"

"About half eight. That's how I know when I saw that kid with the motorcycle helmet, because Keith had only been gone about five minutes."

Perhaps the YDC hadn't done the trick. Perhaps he just didn't get caught these days. "How long was he away for?"

"About an hour and a half or so."

"Could we speak to him?"

"Yeah, sure. I'll get him."

They had a mugging, and a known mugger who had gone AWOL from his place of work at the time, but Tom, usually more than happy to accept things at face value, wasn't content this time with the simple explanation. There was more to it than that, he was sure. Because if it had been a mugging, it had been carried out by an inexperienced mugger, and Keith Scopes certainly wasn't that.

He saw the broad, well-muscled figure emerge from the dimly lit club, and felt old again. Five minutes ago he was a skinny little hooligan who had to have his mum with him when they interviewed him. Now, he was all bulging biceps. He would never have recognized him.

"Keith Scopes? DI Finch, Malworth CID. This is DCI Hill. We'd like to ask you a few questions."

Scopes nodded, his eyes wary. "I remember you, Mr. Finch. Jerry just said police. I was expecting a couple of uniforms—someone said it was a mugging."

"It might have started that way, but it ended in murder," said Tom.

Scopes's eyes widened slightly. "Murder?" he repeated. "Well—yeah, that would explain the ranks."

"You left the club at half past eight or so—why?"

"I came out for a smoke."

"Were you anywhere near Innes Passage?"

"Where?"

"The alley that runs down the side of this building."

"Is that what it's called? I didn't know."

"So now you do. Were you anywhere near there?"

"I was in there. It was snowing then, too. I went in to get some shelter."

"And did you see anyone else?"

"Yeah—a couple of people. Jack Shaw—he's the bloke that looks after the fruit machines for Waterman."

Did everyone in this drama have some connection with Michael Waterman? Of course, Tom thought, the only two establishments open in this part of Malworth on a Sunday evening belonged to him, so it probably wasn't so strange that the passersby were either his customers or his employees. No one else but residents would have any reason to be here, and the residents would be staying in on a night like this.

"Jack was acting a bit weird, now I come to think of it."

"Oh?"

"Stopped in the shadows for some reason. But I noticed he seemed to be limping—maybe he was having trouble with his leg or something."

"His leg?"

"He's got an artificial leg, but you'd never know. He can do anything anyone with two good legs can do." He grinned. "He even does Morris dancing."

"How?" said Tom.

"Badly." Keith laughed at his own joke. "They worked out routines that he could do. I think the whole thing might have been his idea. We never used to have Morris dancers."

"We?" said Judy.

"Stoke Weston," said Keith. "Jack lives there, too."

"You said you saw a couple of people," said Tom.

"Yeah—I saw a woman with Stephen Halliday. He's a steward at the bingo club. He's from Stoke Weston, too, as it happens. They were a little way behind Jack."

Everyone was from Stoke Weston. This was turning into a very weird case, thought Tom. "Could you describe the woman?"

Scopes drew in a breath, blew out his cheeks. "She was just an ordinary woman. Middle-aged. I think she had gray hair. She was wearing a light-colored coat."

That was Mrs. Fenton. She had indeed gone straight home, and she had been with someone. Things were looking up.

"And what does Stephen Halliday look like?"

"He's about my height—five-eight or so, fair hair. He was wearing a leather jacket, and I think he was carrying a motorcycle helmet. They stopped at the door to the flats."

Things had stopped looking up. That was the boy Wheelan had seen, and he was long gone by the time the murder took place. But maybe there were two youths with fair hair. "Did they go into the flats?"

"Dunno. I finished my cigarette, and left to come back here."

"Was this man Jack Shaw still in the alley when you left?" Judy asked.

"No. He stood there for a bit, and then just walked on again."

"Did you talk to him?"

"No—I don't think he saw me."

Or to put it another way, thought Tom, you think he might have seen you, which is why you're so ready to admit that you were hanging about in the alleyway shortly before the murder. "Why not?" he asked. "Were you standing in the shadows, too?"

"Let's just say I didn't draw attention to myself," Scopes said. "He's a bit of an anorak—bores the pants off you if you let him. I told you—he's a Morris dancer."

"So you don't know where he'd been or where he was going?"

"I don't know where he'd been, but he came here and had a word with Jerry, so he might be able to tell you."

"Is there somewhere I can talk to Jerry where there isn't music blaring?" asked Judy.

"Yeah—hang on."

Keith picked up his mobile, and deftly sent a text message. "There you are," he said to Judy. "I've told him to meet you in the office."

"Thank you," said Judy, and went inside.

Tom looked at Scopes for a moment before speaking. "You said you left the alley to come back here," he said. "But you didn't come back here, did you? You were gone for an hour and a half."

Scopes looked a little irritated by Wheelan's indiscretion. "I got a call on my mobile, and I had to deal with something. I didn't get back until about ten to ten."

"Can you tell me where you were?"

"Why should I?"

"Because it might rule you out of our investigation into this incident."

"It was private. Nothing to do with the police."

"A woman has been murdered. It looks as though she was the victim of a mugging—and that's something you know a bit about, isn't it?"

"Oh, for God's sake! I haven't done anything like that for five years. And I didn't mean to hurt that woman I got done for. I just shoved her."

"Maybe you didn't mean to kill this one."

"Am I a suspect?"

"Well, what do you think? You're a mugger, and she was mugged. So where were you at nine o'clock this evening?"

Several emotions chased themselves across Scopes's face as he went into an agony of indecision. He looked angry, scared and bewildered all at once, and had an argument with himself before he spoke. "At nine o'clock, I was in Barton," he said. "I was doing a job for someone."

"Who? Where?"

Scopes shook his head. "I can't tell you that."

"In that case, you'll stay a suspect."

"Fine. When you've got enough evidence to arrest me, I'll worry."

"Right," said Judy, emerging from the club. "If you've finished with Mr. Scopes, I think we can be off."

The snow still fell, less heavy now, but just as persistent, as they walked back toward the alley, quiet and still now that everyone had gone.

"How did you know this was called Innes Passage?" Judy asked.

Tom grinned. "Hitch told me. I thought you'd be impressed."

She rubbed cold hands together as she walked. "Wheelan thought I ought to know that Scopes borrowed a fiver from him earlier in the evening, so he was obviously in need of cash."

"He says he was in Barton at nine o'clock." Tom told Judy what Scopes had said.

"Did you believe him?"

"Yes, I think I did. I think he was frightened to tell me who he was doing this job for. Frightened of something, anyway."

"And Wheelan said that Jack Shaw went to warn him that Waterman was at the bingo club—Waterman doesn't normally work on Sundays, so I gather that everything's a little more relaxed than it is during the week, when he's likely to pop in. He says Shaw arrived at about twenty-five to nine and left again just before Keith came back."

"I'll have a word with him tomorrow," said Tom. "He might have seen something Jerry didn't see. And I want to know if he saw Halliday coming back, and if so, when."

"We'll need to talk to Stephen Halliday anyway," said Judy. "He might know if Mrs. Fenton went into her flat or not. Did she go in and come out again, do you think?"

"If she did, it wasn't to walk the dog," said Tom. "Because it was in the flat, not running round loose in the street."

"If something else brought her out again, we have to know what. Did someone telephone her? Call on her? Had she left something at the bingo club? *Did* Stephen Halliday come back?"

"The phone was checked. The last call to her number was made yesterday evening, so I don't think she got a phone call that brought her out again. Halliday might have come back, I suppose, but it seems a bit unlikely."

"It does indeed."

As they walked back out into the thin, fine snow that still fell on Murchison Place, Judy turned to go to her car. "Right," she said. "I will be talking to Tony Baker—as requested—first thing in the morning. Which means," she added, smiling sweetly at him, "that you have a date with Freddie. Goodnight, Tom."

If Tom had a quid for every time she'd put one over on him, he'd be a rich man. "Goodnight, guv."

"Oh—and tell Liz I've got another load of clothes for her. I should have brought them with me—I didn't think."

"Will do."

Tom and Liz had, with the birth of Charlotte, got close to

Judy and Lloyd. Judy felt less than expert in the matter of bringing up a baby, and Liz had already done it twice, so her advice was
frequently sought. Charlotte's arrival had in its turn made Tom
and Liz think wistfully of when their two were babies, and that
had resulted in twins, born just under a year after Charlotte, a boy
and a girl. And that had been a clever stroke, Tom thought, because Becky got all the clothes Charlotte had grown out of, which
was a pretty fair saving, all things considered.

So she didn't *always* come out on top, he thought, with a
smile.

WHAT HAD BOTHERED GARY ON THE OTHER OBSERVATIONS WAS
that it entailed letting all the deals go down, but at least he had
understood the necessity, because their presence had had to be
covert until they knew they had all the information necessary for
the raids to succeed. But they would be breaking cover tonight
anyway.

Tonight's operation was the culmination of a drug offensive
that had taken eighteen months of painstaking work, he knew
that. The Chief Constable had announced it in his mission statement two years ago. Attacking the drug menace on all fronts, he'd
called it. And it was being handled entirely by Bartonshire drug
squad, because big though the operation was by their standards, it
was still small-scale by national standards. It had cost a fortune,
and the reputation of the force depended on its success. But what
was the point, if all that stuff was on the streets already? Three
people had called at the candy store so far, and they would be sup-
plying any number of minor dealers.

"Why don't we just raid them tonight?" he asked. "Why wait
till morning? Three dealers have been and gone, and they'll have
sold the stuff to three dozen street-dealers by this time tomorrow."

"Oh, no, they won't," said Kelly. "We've been keeping tabs on
them all evening, and we'll continue to do so." He smiled. "This
way we're getting the wholesalers, the dealers, and the small fry

that hang about the pubs and clubs and school playgrounds. I admit I didn't recognize the one that came at nine o'clock, but we've got him on video, and we'll get him eventually. But if we'd arrested him as he left, we'd have blown the whole operation."

Gary realized for the first time just what a huge operation it was, and he might be a very small cog in a very big wheel, but from having felt bored and uninvolved, he suddenly felt elated that he was part of it.

MIDNIGHT. BEN'S TRAIN WOULD BE PULLING OUT OF SHEFFIELD just about now, and his next stop would be Leuchars. He was off back to St. Andrews, and the life that Michael knew next to nothing about.

Michael had left the bingo club at ten, and had come home to his big, empty house. He had asked Jack Shaw in for a beer, but he had said he was going to pop in to the Tulliver before it closed. He had suggested that Michael come with him, but Michael had felt that he would be surplus to requirements, since Jack's sole reason for going there was that he was in love with Grace Halliday. Not that he had ever thought of mentioning this to her, of course. He just worshipped from afar. But he still wouldn't want Michael there, not really.

He wished Ben had been home a bit more often, so that they could have had a proper conversation. They needed to talk about Ben's inheritance, for one thing. And Michael wanted to know how Ben was getting on at university. Was he still enjoying it? Did he know what sort of job he wanted to do when he left? How were his studies going? Did he think he'd come out of it with a good degree?

He wondered what it would have been like to go to university. It was hard for him to imagine adult learning—his tuition had ceased at sixteen, and education to him had been a succession of people telling you what to do and when to do it, and making a hell of a fuss if you didn't.

He had skipped school as often as he'd gone; some money-making scheme or another had always required his attention more urgently than his lessons. He knew that he could have made something of himself at school, could have passed exams and gone on to university like Ben had, but the prospect had been too dim and distant to mean anything to him.

In the here and now, he had thought, with the lack of fore-sight of a teenage tearaway, there was money to be made. But he had always overreached himself, and lost it again. The steadying influence of Josephine had harnessed his potential; once he'd met her, he hadn't looked back. Making money was second nature to him, and Josephine's caution had stopped him sinking it all into some crazy scheme that would fail. She had made him take it step-by-step, and it had worked.

If he hadn't met Josephine he'd have ended up in jail, there was no doubt about that at all. But she had financed him, and she wouldn't countenance anything even faintly illegal being done with her money, so he'd had to play it straight, and it had paid off. People knew they could trust him with their money. Of course, there had always been things that had to be done, but he had had the sense to pay other people to do them, and pay them well enough to keep him out of it if they were caught. Because in his world it wasn't enough to be liked, or respected. A bit of fear al-ways came in handy. And those who crossed Michael knew that they would be in trouble, so no one did it lightly.

He knew he still had a criminal mentality, even if he had been steered away from it over thirty years ago, before he'd ac-quired the criminal record that he surely would have had, and that would have prevented him making his living the way he did. Violence was still a quick and easy answer to most problems, he found. Maybe he should have been more of a disciplinarian at home, he thought. Maybe if Ben had had a clout or two growing up he would have more respect for his wishes now. But he could never have brought himself to lay a finger on Ben.

He'd heard the remark that someone had made about Halliday just as he was leaving tonight. Was it meant for his ears? Did everyone know about it except him? How long had it been going on? It wouldn't be going on much longer, not if he could help it.

He wished Josephine was here. She could have talked to Ben, made him see sense. But Ben barely remembered Josephine; she was just a photograph to him. He had cried all night when Michael had told him that Mummy had gone to heaven and wouldn't be able to come back to him, but Ben didn't remember all that distress now, thank God.

Michael did, and his lip began to tremble as he thought of the little boy he had tried to console while tears coursed down his own face. Some bastard, drunk behind the wheel, had taken away his wife and Ben's mother, and no one had ever come near to replacing her. He had had the odd fling, usually with a married woman. He had never wanted to remarry.

And now he didn't know what to do about Ben, and he wanted Josephine's wise counsel more than he ever had.

TONY BAKER LAY DOWN ON THE BED, SUDDENLY VERY TIRED NOW that the adrenaline had stopped pumping. Twice in one night, he had had a heart-stopping moment. First, the bingo win, and then . . .

For all his expertise in the field of violent crime, he had never before been the first person at the scene of a murder, and he had been within yards of the murderer. At first, he hadn't realized who the victim was. Or that she was dead. He had caught a glimpse, no more, of the figure who ran off.

But he had stopped to assist the victim, discovering first that she was dead, secondly that she was Wilma, and then—to his surprise and some shame—that he didn't really care about that. No— when he found Wilma, he was simply annoyed that it was nothing more interesting than a mugging. That was what he had felt as he had looked at Wilma's lifeless body, while he could still hear her assailant's footsteps in the alleyway. Irritation. Not very laudable, he accepted, as he switched out the bedside lamp, but that was how it was.

By the time the police had arrived, however, he had had time to think, and it looked a little more interesting than it had at first. Tony didn't point out the unusual aspects to the investigating officer, because he felt reasonably sure that the man would find them for himself, and he didn't want to be accused of making a habit of doing the police's job for them.

Finch looked like a slightly harassed cherub, with his mop of golden curls. Efficient enough, though. And he seemed impervious to the weather, so he must be tougher than he looked. Tony had had his gloved hands deep in the pockets of his leather coat all the time they had been talking; Finch, wearing just a suit, wasn't even shivering.

Finch had listened to his story, and had asked him a few questions, not commenting on the answers. It was impossible to tell from his demeanor whether or not he thought he was dealing with more than just a routine mugging. But he had said that his Chief Inspector might want to talk to Tony, so he probably had noticed the oddities.

In his car, Tony had rung the newspaper for whom he wrote his column, and told them of his new adventure—he was just in time to catch the late editions, and the editor was very pleased that he was, especially since news had been slow that day. It would be given a good deal of prominence, because even if some major celebrity was caught with his trousers down right now, Tony thought, with a satisfied smile, it would be too late to make tomorrow's edition.

He felt a shade guilty, but not much. Why shouldn't he make as much of what had happened as he could? All right, someone had murdered the woman, and it might be a touch insensitive to use her death in the way he had, but if he hadn't been able to help her he could at least help himself. After all, he had a TV series in the pipeline, and all publicity was good publicity.

It was only when Stephen came in that Tony realized that he

was the last person he had seen with Mrs. Fenton. It had struck him as odd at the time, because if Stephen's bike was parked round the back of the bingo club, there seemed to be no reason for him to be on foot in Murchison Way.

When Tony told him what had happened, Stephen had said immediately that he had been with her, said that he had walked her to her door, in what seemed like a completely innocent re-sponse to the news. But Tony was having trouble with that. Why had he been running after Wilma, calling her name, desperate to catch up with her, as though his life depended on it? And why had he left at the interval, come to that? Tony had spoken to him ear-lier in the day, and he seemed to think he would be working his normal shift. The decision to leave at the interval had been made after he had started work. After Wilma had won the money? Surely not.

But it was all a bit strange.

CHAPTER THREE

TONY CHECKED HIS BLOOD SUGAR LEVELS, AND USED HIS chart to work out how many carbohydrates were in the breakfast that Grace was even now preparing for him. He supposed this flexible regime would give him a bit more freedom about what he ate and when he ate, but it took a bit of getting used to. He had been on a course, but now he was flying without a net, and that was a bit scary. He gave himself what he hoped was an appropriate injection of insulin, and went downstairs.

Breakfast was always in Grace's kitchen-diner; he ate his evening meal in the pub itself, but with only one guest to cater for, Grace found it simpler just to have him join her in the mornings. Or so she said. Tony thought she liked the idea of him having his feet under her table. And, of course, it was always à deux; Stephen, like most teenagers, never got up until after breakfast.

"Is that you, Tony?" Grace called, as soon as she heard his step on the stair.

"It is," he said, as he joined her in the kitchen. "How are you this morning?"

"Fine, thanks. Are you all right? You were a bit shaken up."

"Oh, I'm all right. Though I honestly thought I was unshockable until last night."

"It was a horrible thing to find."

Yes, he supposed it was. But it had been his own reaction to it, rather than the discovery itself, that had shocked him, though he was reasonably comfortable with it now. When he was thirteen years old he had had to adjust to the fact that he had diabetes; at first, it had frightened him, worried him. Then he had become resigned to the fact that there was a part of him that was different from most people, that it might lead to other serious problems, and that he had to live with it. This was much the same. Perhaps his years of studying crime had made him indifferent to its horror, but so what?

"Your breakfast will be about ten minutes. You just relax and read the paper or something." She looked as though she was going to say something else, but if she had been, she changed her mind, and turned her attention back to the cooker.

He noticed the Valentine card on the sideboard, and took a peek inside when Grace wasn't looking. It was a gently comic one—not vulgar, but not overly romantic, and in traditional fashion, it was unsigned.

He read the paper, but Grace didn't get anything as downmarket as the journal for which he wrote his column, so he would have to wait to see what they'd done with the story. He'd pick one up on his way to the police station.

She joined him at the table with the bowl of muesli that was all she had for breakfast.

"Do you think Stephen will want a lift to the police station with me?" he asked. "It's dodgy weather for an even more dodgy motorbike to cope with, and I think he should talk to them. He must have been one of the last people to see her alive."

Stephen had had a lot of expense lately with the bike, and it was just possible that the temptation of Mrs. Fenton's winnings might have been too much. Tony had no idea if the person he saw running away from the scene could have been Stephen—he really only saw a shadow. And Stephen had seemed genuinely upset when he was told about what had happened. But as far as Tony could see, Wilma had been hit just once, so whoever did kill her might not have realized that he had. And if that was Stephen, that would explain how his distress could be so convincing, if he was discovering that he had murdered someone.

"They won't think he had anything to do with it, will they?" asked Grace, as if she had been reading his thoughts.

"Well—they have to suspect everyone at the outset. I'll be on their list, and so, I expect, will Stephen, once they know he was with her shortly before she died." He smiled. "But unlike me, he at least was presumably somewhere else altogether at nine o'clock."

"But that's the funny thing," she said. "He won't say where he was. I asked him, but he said he was just out somewhere."

Tony frowned. He hadn't known the Hallidays all that long, but Stephen didn't seem the secretive type. "Well—maybe he was somewhere he'd rather his mother didn't know about," he said. "I'm sure he won't mind telling the police."

She smiled, looking reassured, and Tony ate, reading the paper as instructed. But every time he looked up, she would look away. It was distinctly odd, and a little unsettling on the digestion. And now, when he looked up, she looked at the Valentine card, and then back at him, and smiled. "I found it behind the bar this morning," she said. "But it isn't signed, so I don't know who to thank."

Oh, my God, she thought it was from him. He hadn't the faintest idea how to disabuse her of the idea. Denying it when she hadn't even asked him would simply confirm her in her mistaken belief. It seemed that he was getting the thousand shocks that flesh was heir to all at once.

"Oh, I'm sure you have many admirers, Grace—it could be from anyone. That's the whole point of Valentines, isn't it? You don't know who they're from."

She picked up her plate. "Well, if it was you, thank you very much. It really made me smile first thing, and that's not easy when I'm facing a pile of washing-up." She laughed, and stood up. "Tea or coffee?"

"Tea, please."

As soon as he'd drunk it, he was going to the police station— if Stephen wasn't up by then, he'd have to make his own way there. He certainly wasn't staying here alone with Grace thinking he'd sent her a Valentine.

"Well," he said, as he put his cup down. "I'd better make tracks." The tea had almost burned his mouth, he had drunk it so quickly. He made it out into the corridor, but his eye was caught by the open door on the opposite wall. He'd never really noticed that there was a room there before. And Stephen wasn't still in bed. He was up, dressed, and busy, just about to put a newly cleaned rifle back in the gun cabinet attached to the wall. "Good morning, Stephen," he said, knocking on the open door, and going in. "I didn't know you shot."

Stephen turned. "Hello," he said. "Yes—Jack started teaching me not long after we came here." He smiled. "It was great fun. He taught me to fish, too."

"Well, there's two things we've got in common." Tony held out a hand. "May I?" he asked.

Stephen handed him the rifle, and Tony whistled. "This is very nice," he said, squinting through the sight, the rifle pointed at the ceiling. He wondered how Stephen could have afforded such an expensive rifle. Perhaps he made a habit of relieving his customers of their winnings. "Very nice indeed. It must have set you back a bit."

"No," said Stephen. "It was a present from Mr. Waterman."

"That was very generous of him." Tony held out the rifle to Stephen. "Do you hunt as well?"

"Do you mean foxhunting?" Stephen took the rifle, and locked it up in the cabinet. "No. I don't agree with foxhunting."

"Ah," said Tony. "That's because you're a townie at heart—not really a country boy. Very unsporting, shooting foxes. What chance does a fox stand against a rifle? At least they can try to outwit the hunt—and usually do."

"It's pest control. It wouldn't be much good if I gave the fox a sporting chance."

"True. Ever shot deer?"

"No."

"Oh, you should try it. If you enjoy shooting, you would be bound to enjoy deerstalking."

"I don't think I'd want to shoot deer," Stephen said, his face slightly troubled. "I just shoot pests."

Tony smiled. "Then I'd better be on my way," he said. "Unless you want a lift to the police station—I presume you are going to talk to them?"

"Yes," said Stephen. "But no, thanks—I don't want a lift."

"Fine. See you later."

"RAY? MIKE HERE."

He heard a groan at the other end of the line. "I know why you're ringing," Ray said.

"Why is my bingo club splashed all over the tabloids?"

"One tabloid," said Ray. "I can only imagine it's because Tony Baker writes a column for them. You didn't think we told them, did you?"

Oh. Michael felt a little less aggrieved. "Does he? I didn't know. But it's bad enough having this happen to one of my winners without the whole world knowing."

"I understand that. Don't worry, I'll have a word with Judy Hill—she'll set Baker straight. But there's nothing much we can do about it now."

"Can I speak to her? Have you got a number I can get her at?"

There was a rare moment of silence before Ray spoke. "I did say I'd have a word, Mike, and I will."

"No—not about that. It's just that . . . well, I was at the bingo club myself last night, but I'd gone by the time the police were there. I might have some information that will help."

"Oh—right. Okay, I'll tell her to expect a call from you."

He jotted down the number. "Thanks, Ray."

Michael looked out of the window at the cold, bleak morning. Snow lay everywhere still—not thick, but untroubled by the sun, which was presumably up there somewhere above the layers of cloud. It would probably snow again. It matched his mood.

Yesterday had to have been one of the worst days of his life, and his housekeeper's paper of choice had done nothing to make today any better.

"MR. BAKER? DCI JUDY HILL." JUDY SAT DOWN OPPOSITE TONY Baker, and opened her notebook, in which she had jotted down some points on which she wanted some clarification. She had read Baker's statement, written in his own neat, clear hand, which was in all essentials what he had told Tom last night.

She had read something else as well that morning; something that DS Yardley had drawn to her attention. Her phone had rung at precisely one minute past nine, and Yardley had—she had timed him—spoken for precisely eight minutes and twenty seconds before she was able to get a word in. But in essence, what he had told her was that what had begun as a very unfortunate local incident was now going to be investigated with at least one national newspaper's deep interest.

She had caused a copy of the offending paper to be purchased, and laid it on the table. "Your doing?" she said.

Baker put on a look of mock shame, then grinned. "I work for them," he said. "What did you expect me to do?"

She folded the paper and put it down beside her chair. "I would expect you, of all people, to be aware that the police don't always want to release full details of a murder, for very good reasons."

"Oh, come on! I didn't say any more than you'll have said in your very own press release."

That was true. Judy felt that she was probably going to lose this argument—she was only having it because Yardley had insisted that she let Baker know the error of his ways. But what he had said interested her. "What more could you have said?" she asked.

He sat back. "I could have asked why a mugger would take

the quite unnecessary additional risk of opening the envelope and taking the money out while he was still with the victim—but I didn't. I could have said that it would have been very unlikely for the money to have been spread out like that if it had been dropped in the assailant's haste to get away. But I thought you might not want that generally known."

"Anything else?"

"You've got my statement. You know what I saw."

"Yes. But I just want to ask a few supplementary questions, Mr. Baker. I understand you left the bingo club at the interval of the main session, as did Mrs. Fenton. Did anyone else leave the bingo club at the interval?"

"I wouldn't know."

"Can I ask why you were playing bingo in Malworth?" She smiled. "That's the sort of thing that happens in dreams," she added. "Seeing well-known TV personalities in odd places."

He smiled back, and the slightly frosty atmosphere thawed a little. "I'm doing research into people's gambling habits. Bingo's making a comeback."

"Why Malworth?" Judy asked.

"Why not?" He smiled. "The program covers Monte Carlo and Las Vegas, and obviously everyone will expect the British episode to be London. But I didn't want to do the obvious. London clubs and casinos look exactly like the ones in Monte Carlo and Las Vegas. I wanted something contrasting, something different. Something a little more down-to-earth, that the British viewers could relate to, and that might entertain non-British viewers. We are a nation of gamblers—we don't spend as much as some other countries, but three out of four adults in Britain gamble on something, did you know that?"

"But why Malworth?" Judy persisted. For all she knew, the man had had a score to settle with Wilma Fenton.

"Chance. It isn't just Malworth—it's the whole of Barton-shire. I met Michael Waterman at Ascot, and he suggested I come here and sample gambling with the personal touch."

Judy abandoned that line of questioning. He was probably telling the truth anyway. She moved on to her next note. "I know why Wilma Fenton left at the interval," she said. "Why did you?"

"Because I've already played the national bingo game, so I didn't need to do that again. What I hadn't done before was win, and I wanted to get down my feelings about that before they'd gone."

"Did anyone else leave the bingo club at the interval?"

Judy had trained herself years ago to repeat questions while sounding as though she had never asked them before. It irritated people, got under their skin. Unnerved them, as it was unnerving Baker now. His face had lost its urbane been-there-done-that look, and he was failing to meet her eye.

"I can't say I noticed."

He was an attractive man, Judy supposed, but the attractiveness was all a little too false for her. Real people doing real jobs just didn't get their hair done like that. Their teeth weren't that perfect. And real people doing real jobs weren't deeply suntanned in February. Though if he had been to Las Vegas, that might excuse the tan.

"This research is for a television series?"

"And a book. The notes are for the book, really."

"Was anyone else in the car park?"

"Do I need an alibi?" He smiled again. "Sorry—I know you have to suspect me. DI Finch had a rather unsubtle look inside my car last night."

She smiled back. "I'm just trying to find possible witnesses."

"I didn't see anyone else in the car park. But perhaps someone going to or from the nightclub saw something."

"It's unlikely," Judy said. "The nightclub customers either park in the same car park as you did or come by taxi—they don't use the alleyway coming to the club. They use it leaving, when most of the taxi customers walk to the taxi rank rather than wait at the club for taxis that might not turn up."

Baker shook his head. "So the alleyway's deserted most of the evening? That practically invites muggers to do their worst."

Judy nodded her agreement. Maybe Murchison Place and its alleyways would get cameras now—too late, as usual. "You left the car intending to go back to the bingo club. What time would this be?"

"A few minutes to nine, I believe. About two minutes before I rang the police—and you'll have a record of when that was. When I got to the alley, I could see two people—a man and a woman—having some sort of argument, then I saw her fall to the ground. He dropped to his knees beside her. At first I thought he was trying to loosen her clothing or something."

"So he was bending over her?"

"Yes. He certainly seemed to be doing something." He raised his eyebrows slightly. "Arranging the banknotes, perhaps?"

Judy didn't respond, and Baker carried on.

"But when he heard my footsteps, he got up and ran away toward Murchison Place. All I can tell you about him is that he was wearing dark clothing. I went to see if I could help the woman, but . . ."

"Did you touch anything, Mr. Baker?"

"No. I felt for a pulse, that was all. Then I used my mobile to phone the police, and—very commendably, I have to say—they arrived within minutes and began sealing off the area."

Judy smiled. "I'm glad we meet with your approval," she said.

"I was very impressed with the young detective sergeant—Hitchin, is it? He was on top of things as soon as he arrived."

Judy moved on to the next item on her list. "I understand that you knew Wilma Fenton—did you know her well?"

He looked amused. "Hardly," he said. "But I've interviewed a number of people in some depth, and Wilma was one of them. I saw her in her flat, which is how I knew she lived there."

"Oh, I see. Was that a television interview?"

"No. I talk to hundreds of people when I do research. Sometimes I use what they tell me in the books, and at the same time I'm assessing their potential as TV interviewees. Then, when the filming starts, I know exactly what and who we want to see on the screen."

Judy felt a little as though she was interviewing Baker on TV; something about his manner, about his way of answering a question, that sounded very different from the hundreds of other interviews she had conducted.

"Do you often work in your car?"

"No. I usually go back to the office I've rented in Stansfield, and put my impressions on the computer. I can e-mail any photographs I've taken to my colleague in London, and she can produce a first draft of the script for that particular segment. But I was anxious to set down my feelings as soon as I could, as I said, so I used the laptop."

"Did anyone else leave the bingo club at the interval?"

Judy had had a call from Michael Waterman that morning telling her that Stephen Halliday had left the bingo club at the interval, and had run after and caught up with Mrs. Fenton, going into the alleyway with her. They already knew he had been in the alley with her, but what they hadn't known was that he normally worked until half past ten, and had asked if he might leave early just before he made the payouts to Mrs. Fenton and Mr. Baker. They would be talking to young Mr. Halliday. But the part that interested her most was that he lived at the Tulliver Inn. His mother was Tony Baker's landlady. And Waterman had been with Baker when he saw Halliday.

"You've already asked me that twice."

Judy didn't say anything. She just waited.

Baker sighed. "Stephen left at the interval," he said. "Stephen Halliday—he's a steward at the club."

"Why didn't you tell me that the first time I asked? And why didn't you tell DI Finch that last night?"

"I can't claim to know Stephen all that well, but I'm staying with the Hallidays, and I didn't want to drag his name into it, because I found her half an hour after Stephen had left the club. I had no reason to think that he had anything to tell you."

Judy concluded the interview then, feeling much as Tom had. She didn't know what to make of Tony Baker. As they left the interview room, she discovered that a Mr. Shaw was there in response to their appeals to anyone who was in the area, and since everyone else was busy, she saw him herself, leaving someone else to show Tony Baker out.

"I went through that alley not long before it happened," Shaw said once they were seated. "I heard her behind me, talking."

"Did you know who she was talking to?"

"Young Stephen Halliday. He's a steward at the bingo club."

"Do you know Stephen Halliday well?"

"Yes—him and his mum. I work for Waterman Entertainment, servicing the fruit machines. Mr. Waterman supplied one to the Tulliver Inn, and I service it, too. I got to know Stephen first, really. His dad left not long after they arrived in Stoke Weston, and I kind of . . . well, took him under my wing, I suppose. They've been there almost seven years now."

"Could you hear what Stephen and Mrs. Fenton were saying?"

"They were talking about her win. She was excited about it. Stephen was saying it was a pity she'd had to share the prize with Tony Baker—that sort of thing."

"It was quite amicable?"

"Oh, goodness me, yes. Stephen's a very nice lad." He frowned. "You surely don't think he had anything to do with it, do you?"

"We don't know who did or didn't have anything to do with it, Mr. Shaw," said Judy. "That's what we're trying to find out. Did you see anyone else in the alley?"

"No. Mind, that doesn't mean there wasn't someone else there—you can stay out of sight if you want to."

"Yes," said Judy. "In fact, we've been told that you stopped in the shadows for a few moments—is that right?"

Shaw looked slightly alarmed. "Well . . . yes. I was waiting for Stephen, really, but then he stood talking to the lady, so I just carried on." He frowned. "Who told you that?"

Judy smiled, and moved on to her next question. "Did you see Stephen again last night?" she asked.

"Yes—I went to see Jerry Wheelan at the nightclub, and we were standing in the doorway when Stephen ran past us and across the road."

"Do you know when that would have been?"

"Only a couple of minutes after I got there, because after that I sat inside the door to the reception area, out of the cold. It would have been between half past eight and twenty-five to nine, I think."

"So you wouldn't know if and when Stephen came back?"

"No."

Judy made a note. "Can you tell me why you were there?"

"Yes—I was driving Mr. Waterman. He'd been drinking in the early evening, and he won't drive if he's had anything to drink—he lost his wife because of a drunk driver. He wanted me to take him to the bingo club in Malworth and take him home again at ten."

"Did he say why?"

"No. It was odd, because he never works on Sundays. Nothing religious—just that he likes his game of golf and to wind down. I thought he must be doing a surprise spot check or something, so I went over to warn the lads at the nightclub."

Mr. Shaw, having taken refuge from the weather in the nightclub's reception area, hadn't been in a position to see anyone else coming or going along Waring Road. Judy thanked him, and he left.

*   *   *

"STEPHEN, IT'LL BE LUNCHTIME BEFORE YOU GET THERE AT THIS rate! What are you doing up there?"

Stephen had spent a long time in the bathroom, getting himself ready. He'd feel better able to face the police if he looked good. Now back in his bedroom, he was surveying his wardrobe—not extensive, but expensive. He never bought anything that didn't have a designer label. That wasn't easy to do on a steward's salary, but he worked part-time in the bar, and saved up. Eventually, he decided on smart casual.

"You're not going on the bike," his mother said, when he got downstairs. "The snow's frozen hard—it would be far too dangerous. Do you want me to take you in?"

Oh God, no. Turning up with his mother—no, he didn't think so. "I'll get a taxi," he said.

But, he discovered, when his mother answered the knock at the door, he didn't have to get a taxi, because the police had come for him.

KEITH STUMBLED DOWNSTAIRS, HAVING PULLED ON MICHELLE'S bathrobe, and opened the door to the postman, who handed him a pile of stuff done up in two rubber bands.

"Thanks, mate," he said, closing the door and pulling the paper from the letter box. Michelle got mad about that—the boy never put it all the way through. But now that she had a new job she left the house long before it came, so the boy didn't get into trouble so much these days. Keith rarely read it, but he glanced at it as he went into the living room just in case there was anything interesting in it.

The headline was some lame story about a soap star Keith had never heard of being refused a flight because he was drunk, but the column down the side of the front page made Keith's eyes, still half-shut with sleep, open wide. It was all about how Tony Baker, their very own columnist, "the man who in the eighties put the combined might of four police forces to shame," had witnessed a mugger fleeing the scene of what turned out to be not just a brutal assault, but a cold-blooded murder.

Keith put the mail down on the table, and sat down, turning to the promised full story inside.

The double-page spread wasn't, of course, about what had happened last night; there had been no time for them to get much detail about that. It was about how Tony Baker had succeeded where the police had failed, almost twenty years ago. Facsimiles of their own headlines, photographs of a young Tony Baker, of his wife, who had left him during "his relentless pursuit of the truth behind the South Coast murders," were splashed across the pages. Keith had never even heard of the man before yesterday, but then he hadn't been born when these murders had begun.

And now, the paper said, their man had been the sole witness to another murder. According to the paper, Wilma Fenton had been to her regular bingo game, and for the first time in her life she had won a decent amount of money—over four hundred pounds. The murder had happened right outside the street door to the flats where she lived, a door reached via a grim, damp, badly lit alleyway. She had been just moments away from safety when she met her death at the hands of someone lurking in the dank and dismal passageway.

And it happened as Tony Baker had entered that same alleyway; he had seen the victim fall to the ground, had seen the killer flee the scene, had tried to help the victim, but was too late.

An incident that could have happened in any street in any town in Britain, the article went on. An incident that would have made the local paper and the local news, because it was of no great interest to anyone else. But this time, the nation's most outspoken newspaper would be watching to see how the police handled it.

Because their man Baker was troubled—not just because an inoffensive, middle-aged widow had been so brutally slain on a night when she should have been celebrating her good luck, but because it didn't make sense. If Wilma's callous killer was after her winnings, the paper said, he didn't get them. The winnings were left behind, intact. What sort of mugger left his takings behind? Had he ever intended stealing the money? Was there more to this murder than met the eye? That, it said, was what Tony Baker was asking himself, what this newspaper was asking itself, and what the editor hoped the police were asking themselves.

And now, as he laid the paper down with a puzzled frown, it was what Keith Scopes was asking himself. He wanted to know more about these South Coast murders. He went over to the computer, and switched it on. There was bound to be stuff about them on the Web.

"HOW WAS FREDDIE?" JUDY ASKED, WHEN TOM GOT BACK TO THE station.

"Very pleased with himself," said Tom. "Wilma Fenton did indeed have an unusually thin skull. The blow would have been very unlikely to have proved fatal had it been inflicted on someone else. 'Simply a mugging that went all wrong' was how he described it."

"Did he have any idea what the murder weapon could have been?"

"The best he could say was that it had no sharp edges. The indentation suggests something rounded, so I asked if a crash helmet could have done it, but he said no, it was something smaller and much heavier than that. Small, heavy and round."

"Like a large pebble, maybe?" said Judy.

"Could be. The alleyway's cobbled—if one had worked loose, her assailant might have picked it up—" He scratched his head. "But that doesn't explain the half hour, guv. I think someone must have been in the flat with her, and picked something up in there."

Judy nodded. "We'll see what the SOCOs come up with. But if he was in the flat with her, and did it in there, why would she still have all her outdoor clothes on? It doesn't make sense."

"Nothing makes sense," said Tom. "If they weren't in the flat, where were they?"

Judy's phone rang, and she picked it up. "Right," she said, hanging up again. "Halliday's here," she said. "Jack Shaw has confirmed that he was the young man Jerry Wheelan saw, so unless he came back, I doubt that he's our man, but let's see what he has to say for himself."

"He's got no record," said Tom. "But he holds a firearms certificate."

Judy smiled. "It isn't a crime, Tom."

"Well, you know what I feel about guns. If you want to own one, you're not a fit person to do so."

"But you're not one to make sweeping statements."

Tom fought his corner. "It's for a Winchester bolt-action rifle. And the cartridges he uses are the same as the 5.56 NATO cartridges, according to the bloke I spoke to in ballistics."

"5.56 NATO cartridges being what, exactly?"

Tom frowned.

Judy grinned. "You haven't the faintest idea, have you?"

"I might not know what 5.56 means, but they fire the bullets soldiers use, so I know they don't put them in peashooters. That's a serious weapon he's got."

"What does he use it for?"

"Controlling what they call 'pest animals' on the certificate. He shoots on a neighboring farm."

Judy got up. "In theory," she said, "the fact that he has been given a certificate should mean that he is of impeccable character, level-headed, and sane."

"In theory, the bumblebee can't fly."

Judy laughed. "Well, since you think he's Al Capone, you lead."

Despite having been given a very good description by Jerry Wheelan, Tom was still a little surprised when he saw Stephen Halliday. He was dressed in a way that Bobby, his eldest, now eleven, would entirely approve of, and had his hair done in a way that Bobby would certainly have regarded as cool. Tom wasn't sure if it would still be wicked—that might be *so* last year. But cool had stood firm in the slang dictionaries for almost a century, so it was probably still okay.

And Stephen Halliday looked cool. He looked like a normal, fashion-conscious nineteen-year-old. Somehow, since he'd learned about the firearms certificate, Tom had been visualizing a neo-Nazi.

He introduced himself and Judy, and opened the file he had brought with him. "I understand that you're a steward at the Bull's Eye bingo club. Can you tell me what your job involves?"

"All sorts of things. I sometimes work behind the bar, or take drinks and food orders from the tables. And I take people's winnings to the table."

"How does that work?"

"The card's checked off with the caller, and if it's a valid claim, the checker asks for the customer's membership card, and takes it to the cashier for verification. She prints out a winner's envelope with the customer's name on it, and puts the money in it. Then I take it to the table, give the customer his or her card back, and count the winnings again in front of them. Then I put the money back in the envelope, and give it to them."

Tom nodded. They might try to get prints from the money; one of the twenties was brand-new. "We would like to have your fingerprints for elimination purposes," he said.

"Sure."

"Why did you leave at the interval?"

"Something came up. I had to meet someone. I asked the manager if I could leave early, and she said yes."

"Can you tell me what you did when you left?"

"I was walking along Murchison Place, and I could see Wilma ahead of me. Then I saw the envelope with her winnings in it fall out of her bag, so I ran and picked it up. I caught up with her, and walked with her the rest of the way."

"Why?"

"I was going that way."

"You had a motorcycle helmet with you."

The young man frowned slightly. "Yes—I didn't want to leave it at the club. It was expensive—it might have got stolen."

"Are the staff light-fingered?"

He smiled. "No, but you never know, do you?"

"Why didn't you take your bike?"

"It was quicker to walk. I wasn't going far, and the one-way system would have taken me out of my way."

Tom had heard all about the one-way system from Judy when she used to live in Malworth, so that was probably true.

"So you walked Mrs. Fenton to her door."

"Yes."

"How long were you with her?"

"About five minutes or so."

"You didn't go into her flat at all?"

"No. I just left."

"Did she go in before you left?"

"No—she was just getting her key out of her bag. I said good-night, and carried on through the alley. I was a bit late, so I didn't hang about—it didn't occur to me that anything could happen to her."

"Did you see anyone else? Did anyone enter the alleyway?"

Halliday shook his head.

"Did anyone leave the bingo club at the same time as you? Or did you see anyone hanging around when you were walking with Mrs. Fenton?"

"No. Mr. Waterman and Tony Baker were standing just outside, though—they might have seen if anyone followed us."

"What were they doing?" Judy asked.

"Just talking, I think. Oh—Mr. Waterman was using his mobile phone. Not speaking to anyone—just using it, you know? Texting someone, or whatever."

"Thank you." Judy made a note.

"Was that the last time you saw Mrs. Fenton?" Tom asked. "When you left her at her door?"

He nodded.

"You weren't in her flat?"

"No, I told you."

"Who were you meeting?"

Halliday looked down at the table. "I—I don't want to tell you that."

"Well, perhaps you can tell me where you were at nine o'clock."

"No. I don't want to answer that."

Tom stopped the rapid questioning that he favored, and waited. He wasn't as good at waiting as Lloyd or Judy—they could sit it out forever. But he thought he was probably better at it than Stephen Halliday.

"I don't have to tell you, do I?" He still looked down at the table.

"No," Tom said. "You don't have to tell me. But you've admitted being with the victim—"

Halliday's head shot up. "I didn't 'admit' it. I just said it. I was coming here anyway before the police came for me—ask my mum. Or Tony Baker. They'll tell you."

"Fair enough," said Tom. "But you have said that you were with the victim at half past eight, and that she was all ready to go into her flat. But she was found half an hour later, still in her outdoor clothing. So she either changed her mind about going in, or she decided to go out again, and where people were during that time is fairly important."

Halliday just sat staring down at the table, shaking his head.

"Are those the clothes you were wearing last night?"

"No. The stewards wear a uniform. Red blazer and dark gray trousers and a white shirt."

"Were you wearing outdoor clothes as well?"

"I was wearing a biker's jacket."

"What color is the jacket?"

"Black."

"Would you have any objection to letting me have those clothes for forensic examination?"

Stephen frowned. "Why?"

"You were at the scene of what, less than half an hour later, turned out to be a murder. It's possible that the murderer was in Mrs. Fenton's flat with her. You have chosen not to tell me where you were, so I have to find out if that was you. Your clothes might tell me."

"I've told you—I didn't kill Wilma!"

"Do you know who did?"

"No!"

"Then tell me where you were when she died," said Tom.

Still, he shook his head.

"Stephen," Judy said, leaning across the table. "I simply want to be able to eliminate you from the inquiry. Just tell us where you were at nine o'clock. We'll check it out, and that'll be that."

Still no response.

"Was it illegal, what you were doing?" asked Tom.

"No!"

"Because there aren't many things more illegal than murder. So if you weren't killing Mrs. Fenton, you'd be better off telling us what you were doing."

"Of course I wasn't killing her! I had nothing to do with it, so you can't have found anything to say I did, and you're not going to. Why should I tell you what I was doing? It's nobody's business but mine."

Tom sat back. This was the point in the interview where Lloyd would tip his chair back and start rocking gently. It had a sort of mesmerizing effect on the interviewee, who would be waiting for him to crash to the floor, and the distraction was sometimes enough to put the less experienced miscreant off his stroke. But Tom knew if he tried it, he *would* go crashing to the floor.

"Were you with Keith Scopes?" Judy asked.

"No." Stephen frowned, looking genuinely puzzled at the suggestion.

Of course, thought Tom, Scopes and Halliday knew each other. They lived in the same village. Everyone in this inquiry did. He was beginning to entertain ideas of the entire population of Stoke Weston being in on this poor woman's murder. Waterman himself lived there, apparently, in what had once been the manor house.

"Did you see Scopes in the alleyway?" Judy asked.

"No."

"He saw you."

Halliday frowned. "I never saw anyone."

"I think that's who you were with," said Tom. "I think you were both doing something you'd rather the police didn't know about. But this is murder, Stephen. So one of you had better tell us."

Halliday was shaking his head. "I wasn't with Keith Scopes."

Tom had got the impression that Scopes was more afraid of someone else than he was of the police, and he was getting some of that from Halliday. It did seem possible that they had been up to something together.

"All right," he said. "As you have pointed out, you don't have to tell me where you were. So will you let me have your clothes?"

Halliday shrugged. "If you like."

They left Halliday writing out his statement, and Tom arranged for his fingerprints to be taken before Hitchin found someone to take him back to Stoke Weston and pick up his clothes.

"Do you think I chose the wrong approach, guv?" he asked, as they went back to Judy's office.

"Perhaps," she said. "But softly-softly didn't have much effect on him either. I think he's just the wrong man. It's Keith Scopes we should be interviewing."

Tom wasn't sure about that—the whole thing seemed much

too amateur to be his doing. But he did agree that Halliday didn't seem at all likely. "All the same," he said. "I'd like to know what he's got to hide."

"MY CLIENT WAS UNAWARE THAT THERE WERE DRUGS ON THE premises."

Gary suppressed a yawn. He was sitting in on the interview with Cox, the man whose flat they had raided that morning. He was under orders to say nothing; he was there to gain experience by watching the professionals at work.

The problem was that Cox was a fruitcake, and the experience was beginning to lose its appeal. The others had all routinely refused to answer any questions, but Cox was eager to answer, despite his solicitor's attempts to stop him. His solicitor had just stepped in, in the hope of rescuing him from the hole he was digging. But Sgt. Kelly turned back to Cox.

"You are saying you had no knowledge of the drugs found in your flat?"

Cox made a play of considering this, then nodded. "Yes, I think that's what I'm saying. My brother must have left them when he was staying with us."

"And where would your brother be now?"

Cox shrugged.

"And this money? I am showing Mr. Cox exhibit LR2, a large quantity of cash recovered from his flat."

"Nothing to do with me."

"Is it your brother's as well?"

"Must be."

"So you had no knowledge of any drugs, or any cash, or any equipment being in your possession?"

"No."

"So how do you explain the three people who called on you on Sunday night and gave you money?"

Cox smiled. "I'm very popular."

"We have a photographic and video record of these transactions," Sgt. Kelly said. "Would you like to reconsider that answer?"

"They weren't transactions."

"People were giving you money in exchange for packages," Sgt. Kelly said doggedly.

"No. They happened to be giving me money, and I happened to be giving them packages."

"So what was in the packages?"

"Wedding cake. A friend of mine got married, and asked me to let everyone have a bit of wedding cake."

Cox's solicitor leaned toward him and whispered something to his client.

"I hope that's advice to be a bit more cooperative and stop taking us for mugs," said Sgt. Kelly. "We've since arrested two of these people."

Cox smiled.

Gary didn't have the patience for this kind of work. He thought the drug squad was doing a vital job, but he'd much rather they did it without him. This had been the most boring week of his life, and even the nutty Mr. Cox was doing nothing to brighten it up. He'd be glad when his stint with the drug squad was over, and he could get back to normal CID duties. Then he could forget all about Cox and his unsavory activities, at least until he came to trial, which wouldn't be for months. July or August if they were lucky, he'd been told.

"So—you had no knowledge of drugs, there were no illegal transactions going on—can you explain why, in that case, on seeing my colleagues enter the premises, you ran into a room at the rear of the building, upturned a tank containing two live snakes, jumped out of a fourth-story window and climbed down the outside of the building?"

Gary was suddenly wide awake. Snakes? He set snakes on them? What did they do? He would have died if he'd been confronted with live snakes. He would have dived out of the window after Cox. Live snakes?

"All I knew was someone was breaking my door down! I was frightened for my life. How was I to know it was the police?"

Sgt. Kelly sighed. "I would have thought the police uniforms might have given you a clue."

"Police uniforms? You call what they were wearing police uniforms? They looked more like bloody storm troopers!"

That was true, thought Gary. They did. But what did they do about the snakes? Did anyone get bitten? Did they kill the snakes—what? This was like watching a TV with the sound turned down.

"You gave yourself up to the police an hour later. Why?"

"Because I only had my trousers on and it was bloody freezing!"

"Why did you give yourself up to the police if you didn't know it was the police who had raided your flat? How did you know the police were looking for you?"

Cox blinked at him for a moment, then said what his solicitor had been advising him to say all morning. "No comment."

Roll on March, thought Gary. What with interminable interviews with idiots, the possibility of being exposed to snakes, and all night obbos in Transit vans, Gary had decided that the drug squad wasn't for him.

Cox was now saying that he had no idea who the man was that had called at nine o'clock. He peered at the video, shaking his head, as though he wasn't standing there beside him in the still frame. "Sorry," he said. "No idea."

Gary waited until Cox had been taken out. "Snakes, Sarge?"

"Oh, yes—it's not unheard of. It's quite fashionable for drug dealers to use venomous snakes to guard their properties. The ones that are reasonably high up the food chain, anyway."

The sooner Gary was off this attachment and back at Malworth, the better. "What did they do when they saw live snakes coming toward them?" he asked.

Kelly laughed. "Apparently, they were half asleep—one of the lads just sort of scooped them back into the tank with his baton, and put the lid on it."

It wouldn't have been him, Gary thought. No way. He smiled. "I expect they were his brother's snakes," he said.

Kelly laughed. "That story of his would carry a bit more weight if he *had* a brother."

JACK SHAW HAD RUNG STEPHEN AS SOON AS HE LEFT THE POLICE station, but Grace had said that the police had come for him. He had been worried about that all day, and went straight round to the Tulliver Inn as soon as he got home from work, to see how Stephen had got on.

"Fine," he said.

It wasn't like Stephen to be short with anyone, so he obviously didn't want to discuss it. Jack changed the subject.

"Is your mum about?"

"No—she's gone into Stansfield to do some shopping. Did you want her for something?"

Jack shook his head. "Is he about?" he asked.

"Who? Tony? No—he's off being interviewed by Aquarius for tonight's local news."

"Oh."

Baker *had* got himself all over the papers, even though he hadn't caught the murderer. And now he was going to be on the TV news. Grace would be even more impressed than she already was. Jack thought for a moment, then decided to plunge right in. "Are he and your mum . . . you know . . . ?" His voice trailed off.

"No. She'd like it if they were, but they're not." Stephen looked slightly amused. "Did you send her that Valentine?"

Jack felt himself blush. "Fat chance I have," he said. "A one-legged fruit-machine technician."

"Oh, don't put yourself down."

"I'm not, but look at me, and then look at him. Handsome, rich, got all his arms and legs . . ."

"Ah, well—he might have all his arms and legs, but he's got his own problems."

Jack snorted.

"He has. He's a diabetic."

Jack snorted again. "If men our age go to the doctor with an ingrown toenail, they come out diabetic," he said. "If you ask me, it's just something that happens to people as they grow older, but these days they—"

"Well, I don't know anything about that, but he's been diabetic since he was a kid. He takes five insulin injections a day— our fridge is full of little bottles of the stuff. He has to test his blood sugar levels, and carry round stuff in case he goes funny, and tell people what to do if he goes into a coma. He has to work out what he's going to eat, and how much insulin to give himself. He says it's either that or he has to know in advance exactly what and when he's going to eat, and that was always practically impossible, doing what he does. So you see, he doesn't have it all that easy."

Oh. Jack thought about that. Maybe he had been a bit self-obsessed. People never knew about his leg until he told them—it looked like it was the same with Baker. He kept his handicap well hidden. And he really did—he was a strong, active man who seemed to have no health worries at all. But he must have to keep tight control of his condition to maintain that. For the first time, he had a fellow feeling with the man. "Stephen—don't tell anyone else about him being a diabetic, will you?"

"Why not? It's nothing to be ashamed of."

"Of course it isn't. It's just that . . . well, if he's anything like me, he'd rather people didn't know if they don't have to."

"Oh, all right," said Stephen, amiable as ever. "If you say so. But he doesn't mind telling people. In fact, it's hard to stop him once he's started—he thinks everyone's fascinated by anything he does."

That was the first time Stephen had indicated to him in any way that he wasn't a big fan of Baker's.

"And I just thought it might make you feel a bit better," he added.

"It does," said Jack. "It's made me feel a bit guilty, but a bit better, too."

LLOYD HAD MADE DINNER. AT LAST, SOMETHING HE COULD DO TO mark Valentine's Day. True, her mother was there, which wasn't exactly romantic, but that probably suited Judy better. Candlelit meals weren't really her thing.

He hadn't cooked for ages, because unlike Judy, Gina was a good cook. Every morning, she made a bacon and egg breakfast for herself and Judy, and every morning she asked him if he would like something. He had had a cup of coffee for breakfast all his adult life; eating first thing in the morning was something he just didn't do. Unlike Judy, he ate the rest of the time. She sometimes only ate breakfast. But you would think that by now her mother might have accepted that he didn't.

He used to make Judy's breakfast for her, if he was up in time. He often wasn't up in time, but these days no one got to sleep late, not now that Charlotte could make her way from her room to theirs and announce that it was morning. She seemed to wake up with the daylight—another thing she'd got from Judy, who could sleep through anything but sunshine—and Lloyd was positively dreading the coming spring. She'd be getting them up at three in the morning by June.

But Gina made the breakfast these days, so this morning, when he could have done something for Judy to mark the date, however practical and unromantic, he hadn't been given the chance. Then he'd hit on the idea of dinner, and had allowed the three ladies in his life to put their feet up while he slaved over a hot stove.

Now, one of them was in her playpen, happily banging and

twanging the strange thing that banged and twanged, and the other two were coming to the end of what had been an excellent meal, even if he did say so himself.

"What's he like?" he asked Judy.

"Who?"

She knew perfectly well who. She had told him and Gina all about her investigation when she came in last night, and she knew who he was talking about. Lloyd was a little ashamed of his reaction to famous people, but Judy knew as well as he did that he was slightly starstruck, and Tony Baker, of all people, had found this woman's body.

She relented. "He's all right, I suppose. He thinks he's gorgeous, and I'm sure he thinks he knows more about policing than all of us put together, but he's quite pleasant, in a smooth, chat-show-host sort of way."

"You know, I think I recorded that documentary that he did about the South Coast murders—the one he did before they made the TV movie and all that. I must dig it out, look at it again."

"I don't know how you can find anything," said Gina. "I've never seen so many videotapes."

"He's got them all catalogued on his database," said Judy. "On the computer."

Gina looked at him, her eyebrows raised. "Have you really?"

"Yes," said Lloyd, putting on his offended look, but neither of them took any notice. "There wouldn't be much point in having them if I couldn't find what I wanted to watch, would there?"

"Can I look at your database some time?"

"Of course."

"There might be films and things that I'd like to see."

"Oh, there's bound to be," said Judy. "He's recorded every film ever made."

"Ignore her," said Lloyd. "There's not quite that many. But there are a lot, and she's right that there's bound to be something you'd like. I'll get the database up for you now—show you how to find the sort of thing you fancy."

He went into the sitting room and switched on the computer, making ineffectual attempts to tidy the desk while he waited for it to go through its start-up process. It hadn't occurred to him to ask Gina if she'd like to see any of his films—Judy was never interested, so he had assumed that her mother wouldn't be either. Why hadn't she asked before now? Did she really think that he had total recall of where everything was on the tapes? Anyway, he was pleased that she wanted to make use of the tapes. It made him feel slightly less eccentric for having them.

She came in just as he had found out which tape Tony Baker was on.

"Judy's graciously been allowed to bathe Charlotte tonight," she said. "So I've come in for a lesson."

Lloyd showed her how to bring up entries by title, or by category. "You don't happen to like old sixties cult TV, do you?" he asked.

"Oh, yes—I loved some of them. Have you got them, too?"

"Yes. And you're welcome to watch them whenever you like, as long as you don't laugh at me for having the ones you think are rubbish."

"As if I would." She sat down, smiling broadly at the computer screen. "This is great fun," she said.

Lloyd nodded. "I think so, too. She just thinks I'm mad."

"Oh, she would. She thinks if you've seen something once, there's no point in watching it again."

Lloyd laughed. "I know—I was one of the first people in Britain to have a VCR, and she had no idea why I wanted one. Or why I preferred to video some programs even if I could watch them when they were on. I tried to explain how I liked being able to stop and run it back if I missed a bit, and all that, but . . ." He shrugged. "She still doesn't understand. Do you fancy having a look at the South Coast murders thing once we've got Charlotte off to bed?"

"Yes—that would be interesting. I'd forgotten all about that."

Several Taffy the Tabby stories later, Lloyd emerged from

Charlotte's bedroom, found the tape, and put it on. "This was shown just after the trial," he said. "Seventeen years ago. It's hard to believe it was that long ago, isn't it?"

"Look," said Judy. "He had ordinary hair in those days. He puts highlights in it now. And he's had his teeth done."

Lloyd laughed. "Do you think I should put highlights in mine?"

"Your teeth, maybe."

He watched as Tony Baker, with the aid of filmed reconstructions, went through each of the murders.

"Here, at Torquay in Devon," he said, as he walked along the seafront, "five years ago, on the first of July, Carrie Harmsworth was beaten to death in her own home—a little cottage on the edge of town. Lonely, some might have said. Isolated. She and her husband thought of it as peaceful, somewhere she could work undisturbed on her pottery figures, and he could run his mail-order rare book business. He was away at a book fair at the time of the murder."

That had caused the entire population of Torquay to suspect him, if not of carrying out the murder himself, then of hiring someone to do the job for him.

"Nothing was stolen, and the victim had not been sexually assaulted. A small quantity of blood was found at the scene that did not belong to the victim, and though the forensic possibilities of DNA were yet to be discovered, blood could nonetheless prove significant once a suspect had been apprehended."

Eastbourne next, and Audrey Little's murder, on August 1 the following year. The same MO. This time her husband was at work. The similarities had been noticed by the two police forces, as had the fact that in both cases there were travelers in the area. A couple walking their dog had seen someone hanging around earlier in the day, possibly watching the house, but could only give a vague description of the man. Extensive inquiries were made among the Gypsies, but nothing concrete emerged.

"It was in Brighton that the police made what they thought

was their breakthrough," Tony Baker was saying. "When a Mrs. Lillian Evans died exactly one year and one month after Mrs. Little. Now, they were certain that they had a serial killer on their hands. The victims were all married women. They had all been beaten to death in their own homes with whatever heavy object came to hand. The murders had all taken place in broad daylight, in a south coast town, and in each case, Gypsies had been encamped nearby."

Now, he walked along a suburban street. "But this time, the house, as you can see, was not isolated. It stood close to the main London to Brighton line, not far from the railway station. There was a good deal of passing traffic, and they were optimistic of getting some information. And indeed a passing motorist, a visitor to the area, did come forward with information. A Mr. Jason Tebbs Challenger contacted the police to say that he recalled seeing a man running very fast along the road outside Mrs. Evans's house. He'd noticed him because he was wearing work clothes, not running clothes, and he had thought the clothes were smeared with red paint. Was that Mrs. Evans's blood? And was this the face of her killer?"

The screen showed the now-notorious sketch.

"This was the sketch released by the police as a result of the description given to them by Jason Challenger. It was seen on television screens, on posters, in newspapers and cinemas for months. And this . . ."

The picture changed to a photograph of the Gypsy who had been charged with the murders. The man was clearly recognizable from the sketch.

". . . is Joseph Riley, the man they arrested over a year later, having finally run him to earth farther along the south coast. The other travelers had been keeping him out of sight, simply because of his similarity to the sketch, not because they believed he was in any way involved in the murders. He was arrested two years ago, on the thirtieth of September."

Over film footage of Riley's arrest, Baker picked up the story.

"Mrs. Evans had been beaten to death by a spade from her own garden shed, and Riley's fingerprints were on that spade. He had been working in the Brighton area as a jobbing gardener, and his story was that Mrs. Evans had asked him to dig her borders, had paid him, and he had left her alive and well. But he had been in the Eastbourne area in August of the previous year, and in Torquay the July before that, as had all the travelers in his group, and he was not believed."

Well, no, thought Lloyd. He doubted very much that he would have believed him.

"The blood found at the scene of the first murder was of the same type as his. It was type O, the most common blood type of all."

The police had then gone back to the second murder, and arranged for the couple who had been walking their dog to attend a lineup. They each picked out Riley.

"The police were quite happy that they had their man, and he was charged with all three murders."

Baker was now standing on some steps in a churchyard.

"But I wasn't happy. I had no doubt that the couple attending the lineup had picked out the sketch, not the man. Joseph Riley was barely able to read and write, having received little or no education. He lived on the road—he had no use for calendars. He didn't have the acumen necessary to devise some elaborate plan to commit murders one year and one month apart. There had to be a reason for that, but, of course, the police don't need to discover the reason for a crime. They had the physical evidence. The fingerprints. The blood. The eyewitnesses."

The camera pulled back. "It was here in Bournemouth that the next murder took place. On the morning of the first of October, the day after Riley's arrest, Mrs. Nora Green was battered to death in her own home. Nothing was stolen, and there was no sexual assault. But the police would not countenance the idea that they had arrested the wrong man. This murder was different, they said. Her husband wasn't away, as the others had been—he was there with her. He said he had popped out for the morning paper, as was his habit, but the belief—not publicly stated, but very real—was that he had killed his wife in this way in the hope that it would be taken for the work of the South Coast Murderer, not knowing that he had been arrested the night before."

Baker had followed the Bournemouth investigation to the exclusion of all else, taking lodgings in Bournemouth, having to give up his newspaper job as a result. He had pored over all the evidence available to him from the other murders, and had evolved a theory.

"I believed that the murderer had deliberately carried out his attacks in areas where the Gypsies were encamped in order that they should take the blame if necessary. That he, having seen Riley working in Mrs. Evans's garden, had committed his features to memory in order to do exactly what he did—come forward as a witness, produce a sketch so accurate that it might have been a photograph, and throw the investigation in entirely the wrong direction. That he had used the spade Riley had been working with in order that Riley's prints would be found on it. And I believed that his MO had changed in Bournemouth only in so much that he now needed a new scapegoat—in this case, his victim's husband."

Another man the public had decided was guilty of murdering his wife, Lloyd thought. Murder touched so many innocent people.

"I believed that Jason Challenger, who I now knew to be the owner of a fitted kitchen company that operated throughout the south of England, who could be anywhere along the south coast that he chose on any day he chose, for as long as he needed to be there, was the murderer. That he spent months choosing his possible victims, making certain of their habits, of when they were alone . . . But the police dismissed my theory, saying I was letting my imagination run away with me."

Lloyd was uncomfortably aware that he would probably have said exactly the same thing.

"I began following Challenger. If I could watch him make his preparations for his next murder, I could surely convince the police. But after a few months, all I got for my pains was a court order telling me to keep away from him, or I'd go to prison. What now? If I couldn't follow him, how could I prevent another murder?"

A picture now of Mary Shelley's grave.

"It was here that I came to do my thinking. St. Peter's churchyard in Bournemouth, where the ghost of Mary Shelley— someone who really knew how to let her imagination run away with her—might inspire me. Mrs. Green's husband was still under clouds of suspicion, though no charges had been brought, Joseph Riley was serving life imprisonment, and I would go to prison if I went anywhere near Challenger. He must have been laughing his socks off."

He must indeed, thought Lloyd.

"I was running out of time, having spent six months getting nowhere. The first of November was getting close—too close for comfort. That was when I would find out either that yet another woman had lost her life, or that having successfully framed Joseph Riley, Challenger had ceased operations, and an innocent man would continue to pay for his crimes, with no hope of proving that they had been carried out by someone else altogether."

Baker, sitting on the steps now. "These are Bournemouth's very own Thirty-Nine Steps. The number was selected by Bournemouth's first vicar, to represent the number of Articles of Faith in the Church of England prayer book, but I was drawn to them because of their mystery connotation. If Mary Shelley couldn't help me, perhaps John Buchan and Alfred Hitchcock could. And it was sitting here that in desperation I jotted down the years, the months, the victims, one more time, to see if I could find a geographical pattern, something that linked them. I had pored over the facts for months, and I had known that I was doing nothing that the psychological profilers and the forensic teams hadn't already done, but I was doing it with more information, since they had abandoned their task when Riley was convicted. If I couldn't watch the suspect, perhaps I could discover his logic. I could work out who his next victim would be, and watch her instead. But I had failed. In this last desperate attempt, I jotted down the initials of the months: J, A, S, O. The initials of the locations: T, E, B, B. And the initials of the victims: CH, AL, LE, NG . . ."

The initials were written out on the screen as he spoke them, as though they were being jotted down in a notebook.

"And I realized with a shiver of horror that Jason Tebbs Challenger was spelling his name in blood along the south coast of England."

It still made Lloyd's flesh creep, after all these years.

"What's in a name? His forebears must have been challengers, and if ever anyone had issued a challenge, he had. Was I equal to that challenge? I had found my clue, my key into the mind of this man. On the first of November, he was going to kill someone with the initials ER, somewhere on the south coast, beginning with the letter S. And to find out who and where, I had to *become* Challenger. I had to find the perfect victim, just as he had."

Baker explained how he had armed himself with phone books and electoral rolls for everywhere of any size beginning with the letter S, finally producing a short list that he had to narrow down to just one person.

"Realizing that he always wanted someone else to be suspected, I decided that he would pick Ellen Ryland, who lived in St. Austell, Cornwall, in a lesbian relationship. That seemed to me to be the setup that Challenger would find best suited to his purpose. There would be a certain amount of prejudice there from the start, and that would be reflected in the police inquiry, however hard they tried to ignore the victim's unconventional lifestyle.

"So I stalked Ellen Ryland, until one day in October, I saw that I was not alone. Sitting, watching her from a nondescript van, was none other than Jason Tebbs Challenger. I took my now incontrovertible evidence to the police, and they arrested Challenger. His story—that someone else must be doing it using his name—came unstuck when that old blood sample finally came into its own. The previous year, the identification potential of DNA had been discovered, and by the time I made my own modest discovery, DNA testing had already been used to convict someone."

Baker was standing outside the Old Bailey now.

"This is where, after weeks of listening to the evidence, it took the jury just two hours to convict Jason Tebbs Challenger. The circumstantial evidence was almost overwhelming on its own, but it was the tiny clue that Challenger left behind at the scene of his very first crime that proved conclusively that he was indeed the South Coast Murderer."

When the credits had finished rolling, Lloyd switched off the TV, and looked at Judy. "Would you have done any better than they did?" he asked.

Judy shrugged. "I was unhappy, like he was, about the idea of Riley having devised the murders, so I might have been more open to suggestion, but I doubt it. I seem to remember they thought it was some weird ritual that Riley had got involved with, and I might have accepted that. Who knows?" She shivered. "But Baker should have gone to the police when he stumbled on it. What if he'd been wrong? What if Challenger hadn't chosen Ellen Ryland? Some other ER would have died, because he kept that information to himself."

"My initials are ER," said Gina.

"So they are," said Judy. "It's just as well you didn't live on the south coast."

Lloyd frowned. "Are they?"

"Elizabeth Regina. I was named after Good Queen Bess— don't ask, because I never did find out why. I think it was a private joke."

"I didn't know your first name was Elizabeth—why did you drop it?"

"It was my mother's name—it was confusing. I liked Regina better, anyway. But everyone shortened it to Gina, so Gina it is."

Judy stretched. "Am I the only person in this family who doesn't keep their first name a secret?"

Lloyd considered that sentence construction, and decided to let it go, on his new principle of allowing third person plural when one wished to be non-gender-specific. So Judy was saved a lecture.

And he resisted the temptation to warn her to be on her guard. He was sure she was overseeing Tom's investigation with her usual crisp efficiency. He certainly hoped she was, because Baker was no fool, and he would be watching.

CHAPTER FOUR

"Interview with Stephen Halliday," said DI Finch, "Monday, twenty-first February at 10.05 a.m., in connection with the murder of Mrs. Wilma Fenton on Sunday, thirteenth February. Those present DI Tom Finch, Trainee DC Gary Sims, and Stephen Halliday."

They had brought him in for questioning again, and this time they were taping the interview. Stephen felt apprehensive.

"You are not under arrest," Finch said, "and can leave at any time, but I must caution you that while you do not have to answer any questions put to you, it could harm your defense if you fail to mention now something you later rely on in court, and that anything you do say may be given in evidence. You are entitled to legal representation if you wish. Free legal advice is available from the duty solicitor, or you can ask us to contact a solicitor of your choosing."

Stephen blinked at him.

"Do you understand the caution?"

"I'm not sure. I'm not under arrest?"

"No, you're free to leave at any time. Do you want us to contact a solicitor for you?"

It didn't feel as if he was free to leave, but at least he wasn't officially under arrest. "I don't think so, thank you," he said.

"Fine. If at any time during the interview you change your mind about that, tell us, and the interview will be terminated until a solicitor has been found for you."

He really didn't think he needed a solicitor, but he didn't know why he had been brought back. He was soon to find out.

"Mrs. Fenton's handbag had been wiped in a successful attempt to remove any fingerprints," DI Finch said. "But your fingerprints were found in two places on her purse. Can you explain how they got there?"

Stephen swallowed. "She asked me to put the money in it, because her fingers were too cold to open it." He explained about the purse being too small. "So I said just to keep it in the envelope, and I opened her bag, put the envelope into it, and zipped it up. I don't know anything about anyone trying to remove fingerprints."

The two men looked at each other, and Stephen had no idea what that look meant.

Finch looked at him for a long time, then gave a short sigh. "All right," he said. "Interview terminated, 10.10 a.m." He switched off the tape. "You're free to go."

Stephen blinked. Was that it? The interview had taken a great deal less time than all the cautioning and advising that had preceded it.

"We've got your clothes back from the lab," Finch said. "You can take them away with you."

"Does this mean you don't suspect me anymore?"

"It means that I'm satisfied with your explanation as to how your fingerprints came to be on Mrs. Fenton's purse." He stood up. "But it doesn't clear you of suspicion, Stephen, so if you really were somewhere else at nine o'clock, you'd better think about telling us where that was."

No, thought Stephen. If they were letting him go, he didn't need to tell them where he was.

JACK ARRIVED AT THE TULLIVER INN TO DO HIS MONTHLY SERVICE on the fruit machine, to find the lounge bar empty of either staff or customers, but he could hear Grace and Baker talking in the back, so the place wasn't deserted, as he'd thought at first.

Baker didn't seem to have been off the telly. All week, he'd been turning up on some news program or other. The other papers and the TV had picked up the story—the fact that someone who had done what he did with the South Coast business should have actually witnessed a murder had news value, apparently. And Baker was loving it all, you could tell. He would come on, his face somber, saying how shocked he had been, and maybe he had, but Jack doubted it.

He went over to the machine, taking with him a low stool. The control panel was low down at the back, and one of the few things he couldn't do with his leg was kneel—if he ever fell down, it took him forever to get up again, because even kneeling on his good leg gave him problems with the other one. And, since he couldn't kneel, he needed the stool. He could sit on it and work at the machine.

And that's what he was doing when Grace came back into the bar, with Baker in tow. Sitting behind the tall machine, he was invisible.

"They just turned up first thing and asked him to go with them," she was saying, and Jack could hear that she had been crying. "They had more questions to put to him."

"But I don't understand," said Baker. "Where was he at nine o'clock on Sunday? Isn't there anyone who can provide him with an alibi?"

"That's just it—he won't say where he was. He won't even tell me."

"But why not? Doesn't he understand how serious it is?"

"He just keeps saying that since he didn't kill her, they can't have found any evidence to say that he did."

Jack knew they didn't know he was there, but he thought it best just to stay where he was.

"He would never mug anyone!" Grace shouted. "It's ridiculous."

"I don't think it was a mugging," said Tony. "I'm not supposed to tell anyone this, but . . . well, I know the paper said that whoever it was dropped the cash when they heard me coming, but I'd swear it wasn't dropped. It was spread out on top of her. Deliberately."

"What—what do you think that means?" Grace's voice trembled.

"I've no idea, but it makes it even less likely to have had anything to do with Stephen. I think someone was making a point about her, or about the money, or something. But try not to worry, Grace—I'll see if I can find out what's happening. If Stephen really did just leave her at her front door, then he's right—they can't have found any evidence to say otherwise."

"What do you mean, *if* he really did just leave her?"

"Nothing, nothing. I mean that he's told them the truth, and as long as he carries on doing that, he should be all right."

"But they don't arrest people for no reason!"

"Did they arrest him?"

"They took him away!"

"Yes, but did they arrest him? Did they say he was under arrest?"

"No."

"Then he isn't. They're just not satisfied with what he's told them, and if he's refusing to tell them where he was, that's probably why they're questioning him again. Why on earth is he doing that?"

"I don't know." Grace sighed, then caught her breath. "Oh, Tony, your breakfast! I forgot all about that."

"It's all right—it doesn't matter. I haven't taken the insulin yet. And I'm quite capable of making my own breakfast. But I'd better go and do that now. Will you be all right if customers come in?"

She sniffed. "I think so."

"Good."

Jack waited until he was sure Baker had gone before coming out from behind the machine.

"Oh, my God!" Grace nearly fainted. "I didn't know you were there!"

· "I know—I'm sorry if I startled you. But I didn't want to come out while you were talking." He went over to her. "I think it might be my fault that the police are questioning Stephen," he said.

Grace stared at him. "Your fault? How?"

"I was in the alley, too. And I heard Stephen and that woman talking to each other. The police questioned me, and I mentioned that Stephen had been with her—I didn't think anything of it."

Grace managed a smile. "Oh, Jack—no, it wasn't your fault. Stephen told them that himself. No—this is something new. I just wish I knew what."

KEITH WAS IN MR. WATERMAN'S STUDY AT THE GRANGE.

"You got the new rota for March?" asked Mr. Waterman.

"Yes, thanks. I got it on Friday. But you know I'm going on holiday at the end of this week, don't you? I'm not back until the twentieth of March."

"I know. I just wanted to be sure you were clear on what you had to do. When you do it is up to you."

Keith nodded. "Yes, boss." He was puzzled as to why he was here—the question hardly needed asking at all, never mind in person.

Mr. Waterman swiveled round and looked out of his study window, and Keith was beginning to wonder if he'd forgotten he was there when he finally spoke.

"Do you remember coming here when you were a kid?"

Keith smiled. "Oh, yes." They had climbed trees, had bon-fires, played with model powerboats on the lake. And in the cold weather, he and Ben had practically lived in the summerhouse, playing music as loud as they liked, with no one to complain. "I loved the summerhouse," he said.

Mr. Waterman nodded, still looking out of the window. "No one uses it now," he said. "Did Ben ever talk about me?"

Keith felt flustered. "Oh—I don't know, Mr. Waterman. I mean—probably. You talk about your dad, don't you? But I don't remember."

"Did it bother him, not having a mum?" Mr. Waterman turned back to look at him as he asked the question.

Keith was puzzled, and embarrassed, and shook his head. Ben hadn't talked much about his mum, and he said nothing in particular about his dad. Mr. Waterman had always been friendly, and generous, and Keith couldn't remember Ben ever complaining about him any more than all kids complained about their parents. And he had always been good to Keith, almost like a second dad, so he wanted to give him some sort of answer, because he looked like he needed one.

"He liked the lady that looked after him," he said, and wondered if he should tell him what Ben had said about her. It couldn't hurt, not now. "I . . . I do remember him saying he hoped you'd marry her."

"Did he?" Mr. Waterman looked surprised, and a bit concerned. "Did it upset him when she left?"

"No," said Keith. "No—we were teenagers by then. I mean—he was sorry to see her go, but it didn't upset him, if you see what I mean."

He smiled. "Okay, Keith. I'll let you go now."

Keith was very relieved to hear it. He'd never seen Mr. Waterman in this mood.

TONY HAD EATEN HIS BREAKFAST AND WAS TRYING TO ESCAPE BACK upstairs to his room, when Grace called him back. He closed his eyes, and turned to see her holding out a letter.

"This came this morning," she said. "I'm sorry, but the police arresting Stephen just drove everything else out of my head."

There wasn't much in there to drive out, if you asked Tony. He'd already explained to her that Stephen hadn't been arrested, so he didn't bother this time.

"It's got a Bartonshire postmark."

Fan mail, he thought, taking the letter. He'd had quite a lot of fan mail the first time he'd hit the headlines. He smiled his thanks, turning and going upstairs as fast as he could, making it obvious that he didn't want another heart to heart. Just one more week to endure her, he told himself. One more week, and his business here would be wrapped up, at least until the filming started.

In the safety of his room, he turned the key in the lock, and sat on the bed, running his thumb under the flap to open the letter. He pulled it out, read it, and then read it again. And again. Then he picked up the envelope, and looked at the postmark, but, as Grace had said, it was merely stamped with the county. No town. He swallowed, and read the letter for the fourth time, but there seemed to be no doubt about it. The murderer had written to him.

The letter was typed or—more probably—printed in upper case, as was the address label on the envelope, which had the correct postal town, being Barton, rather than Stansfield. Stoke Weston was closer to Stansfield, and the Hallidays's mail was very often addressed wrongly. Did that make it someone very local indeed?

Could it be Stephen? The police seemed to think it could, and there were a lot of unanswered questions. It was hard to cast Stephen in the role of murderer, but Tony knew from experience that murderers came in very assorted flavors, and most of them had close friends and relations who wouldn't believe it of them. Even so, he thought, Stephen just didn't seem to have the inner rage necessary to attack someone in that way. Of course, he did shoot foxes. Not that you needed inner rage to shoot foxes, Tony conceded, especially not on farmland, but it did show that Stephen wasn't totally averse to killing. He smiled. What nonsense, he thought, and closed his eyes, trying to marshal his thoughts. He stayed like that for a long time, and when he opened his eyes again, he knew only two things for certain.

One, there was going to be another murder, and he had to go to the police and warn them. Two, he was going to have to stay here a little longer than he had planned.

JUDY LOOKED UP AS TOM KNOCKED AND CAME IN ALL AT ONCE IN the way he always had.

"I've let him go, guv. What he told us accounted for his prints being on the purse, and if he had wiped the bag, he'd hardly have overlooked the purse, would he? Anyway, there was still money in it—I don't think the assailant touched it, which is why he didn't wipe it clean."

Judy frowned slightly. "He was the last person seen with her, he won't tell us where he was from half past eight to nine o'clock, and now we've found his fingerprints at the scene, despite an attempt to remove them. That sounds quite like evidence to me, Tom. Bringing him in might have rattled him enough to make him tell us where he was, so we could cross him off, if nothing else."

Tom sat down. "Not many muggers take the time to wipe prints."

"I know," she said. "But I think we've established that this isn't what you'd call a professional mugging. And Stephen isn't a professional mugger, so that's hardly an argument."

A week on from Mrs. Fenton's death, and they were no further forward. Conventional wisdom said that if you had no leads within three days, you weren't going to get any, and Judy was beginning to believe it. Forensics had found no sign of Halliday or anyone else having been in the flat, no reason to believe Mrs. Fenton was killed in there and dragged outside, and no traces of blood on anything that could conceivably have been used as the murder weapon. She hadn't thought there would be; it had always been a long shot. Apart from anything else, no one heard the dog barking, and the neighbor had said she was sure Heinz would have barked if anything bad had been happening to Mrs. Fenton where he could see it. She had decided to keep Heinz herself, Mrs. Fenton's brother having said she could, and Judy was pleased about that.

"I want the house-to-house inquiries extended to include the houses at the top of Murchison Place as well as the flats above it," she said.

"But the street was empty, guv."

"Maybe someone was looking out of their window, and saw something. Maybe there's a local busybody."

"Right, I'll ask Hitch to get on to it."

Teams of officers, armed with questionnaires, were producing what seemed to be reams and reams of absolutely nothing, just from the house-to-house already being done at the flats, in the hope that someone came in or went out during the half hour un-accounted for, or heard something, or knew something. In the in-cident room these questionnaires were being sifted through and collated, and the hope was that in among them would be a clue to who had murdered Wilma Fenton.

Posters had been produced and were being put up in all the shops in Murchison Place and beyond, in case Mrs. Fenton had gone off somewhere instead of going into her flat, but so far they had received no credible sightings of her. They had booked some time on the local TV station for an inexpensive dramatic recon-struction and an appeal for witnesses. That would be going out tonight, so maybe, just maybe they would get some information. Someone ran away from the scene—surely someone got a better look at him than Tony Baker did? But it seemed not.

Their thought about a loose cobble being used as the murder weapon had been dashed by the SOCOs, who assured them that there were no missing cobbles. They had found nothing of any note in the alley—like Tom had said, one of the very few things in its favor was that it was litter-free, having been swept on Satur-day evening, and having had little use between then and the time of the murder.

"Not even a cigarette butt," said Tom. "Which is a bit strange. I can't see Keith Scopes being too environmentally aware."

Judy frowned. "Are you saying you don't think he really was in the alleyway?"

"Not really. Why would he say he was if he wasn't? And how would he know who else was there? But I do think it's funny that we didn't find a cigarette butt." He smiled. "Does that count as a little puzzle, do you think?"

In her smoking days, Judy had been known to drop a cigarette and stand on it, particularly if she was smoking when she shouldn't. And every now and then the butt would attach itself to the sole of her shoe, so perhaps Scopes's cigarette butt left the alleyway with him. But while the practice of standing on one's cigarette butts might not be laudable, even that showed more social awareness than she felt Keith Scopes was likely to possess. He would be a thrower-away, rather than a stepper-on, Judy was sure. "I think perhaps it does," she said. "Though I can't see how solving it would help us find Wilma's killer."

"No. Maybe we should be thinking in terms of someone who wanted her dead, rather than a mugging gone wrong," Tom said.

Judy sighed. They'd been through all this before. "We've found nothing at all in Wilma's background that would make anyone want to kill her. And if anyone *had* wanted to kill her, they would have made a proper job of it. That blow wouldn't normally have killed someone—Freddie is absolutely adamant about that."

"Yes, but—" Tom leaned forward, "what if he didn't need to hit her again, because he realized she'd died after the first blow?"

"Why was he hitting her at all, if it wasn't for her winnings?"

"If it was for her winnings, why didn't he take them?" Tom countered. "That money wasn't dropped, guv. It was spread out. You know it was."

"I don't know it was. It looks odd, I'll give you that, but it could just have fallen that way. It's not impossible."

She remembered vaguely something she'd read in a book on logic about yellow blackbirds. How it was impossible to prove that there were no yellow blackbirds. Logically, all that could be said was that no one had ever seen one. And the idea of bank-notes falling from someone's hand and landing separately, scattered over someone's body, none of them missing or going on the ground, was as likely as a yellow blackbird, but it wasn't impossible.

And Stephen Halliday, by all accounts, was a very unlikely mugger, but that wasn't impossible either. He could have come back, gone into Wilma's flat, and then left with her again, on some pretext. When she suggested that, Tom, of course, had an answer.

"Jerry Wheelan would have seen him if he'd come back, guv."

"Not necessarily—he could have been busy with customers."

"But why would she still have her winnings in her bag? Surely if she had been in and come out again, she would have taken them out?"

"If he wanted to make it look like an opportunist mugging, he could have left the envelope for us to find," said Judy, and smiled. "Though that brings us back to why he didn't take the money if he wanted it to look like a mugging, so—yes, perhaps there was some other motive." She sighed. "But whatever the motive for killing her, she must have been somewhere during that half hour, Tom. And her flat seems the most obvious place."

"But Halliday isn't the most obvious candidate. I don't know where he was at nine o'clock, but I don't believe he was killing Wilma Fenton. He's a nice lad, Judy."

"Even though he likes guns?" She smiled.

"Yeah, all right. Even though he likes guns. He's a nice lad who's never been in any sort of trouble. Maybe Wilma did have someone who wanted her dead, but I don't think it was Stephen Halliday."

They had asked everyone at the bingo club if anything at all unusual had happened on Sunday night, or if Wilma said anything to anyone that might throw some light on what subsequently happened to her. Maybe, they had thought, someone had a grudge. Maybe they objected to her winning the money. Maybe they thought gambling was evil, and spread the money out on her as a warning to others.

But the single most unusual thing that had happened was that Michael Waterman had been there, and he never worked on a Sunday. It was odd, and anything odd got noted down. Judy was a believer in Lloyd's theory that if you solved the little puzzles, the big one became less puzzling. It was particularly odd because he had gone there despite the fact that he had had to get someone else to drive him. But they had about four dozen witnesses who saw him come into the club at half past eight, and stay there until ten, so he wasn't hitting poor old Wilma on the head at nine o'clock.

"What we really need," said Judy, "is someone who saw the person who ran away. Or someone who saw Wilma during that half hour."

"All the same," said Tom, "it had to be someone who knew she had won money, so it had to be someone who was at the bingo club."

"Not necessarily. Keith Scopes almost certainly overheard the conversation. Maybe he tricked his way into her flat, and— Come in!" Judy called, as someone knocked, glad that she didn't have to finish her sentence because it was simply going to take her back round the same circle. Why didn't he take the money?

Gary Sims popped his head round the door. "Mr. Baker's downstairs, ma'am—I tried to deal with it, but he says he has to speak to you."

Maybe he'd remembered something, Judy thought hopefully as she went down to the informal interview room.

"What can I do for you, Mr. Baker?"

He took out an envelope, and carefully removed a letter from it, holding it by the very edge, unfolding it with a shake of his hand, and laying it on the table. "My fingerprints are already on it," he said. "You might not want to touch it." He laid the envelope alongside it.

Judy leaned on the table, and read the letter, her eyes widening. "When did you get this?"

"About an hour ago. It could be a hoax, of course. My newspaper colleagues sometimes have a misplaced sense of humor."

GARY WAS GLAD TO BE BACK IN MALWORTH, AND PLEASED THAT he had been put on the murder inquiry, but even they produced dull jobs that had to be done, and he was doing one such. He had spent the afternoon going through the questionnaires from the house-to-house, a task enlivened only by the fact that from the office in which he was working, it was possible to see people arrive and leave, and that had been very diverting. He had no idea what was going on, but something clearly was.

Detective Chief Superintendent Yardley had been the first to arrive, and after about an hour or so, Tony Baker, whose arrival seemed to have triggered all the activity, left. But Yardley didn't go—he was still here, and divisional commanders and CID heads had come and gone all day. Then Yardley, DCI Hill and DCI Lloyd all went off in the Chief Super's official car, driven by a constable who'd told Gary, when he brought DCI Hill back, that they had all had a meeting with the Chief Constable himself.

He was almost a real detective, he told himself. In May he would be going on the course that would give him the full DC rank. He ought to be able to deduce what was happening, but he couldn't. He scratched his head. What could they be about, these meetings that were so secret that no one he had spoken to had the slightest idea why they were happening? Whatever it was, the atmosphere of the whole building was charged, and Gary had been a police officer long enough to know that it wouldn't be long before everyone knew what it was all about, however secret they wanted to keep it.

It was going-home time, and he took his jacket from the back of his chair, half wishing he could stay. But whatever it was, and however intriguing it seemed, even he wasn't prepared to go through any more questionnaires on the off-chance of finding out.

THE NEXT MORNING, TOM ARRIVED AT WORK TO FIND JUDY IN HIS office. If he had been asked once yesterday what was going on, he had been asked two dozen times, and he had no more idea than anyone else. He was sure Gary Sims thought he was lying when he denied all knowledge of the reason for all the comings and goings. But he was about to find out.

"Sorry I couldn't tell you yesterday," said Judy. "But I was told it was on a strict need-to-know basis, and it took me until this morning to convince them that you *did* need to know if you were to be able to do your job properly." She handed him a letter. "This is a copy of a letter Tony Baker received yesterday."

Tom glanced at it, typewritten in capital letters, and his heart sank.

"YOU THINK YOU'RE SO CLEVER, BUT I DON'T THINK YOU'RE CLEVER ENOUGH. YOU COULDN'T EVEN CATCH ME ON SUNDAY NIGHT, AND YOU WERE AL-MOST ON TOP OF ME. I'M GOING TO KILL AGAIN, SO IF YOU'RE ALL YOU'RE CRACKED UP TO BE YOU'D BETTER FIND ME FIRST. DO YOU NEED A CLUE? THE NEXT ONE WILL BE IN STANSFIELD NEXT MONTH. I THINK I'LL STRANGLE THIS ONE. I AM YOUR NEW CHALLENGER. CATCH ME IF YOU CAN."

He looked up at Judy. "Could it be a hoax?" he asked.

"Tony Baker thinks it might be. But I've a horrible feeling it isn't."

A serial murderer. The one thing everyone dreaded, in or out of the police force. And one that communicated his intentions—that was the worst of all.

Judy gave him a brief résumé of the strategy discussed. "We should be getting it on paper today," she said. "It mostly concerns the uniforms. But we can't swamp Stansfield with police officers forever—if he can't do it next month, he'll do it some other time. We simply don't have the manpower to cover every possible contingency, and we don't even know what his problem is yet. So it's up to us to catch him before it matters. We're getting the inquiry team beefed up, but I don't know the details yet."

Tom nodded. "I think we have to assume that it has something to do with Mrs. Fenton having won money at bingo," he said.

"The ACC agrees with you about that," said Judy. "He wants plainclothes officers in all Stansfield's bingo halls until further notice, with an officer to watch for anyone apparently tailing winners when they leave."

A thought struck Tom. "But what if he's lying, and it isn't going to be Stansfield at all?"

Judy shrugged. "Then we're no worse off than if we hadn't heard from him at all. At least it's something positive that we can do."

"I suppose," sighed Tom.

"And apparently Michael Waterman's already put some measures in place in his bingo halls, in view of what happened to Mrs. Fenton. He's now paying out checks only, and if a winner is unaccompanied and has no transport, he's giving them a complimentary taxi home."

Very generous, thought Tom. But in a way, it could work against them. The point of putting detectives in the bingo halls was so that this man would be caught. Giving him no opportunity to follow someone out gave the police no opportunity to follow him. Cure was better than prevention in his book. They needed to catch this person, not merely cramp his style.

And no sooner had he digested this piece of information than it was all happening again, as Judy was once again whisked off to HQ, and he had no idea why. Presumably, once again he didn't need to know.

JUDY HAD ARRIVED AT STANSFIELD TO PICK LLOYD UP AND TAKE him to HQ, to which they had both been summoned.

"Do you know what this is about?" Lloyd had asked her.

"No—do you?"

"No. If we find out that nobody needs to know, can we all just go home?"

Now, they sat in the small conference room. After a few minutes, DCS Yardley and the ACC joined them, sitting down at the table, uttering polite greetings.

Yardley got straight to the point. "This is a fax of a letter received this morning by the editor of the so-called newspaper that Tony Baker works for." He pushed copies across to Judy and Lloyd. "As you'll see, our job is about to be made even more difficult."

Lloyd felt in his pocket for his glasses, then in his other pocket. Finally, he located them in his breast pocket, and read:

I AM THE MAN WHO MURDERED WILMA FENTON IN MALWORTH ON SUNDAY 13 FEBRUARY. SHE IS JUST THE FIRST. I HAVE WRITTEN TO TONY BAKER TELL-ING HIM WHEN AND WHERE AND HOW I WILL KILL AGAIN AND CHALLENGING HIM TO FIND ME BE-FORE MY NEXT VICTIM DIES. IS YOUR MAN UP TO THIS CHALLENGE? I DON'T THINK SO.

The ACC had a degree in business administration, Lloyd knew. He wondered if that had covered madmen who wanted to pit their wits against well-known amateur sleuths in the full glare of the national media.

"They only got this today?" he asked.

"Yes—postmarked Bartonshire, yesterday's date."

"That's odd," said Lloyd. "You'd think he'd have posted them together." He smiled to himself as he saw Judy make a note. He pointed out the oddities, and she wrote them down. They very often proved to be important in the end. Or not, of course.

"Writing to the paper was probably an afterthought," said Yardley.

"Probably. Are they going to publish it?"

"Oh, yes," said Yardley. "The Chief tried to talk them out of it, but without success. They have agreed to let us see any future letters before publication, in case they contain anything of a sensitive nature that we would rather wasn't made public, but they wouldn't agree that this letter contained any sensitive information, since it doesn't go into any detail."

The upshot of all yesterday's meetings had been that they should keep a lid on the letter in order not to panic the public, not a decision with which Lloyd had agreed. In his experience, the authorities panicked, not the public. What the public didn't like was being kept in the dark, and this sort of thing had a habit of leaking out piecemeal. Now, keeping the public in the dark was no longer an option, so he thought they should go whole hog and tell people what they knew.

"The problem is," he said, "that this letter gives the impression that we are in possession of considerably more information than we are. Are we also making public the contents of the letter to Tony Baker?"

"No," said the ACC. "It's still felt that naming the town would cause unnecessary panic, and the media has not been and will not be made privy to the contents of that letter."

"That's all very well, sir," Lloyd said, "but if the press think we've been told exactly when and where it's going to happen, we're going to be given a rough ride if we fail to prevent this proposed murder."

"Our strategy for dealing with the press has already been decided," said the ACC. "DCS Yardley will deal with all press-related issues, including any press conferences, interviews and the wording of press releases. He will liaise with the press officer over any statements that she makes directly to the press, and will be briefed on exactly how much or how little we want the media to know at any given point in time. No other officer should under any circumstances make any comment at all to the media. I'm relying on all line managers making that entirely clear to each and every person for whom he or she has responsibility."

Lloyd was of the opinion that meetings with the ACC would last a third of the time if he would leave out all the unnecessary words. And learning which of the ones he left in were singular and which were plural wouldn't hurt either.

"We have to tread a very fine line between giving the public adequate warning and alarming them," said Yardley. "And between ensuring their safety and going for broke over what turns out to be a hoax. Naming the town would be counterproductive in my view."

"Either way, we won't win," said Lloyd. "If it is a hoax, we'll have thrown too many resources at it. If, God forbid, someone dies, we'll not have done enough."

"If he does kill again, at least we might find a few more leads than we have with Mrs. Fenton," said Yardley.

There was a bright side to everything, thought Lloyd.

"Obviously the ongoing investigation into Mrs. Fenton's death is our best hope of apprehending this person before he carries out his intentions," said the ACC. "To this end, we have doubled the manpower being made available to the murder inquiry—DCS Yardley will give you the list of personnel being seconded." He turned to Judy. "I'm assuming that we're no closer to an arrest than we were last night."

"I'm afraid not, sir," said Judy. "We're hoping that the reconstruction put out on local TV last night will have—"

"I'm not convinced you should have let Halliday go," said Yardley. "The press will have a field day if it turns out to be him in the end."

"I was satisfied with the explanation he gave for his finger-prints being found on the purse, sir. He has never denied that he was with Mrs. Fenton shortly before the murder, and we have two witnesses who saw him leaving the scene twenty-five minutes before the incident occurred. I don't believe we had enough to hold him."

Oh, yes she did, thought Lloyd. She agreed with Yardley that he should probably have been put under arrest and therefore under pressure, so that they could see if he stuck to his story. But she was backing Tom Finch's judgment.

"And Scopes?"

"Well, his record and the fact that he went missing from work for an hour and a half and won't say what he was doing counts against him. But he's always been quite open about being in the alleyway."

"And Baker? For all we know, he wrote that letter to himself."

"There seems to be no possible motive for him to have killed Mrs. Fenton. But he didn't tell us that Halliday left at the same time as she did, so it's possible that he saw or heard more than he's saying." Judy sighed. "The truth is that without independent witnesses, and without the murder weapon, we're up against it."

The rest of the afternoon was taken up with preparations for the invasion of press that was anticipated once the scoop was on the streets, and it was growing dark when Lloyd and Judy finally got back into her car, and headed for Stansfield.

"We're not going to stop this joker," Lloyd said. "Not if he really wants to kill someone. We might delay him, but we're not going to stop him, not unless we find out who he is before he makes the attempt, and we stand very little chance of doing that.

We don't know how much of that note is true—we might be protecting Stansfield bingo players while he's picking off a bookie in Barton."

"That's what Tom said. But I don't think there would be much point in writing the letter if he was just going to tell lies. If he doesn't want us to have any idea where he's going to strike next, wouldn't it be simpler not to write a letter at all?"

Lloyd smiled. "Not everyone has your logical turn of mind. And anyway, the letter's so vague it doesn't matter if he is telling the truth. We can't line the streets of Stansfield with policemen, so the chances are that he will murder again, and the press will be demanding to know why we weren't there with our truncheons at the ready." He thought about what she had said in the briefing. "If you think Baker might know something more than he's telling us about Mrs. Fenton's murder, you should talk to him again."

"I know. But he's an old hand, Lloyd, and he doesn't have much confidence in the police. And talking to him is hampered by the fact that he's still technically a suspect himself, as Yardley pointed out."

"But only because he found the body?"

"Yes. I don't think he killed Mrs. Fenton, because apart from having no reason whatever to do so, he of all people would have done it properly. But he does lodge with Stephen Halliday and his mother."

"Do you seriously suspect Stephen Halliday of murdering Mrs. Fenton?"

"Not really. Tom doesn't think he did it, and he's no pushover."

"If you could cross him off, would you have any reason to suspect Baker of covering up for someone?"

"Well, sort of." She sighed. "Tom thinks he might want to investigate this on his own. That maybe he got a better look at the attacker than he says he did."

"What about Yardley's suggestion that he wrote the letter himself?"

"It crossed my mind," said Judy. "I can't see why he would, though. He doesn't need the publicity, does he? But it's a personal challenge to him, and I think his ego is quite large enough to take it on."

"Ah, then all you have to do is make him feel guilty. If people start dying, it's all because of him. What should have been an isolated and unintentional murder is going to be the first of several, all because he found the body, and this person now wants to challenge him to a duel. And he could have given us a description to go on, and didn't, because he wanted to be a hero again."

"Mm. I'm not sure that being told I was responsible for it all would make me say, 'Oh, did I forget to mention that he's six feet seven and has a tattoo of the Humber Bridge on his forehead?' I think I'd keep quiet."

"Not if it was before anyone else died and you still had time to make amends. And you'd be a little more subtle than I was being," said Lloyd. "You wouldn't go in accusing him of trying to pervert the course of justice. You know how to make me feel guilty—try your technique on him."

"What technique? When do I make you feel guilty?"

"How many times in my life have I apologized to you? Half the time I don't know what I'm apologizing for—I just know I feel guilty."

"Lies. All lies."

"You're making me feel guilty at this very moment!"

"What about?"

"The loft conversion."

"Why should that make you feel guilty? If you want Mum to have her own sitting room, then—"

"See? *That* technique. Already, I'm having visions of your mother sitting alone in her room weeping gently while we're downstairs laughing and joking and cracking open champagne." He shook his head. "So we'll end up doing what she wants. We'll share the house properly, and I'll be begging forgiveness for having said she sometimes gets on my nerves."

Judy laughed. "Of course she sometimes gets on your nerves," she said. "So do I. You don't banish me to my own sitting room."

"You'd give your eyeteeth for your own sitting room—you'd have kept your own flat if you could have afforded it. You always want somewhere to retire to if things get a bit bumpy."

"Like when you're getting on *my* nerves?"

The atmosphere remained slightly frosty after that, and Lloyd was relieved when he was finally dropped off at Stansfield, and she went on her way to Malworth.

MICHAEL HAD CHOSEN THIS ROOM FOR HIS STUDY BECAUSE OF THE view, and tonight, he went in there when he came home from work purely in order to look at that view. He stood in the darkened room, looking out at the sweep of trees sheltering the path that led down to the summerhouse. The lake, the edge of which could just be seen, shimmered in the starlight of another cold, crisp evening.

He could see Ben and Keith as children, racing each other along that path. They had been great friends in those days. Sometimes there had been a whole gang of them there, playing football in the winter and cricket in the summer. They had had a dinghy, and they would take it out on to the lake, and play pirates. Ben had always seemed like a happy child.

Had he really wanted him to marry the nanny who he'd employed? Michael could barely remember her. She had left when Ben turned thirteen, and according to Keith, it hadn't been too much of a wrench, but that was when Ben had started getting into trouble. Aided and abetted by Keith, of course—probably instigated by Keith. But maybe Ben had been missing a woman's influence.

Michael's answer to that had been to send Ben away to boarding school, but that option hadn't been available to Keith's family, so he had just carried on getting into trouble. Michael had taken Keith on in the knowledge that he was no stranger to the police. But he was useful, and loyal, and a risk-taker, which endeared him to Michael, being a risk-taker himself. All bookies were risk-takers, even though they usually came out on top. You had to be prepared to pay out when you didn't, and Keith was prepared to take the consequences if the risks he took didn't come off. No, he had no complaints about Keith.

In fact, he sometimes wished Keith was his son. He understood him far better than he understood Ben. Keith was the sort of son he should have had. Someone who could take care of himself in a punch-up, someone who followed football and knew how to handle a pool cue, both for the purpose for which it was intended and, if he had to, in self-defense.

But Ben was his son, not Keith. He picked up the phone and dialed Ray's mobile number.

"Ray Yardley."

"Ray—sorry, I know you must be busy."

"No—I've just got home, as it happens. It's been nothing but meetings for the last two days, and we're no further forward with Mrs. Fenton's murder, I'm afraid. There have been developments, but none of them good. It'll be all over the pap—"

Michael felt obliged to interrupt him, or he'd be here all night. "I heard that you'd taken young Stephen Halliday in for questioning again, and I wondered what was happening."

"Oh, it was just routine. Something that needed clearing up. DCI Hill was quite happy with his explanation. But he still won't say where he was that night, so I'm not so—"

"Keep me posted about him, will you? I mean—if you have occasion to talk to him again."

"Sure."

"Thanks, Ray." He hung up before Ray could start again.

CHAPTER FIVE

ONY FINISHED HIS COFFEE, AND SAT BACK. "THAT WAS AB-solutely delicious, Mike," he said. "Where did you find her?"

Michael smiled. Tony wasn't the first of his guests to be startled at the quality of his housekeeper's cooking. "I'm glad you enjoyed it. More wine?"

"No—thank you. I honestly can't remember when I had a better Sunday lunch. Grace Halliday is a good plain cook, but I hadn't bargained on eating good plain food for this long. I was supposed to have finished here at the end of February."

Michael frowned. "The police can't make you stay here if you don't want to," he said.

"No, it isn't them." Tony looked worried. "I just don't think I can leave with this nutcase threatening to murder someone because of me. I would feel as though I was running away, or something."

"It might just be a hoax," said Michael. "The papers are beginning to think it is."

"Let's hope so. And that the police catch whoever it is soon, if only because I can't take much more of Grace Halliday. Her food's all right, but she isn't what you'd call stimulating company."

Michael had always found Grace very pleasant and attractive. He'd steered clear of her once her husband left, because he didn't want to be regarded as husband material himself. But that was no reflection on Grace.

"Of course, she's permanently worried about Stephen, because the police questioned him," Tony went on. "Which really doesn't help. I'm glad of the days I get to be in London." He looked out of the French windows at the paved terrace, and the woods beyond. "Is all that land yours?" he asked. "Including the woods?"

"And beyond them," said Michael. "There's a lake down there."

"Is there really?" He patted his flat stomach. "I think I might go out and have a stroll round—work off some of this good food."

"Be my guest," said Michael. "I'd advise you to wrap up warm, as my mother would have said." He would probably benefit from a walk himself, he thought. "If you want company, I can show you where everything's going to be on May Day."

"That sounds like a very good idea."

The Stoke Weston May Day celebrations had traditionally been held on the village green, but twenty-first-century greed had overtaken tradition. The owners of the land had applied for planning permission to build four houses on the green, and when the Stoke Weston Parish Council had objected on the grounds that no building could be erected on a village green, the owners had declared that it wasn't village green within the meaning of the act.

Many months of legal wrangling later, a ruling by the House of Lords had found for the owners. While village activities had been permitted to take place on the green under successive owners, it had never been exclusively for the use of villagers, and there had been no automatic right for this use, merely a toleration of it. And now, it was going to have four luxury houses on it instead.

Michael had been annoyed at the decision, but at the same time pleased that he could do what he did, which was to offer the village his grounds for their festivities. Ben would say he was playing the lord of the manor, and perhaps he was, but he genuinely felt that Stoke Weston village traditions should be maintained. And he'd thrown in a few extras.

The two men stood at the top of the steps from the front door, and Michael pointed to his left, to the grassy area beyond the driveway. "That's where the fête will be," he said. "All the various stalls will be there, and the public car park will be there, too, so people can just pull off the driveway. The maypole, the Morris dancing, and all the traditional May Day stuff will take place on the lawn here." They went down the seven steps from the front door. "This area here," he said, as they turned right and walked along the close-clipped grass, "will have a bouncy castle on it, and a bit fenced off with a sandpit and soft toys and things for the little ones, with someone to keep an eye on them."

They left the house behind, and walked along the lawn.

"Staying at the Tulliver is making things quite awkward," Tony said. "Grace keeps telling me how Stephen can't possibly have had anything to do with it, but I find myself wondering what he was doing there in the first place."

"How do you mean?"

"Well, his motorbike was parked at the back, so wouldn't you have expected him to go out that way?"

"Was it?"

"Yes. So when she's going on about it, I can't help thinking how it looks as though he did follow Wilma Fenton on purpose. I mean—you saw him, too—chasing after her like he did. So, as I said, things are a little awkward."

Michael got the impression that Tony wasn't so much worried about Stephen's possible part in the murder of Mrs. Fenton as hoping that the invitation to stay at the Grange would be renewed, but he wouldn't do that to Grace. It would be far too obvious, for one thing, and he was sure Grace was glad of the extra money that her out-of-season guest was paying.

At the end of the sweep of lawn, he pointed out the meadow where the fair rides would be set up.

"A fair?"

"Why not? I thought I'd make a proper day of it."

Tony grinned. "You're loving all this, aren't you?"

"Yes, I am." Michael couldn't remember when he'd had such good fun. It was almost like being a child again, planning where everything would go, and trying to remember everything that people might want. He was throwing a huge party, and loving every minute of it.

"It must be costing you a bob or two."

"I can afford it. And the marquee for the talent contest has to go there," he said, "right beside it."

A local music teacher was organizing a children's talent contest, with her at the piano. Michael had agreed to judge that, possibly a little foolishly, because he would end up being unpopular with a lot of parents, and he didn't like being unpopular. He smiled, as he saw a way out of this rash decision. Why would they want him when they had a real, live celebrity in their midst?

"It seems it doesn't matter how much space you've got to play with," he went on, "there's always something that you can't put just anywhere."

"Is that a problem?"

"Well, it means that the contest has to be held very early— from nine thirty to about ten thirty, because we can't start the fairground rides until it's over, or the noise would ruin it. But we don't want the rides standing idle for any longer than we can help." Now, he thought. Now, or never. He can only refuse. "Actually, I'm looking for someone to judge the contest," he said. "I wondered if maybe you . . ."

"Me? What do I know about children's talent contests?"

"What do you need to know? Give the prize to the one who does the least damage to your eardrums. You're a celebrity, Tony. That's what you're for."

"Nine-thirty to ten-thirty?"

"Yes. A very short contest. We're not exactly overloaded with talent in a village this size."

"All right," he said. "I expect I can manage that."

"Brilliant. And this path," said Michael, steering Tony across the grass to the rear of the grounds, "leads to the lake, and the tennis courts. This is the path you should take when you come."

Tony frowned. "The path I should take?"

"The tennis courts will be turned into a VIP car park for the day." He saw Tony's horrified expression, and laughed. "They're hard courts."

"I was going to say that there was a limit to how much you should sacrifice," said Tony.

"You can get in from the back road, drive up and park. The public car park will be packed before we know it, and anyway if it's raining, it'll be a sea of mud. So people like yourself, who are helping out, can avoid all that. You see? There are perks." He led Tony down the pathway, lined with trees still bare, but which by May Day would be in blossom. He hadn't walked around his own grounds for years, he realized. It was good exercise, as Tony had said.

"Which way?" asked Tony, as the path forked.

"That's a shortcut to the summerhouse on the right. If we carry on down here, you can see it from the lake." He was very proud of the Grange, but it had never really occurred to him to take visitors round the grounds. He should do that more often.

"Did I hear someone say that you used to have shoots here?"

"We did, when my wife was alive, but I didn't keep it up." Michael smiled, a little sadly. The gamekeeper had been the only member of his staff who he had ever made redundant. "Josephine was the real enthusiast. She was born here—I think everyone shoots in Stoke Weston. It seems to be a sort of local tradition. Come spring, you hear them at it all the time."

"I saw that Winchester you gave Stephen."

That had been Josephine's. Michael had given it to him on the pretext of having bought a new rifle, but it was really because he thought Stephen would appreciate it. He wished he hadn't given it to him now. "Are you a shooting man?" he asked.

"Oh, yes. I've tried my hand at most country pursuits in my time."

"Isn't that a bit difficult? With the diabetes?"

"Not if you don't let it be. Lots of very successful sportsmen are diabetic. But I was more enthusiastic than talented. I'm not a bad shot, though."

The path widened out and the little lake came into view, with ducks bobbing gently on its surface, and Tony stood beside it, shaking his head slightly. "I had no idea there was so much land," he said, and looked across the water. "Is that the summerhouse? It looks more like a bungalow."

"It is. If you want to have a look at it, we can pop along there on the way back. Otherwise you have to take the dinghy, and I don't recommend it—no one's used it for about five years."

They walked back along the pathway, and took the fork to the summerhouse. Michael opened the door, and Tony looked at it the way Michael had when he had seen it for the first time.

"A family of four could live here," he said.

"When he was little, Ben and his friends did live here, practically." Michael closed the door again, too many memories fighting for supremacy. That was why he never used it. Tony made to go back the way they had come, but Michael stopped him. "This way," he said, pointing to the other path that ran into the wood from the side of the summerhouse.

He'd like Ben to meet Tony Baker. He was the sort of man that Ben could be: clever, good-looking, taking on his condition and beating it into submission. Not that Ben had a medical problem, but it was much the same thing. He didn't have to give in to it. And Ben would enjoy Tony Baker's company—he had a fund of stories to tell about his travels, about the hard men he'd faced down when he wanted them to talk to him and they didn't want him around, about the high rollers in Las Vegas, who thought nothing of losing half a million dollars on the turn of a card. Of his days as a newspaper reporter, when he would risk life and limb if it meant getting a story before the next guy. About the women he'd met, some of whom he'd seduced, some of whom had seduced him.

Michael had told him he should write his life story; it would be worth reading. Of course the stories were exaggerated—maybe even invented—but that didn't matter. They were funny, and exciting, and Tony Baker knew how to tell them. He would really like Ben to meet him, but even if Tony was going to be here that long, Ben wouldn't be home for Easter. He was going away somewhere.

They arrived back almost where they had started, beside the house, where the maypole would be erected, and the Morris dancers would do their thing. "That's it," said Michael. "That's the complete circular tour."

They walked back up to the house, and finished off the second bottle of Chablis. Well, Michael did. Tony didn't ever drink very much.

EVERY PAPER IN THE COUNTRY WAS ON MURDER WATCH IN MALworth, but there were still no new leads on Mrs. Fenton, and it seemed to Judy that every time she stepped outside the station, a microphone was shoved under her nose, and she was asked how the inquiry was progressing. Unlike Tony Baker, however, she was unable to make any comment.

In the hope that the publicity would persuade a witness to come forward, Judy had delayed her visit to him, but now she was on her way to see him, having once again run the gauntlet of reporters. She had decided against trying to make him feel guilty, however self-obsessed he was, and however much she felt he probably deserved to feel guilty. He was lapping up all the attention, pontificating on murder in general and serial murders in particular, for anyone who cared to listen, and a lot of people apparently did.

But making him feel guilty wasn't going to get her anywhere. For one thing, making Lloyd feel guilty wasn't something that she could do to order though he seemed to think it was, and for another, she believed that Tony Baker had told them all he could about what he had seen. Or at least—all that he remembered. She was hoping to take him through it one more time, asking specific questions that might fill in some of the blanks.

Grace Halliday, blonde, attractive, but slightly drawn and tired-looking, showed her into the small, comfortably furnished, old-fashioned private dining room of the Tulliver Inn, where Tony Baker came to meet her, hand outstretched.

"Chief Inspector Hill, how nice to see you. Do sit down."

She sat down at the table, as indicated by the wave of his hand. He sat opposite her, where a shaft of bright, cold March sunshine caught him as if in a spotlight, picking out the honey-colored highlights in his hair. She didn't suppose his choice of seat had been accidental.

"How can I help you?"

"I wondered if you would mind telling me again what you saw when you went into the alleyway."

"I'd be delighted, if you think it might help." He twisted round as Grace Halliday came in, this time bearing a tray of coffee. "Ah, Grace, thank you very much. I took the liberty of ordering us some coffee when I knew you were coming."

"Is it you who keeps questioning Stephen?" Grace Halliday put the tray down on the table, and poured coffee as she spoke.

"I've spoken to him once, but DI Finch has seen him twice. We're questioning everyone who was in the vicinity, Mrs. Halliday." Judy waved a hand toward Tony Baker. "I'm here to question Mr. Baker right now."

"But you took Stephen away. Last time you taped the interview."

"It's fairly standard procedure. He was the last person seen with Mrs. Fenton—he could have vital information. He might not even know that he has it—that's one reason we question people more than once. To try to jog their memories. That's why I'm here now, as I said."

"All he did was see that woman safely home."

There was a rather large flaw in that argument, but Judy didn't point it out.

JACK WAS JUST FINISHING HIS ROUTINE MAINTENANCE AT THE casino when Mike Waterman came out of the office.

"Oh, good, Jack, I'm glad I've caught you. I just wanted to talk to you about the boxing evening."

Jack frowned. "I put the confirmations on your desk. Didn't you find them?"

Mike smiled. "Yes—thanks very much. It looks like a great program. You've surpassed yourself. But I need another favor. You produce the village newspaper on your computer, don't you?"

Yes. Jack had had a computer ever since the first home model had come on the market. "I do," he said. "Why?"

"I know you've already done a great job getting these bouts lined up for us," Mike said. "I just wanted to ask one more favor. Do you think you could design a poster for it—you know, with the bouts listed? Only, I don't want to spend any more money than we have to, so that as much as possible goes to the charity, and I know you can do as good a job as any printer."

Jack was delighted to be asked, so the flattery wasn't necessary. He'd enjoy doing that. He already had a thought about how it might look. Like an old-fashioned bare-knuckle fight bill. Or maybe like a cinema poster for one of these martial arts films. "Sure," he said. "No problem."

"Oh, good. Just the design, of course—I can get them printed off. I don't want you going to any expense. But is it possible to do some big ones to go up in sports halls and places like that, and some smaller ones to put up in shop windows and through people's letter boxes?"

"Oh, yes—leave it with me. I'll even give you a choice of design."

Mike beamed. "Thanks a lot, Jack. I hope you've got your DJ dusted off for the night."

Jack smiled. Mike Waterman really did think that everyone had a dinner jacket, even if they didn't get much occasion to use it. He really did. He'd been too long away from the East End, if you asked Jack.

TONY SHRUGGED SLIGHTLY AS THE DOOR CLOSED BEHIND GRACE. "Sorry about that," he said. "She's being particularly irritating at the moment, but I suppose she is worried about Stephen." He picked up his coffee. "And I know you think I saw more than I'm saying, but I really didn't."

"What makes you think that?"

"Because you suspect Stephen, and because I didn't tell DI Finch that I saw him with Mrs. Fenton, you think that perhaps I recognized him in the alleyway. But I didn't. I don't necessarily think I would have, so I'm not saying it wasn't him—I'm just saying that I don't know who it was. And I swear to you, I can't possibly describe him any better than I have. Dark clothes. I don't even know how old he was, except that he could run very fast, so I think he was quite young."

"Well," she said, "I'm hoping I can coax a few more memories from you than that."

Tony smiled. "I think every memory I possess is now a matter of public record."

He was much in demand for interviews with the press and TV since the news of the letter had broken. The interest wasn't quite of the intensity achieved after the Challenger business, but it was getting that way, proving his contention that the public enjoyed following the exploits of serial killers, and this time they were in on it right from the start, which merely added to that enjoyment. And he didn't think enjoyment was too strong a word; when a serial murderer was doing his thing, newspaper sales rose, TV programs netted big audiences, and publishers began looking through the backlists for titles that might benefit from a paperback run. It was murder as entertainment.

Everyone was waiting for this murder to be committed; even in Bartonshire, where the threat was real, there was a sense of anticipation rather than alarm, everyone secure in the knowledge that murder only ever happened to other people. The panic that had so worried the police was strictly confined to the media, where "climate of fear" had become the most overworked cliché in a welter of clichés.

"You might not know you possess these memories," she said.

"How intriguing. Are you a hypnotherapist on the side?"

"No, nothing like that," she laughed. "It's just a technique that sometimes works. What you saw was over in a matter of seconds—you took in images and sounds and impressions all in the blink of an eye. You came to the conclusion in those seconds that the people you saw were drunk, but they weren't, and I'd like to find out, if I can, what made you think that."

Tony really was intrigued. "How does it work?"

"The idea is that you visualize the scene, and then I ask very specific questions about what happened in those few seconds. It doesn't matter whether you have an answer to them or not. If you don't know the answer, just say so. But it might make you remember details."

"All right. Do I have to close my eyes?"

She laughed again, shaking her head. "Open or closed—it's up to you. Whatever helps you visualize the scene."

He closed his eyes, and saw again the entrance to the alleyway. What was his first impression? Just that there were two people in the alleyway ahead of him. "Okay. I entered the alleyway, and I could see two people about halfway along."

"Which way were they walking?"

"They weren't walking. They were just standing there." He opened his eyes. "I didn't tell you that before, did I?"

"No. I realized your statement didn't make it clear. I thought you would remember that easily enough."

He closed his eyes. "Go on. They were standing there."

"Did you think they were drunk straight away?"

No. He had just noticed two people. He told her that.

"Were they standing apart or close together?"

He could see them, as a sort of silhouette, with no discernible space between them. "Close together."

"Was one taller than the other?"

"Not noticeably."

"Were they facing each other?"

No, he thought, they weren't. "No. She was facing the door to the flats. He was behind her."

"Were they touching?"

"Yes."

"How?"

"I don't know."

"Was he embracing her?"

"No."

"Were their heads touching?"

He thought. They couldn't have been, because he had seen two distinct profiles; that was how he knew it was two people. "No."

"Their bodies?"

"Possibly. I don't know."

"Where were his hands?"

His hands . . . his hands were holding on to her. "On her. On her arm." He smiled, his eyes still closed. He didn't realize he'd seen that, but he had. "This is fun."

"What did you think they were doing?"

That was when he'd thought they'd been drinking. No—he thought she'd been drinking. Drunk, he'd thought. The woman's drunk. "I thought she was drunk, and he was trying to get her into the flats."

"Why did you think she was drunk?"

Good question. Because she almost fell. "She stumbled."

"Is that why he caught her arm?"

"No. He was holding on to her all the time."

"Did you think he was drunk?"

"No."

"Why not?"

"He was impatient with her."

"How did you know that?"

Because he was calling her a stupid bitch, Tony remembered. "He was swearing at her," he said, and opened his eyes again, smiling broadly. "I'd forgotten that. Are you sure you're not using hypnotism?"

"I promise I wouldn't know how to hypnotize you. Did you see him hit her?"

Tony closed his eyes again. He turned into the alley, they were there, there was a sort of scuffle, he was calling her names. "I don't know. There was a lot of movement."

"Did he let go of her arm?"

"He must have."

"Before she fell?"

He had seen them both upright, then she was on the ground. "I don't know."

"Did he raise his arm?"

"I don't know."

"Did he kick her?"

"I don't know."

"Did you see his face?"

Yes, side-on, but in shadow. "No features," he said.

"Was he wearing anything on his head?"

He had just seen a shape. "I don't know."

"What color was his hair?"

"I don't know."

"Did you see her fall?"

"Yes."

"How far away were you when she fell?"

He opened his eyes. "Still just inside the alleyway—as you said, it all happened in seconds." He smiled. "After that, I really didn't see anything. He crouched down beside her, but I couldn't see what he was doing, because he was in shadow then."

She picked up her coffee, and sipped it. "Was that when you went to her assistance?"

"No." He felt slightly embarrassed, but he had to tell the truth. He felt a little as though he was on the psychiatrist's couch. "I have to confess that I didn't have any intention of going to her assistance. If it hadn't been snowing, I would probably have taken the long way round rather than carrying on through the alley. But I didn't fancy being snowed on, so I was just hoping to get past them without being spotted. And I took my time getting there. But he heard me coming, and ran. That's when I realized that I'd got it all wrong."

"Do you mind if we carry on?" she asked. "I'd like to see if we can get anything more on what you saw when he ran away."

"Not at all." He closed his eyes. He was enjoying this. "Fire away."

As MARCH WORE ON WITH NO NEW MURDER, THE PAPERS AND TV began to lose interest altogether, and turn their attention to other, more pressing matters, having decided that it was after all just a very expensive hoax.

But Mrs. Fenton's murder wasn't a hoax, and as the sixth week of the inquiry drew to a close, they were still getting nowhere. The lost half hour remained lost; the reason for the attack remained as obscure as it had the day it happened. So despite the lateness of the hour, Tom was still at work, still trying to think of some angle that had eluded him up till now.

The problem with twins, he had discovered, was that you had no sooner got Becky pacified and relaxed and ready to go back to sleep when David would start, and that would set Becky off again. Or the other way round. He and Liz had been up for what seemed like almost all night. It was, these days, unusual for them not to sleep through, but Liz thought they might have caught a bit of a cold. She could just go back to sleep herself afterward, however many times she was disturbed, but he always found himself wide awake, trying to sleep, listening to the clock ticking, knowing he had to be up at seven.

And another long day of dead ends and brick walls hadn't improved his mood. Despite the many calls they'd had since the TV reenactment, and the painstaking work involved in checking them all out, no matter how unlikely, no new leads had presented themselves.

An amateur mugging was the official view, and Stephen Halliday was the closest thing they had to a suspect, but they didn't have anything like enough to charge him. Anyway, it seemed to Tom that he was even less likely now that they had a slightly more detailed statement from Tony Baker. He couldn't recall the assailant wearing anything on his head, or the color of his hair. Stephen's fair hair would have stood out, even in the dim light. If there was one thing they knew, it was that the assailant wasn't a bare-headed blond.

He was in the CID room, empty save for Gary Sims, when he made this observation.

"He could have been wearing his crash helmet at that point, sir," said Gary Sims. "It's black."

"Or it could have been someone with very dark hair," said Tom. Keith Scopes had done this, Tom was sure, however amateur it looked. "Like Keith Scopes."

"I don't know him, sir."

"He works for Waterman as a so-called security officer. He's a bouncer, really." And there *was* an angle they hadn't covered, Tom realized. He went along to Judy's office, knocked and went in to find her putting on her coat. "Have you got a minute, guv?"

"Are you still here?"

"No, I went home half an hour ago."

"Very funny. Does this mean you've got something at last?"

"Not really. It's just a thought. Keith Scopes said he was doing a job for someone, right?"

"Right." She sat down.

"And he works for Waterman. Who was at the bingo club that night, despite having to get someone to take him there, despite the fact that he always takes Sundays off . . ."

Judy held up a hand. "Are you saying that this job Keith was doing was to bump off Mrs. Fenton?" she asked.

He knew she would react like that, but it wasn't so outlandish. "It could have been," he said. "Waterman's the only person with a connection to Mrs. Fenton that we haven't checked out in any real detail."

"Oh, come on, Tom." Judy sat back. "Why would he want to kill Mrs. Fenton?"

"I don't know, guv! Maybe she was blackmailing him or something. So he employs Scopes to get rid of her. He tells Scopes when she leaves—Halliday says he was using his mobile phone. He could even have told him that she'd won money, so he could make it look like a mugging."

"There are several things wrong with that. One, we didn't find any connection between her and Waterman when we checked into her background. Two, how convenient that she won money so that it could be made to look like a mugging. Three, since when would Keith Scopes walk away from over four hundred pounds? It would look much more like a mugging if he'd taken it. Four, if Mrs. Fenton was blackmailing anyone, it's a bit strange that the money she won is the only money she had to her name. Five, if Scopes got tipped off about when Mrs. Fenton left the bingo club, why did it take him half an hour to get round to murdering her?"

That was a pretty good demolition job, Tom thought. But he wasn't going to give up that easily. "All the same, guv, I'd like to go and talk to Waterman. I want to know why he was at the bingo club. If Scopes was doing a job for someone, chances are it was for Waterman. He could have been there to pay Scopes after he'd done whatever it was."

"I don't know, Tom. All right, there might be something in that—but that's a long way from our murder inquiry, if we can't show any evidence of a personal connection between the victim and Waterman. And we've no evidence that this job—whatever it was—was criminal at all, so it's really none of our business."

Tom wanted to do *something,* and he was in no mood to be told that he couldn't. "Are you wary of talking to him because he's Yardley's brother-in-law?"

Every now and then, even though they had become close friends, he overstepped the mark with Judy, and this was one time. She didn't say anything—just looked at him with those dark brown eyes until he felt about two feet tall. He knew her far better than that. "Sorry," he said. "I didn't mean that."

"Good. I'm wary of looking desperate. Michael Waterman has been entirely cooperative with this investigation, he's gone to some expense to put in his own security measures in his clubs, and he seemed sincerely upset about Mrs. Fenton's death. We can't start accusing everyone who happened to be in the vicinity."

Oh, well. At least it was Friday, and he had the weekend off from going through the second wave of so-called sightings of Mrs. Fenton, prompted by a rerun of the TV reconstruction. Tom was of the opinion that if you put a phone number on a television screen, approximately five hundred people in any given TV area rang it for no reason other than the joy of ringing it. And they were having to check them all out.

"Fair enough, guv," he said. "Have a nice weekend." He turned to go.

"However."

He turned back, grinning.

"This inquiry is getting nowhere, and it's true that Michael Waterman did something out of the ordinary that night, and we haven't checked it out. So all right—but be diplomatic, Tom, and do try to make it sound as routine as you can. In fact—maybe you should send Gary."

"Gary? Why?"

"Because he's a trainee, and gets sent on routine jobs. You can go with him and wait in the car so you're on the spot if Waterman doesn't give a satisfactory answer."

It was a compromise, but Tom would take it. He went back along to the CID room. "Come on, Gary," he said. "I've got a job for you. And bring your diplomatic hat with you."

Gary rang first, to make sure Waterman was home from work, and Waterman agreed to be interviewed. The cover story was that they were checking the movements of every male person who had been at the bingo club—believable because the huge majority of people at the bingo club were female, so checking out the males wouldn't be an enormous task. In fact, Tom was going to do just that if this didn't get them anywhere.

Tom waited impatiently on the road outside the Grange while Gary was inside, putting to Waterman the questions they had worked out between them.

At last he came back, and got into the car.

"Well?"

"Sorry I was so long, sir, but he gave me tea and biscuits. He says that he went to the club because his son had gone back to university that evening, and he felt a bit lonely. He knew Tony Baker would be there, and thought they could have a drink to- gether, but as it turned out Baker was just leaving. He'd told Jack Shaw he'd be there until about ten, and Shaw had gone off some- where, so Mr. Waterman stayed and chatted with the staff."

"Mm." It sounded plausible enough, Tom supposed. "Why was he using his mobile phone?"

"He wasn't. At least, he says he doesn't remember calling anyone. He thinks he was probably putting Mr. Baker's mobile number into his phone's memory."

He could check that with Baker. "How well did he know Mrs. Fenton?"

"He didn't. He doesn't have much to do with the bingo halls, so he doesn't know the customers personally, not like at the casino."

It might be the truth, thought Tom. At any rate, it was credible enough for it to be another dead end, at least for the moment. "Let's go then," he said. "I expect you'd like to knock off for the day." Gary didn't have the weekend off, so it would hardly be fair to keep him hanging about much longer.

But Gary was going to be at work for some time yet, as things turned out. As they drove back out of Stoke Weston, Tom saw Keith Scopes coming out of the news agent's, and pointed him out to Gary. "There's our chief suspect," he said. "One thing about this inquiry—it's very handy having all your suspects living in the same village."

He heard his voice going into what seemed like a void, and glanced at Gary, who was twisted round in the seat, looking back at Scopes.

"What's up?"

Gary turned back. "If that's Keith Scopes, sir, he isn't our chief suspect anymore."

Tom frowned. "Why?"

"Because I know exactly where he was when Mrs. Fenton was killed, sir. I was taking a video of him at the time."

"WHAT WAS ALL THE POLICE ACTIVITY AT YOUR PLACE THIS MORN-ing?"

It was Saturday morning, and Keith had been summoned to the Grange as soon as he'd got back from Barton. Mr. Waterman never missed a thing that went on in the village. Now, he was in Mr. Waterman's study, thankful that the police had got to him too late, because Mr. Waterman had very strong views on drugs, and if he'd been caught with the stuff on him, he wouldn't just have gone to prison, he would have been out of a job when he got out.

The police had arrived about three hours after he had gone to bed, waving a search warrant in Michelle's face when she answered the door. At least they hadn't broken the door down, so Keith might conceivably hear the end of it one day. But it wouldn't be one day soon, and he had willingly gone with the cops when they said they wanted him for questioning. Anything was better than Michelle with her rag up. Even this.

"Just a misunderstanding, Mr. Waterman."

They had found nothing in the house—Keith had sold it all before he'd ever left Barton. Besides, he wasn't stupid enough ever to bring stuff home. Michelle thought he'd had a win on the horses—if she knew where the money had really come from for the three-week skiing holiday from which they had returned last Sunday, she would be off like a shot, and he liked having her around. Apart from anything else, she had made the house look really good; she watched all those makeover programs, and she was brilliant at DIY. To Keith, a toolbox was merely an emergency arsenal.

They had got video of him giving money to Cox, and police videos had improved in the five years since Keith had last been in trouble. There was no way he could deny that it was him, but he had insisted that he had owed Cox the money he gave him, and that the package was one that Cox had asked him to put in the postbox for him, which he had done. He had no idea what was in it, and he didn't look at the name and address.

"I expect it was wedding cake," Sergeant Kelly had said. It seemed to be some sort of private joke, because the young trainee had laughed.

They knew he was lying, obviously, but they couldn't prove anything, so they had to let him go. He had almost got away with it altogether—the photograph of him the police had on file was from when he was sixteen, and before he'd started the body-building that had completely altered his physique, so no one had recognized him on the video. But it seemed that the trainee had taken the video, and had spotted him in the street.

He realized that Mr. Waterman hadn't spoken, was waiting for him to say more. "It was nothing, Mr. Waterman, honest."

Mr. Waterman continued to look at him for a long time before he spoke. "I know exactly what the police had on you," he said. "So I know where you were, and I know what you were doing. You got away with it because they couldn't prove you were buying drugs, that's all."

Keith swallowed. Maybe he had lost his job.

"I'll let it pass this time, Keith. But if I ever—*ever*—hear that you're dealing in drugs again, it won't be the police you have to reckon with, it'll be me. And I don't have to follow the rules. Have you got that?"

"Yes, Mr. Waterman."

THAT MORNING, ROBERT LEWIS HAD BEEN FOUND IN ONE OF Stansfield town center's service areas, lying beside his car, by the manager of the card and gift shop next door to the bank where Lewis had presumably intended using the night safe.

Lloyd arrived at the scene, his heart heavy. The bitterly cold wind was blowing flurries of snow into the corners of the service area, tugging at the blue and white ribbon, making it dance and snap. The body lay hidden by a hastily erected tent of blue plastic sheeting to protect it from the elements and prying eyes, awaiting Freddie's arrival. As Lloyd walked over to it, a small crowd was beginning to gather, and the uniforms were trying to move them on.

DC Alan Marshall, Scottish, methodical, and permanently anxious, was standing by the body. "Ghouls," he said, his polite Glasgow drawl making them seem even more ghoulish. "Mrs. Harrison—that's the lady who found the body—is in her shop, sir. She's very shaken up. And you'll want to see this." He carefully lifted up a corner of the tent, and Lloyd didn't have to be a pathologist to see that the man had been strangled. As the blue plastic was pulled farther back, he saw the banknotes spread on the body, weighted down with a polythene bag full of coins.

"His takings, I suppose," said Marshall, letting the sheet fall back. "He owns the BBQ Burger Bar on Oak Street. It looks like the notes were removed from the bag, and placed on the body. We haven't checked yet whether any of it's missing."

"It won't be," said Lloyd. "Whoever this is doesn't want the money." Oak Street, he thought, was where the Bull's Eye bingo club was. And they had had officers in there, while someone was following this man to the night safe, and killing him. He had known it would be like this.

"The FME says he's been dead less than twelve hours, but not much less," said Marshall. "We think it happened shortly after ten-thirty last night, because the burger bar closes at half past ten."

Lloyd nodded. "How come he wasn't missed last night?"

"As far as we can gather, his wife was away somewhere with the children, so there was no one at home to miss him. His next-door neighbor noticed that his car wasn't there, but she didn't think anything of it, because she thought he was away, too."

Lloyd went to see if the card shop lady had recovered enough to talk to him, and she had, but she couldn't tell him anything that he hadn't seen for himself. Soon, everyone involved in the grim aftermath of a murder was there. The white-suited SOCOs, Freddie, the photographer, the video unit, the rubberneckers, still there despite the efforts to disperse them. But after Freddie had had the body taken away, fewer people wanted to stand around in the raw wind than had before. Alan Marshall was right, thought Lloyd. They were ghouls.

The car was taken away for forensic examination, and everything found at the scene was carefully bagged and marked. Dozens of people were already looking for the man's family, questioning his neighbors and employees, collecting evidence from the service area, the burger bar, the man's car. Yet more people would examine that evidence, see what story it had to tell. Freddie would examine the victim, and find whatever there was to find about his assailant. The murder weapon, a dog-chain by the look of it, still tight around the victim's neck, would be examined and its provenance traced if possible. All that evidence would go through to the manager of the incident room, who would assess its importance, log it, keep it under constant review. The statements would be read, the information contained in them collated and acted on.

Lloyd's job was to piece it all together, to narrow the search down, to find in among the general confusion specifics that would channel the effort of his detectives in the right direction. To make some sense of it all, in other words. And he wasn't at all sure that he could. Judy had been trying for over a month to do that with Mrs. Fenton, with no success.

Lloyd had informed both DCS Yardley and Judy, and they arrived with the ACC to visit the scene before all four went back to Lloyd's office in order for the strategy—already worked out in anticipation of the event—to be unveiled.

Yardley's job was even less enviable; they had a serial killer on their hands, and they had no idea even what his hang-up was, never mind who he was. Yardley had to coordinate a major, force-wide manhunt; he had to ensure that the back-up services were available when needed, that as much reassurance as possible was given to the public, that the press was kept informed, and—as the ACC would put it—on the team. The last thing anyone needed was a press that felt it was being excluded, because that way lay accusations of indifference and incompetence as the weeks rolled by without an arrest being made, which they would. No one thought they were going to solve this one any day soon.

"The bulk of the inquiry team will be working at HQ," Yardley said. "We have to assume that he will try again, and that could be anywhere—Barton HQ seems the most sensible place to coordinate operations, and of course, we have a brand-new purpose-built major incident room there. I'll be heading the inquiry, and I will continue to liaise with the press, who will no doubt be back in force. Nothing has changed in regard to the media."

"You'll have gathered," said the ACC, "that I want both of you on this inquiry, since both of your divisions are involved. Besides, you've proved a formidable combination in the past, and I'm hoping that by putting your not inconsiderable talents together, you'll bring this to as speedy a conclusion as possible."

Lloyd smiled. "We'll be working together even though we're a married couple?" he said. "You're not worried that we might put the inquiry on hold in order to throw plates at each other?"

"I have every faith in your joint ability to save plate-throwing for your leisure hours," said the ACC. "You always managed before. Besides, the Chief Constable believes that married couples should be encouraged to work together even on a regular basis, so this should prove him right or wrong." He smiled. "You and your team will also be based at HQ, and will be accommodated in a small suite of offices which is being made ready as we speak." The ACC stood up. "Now, I'll leave you in the Chief Superintendent's capable hands."

"Right," said Yardley, "I've got a printout of the detective personnel being seconded to the inquiry—I think you should handpick people for a small executive team you'll both feel comfortable working with. I suggest the team should be comprised of all the ranks available to you."

"A small executive team," muttered Lloyd, when Yardley had left, and they were alone in the office. "It makes us sound like car salesmen." But it did mean that all the people he liked working with would be back together again, so that was good. "What's that all about, anyway? Why have we got a small executive team?"

"I don't know. It'll be some managerial notion. But you're getting much better. You didn't growl at him when he said that. And you didn't tell him that you don't say 'comprised of,' which you never tire of telling me."

"Well, if you know you shouldn't say it, why do you?"

"Because it doesn't matter," said Judy.

Of course it mattered. But not, Lloyd supposed, as much as catching someone who had just confirmed in the most emphatic manner possible that he was on a mission to kill.

GARY AND SERGEANT HITCHIN WERE ON THEIR WAY TO THE INCIdent room in Barton, having just been to Stoke Weston to interview Stephen Halliday again, because he had been working at the Stansfield bingo club last night. He didn't usually work in Stansfield, but he worked there often enough for this to be simply a coincidence. He didn't have a checkable alibi, however, having said that he was on his way home at half past ten, so once again they had tried to find out where he was when Mrs. Fenton was killed, and once again he had refused to tell them.

The DI was right—it was handy having all the suspects in the one village, because Tony Baker had been there as well, and Gary had asked him where he was when Lewis was killed.

And it turned out that he had been working in his office in Stansfield town center, just a few minutes' walk away from the bank. Gary wasn't at all sure what to make of that.

STEPHEN WAS IN HIS ROOM, HAVING BEEN QUESTIONED YET AGAIN. Where was he at half past ten last night, they'd wanted to know.

Going home from work, he'd told them, but he could see that they didn't really believe him. Maybe he should ring Ben, tell him what was happening. But he didn't want to worry him with it, not now—he was studying really hard for his exams. And he still didn't want to tell the police, because Mr. Waterman would surely find out. And since they wouldn't find anything linking him to this murder in Stansfield, it would be really stupid to run that risk.

Tony Baker had been there when the police came, and they'd asked him where he was, too, so Stephen hadn't felt so bad. And his mum had been out shopping, thank goodness. He had been surprised when he had come home from Jack's to find Tony there on his own—his mother would never normally leave a guest alone in the pub. But she'd left Tony the keys, so he could lock up if he went out. She'd literally given him the key to the door, Stephen thought. That was serious. And she was in danger of making a fool of herself, because it was obvious—sometimes embarrassingly so—that Tony Baker didn't feel that way about her.

Because of that, Stephen was confident that Tony wouldn't tell his mother about the visit from the police, because Tony had had more than enough of his mum wringing her hands the last time. She had already been bending his ear, apparently, after she'd heard about the second murder on the radio, because, Tony said, she was still worried about what Stephen had been up to the night Mrs. Fenton died.

Stephen thought about that, and decided that he was going to tell her where he'd been that night, because it wasn't right, letting her worry like that. She wouldn't tell anyone if he asked her not to. And he wouldn't ring Ben. He didn't want to get him involved. It wouldn't be fair. He could handle this himself, and he would.

CHAPTER SIX

THURSDAY MORNING. TOM LOOKED UP FROM HIS DESK, AND sighed. The small executive team, as Lloyd always called it, had settled into the rooms that had been found for it at Malworth. Lloyd and Judy had a tiny office off a larger room that housed Tom, John Hitchin, Alan Marshall, and Gary Sims. Next door to that was the large, purpose-built incident room, where the large, presumably nonexecutive team was being accommodated, and where the daily briefings, taken by DCS Yardley, were held.

But Tom didn't feel much like an executive, however small. Executives were by definition people who got things done, and despite a great deal of work he was getting nothing done. They had thought that the murder of Robert Lewis would at least be easier to investigate than that of Mrs. Fenton, especially now that the red herring of Keith Scopes had been removed, but they had been wrong.

Lewis didn't seem to gamble at all—as far as they could ascertain, he hadn't even bought lottery tickets, so they had been wrong about gambling being the target. It wasn't impossible therefore that the murderer had hoped to mask his more substantial motive for one of the murders by making it look as though they were the work of a serial killer. Mrs. Fenton's murder might simply have been expedient, because they had found nothing in her background to suggest that anyone would want her dead.

On this premise, they had started out with reasonable hopes of finding something in Lewis's life that would give them a lead to his killer. But four days on it seemed to Tom that they had spoken to everyone who had ever so much as nodded to Robert Lewis in the street, and they could find nothing at all that explained his death in terms of anyone specifically having a grievance against him.

The discovery that Tony Baker had been in his office in Stansfield town center when the murder took place had caused a lot of speculation, but with no evidence to either implicate or clear him, speculation was what it had to remain. His proximity to both murders could simply be coincidence, though no one really thought that it was, and Alan Marshall, naturally, had been set on the task of going into the backgrounds of the victims in case they had a common connection with Baker or, indeed, anyone else so far involved in the inquiry. He had drawn a blank.

But had they themselves attended the same college or school, or worked for the same company, however many years apart? No, of course they hadn't. They had been born in different towns, they had lived in different towns, and they had gone on holiday to different places. If they had an acquaintance or a tradesman in common, no one at all had been able to find him or her.

Mrs. Fenton lived alone, and had no dependants—Robert Lewis had had a wife and two children. Mrs. Fenton was sixty-two, Lewis was forty. They didn't belong to the same church, the same club, the same bank, they didn't shop at the same places, go to the same pub . . . in short, their lives had nothing at all in common. Yet they had both been murdered, both had been carrying a sum of money, and in each case the banknotes had been removed, from an envelope in the first instance and a bag in the second, and laid out on the body. To what end? The victims were far from rich—it could hardly be a statement about greed.

The letters received by Tony Baker and the newspaper had been through the forensic mill, and had revealed precisely nothing. The paper was available everywhere, the letter used a font that was in virtually every word-processing program in the world, the envelope was self-seal, the address label was self-seal, and, the forensic report had concluded, since it wasn't even necessary to lick the stamps anymore, DNA would not be forthcoming. The

envelopes had been handled by too many people to be worth
fingerprinting, and there were no prints on the letters other than
those of the people known to have handled them, being Tony
Baker and the newspaper staff. It was someone literate, that was all
they knew. All the apostrophes were in the right places, according
to Lloyd—Tom wouldn't know for certain whether they were or
they weren't, not without looking up the crib sheet that he'd written out years ago, after a lecture on the subject from Lloyd.

The postmortem examination had provided nothing new,
other than Freddie's belief that only a man, or a woman with unusual strength, could have strangled Lewis without his having the
chance to fight back. But they already knew they were looking for
a man, so that didn't really help. Nothing found at the scene of either crime had proved to be of the slightest use, or at least, no use
that they had been able to determine, and while the press office
and DCS Yardley were manfully keeping the press supplied with
progress bulletins, the truth was that six weeks after Wilma Fenton's murder, and almost a week after Lewis's, the inquiry was all
but at a standstill.

Lloyd, never a great believer in experts, was, despite his reservations, and the fact that Tony Baker was still a suspect, on his
way to see Baker on the grounds that he knew more about the
workings of a serial killer's mind than did the average man. And
perhaps Baker could make some sense of what seemed to be entirely random murders, except for the amount of cash that was so
ostentatiously not stolen. Tom certainly hoped he could, because
the small executive team was at a loss.

THE PUB WAS OPEN FOR BUSINESS, AND LLOYD WENT INTO THE
small lounge bar, introducing himself to the lady he discovered to
be Grace Halliday. She went off to fetch Tony Baker, leaving
Lloyd with the barmaid, and the food. Lloyd's habit of not break-
fasting didn't often bother him, but there was a delicious smell
permeating the little pub, and Lloyd saw the small batch of sliced

pork sausage under the glass of a hot food display cabinet, and the pile of thickly buttered rolls. His stomach gave a less-than-discreet rumble, and he smiled. "I think I'm going to be very un-professional, and have one of these in a buttered roll," he said to the barmaid.

"Ah, pork burgers are Grace's specialty, aren't they, Rosie?" said Baker, as he joined him in the lounge bar. "People come here for their elevenses just because of them."

"Pork burgers!" said Grace, following him in. "It's just some fried sausage in a bun."

Three people came into the pub, to prove Tony Baker right about their popularity; Lloyd watched the little batch disappear before his very eyes.

"Don't worry," said Grace Halliday, with a smile. "I've got more on."

"Oh, good. Then I'll have one, please," said Lloyd, taking out some change.

"Have it on me, Chief Inspector," said Tony. "And I think I'll have one, too, Grace—it's been a while since breakfast."

"Just take Mr. Lloyd through to the dining room," said Grace. "I'll bring them in. About ten minutes—will that be all right?"

"Perfect."

Once they were in the dining room, Lloyd got round to the reason for his visit. "I'd like to pick your brains about serial killers," he said. "I've never had any dealings with one before. Can you give me any pointers about what sort of man we're dealing with?"

Baker sat back. "In my experience," he said, "serial killers come in a number of varieties—at least the ones I've met and talked to in any depth." He thought for a moment before con-tinuing. "There are the ones who think they have been com-manded by someone—often God—to rid the world of some class of person—often prostitutes. Jack the Ripper was probably one such. They don't want to be caught, but are often relieved when they are, because they don't particularly want to kill. They simply feel compelled to."

"I think we can rule that out. There's no class into which both Mrs. Fenton and Mr. Lewis can be slotted."

"Okay. So then there are those who kill for gain, like John Joseph Smith, the brides-in-the-bath murderer." He shook his head, almost indulgently. "God knows how he got away with it three times. It seems that everyone who met him found him repugnant, except the women he targeted—they would marry him within days of meeting him and sign over their life savings to him. The odd doctor has gone in for that line of serial murder too, persuading elderly women to put him in their wills before quietly ending their lives. They, of course, have no desire whatever to be caught. They are far and away the least interesting to converse with."

"It doesn't seem possible that there's any sort of gain," said Lloyd.

"No, so I expect you can rule that out too. Then there's someone like Challenger, who hated women and wanted the world to know it. He wanted to be caught all along, otherwise how would anyone know what he'd done? But he had hoped to finish the job first, I expect. I never got the opportunity to talk to him."

He paused for what seemed to Lloyd like dramatic effect. He supposed if you gave talks on the subject, you got used to delivering them to an audience. He knew how Queen Victoria had felt when she said that Gladstone addressed her as if she were a public meeting.

"And I imagine," Baker continued, "that in effect, that's what you've been looking for so far. Someone who had a reason to kill these two people, however bizarre." He took out of his pocket what looked like a spectacle case but which proved to contain two little bottles of insulin and a hypodermic needle. "Do you mind if I do this here?" he asked.

"No, not at all," said Lloyd, not sure if he minded or not, but it didn't seem to be good etiquette to demand that your host take his insulin injection elsewhere. "Actually, I was wondering about that—I didn't think you'd be able to have a snack just because you felt like it."

"I couldn't, before," said Baker. "But I'm part of a clinical trial for a new way of taking insulin. It's called DAFNE—the letters stand for Dosage Adjustment for Normal Eating, and that's exactly what it is. If I fancy a snack, I just take an extra shot to cope with it."

Lloyd smiled. "I suspect it isn't as simple as you make it sound."

"Well—you have to learn how to do it. And the drawback is that I have to have four or five injections a day rather than just two. I have to inject at lunchtime, for instance, which I never had to do before. But before, I had to have lunch at lunchtime, and believe me—that was more restrictive. Now, if I miss a meal, I just don't take the insulin."

"I doubt if I could be as sanguine about it as you seem to be," said Lloyd.

"I've lived with it a long time. And if you spend your life worrying about what might be going to happen, you forget to live at all. But to get back to the subject at hand—there is another variety of serial killer."

Their variety, presumably. Doubtless the variety you really don't want to have to deal with at all.

"These are the ones who kill randomly, and without motive, and this could be one of them. It's—if I might put it like this—the purest form of murder. Killing for the sake of it. No motive, no link, no pattern. They simply kill. And as I'm sure you know only too well, murderers like that can get away with it for years and years sometimes, because traditional investigative methods simply don't work."

Oh, that was what Lloyd really wanted to hear.

"And since this one seems now to be killing purely as some sort of challenge to me, I think perhaps that's what you've got. Though in a way you're lucky, because he's made his intentions known. With killers like that, the connection is sometimes simply not made, not for decades sometimes."

Despite himself, and rather impolitely, Lloyd watched, fascinated, as Baker expertly filled the hypodermic, and, through the polo shirt he wore, gave himself the injection.

"Is it all right to inject through your clothes like that?"

"It isn't recommended, but there's no reason why not. I find it a little more socially acceptable than baring my skin."

"I think I always assumed that you would inject it into your arm," said Lloyd.

"You can—but not into a vein. Or muscle. The upper arms, the thighs, the calves—they're all acceptable injection sites, but the abdomen is more usual. The time the insulin takes to work varies with where you inject it."

"Does it hurt?"

"No." He put the needle in a container, and put the insulin back in its case. "I'll tell you what does hurt, though—checking my blood sugar levels. You have to prick your finger to get the blood sample, and that can hurt like hell. With this new system I have to do it more than ever." He smiled. "What were we saying?"

"That Lewis's murder might be entirely without motive other than the desire to outwit you," said Lloyd.

"Yes," he said, his face growing somber. "And I'm very sorry if I precipitated this. But I don't honestly believe that my presence at the scene of Mrs. Fenton's murder *caused* him to kill again. I believe that serial killers are born, not made. I think it's in them all along. Something will trigger it sooner or later. In this instance, my presence at the scene of the first murder."

"But what about the money? Surely that means something?"

"Perhaps." Baker elegantly scratched his coiffured head, then smoothed the hair down again. "But it could actually be quite meaningless."

Lloyd was beginning to wish he hadn't come at all. "Meaningless?" he repeated.

"Just something he does to let you know that it's his handiwork." He sat forward again, elbows on the table, his chin resting on intertwined fingers. "There have been cases where the murderer leaves something at the scene of the crime—a tarot card, let's say. It's an ego thing—the police, as I'm sure you know, often leave that sort of thing out of any information they give the public, as you have left out the detail of the notes being spread out on the body. The presence of that signature proves that the killer is still in business, and you haven't got a copycat. That kind often want to get caught, whether they realize that or not."

Well, that was good, thought Lloyd. But *when* did he want to get caught?

The pork burgers came, and Lloyd discovered that he agreed entirely with the locals, as he continued listening to Baker's dissertation.

"However," said Baker, in a warning tone, "today's psychopaths are scientifically aware. They know that if they introduce anything to the scene of the crime, forensic examination can often trace it back to its source and the police can in that way narrow their search down. Once they've done that, the net will begin to close in. So if you don't want to get caught, it's much better to use something that the victim already has on him. Money is as good as anything else—everyone carries money."

Now he was saying that he *didn't* want to be caught. But then, wasn't that what experts always did? Freddie did it. On the one hand this, on the other hand that.

"But they were both carrying a *lot* of money. Is that significant, do you think?"

"It might be significant, and it might not. Mrs. Fenton's murder could have been for gain, and I could have frightened him off, making him drop the money. And now that he's killing for the sake of it, he's using that as his calling card. Or it could have tremendous significance. The problem is that you don't have enough data on which to base a hypothesis, as Sherlock Holmes would have said. To be brutally honest, what you need is one more murder."

Lloyd had an argument with his waistline as he digested his last mouthful, then remembered that his snack was going on Tony

Baker's tab. Unlike Oliver Twist, he didn't have the chutzpah to ask for more, so he was forced to curtail his carlie intake. "So," he said, "you're telling me that in your opinion I've got no hope of catching this man unless he murders again?"

"Well . . ." Baker looked a little uncomfortable. "Yes, I suppose that is what I'm saying, but I think you knew that already, or you wouldn't be here. You need to know if there's any sort of pattern."

Lloyd nodded his agreement with that.

"There is the fact that he wrote that letter," said Baker encouragingly. "There's no point in winning a challenge if no one knows who you are, so he might subconsciously want to get caught, like the tarot card brigade."

"But not by you, presumably, or he would have lost."

"Quite. I'm the one he wants to outwit, not the police. He could start taking risks. And that could mean that he's caught before he does the deed, because he obviously did some homework on Lewis, and he might do that again. He could behave sufficiently suspiciously to attract attention. At the worst, it could mean that you at least have some witnesses if he does do it."

"Have you accepted the challenge?"

Baker frowned slightly. "Sorry?"

Lloyd was sure he knew perfectly well what he meant, but he reworded the question. "Are you actively trying to find him?"

"Yes," Baker said. "I am."

"How?"

"To quote Sherlock again—I have my methods. They probably won't work, but I will be happy to share anything I find out with you. I suspect, however, that we've all drawn a complete blank so far. I know I have."

Lloyd drove back to Barton, feeling that he had learned a great deal more about diabetes than he had about the psyche of the serial killer, but that was hardly Baker's fault. There was clearly no such thing as a stereotypical serial killer, and only he knew what his next move was going to be.

*　*　*

THE NEXT MORNING, GARY WENT INTO WORK EAGER TO TRY OUT A
theory. When he had found out that Tony Baker had been working in Stansfield town center the night Lewis died, he had what
he thought was an idea, something no one else had considered.
Jason Challenger had been sent to prison for life, with the recom-
mendation that he serve at least twenty-five years, but no one
had checked to see if he was really still in prison. People often
appealed against minimum sentences, and there was a lot of talk
about them even being unlawful, so perhaps he was out. And
perhaps he was challenging Tony Baker again, because both murders had been carried out close to where Baker happened to
be working. It had seemed promising, until he discovered that
five years ago Challenger had had a heart attack and died in
prison.

But last night he had realized that he didn't need to abandon
the theory just because it wasn't Challenger. "Alan?" he said, as
he went into the office.

"Mm?" Marshall raised his head and regarded Gary with the
look of one whose mind was still on what he was doing before he
was interrupted. "Good morning, Gary."

"Oh, yes—sorry. Morning, Alan. Do you think we should
maybe be checking into who Tony Baker's been involved with
since he's been here?"

"Why?"

"Well, we haven't been able to find a link between the victims, so everyone's assuming that this man decided to challenge
Baker just because he happened to witness him killing Mrs. Fenton. But what if he was *meant* to witness it? What if someone
intended killing her just because he knew Baker was there?"

Marshall frowned. "But how could the killer have known that
Baker would go into the alley? He only went back through it because he wanted to ask Waterman something."

Gary knew that. But there was the missing half hour during

which Wilma Fenton had not gone into her flat, and they had not had a single confirmed sighting of her anywhere else. Not one. So she had stayed in the alley, and something or someone had stopped her going into her flat. It seemed to him reasonable to suppose that it was the killer.

"If he knew Baker would be working in his car, maybe he was going to get Mrs. Fenton to go with him and do it where Baker would see it happening. He goes into the alley and hides, waiting for Mrs. Fenton, because he knows that she'll come home at about half past eight."

"So he's been planning this for some time, has he?"

"Why not? Baker had been doing this research for a while."

"All right." Marshall smiled slowly. He did everything slowly. "But how was he going to get her to go with him?"

"He must have been talking to her for about twenty minutes— maybe he was going to offer to walk the dog with her or something. But when that didn't work, he started trying to make her go with him—Baker said he was hanging on to her arm. Then he realizes that Baker has come into the alley, and he can do it there, so he does."

Marshall thought about that, then shook his head. "If he wanted to kill someone purely for Baker's benefit, why didn't he just follow Halliday and kill him? That would be a lot easier than getting Mrs. Fenton to go with him."

"Because Halliday was running. Maybe he was too fast for him. And a lady of sixty would be an easier prospect than a boy of nineteen."

"But if whatever story he was giving Mrs. Fenton wasn't working, why wouldn't he just give up and wait for someone to come through that he could follow and take unawares?"

"Because by the time anyone else wanted to use the alley, Baker would be gone."

Marshall didn't seem impressed, but he wasn't dismissing it out of hand just yet. "How did he know he'd find that money in her bag?"

"Because she was talking about it to Halliday."

Marshall's eyes had lost their look of utter disbelief, to be replaced by a look of what Gary liked to think was thoughtful disbelief. "Oh, what the hell," he said, eventually. "It's worth a try. We'll run it past the DI when he comes in."

JUDY LISTENED TO TOM AS HE TOLD THEM THE THEORY ADVANCED by Gary Sims, and groaned. "Not another one," she said, glancing at Lloyd, with whom she was once again sharing an office, something they hadn't done for years. "One scenario-producer is enough for any small executive team."

Tom grinned.

"That's obviously why you asked for him," Judy said to Lloyd. "You're soulmates."

"Are there any immediate holes in it?" Lloyd asked.

"Well, it was freezing that night—I can't see Wilma standing chatting to someone in the alleyway for twenty minutes. And Tony Baker didn't usually work in his car." She had nevertheless jotted down the salient points. She didn't know Gary Sims well enough yet to know how useful his scenarios were, but Lloyd's usually had some grains of truth in them, and so might Gary's. "Plus, he only left at the interval because he'd won, and he wanted to record his feelings."

"But it could still have been done for his benefit, guv. If someone saw him working in his car, it could have happened more or less that way."

The phone rang, and Lloyd picked it up. "Send him up," he said, and looked at them, his face grim. "Talk of the devil," he said. "Baker's here. And he says it's urgent, so I imagine he's brought us bad news." He sighed. "Or good news, depending on how you look at it. We need another murder, according to him."

Tony Baker was shown in, and his apologetic glance took in all three of them before he took out another long envelope, and removed the letter, placing it on Judy's desk. He put the envelope beside it.

Lloyd came over and perched on her desk. She had forgotten that particular irritation of sharing an office with him, as he took out his glasses and leaned over her in order to read the letter.

ANOTHER ONE MURDERED RIGHT UNDER YOUR NOSE. I THOUGHT YOU WERE SUPPOSED TO BE GOOD. BUT I'M GIVING YOU ANOTHER CHANCE TO CATCH ME, SO DO TRY HARDER THIS TIME. THE NEXT ONE WILL BE IN BARTON, IN APRIL. FROM YOUR NEW CHALLENGER.

"As an expert," she asked Baker, "how much faith can we place in what he writes in these letters?"

Lloyd didn't exactly tut out loud. He didn't even produce a sharp intake of breath—indeed, Judy would be hard pressed to describe what it was he did do, because no one else in the room would know that he'd done anything. But she had committed some grammatical solecism, and he was letting her know that she had. Another drawback about working closely with Lloyd that had slipped her memory.

Baker sat down. "There would be little point in writing them if he was going to lie," he said.

That was what she'd said herself, but she had hoped, irrationally, that Baker would disagree. Because this was March 31, so the murder could take place tomorrow. What could they do in that time? But it hardly mattered. Throwing resources at Stansfield hadn't worked, and she didn't suppose that it would work in Barton either.

"But it's not much to go on, and Barton's a fair-sized town." He smiled. "Sorry—city."

"It's been suggested," said Lloyd, "that Mrs. Fenton's murder might have been engineered for your benefit."

Baker frowned. "I don't see how. I didn't know myself that I was going to go back to the—"

Judy held up a hand. "We've been all through that, Mr. Baker, and we know it's very unlikely. But it is just feasible. Has anyone shown a particular interest in what you did in the South Coast murder business?"

"No—in fact, I don't honestly think anyone I met even remembered about it until it was all over the papers again, and that was after Mrs. Fenton's murder, obviously. A few people know my face, but that's from the TV programs, and even then they can't very often place me. 'You're that bloke off the telly,' that's what they usually say if they recognize me at all. And they're quite often mixing me up with someone else."

Tom pulled over Lloyd's chair and sat down. "Have you noticed anyone taking a particular interest in you yourself?"

There was a moment when Baker looked almost embarrassed, then he shook his head.

"Are you sure?" Judy asked.

"Quite sure."

"Only—that seemed to strike a chord with you."

This time he actually flushed a little. "Well, not unless you count my landlady," he said. "But she isn't interested in me as a catcher of serial murderers. Just as a catch."

Lloyd smiled. "She's a good cook," he said. "You could do a lot worse."

"She can fry sausage. I wouldn't say that was an indication of her prowess in the kitchen. She's not what you would call my type. And I don't think she's your killer," he added, looking back at Judy.

"No," Judy agreed. Apart from anything else, Grace Halliday had been working in the pub at the time of both the murders. Her interest in Tony Baker was presumably purely romantic, whether he liked it or not. And he probably did like it, she thought, sure that his ego didn't object to being massaged, even by Grace Halliday, whom he seemed to regard as beneath him.

"Has anyone deliberately avoided you?" asked Lloyd. "Have you noticed anyone who goes out of his way not to talk to you—when you're in the pub, say?"

"Well, village people tend to regard any outsider with some suspicion," said Baker. "I can't say I've noticed one more than any other."

After he'd gone, Judy informed Yardley that they had a new letter, and it was borne away to the lab, doubtless to prove to be as uninformative as the first two.

"I suppose he'll be writing to the paper again," Tom said.

"Probably," said Judy, gloomily, then turned an accusing eye on Lloyd. "Okay," she said. "What did I do wrong this time?"

For once, he didn't feign innocent bewilderment at her question. He grinned at her. "A dangling participle," he said.

"What's that when it's at home?"

Lloyd smiled. "Look it up."

BARTON, TONY DISCOVERED, AS HE SNAPPED YET ANOTHER UN-lovely scene, was full of places where a murder could be carried out in comparative privacy. It didn't have Malworth's alleys, or Stansfield's pedestrianized town center with its concealed service areas, but it did have back streets, where no one would choose to be if one could just as easily be on the main streets.

The back streets tended to be lined with the yards of commercial properties, some walled off, with cast-iron gates leading down to basement entries, but some open to the street. It was here that the detritus of restaurants and food shops was thrown into bins and Dumpsters to be picked up by the refuse collection vans that worked the area during the night, something they could do because there were no residents to disturb, unless you counted the vagrants who huddled round the heating vents.

Now, on a bright, sunny afternoon, the backstreets were busy, being used by the cars and vans that knew how to avoid the endless traffic lights on their journey through the city. Too many pairs of eyes to add to the ever-vigilant cameras, so the murder would have to be carried out at night again.

But even at night, even given the tawdry desolation of the backside of any city, it would be riskier to murder someone here than it had been in Stansfield, and the encouragement that he had given Lloyd had not been misplaced. There was no way to ensure that no one would see what was going on. Leaving out the information, given freely last time, about how the murder was going to be done, had been a wise decision; any plan would have to have a back-up, with so many variables to take into account.

It could even be simply opportunistic, but that carried its own risks. What might seem like an opportunity could turn into someone raising the alarm, because people were on their mettle now. And the cameras might pick something up, if the murder wasn't planned to exclude them.

He had confined his research to the streets on either side of Mafeking Road, a long, wide road that had given a section of itself over to the very kinds of human activity that Tony investigated in his TV series. Gambling, drinking, drugs, sex. Mafeking Road itself would be busy, but passersby would tend to be otherwise engaged, either wrapped round a companion or in large groups, all under the influence of some intoxicant or other. They would have little reason to venture down the streets on either side. Streetwalkers would be abroad, but they would be borne away in their customer's cars. And the victim wasn't going to be a prostitute—cars were far too easy to trace. Not like in Jack the Ripper's day, when his hansom could disappear into the London fog. A prostitute would be much too risky a proposition.

Whoever was chosen as the victim, there was a risk to be run. The buildings would be active, all of them, unlike the shops and offices farther up. But while that area was much more secluded, it didn't afford the opportunity that this one did. The victim would have to be lured to the quieter area, and that meant spending time with him or her, something to be avoided at all costs.

But here, with the booming nightlife, there were other dangers. Someone could be looking out of a back window, or taking rubbish out to one of the bins, and the police were always around where there were drink and drugs to be had. The frequency of the patrols would be increased, no doubt. This murder had to be planned, he was sure of that, but the most careful planning wouldn't by any means eliminate all the hazards.

Barton wasn't somewhere that Tony would choose to commit a murder, however easy it would be to get lost in the crowd moments later. It would be a riskier business altogether to commit a murder in a city that, like most cities, never really slept.

Stansfield could have been a coincidence—Stephen could have just happened to be working there on the night of Lewis's murder. And that was surely the case, Tony told himself, because even his writer's imagination couldn't conceive of Stephen Halliday as a murderer. But always at the back of his mind was his first-hand knowledge of the breed, some of them the most mildmannered people on earth.

And in all the time Tony had been at the Tulliver Inn, Stephen had never worked in Barton, so if nothing else the Barton murder would prove if it really was Stephen who had written him those letters.

IT WAS UNSEASONABLY WARM FOR THE MIDDLE OF APRIL, IN STARK contrast to March, when sleet and snow had been the order of the day. Keith ran a finger round his stiff, starched collar, as he left the open fire doors at which he was posted, and moved farther into the room, casting a fleeting look at the perspiring boxers in the ring, glad that at least he wasn't having to do that for the amusement of the Bartonshire nobs.

He looked round the room, his glance taking in the top table, and caught Mr. Waterman's eye. Waterman gave a nod that was really no more than a slow blink, and Keith wandered on toward the bar.

"Can you get someone to cover me for fifteen minutes?" he asked the bar manager. "I've not had a break yet."

The manager looked at the clock. "Fifteen minutes," he said. "Exactly. You'll have to be back here by ten forty-five—no later. I'll need you on the bar from then."

"I'll be back," said Keith. "Don't worry."

MICHAEL WATERMAN WATCHED KEITH AS HE WALKED FROM THE bar to the big doors that stood open at the back of the hall.

"Good little scrapper, that black lad," said Jack Shaw, just as his opponent went down for the count. He grinned. "What did I tell you?" He looked at his watch. "Well—that's it, for me. It was a good night, Mike. Thanks for inviting me."

Michael smiled. "You're welcome, Jack—no one's done more than you to make this evening a success. I don't know how you persuaded them all to come, but it's been a great program so far."

"Oh, I enjoyed twisting the boxing clubs' arms. And by the look of the tables, we've made a fair amount for the charity."

"You know this do is going on until the small hours, don't you? There's no need to go yet."

"I need my beauty sleep."

Tony Baker stood up, and leaned awkwardly over the table to shake Michael's hand. "Me, too," he said. "I think I'll call it a night. Thanks, Mike. It's been a very interesting evening."

As soon as Michael had realized that Tony Baker had bought a ticket for the boxing evening, he had arranged to have him at the top table, so he could show him off to his other VIP guests. It was a shame he was leaving early.

"I had no idea that so much betting went on at things like this," Tony added, and grinned. "Are you opening a book on the talent contest, too?"

Michael laughed. "Oh, I forgot," he said. "Another perk of coming to the May Day do is that you'll get to see this one make a prat of himself Morris dancing." As soon as he'd said it, he wished he hadn't—Jack looked less than pleased with him. He'd always made fun of Jack's Morris dancing—it never usually annoyed him.

"I look forward to that," said Tony.

Having made their way through the tables, both Jack and Tony made for the nearest exit, being the fire doors, but whereas Jack made it, the mother of one of the talent contest hopefuls waylaid Tony, and she didn't seem inclined to let him leave, so Jack went on alone. Poor Jack—Michael imagined that he would be all too aware that he could leave a room any time he chose without anyone begging him to talk to her before he left. Another black mark against Tony, Michael was sure. But he was equally sure that Tony would just as soon leave as be set upon by females— he was trying to edge closer to the door, but without success.

At quarter to eleven, Keith returned. Once again they caught each other's eye, and this time, the merest movement of Keith's head from side to side told Michael what he wanted to know.

He realized, a fraction late, that he was being addressed by one of the people at the table, and tried hard to look as though he had been listening to what she had been saying. What with not knowing what she was talking about, and finding it difficult to hear her above the noise of those watching the next bout, he didn't think his attempt was entirely successful.

He signalled a waiter, and ordered more wine. Clearly, most of his guests had every intention of staying until the end and getting their money's worth, and who could blame them? He smiled as he saw Tony Baker finally making it to the door, and leaving, at ten to eleven.

OUTSIDE THE BARTON BINGO CLUB, STEPHEN TRIED ONCE MORE TO start the bike. The bingo had finished at half past ten, and he had been about to leave when the caller had made an announcement.

"Before he goes, we want you all to sing Happy Birthday. Stephen—where are you, Stephen?"

A spotlight had found Stephen, who had smiled winningly.

"He's twenty years old tomorrow—remember when you were twenty, ladies? Of course you do—King John had just signed the Magna Carta, hadn't he? In 1215, wasn't it? It was supposed to be at twelve, but he got held up in traffic."

Oh, God, Stephen had thought. Was he going to go into some comedy routine? But he had confined himself to that one unfunny joke.

"Anyway—he's only here tonight, so we're celebrating a day early. Now—all together, let's give Stephen's teens a rousing Bull's Eye club send-off."

". . . happy birthday, dear Stephen, happy birthday to you!"

Stephen had waved, and smiled, and had very nearly made it to the door when two ample ladies practically jumped him.

"Are you new here? I haven't seen you before," said one.

"I don't often work in Barton."

"Oh, that's a shame," the other one said. "Will you be working here in the future?"

"I don't know—I'm mostly in Malworth, and now and again in Stansfield. The rota goes up on the wall, if you want to look out for me coming back here."

"Oh, I think I'll have to move to Malworth, if that's where you usually are! Is that a crash helmet? Do you ride a motorbike?"

"Yes." If he didn't, it would be an odd sort of fashion accessory, thought Stephen.

"You don't fancy a pillion passenger, do you?"

"Get on!" said the other one. "He'd be doing wheelies whether he wanted to or not, with you on the back."

And so it had gone on, with Stephen smiling gamely and laughing at their ever more risqué jokes until at last they reluctantly let him go.

He would have been home by now if it hadn't been for them, he thought, as the bike, after several attempts, reluctantly fired into life.

*   *   *

JACK HAD BEEN FURIOUS WHEN TONY BAKER HAD GOT UP AT THE same time and said he was leaving, too, and blessed Mrs. Turner for stopping him when she did. Patsy Turner went in for every talent contest ever held, and was presumably going in for this one that Baker was judging, so Jack imagined that he would be held up for some time. Presumably he would have a little while in which to try to impress Grace before Baker got here.

He had never worn a dinner jacket and bow tie before; looking at himself in the long mirror of the plush private toilet in the casino, he had been startled to see what a difference it made to him. And maybe, just maybe, so would Grace.

He had been in one of the cubicles when Tony Baker had come in, and had met someone who'd said in fun that he had it made, staying at the Tulliver, because an unattached good-looking blonde with a pub was every man's dream. And he'd listened as Tony had dismissed Grace as nothing more than an empty-headed irritation. He'd waited until they'd left before he came out, and decided to go home when the next bout finished. Not that he would dream of telling Grace what Baker had said, but she shouldn't be wasting her time with Baker and his overblown ego, and maybe if she saw Jack in his finery, she'd find him not so bad after all.

He had walked into the pub to find it empty, not an unusual occurrence. Stoke Weston people had to get up early, and it wasn't yet that time of year when people came from the surrounding towns to spend their evenings in country pubs. Grace had come through as soon as she had heard the bell, run past him, locked the pub door, grabbed his arm and practically dragged him upstairs. He had a feeling that the dinner jacket was unlikely to have produced that effect, and anyway, she was gabbling something about Tony Baker all the time she was doing it. It took longer to get upstairs than she would have liked, because steps were another thing that gave Jack a little trouble.

Now, they were in Tony Baker's room, and she was showing him what she had found.

"I don't pry, Jack, I really don't. But he locks the door all the time, and I hadn't cleaned in here for over two weeks, so I just let myself in with my key, and I was dusting this table when this file fell, and things came out, and—look. Look what I found."

She thrust a printout of a photograph into his hands. "Look," she said. "That's that bit behind the bank in Stansfield where that man was killed."

Yes, Jack had recognized it. "Well," he said, "he's a journalist, isn't he? Maybe it was for his paper or something."

Grace made an impatient noise. "Look at the date!" she said. "The date's on it, along the bottom. Look at it. That photograph was taken in February, and the murder happened in March. And look at this." She handed him a sheet of paper on which a list had been ticked off.

Jack read, and what he read certainly did make disturbing reading. *No cameras. Room for two cars only. Secluded. Poor lighting. No residential buildings* . . .

"Jack—do you think it's him?" Her voice was no more than a whisper. "Do you think he's the one who killed these people?"

It was clearly what she thought, and that rather suited Jack, but he thought it best not to reply.

"What else could that mean?" she demanded. "It must be him. I don't want him here—should I call the police?"

Jack looked at it. "I don't know what to make of it," he said. "But calling the police might be a bit strong, without hearing his side of it."

"But what's it all about?"

"I don't know," Jack said. "But I think you might be jumping to conclusions. Let's look at the other stuff."

They spent some time going through the papers, and everything they found made Grace more and more suspicious.

"I'm going to call the police," she said.

"I really think you should wait and see what he says."

"Are you going to wait with me?"

"Yes, of course I will."

"Maybe we should put on his laptop," she said. "See what else he's got."

"I think that might be a bit—"

"He could be sending these letters to himself! How do we know he isn't?"

Jack didn't have the chance to respond to that, because Tony Baker himself was in the doorway.

"Is there a problem?" he asked.

For a moment, neither he nor Grace spoke, then Jack felt that there was little point in trying to be diplomatic, and plunged in. "Grace is a bit bothered by what you've got in this file," he said.

"It fell open," Grace said quickly, her voice scared. "I couldn't help but look at it."

Baker looked puzzled. "Did I forget to lock the door?"

"No, but the room has to be cleaned."

"Of course it does. I'm sorry, I didn't think." He came in, and picked up the file. "And I'm not surprised you're worried about me, if you've been looking at this," he said. "But I can explain. Shall we go down?"

Baker led the way, and Jack stood aside to let Grace go ahead of him. "Don't worry," he said. "I'm right behind you."

Well, he was behind her, at any rate. Not exactly right behind her, since it took him rather longer than it took her to get downstairs again. Grace waited at the foot of the stairs for him, and they went into the sitting room together. Tony Baker was standing by the fireplace, looking penitent.

"I'm glad you've decided to hear me out," he said.

Jack sat beside Grace on the sofa, and waited to hear what he had to say for himself.

"I'm really sorry that you got such a shock," he said. "But that's how I hope to find out who the murderer is."

Jack frowned. "How come you've got a photograph of the very place that bloke in Stansfield was killed? Taken three weeks before it happened?"

"It's in the file because it *did* happen," said Baker. "I took photographs of a dozen places in Stansfield, and one of them turned out to be where it happened, as I thought it would. And now it's in that file, because I can study it, and that lets me know his preferences."

"I don't understand," said Grace.

"I know how this man thinks," said Baker. "I've met him a dozen times in my career. I knew from what happened in Malworth what sort of place he would choose in Stansfield. And I tried—unsuccessfully—to narrow it down to one place. Because if I can do that, there's a chance that I will even be able to work out who his victim might be."

"What good would that do?" asked Jack.

"If I can find his likely victim, I can find him, and stop him before he does any harm."

Grace still looked at him suspiciously. "How?"

"I don't have a clue who the murderer is," Baker said, "so I have no suspect to tail. But if I can work out who he might have down as his target, I can tail the potential victim, like I did before. If I'm wrong, then it makes no difference to anyone. But if I'm right, then I can prevent him killing again."

"Covering yourself in glory while you're at it," Jack said.

"Yes."

Jack was startled by the candid answer.

"I'm quite prepared to admit that I'd like to find him myself, and beat the police to it for the second time. It would do me no harm to win this challenge, and my pride is even a little bit at stake." Baker sat down in the armchair opposite them.

"Do the police know what you're doing?" Jack asked.

"They know I'm trying to find him. They don't know how. And they would laugh at me if I told them, but—as you see—it was partially successful. I really do know quite a bit about this sort of thing."

Grace had never lost the look of distrust. "But how could you know where he was going to kill that man?" she asked.

"I just . . . think myself into his mind. I knew it would be somewhere like the alley in Malworth—somewhere that wasn't overlooked by houses, that didn't have strong lighting. I thought it would be carried out at night again. But there were about ten places that it could have been—that was just one of them. I can show you all the other photographs if you don't believe me."

Grace didn't respond.

"But the second murder gave me a lot more to go on than the first, and I might get closer this time." He smiled. "I don't stand a hope in hell of succeeding, but to be honest, I'm almost enjoying the challenge. No—if I'm really being honest, I *am* enjoying it. I know people have died, and I know it isn't a game, but it's much more my thing than documenting people's gambling habits."

Jack looked at Grace, but despite the frank explanation she still looked thoroughly scared by what she'd found, and totally unconvinced. He would wait until Stephen was home before he left, he decided. She would be afraid to be left all on her own with Baker. Jack was surprised when he saw the time; Stephen was a creature of habit.

"Stephen's late tonight, isn't he?"

"What? Oh, yes. He was working in Barton tonight." Grace looked at the clock. "All the same," she said, "he is late." Her eyes suddenly widened in fear again. "You don't think anything's happened to him, do you?"

Jack wished he had kept his big mouth shut. "No, of course not. He'll just have been held up. How come he's in Barton? He doesn't usually go there, does he?"

"Not usually. But he finishes at half past ten. What if something's happened?"

"I'm sure nothing's happened," Jack said. "Maybe he went out for a drink to celebrate his birthday."

"He wouldn't do that—he's on the bike."

"Well, it wouldn't have to be alcoholic, Grace. Like I said, he'll just—"

As he spoke, the back door of the pub opened and closed, and

Stephen appeared in the sitting room, looking a little startled at the threesome he found there, as well he might, thought Jack.

"Where have you been?" said Grace. "I was worried about you."

"I got held up at the club. And then the bike wouldn't start, *and* it broke down on the way home."

"You could have phoned."

"Sorry."

"It'll be your birthday in twenty minutes," said Baker. "Would you like your present now?"

Stephen looked for a moment as though he was going to say that he didn't, but then he smiled. "Why not?" he said.

And thus it was that Jack found himself at an impromptu and rather strange birthday party, with everyone trying to look as though that was what they wanted to do. But Grace opened a bottle of champagne, and that seemed to relax her a little.

"Well, I'll be off then," said Jack, when Stephen had opened his presents, and the champagne had been drunk. "I'll give you my present tomorrow, Stephen. I'll see myself out, Grace."

But Stephen followed him to the door. "What's going on? Mum looked as if she'd seen a ghost when I came in."

"Just a misunderstanding. She'll tell you herself if she's a mind to."

Stephen looked puzzled, but he didn't inquire further. "Okay," he said, his voice doubtful. "I'll see you."

"Yep. See you, Stephen."

Jack went out into the still balmy night, and began the short walk home. Thinking that Tony Baker was the murderer had meant that for once Grace wasn't making eyes at the man, which was better than nothing, he supposed. But his own new suave image hadn't exactly taken her breath away.

Still, she had turned to him when she needed help, so things were definitely looking up.

CHAPTER SEVEN

S TEPHEN HAD GONE TO BED NOT LONG AFTER JACK HAD LEFT, but he hadn't slept. Ben had rung to wish him happy birthday, and had asked him all about the murders, which were national news once again. Stephen still didn't tell him that he had been questioned about them.

They had talked for a long time, until Ben had to go to bed. He had lectures to attend in the morning, he'd said. It was all right for Stephen, working the odd hours that he did—he could stay in bed in the morning, but Ben couldn't. So Stephen had finally let him go, but not until he'd asked him what he thought about his dad playing host to Stoke Weston's May Day celebrations—Ben always found his father's grand gestures a bit much. But it turned out that Ben didn't know about it. When Stephen explained, Ben said that it would give him an excuse to come down that day, so they could see each other. He couldn't get away over the weekend because there was something he had to do at university, but he had the Monday off because it was a holiday in Scotland, too.

He found it hard to sleep after that, as he always did when they had spoken. He wished Ben was here, that he hadn't had to go to university so far away, and he was excited about May Day. But another reason that he couldn't sleep was his awareness that his mother and Tony Baker were both still downstairs, though it was now well after three o'clock in the morning. He could hear the rise and fall of their voices as they spoke quietly, though he couldn't make out what they were saying. It was unusual for his mother to stay up so late, and it was unheard of for Tony, who usu-

ally shut himself in his room as soon as he came in. But the
evening had been strange—finding Tony and Jack and his mother
in the sitting room had been odd, to say the least. Tony and Jack
had been in their tuxedos, so they must have come to the pub
from the boxing thing that Waterman had put on. Whatever this
misunderstanding had been was presumably still being discussed,
far into the night.

It was after four when they at last came upstairs, and Stephen
might have managed to sleep were it not for the fact that the talking continued, now in whispered exchanges, on the landing, and
finally in the room next door to his. It was embarrassing, knowing
that Tony was with his mother in her bedroom, as it could only
mean one thing: she had finally achieved what she had been aim-
ing for ever since Tony Baker had arrived in Stoke Weston. Perhaps Wilma had been right after all; perhaps he was going to get
a stepdad. The idea of Tony Baker as stepfather didn't appeal to
Stephen at all.

It went quiet then, and Stephen tried to go to sleep, but after
a little while noises could be heard through the wall that made
him blush a painful deep red, as he tried not to imagine what was
going on. They weren't particularly loud, but they were quite un-
mistakable, and while he could just about take his mother's union
with Baker as an abstract notion, the audible confirmation of it
was too much. He buried his head in the pillow, but though that
blocked out the sounds, it didn't block out the images that kept
forming in his head whether he wanted them to or not.

In desperation, he picked up his Walkman, and jammed in
the earphones, switching it to radio. Any radio station, any kind
of music, anything at all to take his mind off what was happening
next door. Music of some sort was playing; he turned the volume
up as far as his ears could stand, and lay in the dark, trying to concentrate on the words of the song, to let the images it produced
override the ones already in his mind.

He hung on the DJ's every word, listened intently to every
track, and gave his undivided attention to the six o'clock news

when it came on. It was international news first, and Stephen became more aware of the state of the world's wars and politics than he had ever been. The first item on the home news was also political; Stephen didn't know what they were talking about, but he listened to the minister for something or other as though his life depended on what she had to say. And then came something in which he really was interested, as everyone in Bartonshire would be, when they awoke to it.

"Bartonshire police have confirmed that a man found stabbed to death in the center of Barton early this morning is believed to be the third victim of the man they are hunting in connection with the murders of two other people in the county in the last two months. The victim, whose name has not yet been released, is thought to have lived rough in the city for many years, and was found dead shortly after two o'clock this morning.

"The killer is believed to be the author of anonymous letters being sent to Tony Baker, the journalist and broadcaster who solved the case dubbed the 'South Coast Murder Mystery' eighteen years ago, and to the newspaper for which Mr. Baker is a columnist. The most recent letter named Barton as the intended scene of his next murder, and police patrols were stepped up in the city as a result, among other measures. The man leading the murder hunt, Detective Chief Superintendent Yardley, went immediately to the scene of this latest killing, and read this statement to the waiting reporters.

" 'Bartonshire police very much regret that the extra precautions taken in Barton in light of the communication received failed to prevent another murder. Every effort is being made to find the person responsible for these tragic deaths, and we would like to talk to anyone who was in the Mafeking Road area of Barton at any time last night or in the small hours of this morning.'

"Detective Chief Superintendent Yardley added that the area in which this latest killing took place is very busy at night, having several wine bars and various places of entertainment, and that the police are hopeful of finding witnesses with information that will lead to the capture of whoever is responsible."

Stephen switched off the radio, and removed the earphones, relieved to discover that everything was now quiet in the room next door. Finally, at ten past seven in the morning, he fell asleep.

"THERE ARE EMPTY PREMISES ON MAFEKING ROAD," SAID YARDLEY. "I've arranged for an incident room to be set up."

"Hitchin and Sims should be available to man it as soon as it's ready," said Judy.

"Good. Well, now that you and Lloyd are here, I think I'll get back to HQ—let me know if you get anything worthwhile." He looked around. "Where is Lloyd?"

"He's talking to Freddie."

"Oh, right—I just wanted to say that if you need more personnel, let me know. And find out where Tony Baker was last night—if the first two are anything to go by, I don't suppose he was too far away."

"Yes, sir. I'll tell Lloyd when he comes back."

"We've got to get this man," Yardley said, looking suddenly haggard. "We can't go on letting him lead us by the nose like this. He's getting cocky now—killing someone in a place teeming with people, wrapping up the murder weapon for us. And telling the paper that it was going to be Barton—he didn't do that last time."

Once again, the newspaper had received a letter the day after Baker had received his, and unlike the first one to the paper, it had named the scene of the next murder. Ignoring the gentlemen's agreement to let the police see any communication from the murderer before going to press, the newspaper had published it in its entirety, so this time, the special measures had had to be taken with the press watching their every move. None of the papers had revealed anything about those measures that they had asked them not to reveal, but it had made their lives a little less easy, nonetheless, to have the press breathing as closely down their necks as they were. But, as Lloyd pointed out, it did mean that the papers knew the limitations of anything they did. They couldn't, for instance, assume that Barton really would be the scene of the next attempt, so resources were being stretched, even if they were being forewarned.

Patrols had been stepped up in secluded areas of Barton, which had included the rear of the properties along Mafeking Road, but the patrols couldn't be in two places at once and it would have been an easy matter to wait until they had passed before carrying out the murder. Warnings had been issued to people not to go out alone in secluded areas day or night, but no amount of warnings could reach someone like this victim.

Freddie had let them take the body away, and Judy was watching the white-suited scene-of-crime officers remove the pathetic collection of odds and ends that constituted the worldly goods of Davy Guthrie, the vagrant whose life had been ended, not by the cheap alcohol that he had consumed at a frightening rate, not by the many bitter winters that he had endured on the streets of Barton, not by the tobacco that he rolled into the thin, foul-smelling cigarettes that he smoked continually, but by someone with a knife and a desire to kill.

It had occurred to no one that someone like Davy would be a target, least of all, Judy imagined, to Davy himself. But a target he had been, and the small change that he had begged in order to buy his next day's supply of cheap booze had been left on his body, sorted into piles of differing coins.

He had been found by the two police officers part of whose duties included moving on the derelicts who took up residence on the side streets of Mafeking Road at night, most of them having begged money during the day and evening from the people going into the clubs and bars on Mafeking Road itself. Davy was a regular, and this had been his spot. The police would let him sleep off the alcohol and move him on at around two in the morning, to forestall the complaints of those who had to service the streets at night.

Knowing that he would be wakened at this early hour, Davy, in common with the other street dwellers, had always settled down early. The officers had checked that area at intervals during the night, but by the light of sodium streetlamps Davy dead was indistinguishable from Davy asleep, and it wasn't until they had tried to rouse him that they had realized what had happened.

It was entirely understandable if you had ever walked the beat in a city where homeless drifters slept in the street; a tolerant attitude toward them meant that they weren't harried and shifted when there was no need, because they weren't actively begging, and they were getting in no one's way. Compassion rather than a lack of concern had prompted them to leave Davy alone. But the newspapers wouldn't see it that way; already the TV crews were unpacking their equipment to film the mean little street in which Davy had made his home. The police had passed by as this man lay dying, that's what they would say.

And they would ask the inevitable questions. What were the police doing to catch this man? How many more had to die before they got their act together? Did the murderer have to sell tickets, or what? He told them when and where he was going to do what he did—how much more did they need?

And Judy wouldn't blame them for thinking that too little was being done. They didn't understand about the boxes and boxes of filed statements, about the hours spent poring over them in the hope that one of them contained something that had a bearing on the investigation. They didn't know about the exhaustive searches into the backgrounds of the victims, of the hundreds of man-hours spent knocking on doors, asking questions to which no one had an answer. They didn't know about the dozens of cars whose owners were traced, checked, and ultimately eliminated from the inquiry, about the false leads and dead ends, and the endless interviews with likely candidates, all of which came to nothing. This man apparently killed randomly, and for no reason other than to get away with it. And when getting away with it *was* the motive, then it wasn't particularly difficult to do just that.

But this time, things were a little more hopeful. It had been a warm night, unlike the nights on which the other two murders had taken place, so there had been people about on the streets—people who could help them narrow down the time of death, who could describe the others they had seen in the vicinity. There was a camera on one of the buildings, though Judy doubted that this man would make as elementary a mistake as to be caught on it. But perhaps he had.

And, as Yardley had mentioned, they had found what appeared to be the murder weapon in one of the big industrial-sized bins at the rear of the restaurant on the corner of Mafeking Road and Ladysmith Avenue, the latter being where Davy had chosen to make his sleeping arrangements. It had, for reasons known only to whoever put it in there, been sealed in a padded bag. Perhaps he had thought it would escape detection, but the presence of a brand-new sealed padded bag in a wastebin had naturally excited some interest, so it seemed unlikely that he would have believed that.

Yardley hadn't told the papers about the discovery—it still had to be confirmed that the blood on the six-inch blade of the curved, fisherman's trout-filleting knife was Davy's. But if it wasn't, Judy thought, they'd better start looking for another body. She doubted that they would find anything as useful as fingerprints on the knife, its sheath or the padded bag, but knives could sometimes be traced.

Mafeking Road ran for three miles through the center of Barton, and a mile of its length had become known locally as Sunset Strip, because coffee bars, restaurants, wine bars, clubs, amusement arcades and pubs had, over the years, become established. Michael Waterman's Lucky Seven Casino was about a quarter of a mile away from where Davy's body was found, and Judy felt that the Waterman connection could no longer be a coincidence.

The Bull's Eye bingo club, however, was a fair distance away, so it wasn't exactly the same setup as before. Even so, they were checking to find out where Stephen Halliday had been working last night. He was their only suspect now, and that on so little evidence as to be laughable, but he had to be checked out.

Ladysmith Avenue ran off Mafeking Road at a right angle, running down the side of the big corner restaurant called Forty-second Street, and at night served as an unofficial car park to the various businesses on Sunset Strip. Railings separated the pavement from the strip of grass at the side of the building, and it was under these that Davy had bundled himself up for the night in the filthy blanket that the SOCOs were taking away, now stained with blood as well as the many other bodily fluids it had had to absorb over the years.

Ladysmith Avenue intersected with Kimberley Court, the cul-de-sac onto which the buildings on Mafeking Road backed, where the other down-and-outs slept, then carried on, taking traffic to the ring road that skirted Barton, and out of the city. The chief attraction of Kimberley Court was the refuse bins and the food scraps they contained. As they closed for the night, one or two of the restaurant owners even brought out their surplus food for the human flotsam that fetched up on their doorsteps, despite being asked not to do so by those who seemed to think that living on the street was a soft option.

No one knew why Davy had remained aloof from the others; he was the only one who chose to sleep round the corner on Ladysmith Avenue, and this had proved to be his undoing, because it had made him the softest target of all. But he slept on the pavement between Kimberley Court and Mafeking Road, so it did mean that two of the buildings across Mafeking Road had a clear view of him. These were the Queen Bee, a gay club, and Chopsticks, a Chinese restaurant. People must have been coming and going from both these establishments, and they were optimistic of getting something positive from one of them.

Judy heard Freddie's car take off, and after a moment, Lloyd joined her, shielding his eyes against the morning sun that promised another warm day.

"He died some time after nine o'clock last night, according to

Freddie. He's doing the postmortem this afternoon. Toss you for it."

"He who speaks to pathologist attends autopsy," she said. "Old Chinese proverb—ask the people in Chopsticks, if you don't believe me."

"That's not fair. I got Lewis's."

"Life isn't fair." She passed on Yardley's message as they walked down Ladysmith Avenue toward Mafeking Road, where the incident room was already being furnished. When Yardley arranged for something to be done, it obviously *got* done, Judy thought. That was refreshing, and presumably meant that if they did need more people, they would get them.

"I'm a bit surprised that Davy had any money on him at all," Lloyd said. "I'd have thought he would spend the day's takings before going to sleep."

"Does it constitute a little puzzle?"

"Probably not."

They crossed the busy road, and Judy looked down toward the casino as they walked to the incident room. "Another Waterman establishment just five minutes' walk away from the crime scene," she said. "Or am I just getting paranoid?"

"It is beginning to seem relevant," said Lloyd. "But the last two victims had nothing to do with Waterman that we know of. We might find out that Davy is his long-lost cousin, but I doubt it." He looked at her. "Since Scopes has been crossed off, am I right in assuming that it's Waterman himself you're wondering about?"

"Frankly, I'm beginning to wonder about you. Anyone. Someone's killing these people. Why don't we have a single lead?"

"Because whoever it is knows what he's doing." He shook his head. "And what are we to make of the murder weapon being neatly parcelled up in a padded bag?"

"God knows. Tom thought they'd stumbled on a blackmail drop—the last thing they expected to find in the envelope was the murder weapon. Yardley thinks the murderer's just getting cocky." Judy looked at her watch. "I've got the owner of the restaurant coming to let us see his CCTV footage, because that seems to be the only camera that takes in Ladysmith Avenue. And I'd better get back over there. I got the poor man out of bed, so the least I can do is be there when he arrives."

"That's the problem with this area being active at night," said Lloyd. "People who are working or playing until two and three in the morning aren't around much during the day. I think the incident room should be manned until about eleven o'clock at night if we're going to get anything useful. Do you think Yardley will go for that?"

"I think he'd go for twenty-four-hour manning if he thought it might get a result."

Judy hurried back across the street, and was waiting outside the restaurant just in time to see the owner's car pull up.

"I'm sorry to have to put you to this inconvenience," she said.

"No problem," he said, unlocking the door. "Just go straight on through to the back," he said, waving her ahead of him as he cancelled the burglar alarm. "I have to warn you that the camera isn't set up to take in Ladysmith Avenue—I mean, it does, but that's not what it's for, really. It's there so that we can keep an eye on the back court—that's where we're vulnerable to break-ins or whatever. And we can watch deliveries being made, and keep an eye on our cars. Most of the staff park in Kimberley Court."

There was just one camera, and Judy found to her disappointment, but not to her surprise, that it took in the wrong part of Ladysmith Avenue, the part that carried on away from Mafeking Road after it had passed Kimberley Court. That had seemed likely to be the case when she had looked at its position, but it had been high enough up on the old building to make her believe that it might get the near corner of Kimberley Court and Ladysmith Avenue in the shot. And it would have, but for the sloping roof of an open porch affair that the restaurant had had built onto the exterior of the building. It also obscured the view of the bin in which the weapon had been found. Now, why didn't that surprise her?

"Is it possible for customers to see the output from your security camera?" she asked.

"Yes—they pay at the kiosk, and there's a screen in there."

If he'd said no, they could have looked with some degree of enthusiasm at his staff, but it could just as easily have been a customer who worked out exactly which of Barton's homeless he could most easily and efficiently eliminate without the camera seeing anything. But the murderer might have walked along that part of Ladysmith Avenue that the camera did pick up, so she asked for the tape.

"Were you out of the restaurant at all last night?"

"Not me, no, but some of the staff would be—taking out the wastebins, and probably nipping out for a smoke. But they would stay in the yard, I expect. They wouldn't actually go out onto the street unless they had to get something from a car."

"Someone will probably be here this evening to have a word with them," said Judy. "If you could let me know who was working last night, that would be a help."

"Sure."

"And maybe a list of customers?"

"Well, we do a lot of passing trade, but a few people booked. I can give you their names and telephone numbers."

Oh, well, she thought. Her day might have begun with an early morning call from Yardley, but at least it was warm and sunny, and the first member of the public with whom she had had dealings had proved to be friendly and helpful. She couldn't ask for much more than that.

GRACE HAD TOLD STEPHEN ABOUT THEIR ALTERED STATUS, AND Tony was now having lunch with both of them, in Grace's dining room, as proof.

She had been so frightened, so suspicious, so ready to call the police, that Tony hadn't known what else to do. He had waited for what seemed like an age in the sitting room while she and Jack doubtless held a conference about how to proceed before coming down and joining him. After he'd offered his explanation to them, and suggested the midnight celebration of Stephen's birthday, she had seemed to become slightly less wary. But when Stephen had gone up to his room, she had asked him again to explain to her how he could pinpoint where a murder was going to take place when it was obvious that the police couldn't.

He was tempted to say that it was because he was considerably brighter than anyone on the police force, but thought that wouldn't go down too well. Instead he pointed out that unlike the police he had only one problem to think about, and that he was perfectly capable of thinking about it and working on it to the exclusion of everything else, including, in the case of the South Coast murders, his marriage.

He had told her then about that single-minded, obsessive investigation into the South Coast murders, and how his behavior had been so suspicious that Challenger had managed to get a court order stopping him going anywhere near him, basically on the grounds that he was barking mad. He had explained exactly how he had worked out who Challenger's next victim would be, and how he had stalked her instead, thereby saving her life. He had done the same thing then, he'd said. He had put himself in Challenger's mind.

He had talked for hours, and sometimes it seemed that he was winning, but then the suspicion would come back into her eyes, and he would get nervous again. The lowish profile that he had enjoyed for the last decade, doing TV series shown on minority channels, had suddenly become a high profile; he was still not someone that people recognized in the street, but the papers certainly knew who he was, and his name was one that everyone now knew. Being asked to leave his temporary lodgings would be something that his fellow journalists would find highly diverting, and his landlady calling the police and accusing him of being the

Anonymous Assassin—an epithet chosen by his very own newspaper, and used by all the other tabloids—was something that
didn't bear thinking about. Desperate measures were required.

It wasn't as if he had never betrayed his intellect before; he
had betrayed it when he had accepted the huge sum of money offered to him by the paper for his story. He had betrayed it again
when he had agreed to write the column, using the overheated
prose and shameless hyperbole favored by its owner, and therefore
by its editor. He had never betrayed his principles, but that was
mainly because he wasn't at all sure he had any, so the fact that
Grace's only son was someone he believed to be a murderer with
whom he was engaged in a duel was no stumbling block to what
he intended doing.

He had gradually raised the charm level to maximum, the
anecdote rate to high, the self-mockery to full volume, and with
the single-mindedness that had got him where he was, had worked
on her until the suspicion had turned to mere doubt, and the
doubt to a smiling acceptance of her overreaction.

The smiles had turned to kisses, and the kisses to a night of
passion—albeit a short one, given how long the overture had
taken, and the fact that they both had things to do in the morning. And he had to admit that as sacrifices went, having sex with
Grace was one of the more enjoyable ones.

Having lunch with her son in his current mood was not, especially since there was now no doubt at all in Tony's mind that he
had witnessed Stephen Halliday murdering Wilma Fenton.

THEY HAD COME INTO THE INCIDENT ROOM IN DRIBS AND DRABS
throughout the morning, but the trickle seemed to have dried up,
and of the ones who had come in, two had asked what they were
selling, and one had asked for directions. So far, none of them
seemed to have had any useful information, but at this stage you
never really knew what would turn out to be useful.

Gary was looking idly out of the plate-glass window at the

casino opposite, wondering if Stephen Halliday really was the Anonymous Assassin. Apparently, he'd been working in Barton last night, and DI Finch had gone over to Stoke Weston to interview him yet again.

"Do you think anyone's thought of relieving us for lunch, Sarge?" he asked.

"I doubt it," said Hitchin. "I think it'll be thee and me until further notice. That's why I've brought sandwiches. See? Experience tells."

"Do you mind if I go and—" Gary broke off as he saw a familiar figure passing the front of the building. She wore a man's raincoat, two sizes too big, over a tweed skirt and a cotton shirt. She wore socks and boots. Her gray hair was swept back from her face, and fell straight to her shoulders. It was Dirty Gertie. She pushed a pram that contained her other clothes; unlike some, Gertie washed both herself and her clothes whenever and wherever she could, which made her nickname a little cruel, but Gary thought it had perhaps referred to her morals rather than her cleanliness. Not anymore—Gertie was too old to earn any money that way. But she didn't beg; she lived on her old age pension. And she wasn't, technically, homeless; she had an address to which she had occasionally been taken, but from which she always fled at the first opportunity.

"Gertie!" he called, getting up from the desk, and going out to catch her before she walked briskly past. Gertie always walked briskly, as though she had somewhere to go and despite being permanently sozzled. Drinking was so much a way of life that she needed alcohol to function.

She frowned, and pulled her head back slightly to look at him. "I know you," she said.

"It's Gary."

"Gary," she said, the frown deepening. "Gary."

"Yeah—don't you remember? PC49, you called me, but I think maybe you called everyone that. I used to give you your wake-up call. About two years ago?"

"Years," she repeated, in a faraway tone. "Years mean nothing to me, Gary."

She spoke like a dame of the British theater, with perfect vowels and no dropped consonants, and only the faintest slurring of speech, except now and then, when a word proved to be too difficult.

Her address was a posh one, Gary knew; she came from a long line of wealthy aristocrats. Apparently, when she had first appeared in Barton about ten years ago and had told stories of her father being the younger son of an earl, everyone had assumed that she was fantasizing, but she wasn't. And the family, regardless of its makeup at any given time, always took her in if she was taken back to them. But she wouldn't take their money, and she wouldn't accept any help for her alcoholism or her other problems. No doctors or priests for Gertie.

"Do you still sleep round the back of the restaurant?"

"I do." She swayed slightly.

"Will you come in and talk to me and my sergeant for a little while?"

She looked in the open door at DS Hitchin. "A sergeant? That's good. That's very good."

"What is?"

"He's black. That's good."

"Is it?"

"Once, you know, Gary, once they wouldn't have made a black man sergeant."

"No? It makes no difference these days."

She smiled. "Good. I never held with it myself. Skin comes in different colors—like hair. And eyes. And cats."

"So does that mean you'll come in and talk to us?"

She went in, pram first, and swayed in front of Hitchin.

"This is Gertie, Sarge," said Gary. "Sergeant Hitchin," he said to Gertie.

"Call me John." Hitchin smiled at her. "Could I have your last name, please?"

"Hatton, née Gore. My husband left me—do you blame him? But I kept the name. Gore has such unpleasant connotations, don't you think?"

"Would you like to take a seat, Mrs. Hatton?"

Gertie sat down on one of the plastic chairs, and looked hazily at Gary. "How do I know you're policemen?" she said. "Neither of you is in uniform. You might be conmen."

Gary and Hitchin took out their IDs, and Gary took them to her. She tilted her head back to look at them. "That," she said, "doesn't do you justice, John. You're a much more handsome man than that would suggest."

"Thank you."

His did do him justice, Gary supposed. Oh, well. He'd never claimed any sort of position in the handsome stakes. He sat beside her. "Would you like a cup of tea?"

"Thank you, dear, but I don't think I have the time."

"Oh, surely you've got time for tea, Mrs. Hatton," said Hitchin. "Gary was just going to put the kettle on, weren't you, Gary?"

She smiled. "Oh, well, if you insist. Thank you."

Gary switched on the kettle, and put a tea bag in a mug. "Did you hear what happened to Davy?" he asked.

"Ah, yes, tragic. Tragic—he couldn't have been more than forty-five. Why not me? That's what I asked myself. I'm old. I'm disp—" There followed an attempt that was a cross between disposable and dispensable, then she gave up on that. "Well, I'm old, anyway. Two spoonfuls of sugar, dear."

"You're not old," said Gary. "How old are you?"

"Oh, darling, how should I know?" She held up her hand, her forefinger extended. "But I can give you a clue. I was named after Gertrude Lawrence—now, she was at her height in the late twenties and early thirties—so you can work it out. I think I must be past my three score and ten, don't you?" She clasped her hands, and looked blissfully at Gary. "Oh, I remember . . ." she began, then frowned. "What was I talking about?"

"Davy."

"Tragic."

"Did you see him last night?" Gary brought the tea over, dragging with him the small table with the posters on it, so Gertie didn't have to hold on to a hot mug for any longer than was necessary.

"No. I wouldn't, you see, because I retire even earlier than he does. Thank you, darling. That's lovely." She picked up the mug, and blew gently at the steam. "And he never joins the rest of us in the evening."

Gary loved the image of the country house that her language conjured up. "Did you see or hear anything?" he asked. "Anything unusual?"

She nodded slowly. "I saw something very unusual," she said.

Gary and the sergeant waited, but she sipped her tea, and didn't seem to be going to say anything else. Please, please, thought Gary, please don't let her have forgotten what she's saying.

"What?" he asked. "What did you see that was so unusual?"

She put the mug down, and leaned forward, her eyes glazing slightly. "I saw someone in a DJ rummaging in one of the bins—at least that's what it looked like."

Gary's mouth had gone dry. "Someone in a DJ?" he repeated, to make certain he had heard correctly.

"Dinner jacket, dear. Dinner jacket. A tuxedo, if you prefer."

"Yes. Could—could it maybe have been a tramp? Wearing someone's castoff? Looking for food?"

"No, no, darling. A dinner jacket, bow tie, shirt, shiny shoes—the lot. All black—or at least very dark. Could have been navy or gray. Except the shirt. It was white. He was a regular size—not fat, not thin—a proper manly bearing. And he was wearing gloves—odd, I thought, on such a warm night."

"Can you describe his face, Mrs. Hatton?" asked the sergeant.

"Sadly, no."

"Anything you can remember."

"I've told you what I remember."

"Was he black or white, for instance?"

"I don't know, dear. I couldn't see his face. And he wore gloves, as I said."

Gary took over again. Hitchin was too polite. "Gertie—how could you see exactly what he was wearing, and not be able to see his face? Was he wearing a mask?"

"I wouldn't know, Gary, darling. I couldn't see his head."

The *headless* assassin? That would sell some newspapers. Gary looked baffled.

"If you go and lie down where I sleep, you'll see."

Gary decided to leave the practical demonstration as a last resort. "Can you explain to me where you sleep?"

"I sleep under the canopy thing."

Canopy thing, canopy thing . . . Gary couldn't think what the canopy thing was. He couldn't remember a canopy thing, and he hadn't actually been to the scene—he should go there and get the lay of the land. But not literally.

"It's a sort of roof thing that someone had built on not long ago. It slopes right down." Gertie held her arm at a forty-five-degree angle. "So they can store things outside without them getting wet."

Gary was beginning to get the picture.

"And I sleep under it on the same principle." She repeated the last word to make sure she'd got it right. "I'm the oldest resident, you see. So I got first choice. And when people come into the court, I can only see them from here down." Her outstretched hand went to her throat. "Unless they're very small indeed."

Gary smiled. "Well, at least we know that he isn't very small."

She looked at him unsteadily. "Is it important?"

"It could be very important. Did you see where he came from?"

"He came from Ladysmith Avenue, where Davy sleeps."

"Which bin did he go to?" asked Hitchin.

"The big one on the corner, right beside where I sleep."

Gary didn't know if that was the one where they'd found the knife, but judging from Hitchin's expression, it was. Damn the canopy. Gertie would have described him perfectly if she'd seen his face.

"Can you remember what kind of bow tie it was? Was it a normal one, or one of these that's practically hidden inside the collar?"

"A normal one. But it looked too neat to be a real one. A clip-on one, I'd say."

"And could you see what he did after he left the bin? Where he went?"

"He went back the way he had come, got into a car, and drove off."

"Which way? Toward Mafeking Road or away from it?"

"Toward Mafeking Road."

"Did you hear the car arrive?" asked Hitchin.

"No."

"Do you know what sort of car it was?"

"Oh, no, darling. I don't know cars."

"Did you notice what color it was?"

"No. All the cars look the same color in the streetlights. A sort of dark color."

"That's great, Gertie," said Gary. "You're being a big help. Did you see any of the number?"

"No."

"Not even a letter?"

"Nothing." She put a hand on his shoulder. "Sorry. But the eyes aren't what they once were."

"Do you know when you saw this man?" asked Hitchin.

"Time . . ." She lifted her shoulder in a shrug, her hands, upturned, held out in a gesture of helplessness.

"Was it long after you retired?"

"Mm . . . yes. I think something woke me. That could have been his car arriving, I suppose. But I do wake up from time to time anyway. And I don't know when it was."

"Oh, well," said Gary, "never mind."

"And," she said, drawing the word out to command their attention, "I heard something unusual, too. Some time after I saw the man at the bin. I heard this . . . clicking noise."

"Clicking noise?" said Hitchin.

"Click, click, click. It was quiet, but I could hear it."

Gary and Hitchin exchanged baffled looks.

"I didn't imagine it—there's nothing wrong with my ears. It was coming from Ladysmith Avenue, too."

"What did you think it was?" asked Hitchin.

Gertie looked at him sorrowfully. "A clicking noise," she said.

Gary wasn't sure what to ask about that. "How long did it go on for?" was what he came up with.

"A few moments, then it stopped and started again."

"Had you ever heard it before?"

"No. That's why it was unusual. Then it just . . . faded away." She shrugged. "That's it," she said. "I slept then till the police came and told us about Davy."

Hitchin stood up, and came round to where Gertie sat. "Well, thank you very much for coming in, Mrs. Hatton." He held out a statement form. "While you were talking, I took the liberty of writing down what you've told us. Would you mind reading it, and if you agree that I've got it right, could you sign it?"

She looked at him for some moments, as she processed all those words. "Certainly," she said.

As she read her statement, Hitchin went into his briefcase, and took out some cling film–wrapped sandwiches.

Gertie looked up. "Oh, John," she said. "Spelling, dear. I think you'll find that 'rummaging' has two m's."

"Sorry," said Hitchin, making the correction. "If you could initial that?" he said.

Gertie stood up, put the statement on the desk, initialled the correction, and signed her name with a flourish. "There you are. No more spelling errors."

"Thank you. One more thing, Mrs. Hatton," Hitchin said.

"I've got these sandwiches, and they're going to go to waste, because I've been invited out to lunch, and Gary says he doesn't like ham and tomato. Could you use them, do you think?"

She smiled, entirely aware of what Hitchin was doing. "I'd be delighted to take them off your hands," she said. "Thank you, dear."

With that, she pushed her pram back out into Mafeking Road, and walked briskly off.

"Gary—go and get us some sandwiches."

KEITH OPENED HIS EYES, AWARE THAT SOMEWHERE THERE WAS A tune playing incessantly. It took his sleep-clouded mind a moment or two to realize that it was his mobile phone, and he sat up on one elbow while he tried to work out which of the things on the bedside table his mobile phone actually was.

"Keith Scopes," he said, his voice heavy.

"Rise and shine, Keith—it's your boss."

"Oh, Mr. Waterman. Er . . . yes. What time is it?"

"One o'clock."

"Oh, right. Time I was up anyway."

Keith felt aggrieved, since he'd been working until after two o'clock in the morning, but then he remembered that Mr. Waterman had, too. At least he'd been entertaining his guests until then, if that counted as working, and Keith supposed that it did. How come he was so bright and breezy?

"I just wondered if you fancied working the May Day bank holiday."

Keith was still trying to work out what day this was, and he was talking about a bank holiday that wasn't for . . . well, a long time. But he wasn't going anywhere, as far as he could remember. Wasn't May Day that weird one that came between Easter and the spring bank holiday? No one went away for it, did they? Michelle wouldn't have arranged for them to go anywhere.

"Sure. Where?"

"My place. Stoke Weston is having its May Day celebrations there this year."

"Oh, yes," said Keith. "They've nicked the village green, haven't they?"

"It's going to be a great day. And I want you to be the chief security officer. I'm rounding up a few others, but you'll be in charge."

"Great. When is May Day?"

"Oddly enough, it's on the first of May this year."

"Well," said Keith defensively. "I didn't know if that was always the day we got off for it."

"No—I wasn't being sarcastic. It isn't usually. It's usually the first Monday in May. But this year the first Monday in May is the first of May. So I'm pushing the boat out a bit to celebrate May Day being on May Day, if you see what I mean."

"Right. Good—yes, I'll do that."

"Good. Don't go back to sleep—you said it was time you were up."

"No. Thanks, Mr. Waterman. See you."

He lay back on the pillow. Chief security officer—that sounded good. He stumbled out of bed before he fell asleep again, and went downstairs, automatically switching on the TV as he passed it. It was the regional lunchtime news, and he stopped to watch.

". . . forty-three-year-old Davy Guthrie was a well-known figure in Barton, and many people were shocked to hear of his murder. Police believe he was stabbed while he slept, in a side street off the area known as Sunset Strip to Barton's clubbers . . ."

"SO WHEN DID YOU GET BACK HERE?" ASKED TOM. HE ALREADY knew the answer—Stephen's bike arriving in the village was something the neighbors noticed, and one of them had already mentioned what time Stephen got back.

Stephen Halliday sighed. "About half past eleven," he said.

"My bike broke down, and it took me about a quarter of an hour to get it started again."

"Oh? What's wrong with it?"

"I don't know—I've had it fixed once. Well, I thought I had. But it's doing the same thing again. If I stall it, I can't start it again."

"So what made you stall it?"

"Something ran out on the road. A rabbit, or something. I braked, and stalled the engine."

Tom wanted to believe him, but it was beginning to look a bit dodgy for Stephen Halliday. According to Waterman Entertainment, he had only ever worked at the Barton bingo club once before last night, so the coincidence factor that had been present at Stansfield didn't apply. He had, according to the staff at the club, left the building at five minutes to eleven, and it was a twenty-minute journey to Stoke Weston. Fifteen minutes gave him plenty of time in which he could have driven to Sunset Strip and stabbed Davy Guthrie. But he still couldn't see it himself, and they were very far short of having any evidence against him.

"I thought you shot rabbits. But you braked to avoid this one?"

"I do shoot them—that doesn't mean I want to run them over. Anyway—it could have been a cat, or anything. I don't know what it was."

"Can I see the clothes you were wearing last night?"

"If you want. Do you want to take them away again?"

"If you don't mind."

"Well, it's my night off tonight, but is there any chance of letting me have them back tomorrow? Last time I had to borrow someone else's blazer, and it didn't really fit me."

Tom could see how that would upset Stephen, just as it would upset Bobby. "Well—I kind of doubt that they'll be that quick. Sorry." It would be a waste of time, Tom knew. There was a slight chance that the assailant had got blood on his clothes, but it was more likely that he hadn't.

And a less likely serial killer than the patient, obliging, slightly baffled Stephen Halliday he had yet to meet. If only he would tell them what he was doing the night Mrs. Fenton died, they could stop bothering him.

"BEN! I DON'T OFTEN GET A CALL FROM YOU." MICHAEL SUDDENLY realized that he didn't ever get a call from his son. "What's happened? Is something wrong?"

"No, nothing like that. But I've been hearing about the May Day festivities at the Grange—I thought I might make a flying visit. Why didn't you tell me?"

"Because I thought you'd go on about me being Lord Bountiful."

"No—it sounds like fun. I don't think I've ever seen maypole dancing."

"Well—no," said Michael. "I mean—if your mum had been around, maybe, but it's not the sort of thing a man and his son would go to, is it?"

"No, I suppose not."

There was an awkward silence, generated, Michael knew, by his embarrassment, not Ben's.

"Well—that was all, really. I don't think I'll get down before then, so I'll see you on May Day."

"Oh—you can't make a weekend of it?"

"No, I wish I could, but we've got someone coming that weekend to give us extracurricular talks, and I'm expected to attend. I'll get the train down on Sunday evening, and go back on Monday evening."

"Well, if you think you can do that."

"Oh, yes. I sleep like a log on trains. I'll see you then. 'Bye."

Well, that was something, Ben making a special trip like that to see him. Michael didn't suppose it was really the May Day shindig that was bringing him home. Of course, his twenty-first was on May 8, so perhaps he wanted to talk to him about the money, and how best to invest it. But whatever the reason, Michael was very pleased that he was coming.

His secretary came in then and told him that there was a police officer waiting to speak to him.

"Show him in," he said.

"Her," said his secretary.

His next assumption was also wrong, because it wasn't the uniformed constable he had been expecting, but the very Detective Chief Inspector Judy Hill that Ray had told him about. He was right; she was attractive, and was managing somehow to look cool and smart despite the mini–heat wave, which was more than could be said for him. His suit had started crumpling the moment he'd sat in the car that morning.

Once he'd got her seated and established that she didn't want a cold drink, despite the warmth of the day, he asked how he could help.

"We have a witness who saw a man in a dinner jacket behaving a little oddly in Kimberley Court last night. And I think that your casino is probably the only place in the area that would have customers wearing dinner jackets. Might some of your customers have been wearing dinner jackets last night?"

Michael bit his lip. "I'm afraid they were all wearing dinner jackets," he said.

Her eyes widened. "All? Do you insist on it?"

"No. The casino was host to a charity boxing program—formal dress, four hundred pounds a table. We did very well indeed—made thousands for the charity."

Judy Hill closed her eyes. "I hardly dare ask this," she said. "About how many were there?"

"About three hundred and fifty. It's a big place, Chief Inspector."

"If it was an all-ticket evening, I take it you'll have their names and addresses?"

"Oh, yes." Michael smiled. "Maybe I can be a bit more help

than that, though—about what time was this man seen behaving oddly?"

"That's just it, I'm afraid. We don't know. But if you have anything that might help . . ."

"No—it was just that I don't think anyone left until some time after dinner—I can't be certain, of course, but the earliest to leave the top table went at about half past ten or so. If you'd said it was any earlier than that, then it might have been quite easy to ask around about who went out. But if it was after half ten . . . well, people did start drifting away, except the hard core ones who stayed until two a.m. And even they went out occasionally for a breath of air—it was extremely warm."

"And there were presumably about . . . what? Ninety tables?"

"Eighty-five. There must have been, because it came to seven dozen bottles of sparkling wine, plus a few bottles of the real thing for the top table."

She smiled.

"And for all I know their occupants all nipped out at one point and behaved oddly."

"Did you, by any chance?" she asked, smiling.

The smile didn't fool him. She wanted to know. They'd already checked up on his movements with the first two, so he had been expecting this.

"No—I was at the table throughout, except for two visits to the gents', which didn't necessitate leaving the building. I've got witnesses who can confirm that was where I went, and your own chief constable will confirm that I was at the table all the rest of the time. Will you be interviewing him?"

"I will," she said crisply. "Well, thank you, Mr. Waterman. If you can let us have the list of guests, we'll do the rest."

"WE'RE LOOKING FOR A MAN OF REGULAR BUILD BETWEEN FIVE foot seven and six feet or so," said Yardley. "Who was wearing a plain white shirt, and a dark suit. He wore a traditional, dark bow tie, which might have been a clip-on, and he drives a car—the color is fluid, but it's more likely to be dark than light. So there's no point in talking to a five-foot-two ex-jockey with a pronounced paunch. And be polite. These people paid a hundred pounds a ticket, so just make sure that they are approached with tact and diplomacy."

They were assembled for the evening briefing, and Judy could feel Lloyd wanting to point out that he didn't reserve tact and diplomacy for people who could fork out a hundred pounds for a seat at a boxing do, but even he knew better than to criticize a chief superintendent in a briefing.

"Do you mean don't go accusing them of being the Headless Assassin, sir?" asked one of the DCs, with a laugh.

That was how he had immediately become known once Gary had told his story.

"I wouldn't put it past this man to have worn a dinner jacket just so that we'd suspect someone from the casino," Tom said.

"Good point," said Yardley. "It seems obvious that he knew exactly which bin wasn't overlooked by that camera, and exactly which person he could murder without too much difficulty, so the evening clothes could have been deliberate. But we have to start somewhere."

They did indeed. Her friend the restaurant owner had said that none of his diners had been wearing formal dress, so the casino was, as Tom had said, the only game in town.

"Would he know that Gertie couldn't see his face?" asked Lloyd.

"I don't think he'd even know she was there, sir," said Gary. "I met her later in the afternoon, and she insisted on showing me where she sleeps. She's behind all those empty cardboard boxes that they store in that shelter thing—she disappears."

"What do we think about the car?" asked Yardley. "Was it parked there all along, or did its arrival wake Gertie?"

"Chances are it was parked there all along, sir," said Alan Marshall. "Both sides of that road are chockablock at night, which is how Headless could keep out of sight of the patrols. I can't see him being lucky enough to find a parking space convenient to the murder location."

"Good point," said Yardley again. "So we're saying that Headless was in the vicinity all evening, and at some time after nine, he stabbed Davy Guthrie to death, put the knife in the bin, first popping it in a Jiffy bag, and drove off toward Mafeking Road."

"Which could mean that he actually lives in Barton, sir," said Gary.

"Well," said Yardley, "I don't think we should read too much into which way he went, because I'm sure he would know that he would be picked up by the restaurant camera if he went toward the ring road."

"But if we can get a time," said Lloyd, "he will have been picked up by the traffic cameras on Mafeking Road itself. We'll check both sets of lights, obviously. But Alan would stand a better chance of picking out his car if we could find out roughly when all this took place."

Everyone laughed. Alan Marshall was always first choice for jobs requiring dogged diligence.

It was such a relief to be in a briefing where people were able to offer suggestions and produce queries—it seemed to Judy that they had spent weeks contemplating their navels until now. A real witness, with real information was just what they needed. And Tom had cheered up on hearing about Gertie's encounter with Headless—it considerably lengthened the odds on Stephen Halliday, who would have had to change into and out of full evening dress as well as doing away with Davy in the fifteen minutes at his disposal. Possible, but extremely unlikely. And he would have had to get rid of the outfit, because it wasn't in his wardrobe—Tom had checked. It could, in a pinch, have been hired and taken back this morning. But Stephen was a very long shot now.

"And what about this clicking sound?" said Yardley. "Any ideas?"

A silence descended.

"A clock?" someone suggested after a moment.

"That would be a ticking sound, not a clicking sound," someone else objected.

"Dolphins make a clicking sound, don't they?"

"Yeah, good thinking—maybe she heard a dolphin. They're a real problem round there. Worse than pigeons."

"Or a death-watch beetle," said someone else. "They click."

"And there's that tribe in Africa that talk in clicks. Maybe it was two of them she heard having a conversation."

"Or just one of them, on a mobile phone."

"All right, all right," said Yardley. "Any sensible suggestions?"

There were, it seemed, no sensible suggestions. The ongoing inquiries into all three murders were discussed and updated, tomorrow's tasks given out, and the briefing was over.

Yardley waited until everyone but Lloyd and Judy had gone, then sat down at one of the tables, beckoning them over.

"I've decided to bring in a psychological profiler," he said. "All right—maybe Gertie's got us on the right track at last, but maybe she hasn't. She's an alcoholic who lives on the streets, and who knows what her mind conjures up when she's asleep. We don't know if she saw any of that. It sounds to me like she was dreaming about the Invisible Man."

"Gary Sims says she knows how many beans make five," said Lloyd. "He knew her quite well when he was on the beat here, and I trust his judgment."

"Good. But a lot of booze has flowed down Gertie's throat in the last couple of years. So let's get someone in to give us some indication of who we're looking for—someone who isn't a suspect himself."

This was a dig at Lloyd for talking to Tony Baker, which had not gone down too well with Yardley. It turned out that Tony Baker had been a guest at the boxing evening, so he remained a suspect. Of course, it was equally possible that the letter writer was killing where he did purely because of Tony Baker's presence in the area, as Gary Sims had suggested.

And Lloyd's action in consulting him wasn't so terrible; he had told him nothing he didn't already know, and they were desperate for any sort of lead. They all knew how Yardley felt, however. There was something about Tony Baker's account of that night in the alleyway that didn't ring true, which was another reason that Stephen Halliday remained a suspect, however unlikely, because Baker might be trying to protect him.

She would doubtless be treated to Lloyd's views on psychological profilers when they got home. How wonderful. But it would at least make a change from the loft conversion.

THE LITTLE PUB HAD THE USUAL CROWD IN WHEN JACK WENT FOR his evening pint, hopeful that last night had put him on a different footing with Grace, but it was Stephen who was behind the bar.

"Is it your night off from the bingo?" he asked.

"Yes—I'm having a wonderful time. I'm stuck behind the bar, I've had that detective inspector round here wanting to know where I went when I left the bingo club last night, and my bike's died altogether now. Best birthday I ever had."

Oh, dear. Jack wasn't sure what to say. It wasn't like Stephen to be like this, even if he had had a rotten birthday. "I'll have a pint, please. What did the inspector want with you this time?"

"He took my clothes away again, but then he brought them back and wanted to know if I had a dinner jacket. I had to take him upstairs and let him look in my wardrobe."

"Couldn't you have refused?"

"What would be the point? I don't have a dinner jacket."

True. All the same, Stephen was a lot more accommodating than Jack would be in his position. He was surprised Grace wasn't here shouting about harassment. "Where's your mum?"

Stephen pulled his pint, slowly, carefully. "Don't ask," he said, his voice low, so that the other customers couldn't hear.

"Why not?" Jack automatically lowered his own voice. "Where is she?"

His pint was put down a little too vehemently, sloshing over the glass and spilling over and off the drip mat. "Have that one on me," said Stephen, swiping at the beer with a cloth. His cheeks grew a faint pink, and he answered Jack's question. "She's with him."

Jack frowned. "Who? The inspector?"

"No! Tony Baker."

"Is she?" Jack sipped what he'd been allowed of his pint, puzzled, in view of how she'd felt about him last night. "I thought she'd gone off him a bit."

Stephen laughed without humor. "A great reader of a situation you are," he said.

"Why? Where have they gone?"

"Nowhere. They're in the sitting room. But if you're thinking of popping in to say hello, knock before entering."

Jack blinked at him. Last night she had been all for calling the police—if he hadn't told her not to, she would have. "Are you saying that they . . ." He finished the sentence with a waggle of his head.

"Yes. I told you she'd get her own way in the end."

"Are you sure?"

"Yes, Jack, I'm quite sure."

"When?"

Stephen's eyebrows rose. "Last night, if you must know," he said. "And I don't know why I'm whispering, because they're making no secret of it, believe me."

No. No, Jack wouldn't—couldn't—believe it. But Stephen wouldn't be saying it just to wind him up—he wasn't that kind of boy. So it had to be true. Stephen seemed to be blaming his mother for the situation, but Baker must have worked very hard to achieve that turnaround.

Fortunately, Stephen was in no mood for idle chatter, so Jack was able to drink his pint in stunned silence, and leave. He looked back at the little pub as he made for home, at the curtained sitting-room window. He wished now that he had let her call the police last night. They might not have been as ready to believe Baker's explanation as Jack had been.

But then, he thought, Grace hadn't been as ready to believe it. So what had changed? Why was this happening?

CHAPTER EIGHT

THE BARTON MURDER HAD TAKEN PLACE BETWEEN 9 P.M. ON Monday, April 17 and 2 a.m. on Tuesday, April 18, when Davy was found dead. On Wednesday, April 19, Tony Baker had brought them a new letter, one that gave even less information. The next one would be in May—that was all it said. No place, no method. They had no idea whether this reduction of information was all part of the plan. If it was, it could mean that they would be given no warning at all about the one after that, and in a way, Judy would be relieved if it did, because that was how she was used to crime being committed.

As the inquiry rolled on without any breaks, the press had become less friendly to the police—even downright hostile on occasion. There were rumors that Yardley was going to be taken off the inquiry, because the Waterman connection had become clear to everyone, and his family relationship with Michael Waterman put him in an awkward position.

On Thursday, April 20, the newspaper had duly received its letter, taunting them about "their man" failing to stop the writer. Why he wrote to the paper the day after he wrote to Tony Baker was still a puzzle, but it was one firmly on the back burner of this inquiry, because despite Gertie's evidence, they were, one week on from Davy's murder, no further forward, a situation their bad press was simply making worse. This Monday morning was one that Judy would happily have slept through; for once, Lloyd had had to get her up for work. Even Charlotte had been unable to stare her awake as she usually did.

She looked at the ever-increasing pile of statements, and sighed. The dozens of people working on the case in Barton were in the process of checking every one of Waterman's boxing-evening guests who matched Gertie's description, and most of them could have been her headless man. The great and the good of Bartonshire favored plain, simple evening dress—or at least, the clothes rental shops did. There were very few ruffled shirts or colored waistcoats to cut down the number of people whose movements had to be investigated. The clothes that had been hired out had all come back minus sinister bloodstains, but that didn't mean that those who had hired them could be crossed off, because Davy had died almost instantly from a single knife wound to the heart, and there was no reason to suppose that his murderer had got any blood on his clothing. Davy, bless him, hadn't got all that much blood on his own clothing.

With, Judy was sure, immense tact and diplomacy, the bulk of the ever-growing investigation team was sifting through the list to reduce it to those who roughly answered Gertie's description, who had parked on Ladysmith Avenue, and who were in a position, after nine o'clock and before two o'clock, to have left the casino by either the front door or the open fire doors, walked down either Kimberley Court or Mafeking Road, turned onto Ladysmith Avenue, killed Davy and put the knife in the bin before driving off. This was the list that the small executive team was to work on.

It included Tony Baker, who had left the casino at ten-fifty. Michael Waterman, however, of whom Judy had been becoming ever more suspicious for no good reason whatsoever, had, from eight o'clock in the evening until half past two in the morning, been sitting at the top table, or talking to people at the other tables. He had indeed had his alibi confirmed by the Chief Constable, of all people, so she supposed she had to forget him.

The people on the slightly reduced list were having their movements on the nights of the other murders investigated, which would at least reduce it further, but in Judy's experience very few people could furnish cast-iron alibis for what they had been doing two months ago, so she doubted that the exercise would reduce it all that much. But it might reveal someone who was less than forthcoming when questioned.

A new questionnaire had been devised that took into account dog ownership, fishing and other hobbies in the hope that someone who might have ready access to dog chains and fishermen's knives could be examined more closely. The dogged and indefatigable Alan Marshall was going through the completed questionnaires, and his findings would be reported to her and Lloyd. It all took a great deal of time, and May was fast approaching.

The knife had indeed proved to be the murder weapon, but it was available by mail order, on the Internet, in fishing tackle shops, sporting goods shops and everywhere else, as far as Judy could see. It was not going to be possible to trace it back to a particular outlet, and there were, of course, no fingerprints. They were checking the Barton outlets for anyone who had bought such a knife recently, with no joy so far.

She was beginning to believe that Headless really was the Invisible Man.

"Tony?"

"Speaking."

"Mike Waterman here. How are you doing?"

"Very well, thanks, Mike. What can I do for you?"

"Nothing. But you know how you're going to be here on May Day to judge the talent contest? Well, my son Ben's coming down from St. Andrew's on a flying visit, and I'd very much like you to meet him." Michael couldn't believe it had taken him this long to realize that Ben could after all meet Tony Baker. He just hoped he hadn't left it too late.

"I'd love to meet him."

"Good. I thought if you could come to lunch, that would be ideal. I hope you don't have other lunch plans."

"No, none. I look forward to sampling your housekeeper's cooking again." There was a heartbeat before Tony continued. "Is this a stag lunch?"

Michael smiled. So Tony had met someone, had he? "No, not at all," he said. "Please bring anyone you like."

Another silence. It was a bit like when he'd spoken to Ben, only this time the embarrassment was from the other end. Surely he wasn't another one? If he was, he'd be the last person he wanted Ben to meet. No—no, he'd indicated that it was a female person he wanted to bring. And that would be all the better. Maybe it was because Ben had lived in an all-male household, and then he'd sent him to an all-male school—you heard things about these places. He should have known better. Yes, it would be good for Ben if Tony brought a lady friend.

"I'd better come clean," Tony said. "I take back everything I may have said to you about Grace. We've become something of an item in the last week or so."

"Really?" Mike was delighted, if a little surprised. He'd always been fond of Grace himself, but Tony had seemed to find her less than appealing. And Ben liked her, so he'd be pleased to have her company. "Is it serious?"

"Oh, who knows. Perhaps."

"Well, well—that's brilliant. What happened? Did she take off her glasses and you realized she was lovely?"

Tony laughed. "Something like that. Maybe I was falling for her all the time, and putting up obstacles. I think I like my freedom too much."

"Oh—that does sound serious. Well, of course you must bring her. Make a day of it—she could do with some time off from that pub. Let Stephen look after it."

"I might just do that. You're right—she works much too hard. And Stephen's no help. Expects her to do everything for him. Cook, clean, wash, iron. He's a nice enough lad, but he's been spoiled rotten."

Michael had no wish to discuss Stephen, but it was at least

cheering to hear someone who wasn't singing his praises. Of course, he too had sung his praises in the past, but that was before he knew what was going on. Now, all he wanted was to get Stephen Halliday out of Ben's life.

And until he could do that, he had to keep them apart, which was what had prompted his suggestion that Tony and Grace make a day of it—the kind of on-the-hoof inspiration that had made him a rich man. Because if Stephen had to look after the pub in the morning, then get to work as soon as it closed for the afternoon, there would be no time for him and Ben to sneak off somewhere together. He made a mental note to make sure that Stephen was told it would be impossible for him to take the bank holiday off. He knew Stephen well enough to know that he wouldn't feign sickness or anything like that if he believed he was needed at work. He was a very conscientious boy, Stephen. There was a moment, when that thought crossed his mind, that his own conscience pricked him, but it passed.

"I take it you're not in the pub at the moment," he said. "You'd be in trouble if Grace overheard you talking about Stephen like that."

"No—I'm in the car, just turning down toward Stoke Weston now."

Michael literally bit his lip to stop himself from lecturing Tony on the evils of talking on a mobile while driving. Anything that took your mind off what you were doing was criminal, as far as he was concerned. But he tried not to lecture people, aware that his experience had colored his opinion of these things. He would never allow anyone to drive when they were over the limit, which was fair enough, but you couldn't go pulling people up on every bit of inconsiderate driving.

"So that's a date," he said. "Half past twelve for one o'clock on the first of May. I look forward to it."

"As do I. See you, Mike."

*   *   *

"I'M GOING TO SEE IF I CAN GET A FOX—DO YOU WANT TO COME?" said Stephen, opening the gun cabinet as he spoke on his mobile, and taking out both rifles. Jack kept his in Stephen's gun cabinet, because it was more secure.

"Sure," said Jack. "But it's not quite dark enough yet."

"I'm not spending my evening off looking after the bar so that they can bond all over the place. I'm going out while the going's good."

"Oh, right. Well, come over here then. I'll make us a spot of supper, and then we can go out."

Stephen arrived at Jack's, and flopped down on his big com-fortable sofa. "They're like a couple of kids," he said.

In fact, it wasn't as bad as it had been, now that everyone had had a little while to get used to the idea, but the setup was still one he couldn't enjoy. "Do you want a lodger, Jack?"

Jack didn't reply; he got up and went toward the kitchen. "What do you fancy?" he asked. "A fry-up?"

"Yeah, that would be great." After a few moments, he got up and went into the kitchen. "He's even started trying to boss me around now," he said. "The other night he told me to go and clean the floor in the gents' toilet. It's like he thinks he's in charge now. He's persuaded Mum to go to this May Day do that Mr. Waterman's having at the Grange, and he had the nerve to tell me to look after the pub."

"What did you say?"

"I told him I was going to the May Day celebrations too, so if she was going, they'd have to see if Rosie could man the pub."

"Is Grace going, then? She's never shown much interest in May Day before."

"Of course she's going—they couldn't bear to be separated for a whole day, could they? Anyway, he's taking her somewhere after he's judged the talent contest. And they've been invited to lunch by Mr. Waterman."

Jack turned the sausages, and went into the fridge for bacon.

"So you've condemned yourself to watching me Morris dancing just to spite them?" he said.

"Something like that."

It wasn't to spite them. He'd said he was going to the May Day thing to make sure that he wasn't stuck behind the bar if Ben thought of a way out of what seemed to Stephen like an impossible situation. Ben was good at that.

Stephen was having to work the bank holiday, which meant that he had to be at work by half past three, and now Ben was apparently supposed to be at this lunch that his father was arranging. Stephen had tried to see if he could get at least the afternoon off, but it wasn't possible. They had given him Sunday evening off as compensation, but that wasn't going to be any good to him, because Ben's train wouldn't get him here until the early hours of Monday morning.

He and Ben had arranged to meet at the Tulliver at eleven and take the bike, now once again reportedly fixed, into Barton. They had planned to go to a motel or something for the afternoon. And even if Stephen had to be at work by half past three, it would have been all right. But that was no good now, because Ben had to be back at the Grange by half past twelve for lunch at one; they would have fifty minutes in Barton before he had to leave. That would mean they couldn't go anywhere that they could be alone, which would be worse than not seeing him at all.

He hadn't rung Ben yet—he didn't think he could know about this lunch, or he'd have been in touch. He'd ring him tonight. Maybe he'd be able to get out of it, but apparently it was all so that Tony Baker could meet him, so that seemed a bit unlikely.

Everything in his life had started going wrong the moment his mother had met Tony Baker.

"Cheer up," said Jack, putting two heaped plates on the table. "Get that down you."

"It's all my mum's fault," Stephen said, picking out knives and forks from the drawer.

"What is?"

"Everything."

Jack frowned. "Don't you go blaming your mum because she's taken a shine to Tony Baker," he said. "It's not her fault he bosses you about. Tell him to pack it in."

"I can't."

"You want to learn to assert yourself."

GARY WAS ON LATE SHIFT AT THE BARTON INCIDENT ROOM WHEN she came in. At first, he thought it was a hooker, since she seemed to be very overstated. Plunging neckline, dramatic eye makeup, lipstick you could carve with a knife. Then as this apparition approached, he realized it was a man. He was good—there was no doubt about that, but close up, you could see the faint suggestion of five o'clock shadow.

"Hi," he said, in a Yorkshire baritone. "My name's Dolores Van Doren."

Gary looked at him, his eyebrows raised. "Come again?" he said.

"I could make a rude joke, but I won't. All right, my name's William Eckersley, but that wouldn't go down very well with the punters."

"Trainee DC Gary Sims. Take a seat, Mr. Eckersley."

He sat down, crossing one elegant leg over the other. He had good legs, Gary noted. Better than a lot of women he knew. And Gary couldn't imagine how he could walk in those shoes.

"I work at the club down the road," he said. "The Queen Bee."

"Oh, right. You're a drag artist."

He smiled, showing impeccable white teeth. "I can see why you're training for detective work," he said. "Not a lot gets past you, does it?"

Gary laughed. "Have you got some information for us?"

"Yes, I think so. I've been away, you see. In Spain. I only

found out about Davy tonight. Poor little inoffensive Davy. What did he ever do to that sod that he picked on him?"

Gary shrugged.

"Anyway, I don't know if I'm just being . . . well, you know, if I'm making something out of nothing. Summit out o' nowt, as we say up north. But the last night before I went away, I was doing my act, and I get a fifteen-minute break. Well—it was hot in there that night, I can tell you, and when you've got all this clobber on—I'm not kidding, I thought I was going to faint. So I came out for a breath of air. And you can see right along Ladysmith Avenue from the door of the Bee."

Gary sat up. "What did you see?"

"Davy was in his usual position, propped up with his head against the railings, covered in that filthy blanket." He shuddered. "Oh, just thinking of that blanket makes me want to heave," he said. "Anyway—Davy was there, and I could see this old guy walking toward him."

"Which way was he walking?"

"Up toward Kimberley Court. He was carrying a white stick, and I'd never seen a blind man round here, so I thought—if he doesn't know there's a destitute drunk lying across this pavement, he's going to come a cropper. But he didn't, because he was tapping his cane on the railings, you see. When he got to Davy, he stopped, and I saw him bend down."

Gertie's clicking sound. It was the blind man's cane on the railings. Good old girl—Gary knew she hadn't imagined it.

"He stayed like that for . . . I don't know . . . maybe half a minute. And then he turned round and came back down to Mafeking Road again. Well, it seemed a bit odd, but I didn't think anything of it at the time, not really. Then when I heard tonight what had happened, I thought—well, he could have been stabbing him for all I know."

The thought had occurred to Gary, too, but then he realized that Gertie had already seen Headless disposing of the weapon by the time she heard the blind man's cane clicking on the railings. Davy was already dead when the blind man got there.

"Do you know what time this was?"

"Oh, yes—like I said, I only had a fifteen-minute break. I got offstage at ten forty-five, and I had to be back on at eleven. I saw the blind guy about five minutes after I came out."

"Did you see anyone else approach Davy before or after he did?"

"No, no one."

"What time did you go back in?"

"I waited until the last minute—literally. About a minute to eleven. It was like walking into a sauna."

"Did Davy look any different after this man left him?"

"Do you mean did he look dead? Well, yes, but he always did, didn't he, Davy? Even when he was walking about. Did you know him?"

"Oh, yes."

"There was never any color in his cheeks, was there? So he looked the same as ever when I saw him to start with, and he didn't look any different after the blind guy left him, or I would have known something was up."

"Did you notice what the blind man was wearing?"

"Not really. Shirt and trousers, but I don't remember what color or anything. A light shirt—maybe white."

"He wasn't wearing a jacket?"

"No. No, he definitely wasn't wearing a jacket—or a tie, because I was thinking how nice and cool he looked in his shirt-sleeves and open neck, and then I realized I was envying a blind man."

"Was he carrying anything?"

"Just his stick."

"Which way did he go when he came back down to Mafeking Road?"

"He turned to my right, his left." He twisted round. "Walked down past here, on the opposite side of the road," he said, pointing out of the window. "Past the casino. I got a good look at his face, if you want me to pick him out of a lineup. I'd definitely know him again—I'm good at faces. But not at nondescript clothes."

"Can you describe him?"

"He seemed to be about my height—five ten to six feet. Quite erect, but he wasn't young, I can tell you that. In his seventies at least. Gray hair, brushed back from his forehead, but not a lot of it. A thin face. He was quite skinny. He wore dark glasses."

"Did you see anyone in a dinner jacket? Not necessarily approaching Davy—just anyone at all?"

"No. You'd notice, wouldn't you? It's all jeans and T-shirts round here. Though they did have some sort of do on at the casino that was black tie, I think, but I didn't see anyone come out of there."

Gary got a statement form. "I'd like you to make a formal statement," he said. "Would you like to write it yourself, or do you want me to do it?"

Eckersley waggled his fingers at Gary, who could see two-inch-long false nails, and the difficulty.

"I'll write it for you," he said.

Sgt. Hitchin came in while he was doing that, and after William Eckersley had gone, he looked at Gary. "What did Danny La Rue want?" he asked.

Gary told him. "It looks as though the blind man couldn't get past Davy. And if the beat men couldn't tell whether he was alive or dead, the blind man certainly couldn't, could he? When he couldn't make him move, he just turned round and came back to find some other way to where he was going rather than have to step out into the road."

"We'll have to try to trace him," said Hitchin. "He might have seen—" He stopped, and hit his head. "No, probably not. He might know something that would help."

"I can start asking around now, Sarge." Gary got to the door, and then realized something else that Dolores had told him. "This puts Stephen Halliday in the clear," he said. "Because he didn't leave the bingo club until five to eleven, and Davy was dead by then."

JACK AND STEPHEN GAVE UP AT ABOUT HALF PAST NINE. THE shots, even with the moderators on the rifles, eventually sent all the other predators running for cover. And people tended to complain if you carried on much later than that, though not as many as complained before they were allowed to have the moderators. But they'd got a fox.

"Do you want to try again on Sunday night?" asked Stephen, as they arrived back at the Tulliver.

"Yes, why not?" said Jack. "I'll come in and have a pint before I go home." He followed Stephen into the small back room, then heard someone ringing the bell and shouting for service. "I don't think there's anyone on the bar," he said.

Stephen sighed, and handed Jack his rifle. "Lock that up for me, will you, Jack? I'll go and serve them."

Why was there no one on the bar? That wasn't like Grace at all. No wonder Stephen was a bit fed up. As he turned to put the rifles away, Jack could see Grace with Tony Baker, coming out of the kitchen, laughing.

"I'm supposed to be serving!" she said. "I'll have a riot on my hands if I don't get back to the bar."

"Well, Stephen's back now." Tony Baker looked across at Jack. "See? Jack's here." He walked across the corridor to the doorway. "I take it Stephen's come back with you," he said.

Jack put the rifle back on its rack, and locked up the cabinet. "He's gone to serve someone," he said.

"Good," said Baker. "That's what I was going to tell him to do."

"Hello, Jack," said Grace. "Did you have a good night?"

"Not bad. Got one."

He didn't want to stay now, but Stephen would be expecting

him in the bar, and the lad probably needed moral support. He could see what he meant about Baker.

"I'll just go through," he said. "I think Stephen will have pulled me a pint."

"Tell him I'll be through in half an hour," said Grace. "There's something on the telly that Tony wants me to watch, and I can, now that Stephen's back."

Of course there was something on that he wanted her to watch. Anything to keep her to himself. Jack went into the bar to find Stephen trying to serve a whole load of hikers who had obviously decided to undo all the good that their day's hiking had done, and had spent the evening getting merry. Now they wanted the same again all round. He sighed, and lifted the bar flap. "I'll give you a hand," he said.

A grim twosome greeted customers who ventured into the Tulliver Inn that night, and Jack was very aware of the impression they must be giving. Stephen was normally the most amenable of lads, the most easygoing, friendly, cheerful boy you could ask for. Not lately. Not since Tony Baker had come here. And he was blaming his mother, which wasn't right, and not like him at all. And Jack had always just taken what was handed out to him, which had never been much, but he hadn't seen any reason to complain, until Baker had come and disrupted what he chose to call his life.

It wasn't much of a life, living alone and wishing he didn't. Mending fruit machines when he was capable of so much more than that. But he'd never had the confidence to make anything of himself. He'd had the nerve to tell Stephen to assert himself—that was a laugh.

The way Grace had thrown herself at Baker had made him realize just how empty his life was, coming in here night after night just so she would talk to him, happy just to be where she was. She had never once thought of him as anything but a confirmed bachelor who had taken a shine to her son, who liked teaching him how to shoot and fish. She humored him, if she did anything that positive about him at all.

But then along came Baker with his tan and his haircut, and she stopped doing even that. He might be the only man in the room for all she cared about anyone else. And Jack remembered those things he'd heard Baker say about her, his frown growing deeper as he thought about them together, thought about Grace, believing Baker actually cared about her. She would regret taking up with him.

And why had Baker done it, if that was the way he felt about her? Just to make Jack look like the pathetic fool he was? Why snatch away the one thing he had ever really wanted? Why? What difference could it possibly make to him?

Jack stopped in the middle of pulling a pint, as his eyes widened slightly. It did make a difference to him, he thought. It really did. It all became clear, as he stood there, staring down at the amber liquid in the glass as though he were looking into a crystal ball, and he knew what he had to do.

"Are you going to pull that or hypnotize it, Jack?"

Jack snapped back to the here and now, and finished pulling the pint. "Sorry," he said.

"You're miles away."

No. He wasn't miles away. And he wasn't going to be miles away. He would be right where it mattered, when it mattered, because Tony Baker was never going to take Grace Halliday away from him. Never.

THE PSYCHOLOGICAL PROFILER HAD BEEN BROUGHT IN, AND HAD been studying both the murders and the letters to see if he could narrow their search down. He had been working on the problem for a very short time, but Yardley had persuaded him to give them some of his findings so far, since their one and only suspect had now been cleared.

Yardley was a product of everything that had gone wrong with policing, in Lloyd's view. He was a pleasant enough man, but he had whizzed through the ranks, barely stopping long enough to find his feet in one before being promoted to the next one. He was given to using phrases in his memos like "customer interface," which set Lloyd's teeth on edge, though at least he didn't actually speak like that. His latest wheeze was a campaign with the slogan "Give the Fuzz a Buzz," encouraging people to ring up if they suspected any wrongdoing of any sort—the sort of thing they would once have mentioned to the bobby on the beat, he'd said. Since when?

He hadn't immediately e-mailed him back saying that, because Judy had trained him out of opening either his mouth or his e-mail and telling people what he thought of them, especially senior officers. He hadn't even said anything when Yardley had gone on to call what he was hoping to get from this campaign "popular intelligence input," and that restraint had been positively manful.

And as soon as they knew they had a serial killer on the loose, Lloyd could have put money on him wanting to bring in a psychological profiler, a breed for whom he had little time. Now he wasn't even letting the man do his job properly before demanding results.

But before that meeting, Judy and Lloyd had been summoned to the ACC's office, where he and Yardley were waiting for them.

"As you know," the ACC said, "there has been considerable press speculation about the appropriateness of Detective Chief Superintendent Yardley's position as head of this inquiry, in view of the apparent connection between these murders and Waterman Entertainment outlets. Mr. Yardley has this morning told me that he would feel happier if he were to step down from heading the inquiry, and indeed, from actively engaging in it, until such time as the supposed connection is proved or disproved. He will, of course, continue in his normal duties as head of Bartonshire CID, but he will not take any further part in this investigation."

Yardley smiled, more than a little ruefully. "I'd much rather not leave you in the lurch," he said. "But I can't blame the press for thinking that I'm too close to Mike Waterman—this could turn out to be one of his employees, or could even involve Mike himself in some way, either as an indirect victim or an indirect perpetrator. At least the Chief Constable himself has vouched for the fact that Mike didn't personally kill Davy Guthrie." He smiled again. "I'm inclined to the view that someone is deliberately making it look as though Waterman Entertainment is involved. But I wonder if I would be thinking that if I weren't Mike's brother-in-law and his friend."

The ACC cleared his throat. "If I were to head the inquiry myself, there would be a great deal of background that I would have to be made aware of, and I feel that this would be counterproductive. Therefore it has been decided that for the duration of this inquiry, DCI Hill will take the rank of Acting Detective Superintendent, and will head the inquiry from now on."

Lloyd was very, very good at not letting his face slip, and he called on all his acting skills to come to his rescue now as he congratulated Judy. Not that she didn't deserve this chance to prove herself; she certainly did. But the inconvenient male chauvinism that he tried so hard to keep submerged had bobbed to the surface like the idiotic inflated beach ball that it was. Judy had gone slightly pink, but not so anyone but him would notice.

"I take it that neither of you will have a problem with that? I do hope I'm right, because I argued very persuasively that you wouldn't, and that we would be making a little bit of history in a good cause."

"No problem whatsoever," said Lloyd.

"No," said Judy. "No problem. I just hope I can justify your faith in me."

"No one's expecting miracles, Judy," said Yardley. "One would be nice, though."

"So what happens if I beat someone up in the cells?" asked Lloyd. "Or sexually harass a WPC?"

"The complaint will be dealt with by a senior officer to whom you're not married," said the ACC.

That seemed sensible, Lloyd supposed.

"I expect you'll want a few minutes to get used to the idea— I've asked Dr. Castle to meet with you in fifteen minutes."

"So how do you feel about it?" Lloyd asked, as they got back to their office, having walked the short distance in silence.

"Guilty."

Lloyd frowned, and sat on the corner of her desk. "Why?"

"Because I know you're having a hard time with it, however much you pretend you're not. And because it's all very well having a Chief Constable who wants more women in the senior ranks, but I seem to be the only woman he ever wants there. He keeps handing things to me on a plate."

Lloyd snorted. "For one thing, it's pretty obvious that it was the ACC who pushed this through, despite the Chief Constable's reservations. And for another, what he's handed to you on a plate is one very hot potato."

"Do you think he's setting me up to fail?"

"No—that isn't what I meant at all! I'm just pointing out that he isn't handing you this chance because you're the token female—it's because he thinks you'll get things done and say all the right things to the media at one and the same time." He grinned. "Even though you *are* the token female," he added, and got hit.

"Get off my desk," she said. "That's an order."

Lloyd smiled, and went back to his own desk.

"So how hard a time *are* you having with it?" she asked.

In a way, he was having a harder time with his reaction to it than to the situation itself. Some rogue gene passed down through generations of male dominance made him feel emasculated because Judy was going to be his boss, and that made him feel ashamed. He had found himself hoping that the press didn't find out that they were husband and wife, which they hadn't, so far, but as the ACC had said, they would be making a little bit of history, so he didn't suppose it would be too long before they did find out.

"I'll get used to it."

"I'm hoping you don't have time to get used to it."

KEITH SAT ON THE EDGE OF THE SOFA, HIS FISTS CLENCHED AS IF holding reins, as the runners and riders streaked past the camera.

It turned out that Michelle had indeed arranged for them to go away this weekend, and she had been anything but pleased when he told her he'd agreed to work on the Monday. And he'd no sooner smoothed things over with her about the day lost from their weekend break than he'd seen the runners and riders for this race. It had seemed like too good an opportunity to let pass, so now their holiday money was galloping toward the finish, and he was wondering why he wanted to live so very dangerously.

"And it's Mayday from Baby's Done It, with One More Time coming up fast on the outside. Still Mayday from Baby's Done It, Mayday from Baby's Done It . . . One More Time is challenging hard for second, and it's Mayday from One More Time now, with Baby's Done It beginning to lose ground to Jumpandjive. It's still Mayday, holding off a strong challenge from One More Time, as Jumpandjive moves into third, with Baby's Done It continuing to lose ground, being caught now by Between the Sticks. And, at the line, it's the appropriately named favorite Mayday who wins the seventeenth Heaven's Gate Maiden Handicap, followed by One More Time second, Jumpandjive third, with Between the Sticks just overtaking Baby's Done It to get fourth place. The favorite, Was She Worth It, is just crossing the line now, in a disappointing sixth place, with Strive'n'strive and When I'm Sixty-Four bringing up the rear. So, to recap, first, Mayday, ridden by . . ."

Keith smiled, and sat back, his hands behind his head. Perhaps it was an omen, because he was gambling on May Day in more ways than one.

*   *   *

TOM HAD BEEN TOLD ABOUT YARDLEY'S DEPARTURE, AND JUDY'S promotion, and had passed the news on to the small executive team. Now, he sat round the table with Judy, Lloyd and the profiler, thinking of all the things he could be doing with his time instead of listening to the pedantic Dr. Castle. Like finding out how Lloyd had taken it, for one.

"I have to stress," Castle began, "that anything I say now could be contradicted by something that I discover tomorrow. Profiles are arrived at by analyzing the type of crime committed, the method, the areas in which the crimes take place, the actions of the criminal himself, the observations of witnesses and victims, the physical evidence and so on. I have only had time to make what I would hardly dignify by calling even a rough analysis."

"That's understood, Dr. Castle," said Judy. "But even the roughest analysis could point us in the right direction."

"And it could point you in entirely the wrong direction," warned Castle. "Arriving at a profile without an in-depth scrutiny of all the available data is the next worst thing to simply jumping to conclusions."

"I think," said Lloyd, his face entirely serious, "that at the moment, we would simply like your theoretical input to add to our own empirical data. A sociopsychological overview, if you will."

Tom didn't dare catch Judy's eye. Lloyd would have been in trouble with her for that before she was his boss.

"Very well," said Castle, entirely unaware of Lloyd's mockery. "If we can look, in the first instance, at where the crimes have taken place, we see that in each case they occurred in an area where commercial businesses operate in the evening. And in each case, one or more of those businesses is owned by Waterman Entertainment. That suggests, on the face of it, that the perpetrator may have some connection with Waterman Entertainment."

"Do you think he's more likely to work for Waterman than to be a customer?" asked Tom.

"There is little data from which to extrapolate a possible socioeconomic group for the perpetrator, and it seems that Waterman Entertainment prides itself on appealing to all strata of society, so the status of the perpetrator is fluid."

Heaven help us, Tom thought, sneaking a look at his watch. I only asked a simple question.

"But I tend to think it's an employee for the simple reason that people usually go out in couples or groups for an evening's entertainment. I think that the perpetrator would find it difficult to explain an absence to a companion, whereas absences from work, while more difficult to achieve, could be more easily explained. However, the dinner jacket—unless it was worn to confuse us—does seem to suggest a customer rather than an employee. But the whole thing is highly speculative, as Waterman Entertainment outlets seem ubiquitous in Bartonshire, and their proximity could be mere coincidence."

If Tom had followed that, then it was nothing more than they had arrived at themselves without using so many syllables to do it. Lloyd made a business of noting something down, and looked with feigned, deeply concerned interest at Castle, as he continued. Judy would kill him if he kept this up.

"But it's also the case that this person has an intimate knowledge of the areas in which the murders occurred—the avoidance of any surveillance cameras, the knowledge of his victim's habits, and so on, shows that. Now, either this is as a result of having worked in those areas for some time and getting to know them and their inhabitants, or of careful and lengthy reconnaissance by someone not connected with these areas. The latter would require the perpetrator to be away for very long periods of time, and if that is the case, he is, I suspect, answerable only to himself."

Oh, here we go. He's a loner with a chip on his shoulder. Well, you could knock me down with a feather, squire, honest you could. How do you boffins do it? Tom knew exactly how Lloyd felt.

"But even so," Castle went on, "to acquire such intimate

knowledge of every single one of the factors involved in avoiding detection would be a very tall order. I tend to come down on the side of its being someone who has personal and detailed knowledge of the area already, and who only has to pick his victim, as it were. Which again points to someone who works or has worked in all three areas, in the evenings."

"A Waterman employee," said Judy.

"Possibly, but there are other interpretations, even at this early stage. The perpetrator is a man, I think, partly as a result of the witness to the first murder saying that he saw and heard a man, partly because the tone of the letters suggests a male writer, but more in view of the pathologist's reports on the second and third murders. In the second murder, he noted that a woman would be unlikely to have the necessary strength to disable a healthy, fit man quickly enough to prevent his fighting back, and there is no physical suggestion that he did. And he was of the opinion that a man—a right-handed man—was likely to have inflicted the stab wound on the third victim."

"What about the fact that he's used a different method of killing each time?" asked Judy.

"Ah—now that is very unusual indeed, and of course makes my job more difficult, because the method is one of the pointers to the personality of the perpetrator. I think he's adopting what we might call a best-practice policy."

Yardley certainly might call it that, thought Tom. He doubted that Judy would. But maybe it was some sort of infection that got you once you reached the higher ranks. Still—she was just an Acting Superintendent. Perhaps she was immune. He hoped so.

"He is asking himself what the best way to kill this particular person would be. A man reaching back into his car for the bag of money he intends depositing in a night safe puts himself in a perfect position to be strangled from behind. A man lying semiconscious, leaning against railings, would have to be handled in order to be strangled—his head would have to be lifted, or he would have to be strangled manually. Either way, it would require direct contact, and he could wake up, bite, fight back. Even if he didn't, handling him directly means that traces could be left at the scene, and on the perpetrator's clothing. Much simpler, quicker and easier just to stab him."

"You're making him sound like a professional killer," Judy said.

Castle nodded. "I think in a manner of speaking, he could be. You've been asking people about their hobbies, I believe, and there are those whose hobbies include killing. Look at the physical evidence—the fishing knife used in the third murder, and the choke-collar used in the second. The knife speaks for itself and the choke-chain could suggest a familiarity with training dogs— something a huntsman might well use to train foxhounds. Of course, anyone could buy the items used, but not everyone intent on murder would make those their weapons of choice."

Tom was very glad that young Stephen Halliday had finally been cleared of suspicion, because that would have been another nail in his coffin. He dispatched animals. But not rabbits that ran out in front of his motorbike. And anyway, everyone seemed to shoot in Stoke Weston. "Waterman employs a lot of people from the village he lives in," he said. "And that's real hunting, fishing and shooting territory. Farming, too." Despite himself, Tom was growing genuinely interested in what this man had to say, and he could see from his face that so was Lloyd. "So there's no shortage of candidates there."

"The victims seem random," Dr. Castle went on. "Male and female, no sexual assault, no theft. That, and the circumstances surrounding the murders, suggests that they are chosen purely for ease of killing, which in turn suggests that the murders themselves are almost incidental. They are like moves in a game. And that leads us to the letters."

"What do you make of them?" asked Judy. "Psychologically?"

"What they say is unimportant, I think. The most significant point is that they are addressed not to the police, but to a man who came to prominence by solving a series of murders for which the wrong man had been arrested, tried and convicted. We have to ask ourselves who might want to challenge him to this sort of duel."

"He did witness the first murder," said Tom. "Couldn't that be what prompted the duel?"

"It could. But I believe you have entertained the idea of the first murder having been engineered in order that he might witness it. If that is the case, we would be looking for someone who perhaps had a score to settle in the first place."

"We've eliminated the possibility of anyone connected with Challenger," said Judy.

"Have you looked at any of the police officers connected with the original inquiry? Could one of them be working here now?"

There was a silence as they digested the possibility that one of their own was murdering these people. Tom wondered briefly about Yardley himself, but no—he hadn't worked on the south coast. Had he? He'd read his profile when he'd been appointed, but he couldn't be sure. Was there more to his stepping down from this inquiry than they thought?

"No," said Judy. "We haven't."

"It's something you might want to check. If this man transferred, he could have worked in Bartonshire for almost twenty years, walking the beat, perhaps, in those towns. He would know forensic procedures, and how to avoid them. He would have the theoretical knowledge at least of how best to kill with the least likelihood of detection, and he could well harbor resentment for having been made to look foolish. Given that we are dealing with a disturbed personality—when he heard that Mr. Baker was here, he might have devised this plan to get his own back."

They all looked at one another, all, Tom knew, trying desperately to think if any of their long-time colleagues had worked down south at any time.

"But while it's worth checking out, I think it's probably fanciful," added Castle. "For one thing, I seriously doubt that the first murder was part of this challenge, or I think a letter would have preceded it. The fact that the first letter came *after* that murder suggests, as DI Finch said, that Mr. Baker's presence at the scene prompted what followed. I offer it merely as a line of inquiry that you might want to check out."

"Do you have a theory as to what this challenge is all about, if it isn't someone with a score to settle?" asked Tom.

"Hardly a theory. But it seems likely that the perpetrator is local, and it could be from someone who resents Mr. Baker, not because he solved a series of murders twenty years ago, but because he is in some way interfering with the perpetrator's life here and now. But it would have to be resentment to the point of obsession to cause the murder of three innocent people."

Judy looked up from the notes she was making. "I'm not clear on how murdering three people who have nothing to do with Tony Baker means that the perpetrator is getting some sort of satisfaction, whether it's a personal or a professional resentment. How does that affect Tony Baker? No one expects him to solve these murders—not even the press. We're the ones who are getting it in the neck for making no progress. So what's the point of this duel?"

"We're dealing with a disturbed mind," said Castle. "He possibly feels that it will diminish Mr. Baker in the public's eyes if he can do nothing to prevent murders being committed 'right under his nose' as the letter says."

"I understand Baker *is* actually trying to solve these murders," said Lloyd. "If the perpetrator knew that, once challenged, Baker would feel compelled to do that, would it make any more sense?"

Castle shook his head. "Not to me," he said. "Not as things stand. It can't harm Mr. Baker if he fails to apprehend the murderer, and can only raise his stock if he does. But, as I said, we are dealing with a disturbed mind, and the logic of it might have no bearing on his actions. My personal belief is that the challenge will have a purpose, and that discovering that purpose might lead you to the perpetrator."

"Could Baker himself be writing these letters?" Judy asked.

"Well, that's obviously a possibility, but I come back to the fact that I believe the duel will turn out to have a specific purpose. The murderer carrying on a duel with himself would seem to be even more pointless."

"It's got him on the TV a lot," Tom said.

Castle nodded. "It has, but it did that as soon as the first letter was received—there would have been no reason for him to kill again, if that was the motive. And Baker is a very successful man—I doubt that he was in need of a career boost."

"What about the disposal of the weapons differing each time?" asked Judy.

"I'm inclined to think that expediency rules the day with this man," said Castle. "If I'm right that the first murder wasn't part of this challenge, he may not have taken the elaborate precautions he took with the subsequent murders. He may have been fearful of fingerprints being found, so he removed the weapon from the scene. In the second incident, it was undoubtedly expedient to leave the choke-chain in situ, rather than run the risk of it being found on his person, should he be seen in the vicinity of the murder. A choke-chain minus a dog would be hard to explain away, and could easily be matched to the injuries received by the deceased. It was definitely best to leave it where it was."

"Then why put the knife in a padded bag and dump it in a bin that he must have known would be searched, rather than leaving it where it was?" Judy asked. "He was seen putting the package in the bin, and that was a risk he needn't have taken."

"That point is significant, I am sure. Why it should have been a more desirable thing to do than leaving the knife with the body, I don't know. But I think he believed that it was. Everything about this man says he does nothing without a purpose, and never acts without thinking, which is why I'm certain the duel itself has a purpose. He makes meticulous plans, and follows them, I'm sure, without deviation, no matter what. Indeed, your best chance of catching him might well be if something goes wrong with his plans that he was unable to foresee—I don't believe he's someone who can think on his feet all that well. Everything has been carefully thought out beforehand."

"But the first murder is different, isn't it?" said Lloyd. "Whatever its motive, it seems to have been opportunist, spur-of-the-moment. You think that he had to remove the weapon because it would have his fingerprints on it. Would a man such as you describe—one who does nothing without a reason and without careful forethought—would such a man commit such a crime?"

"Now you come to mention it, Mr. Lloyd—no, I doubt very much that he would." He looked irritated at having been caught napping. "This is the sort of thing that I thought might happen if I had to report to you earlier than I would choose."

"So the first murder probably wasn't committed by the same person at all," said Lloyd.

"Two murderers?" said Judy. "We're having enough trouble finding one."

"But it makes sense, doesn't it?" Lloyd turned to her. "You said yourself that it looked like a mugging gone wrong. Freddie said that the assailant was very unlikely to have intended to kill Mrs. Fenton. So what if that's just what it was? What if the mugger was scared off by Tony Baker, and did just drop the money, which happened to fall the way it did?"

"Well—I did concede that the money falling the way it did was about as likely as a yellow blackbird, but go on," she said.

"Tony Baker tells his editor that he's witnessed a murder, and something that would have been strictly local news is splashed all over the front page of a national. And then . . ." Lloyd tipped his chair back, swaying gently as his theory evolved. "And then someone who might never have heard of the South Coast murders, or of Tony Baker, reads all about it, and is excited by the idea—Baker says that serial killers are born, not made. Something triggers it, he says. What if that was the trigger?" He swayed gently back and forth as he thought. "This person thinks what fun it would be to kill people right under Tony Baker's nose, and that's what he does. He kills people when he knows Baker is in the vicinity, making it look superficially like Mrs. Fenton's murder by not stealing whatever money he finds, and making that obvious by scattering it on the body. When he writes to Baker, he takes the credit for the first one while he's at it, so that it looks as though he knew Baker was there all the time, and was already one step ahead of him."

It was true, thought Tom, that neither Judy nor Freddie had been happy with the first one being deliberate murder. His own theory had been that since one blow had done the job, the assailant didn't bother hitting her again, and in view of subsequent events everyone had gone along with that, but murderers generally preferred to make certain. Lloyd seemed to be on to something.

"He might not even be local," said Lloyd.

"No," said Judy, the flaw-spotter. "He has to be local. If he didn't commit the first murder, how did he know to leave the money on the victims' bodies? Someone must have told him about how Mrs. Fenton was found."

"It's certainly more than possible that someone else committed the first murder," said Castle. "In which case, the Waterman connection could be quite spurious—the locations being chosen simply because they mirror the original murder."

Judy nodded. "So . . . to sum up?"

"Well, it's summing up in the middle of the trial," said Castle. "But you could—I stress *could*, particularly in view of Mr. Lloyd's contribution—be looking for someone—perhaps, but not necessarily, a Waterman employee or customer—who works or engages in recreation in the evenings, in all three towns, who is literate, with a knowledge of killing, possibly as a participant in field sports, and with what amounts to an obsession with Tony Baker. But it's quite possibly nonsense, I warn you." He closed the file in front of him, and sat back.

"Well, thank you, Dr. Castle," said Judy. "That's been very thought-provoking."

"If you have any other questions, I'll be pleased to try to answer them, but what we have discussed covers everything I have in my notes. And I beg you not to act precipitately on anything that we have discussed here today, because this is a crude, fuzzy snapshot, and it could be a snapshot of the wrong man."

Tom left the meeting finding it quite difficult to come to terms with the fact that he thought Dr. Castle had made a useful contribution to the investigation. Damn it, he'd be worrying if he was sufficiently highly customer-oriented any minute.

"So that puts Scopes back on the list," said Judy, as they walked along to their offices. "Though I hardly think he's serial-killer material, and only half the snapshot applies to him. Tom, I think you should speak to him and Tony Baker tomorrow. Lloyd's volunteering to spend the day going through the staff records with me to see which of our colleagues worked on the South Coast murders, aren't you, dear?"

"If you're sure I'm not too humble for that job, ma'am," said Lloyd.

"I'm going to get this all weekend," she said to Tom. "Because he feels miffed. Can I come and stay with you?"

"Actually," said Lloyd, "I'm feeling rather smug."

"Why? Because the psychological profiler agreed with you, or because he didn't realize how very rude you were being to him earlier?"

"Neither. Because didn't I tell you years ago that you'd end up as my superintendent?" He beamed. "And I'm always right."

"He's always right," said Tom.

"I'LL COME STRAIGHT TO THE POINT," SAID DI FINCH, AS HE CAME into the sitting room.

Tony felt a little apprehensive. A Sunday afternoon visit must mean that something was up, and Finch seemed very serious. Of course, what they were investigating *was* very serious, but his relationship with them had been almost colleague to colleague. This felt much more like a visit from the police than any of the previous interviews had.

"Please do," he said.

"Have you told anyone at all about the money being scattered on Mrs. Fenton's body?"

Ah. They must be working on the idea that the subsequent murders were copycat affairs. Tony wondered if he should lie, but decided that it would be pointless. "Yes," he said. "I'm very sorry—I know I promised. But I did tell Grace."

"Why?"

"It was because you took Stephen in for questioning over the Fenton murder. She was worrying herself to death about it. He wouldn't tell even her where he was at nine o'clock that night, and that was really bothering her, because she thought he must have done something wrong."

"And how did telling her about the money help?"

"She was actually beginning to think that Stephen might have mugged Mrs. Fenton, and—I didn't really mean to say it, but I told her I didn't think it *was* a mugging. I told her I thought the murderer had some sort of personal grievance with Mrs. Fenton, which *is* what I thought at the time. And I told her why I thought that. But I said that I wasn't supposed to tell anyone, and I'm certain she won't have mentioned it to anyone else."

"If you've told Mrs. Halliday, how can we know that you haven't told anyone else?"

Tony thought, much as he had with Waterman, that he had better tell them about his altered circumstances, in the hope that it made his betrayal seem less idiotic, which it had been. There had been no need to tell her at all, but he had thought that she might calm down a bit if he did. "Things have changed since I saw you last," he said. "Grace and I have begun a relationship. I think it was brewing all along, to be perfectly honest. I was protesting too much, now I come to think about it. And—well, I suppose I told her as one does when one is close to someone, and has knowledge that will make them feel better. I didn't want her worrying about Stephen."

It had been true at the time, at least to the extent of wanting to stop her going on about it all the time. He had genuinely believed that Stephen had had nothing to do with it. Now, he wished he'd kept his mouth shut, for two reasons: one, his reassurance had been badly misplaced, and two, he had put himself in bad odor with the police. "She is absolutely the only person I told," he said, and that much was entirely true.

"Then we'd better find out how many people *she* told, hadn't we?"

Grace was asked to come in, and she assured Finch she had told no one at all. "Tony said that it was important that no one knew," she said. "I didn't tell anyone."

After Finch had gone, Grace looked at him, her face worried, an expression that he had had lots of time to get to know, and which grew no less irritating with the passage of time. "Are you in trouble over that?"

He took her in his arms. "It's not against the law to tell someone something you saw with your own eyes," he said.

She moved closer to him, and he wanted her, instantly. Her ability to do that to him irritated him a little; it put her in control, and he didn't like that. But he had been celibate for some months before his great sacrifice, and perhaps his libido was just making up for lost time.

"By my reckoning," he said, looking at his watch over her shoulder, "we've got two hours before you have to open up again."

She smiled. "You're awful," she said. "I've got things to do. You can keep me company while I do them."

"Leave them."

"It's half past three in the afternoon, Tony."

"I know. And Stephen is safely at work, and will be until seven o'clock, so you don't have to worry about him hearing anything."

"I'm sure he *can* hear us—that bed squeaks. I'm certain that's why he's been so moody."

"It very probably is why," Tony said. "So let's go up now, and then tonight we can lie asleep in virginal purity, and not disturb Stephen at all."

"But we won't! I know you."

"Go on. Up those stairs, woman." He playfully smacked her, and she led the way upstairs.

At the top, she stopped, and turned. "I forgot," she said. "Jack Shaw knows."

Tony frowned. "Knows what?"

"About the money."

He stared at her. She had forgotten telling someone about the money? He couldn't believe what he was hearing. He really had impressed on her the importance of keeping it to herself. And why would she tell Jack Shaw, of all people?

"What on earth made you tell him?"

"I didn't. But he was working on the fruit machine when you told me—I only realized he was there after you'd gone. So he must have heard what you said." She bit her lip. "Should I ring the police and tell them?"

Tony smiled. "If you think Jack's the Anonymous Assassin."

Grace laughed.

"Quite. So let's just do what we were going to do, and forget all about this business."

CHAPTER NINE

MAY DAY. STEPHEN WASN'T USED TO GETTING UP THIS early in the morning, but he had hardly been able to sleep anyway, so he was up, showered, shaved and dressed by eight o'clock. By half past, he had negotiated breakfast with Tony Baker and his mother, and excused himself, getting up from the table just as there was a knock at the door.

"What's happened to you?" he asked, as he opened the door to Jack, resplendent in his Morris dancing costume with its white shirt, its scarlet sashes, its black knee-britches, white stockings and bells, but supported by old-fashioned wooden crutches.

"Let me in and I'll tell you."

Stephen opened the door wider so that Jack could negotiate it more easily, and watched as he swung himself, the bells tinkling merrily, along the corridor to the sitting room. Following him down the corridor, Stephen could see that Jack's ankle was badly swollen, and he almost laughed. There was something funny about someone who could do practically anything with his artificial leg finding that his good leg couldn't take the strain. But he supposed it was having to take a lot more strain than it should, so it really wasn't funny at all.

Jack sat down heavily in a tiny peal of bells, propping the crutches up against the wall. "I was with the lads up at the Grange—we were doing a final rehearsal, and everything was fine, and then I felt my ankle go. Just like that. My good ankle—would you believe that? Swelled up like a balloon after they got me home. I put an ice pack on it, but it didn't help much. So I just bandaged it up and came over here." He stuck out his foot. "Could you buckle that properly for me, Stephen? It's awkward for me to reach."

Stephen buckled the clog, and looked up at him. "Are you all right with the crutches? I mean, with having to put your weight on your artificial leg?"

"I can manage short distances, like from my cottage to here. I'm used to putting my weight on it with the dancing."

"I hope you're not looking for a substitute. I don't know the first thing about Morris dancing. Or is that another thing that the fabulous Baker boy can do?"

Jack smiled. "I doubt it. No, they can manage without me— one of the musicians will stand in. Anyone who knows the moves can do it—no leaps or bounds to execute." He sighed. "It's not really Morris dancing, you know. You need six able-bodied men for the real thing. Most teams have twelve legs."

"Oh, come on, Jack," said Stephen. "None of the others would be much good at the real thing either—it's just a bit of fun." The village's Morris team was made up entirely of men who were decidedly past their prime—Stephen was certain the others were glad of the excuse not to have to do anything too athletic. "Stop putting yourself down."

"Anyway—I'm here because I'd like to go back up to the Grange now I've got myself sorted out. It looks as though it'll be a better way to spend the day than sitting looking at my foot. I thought maybe I could cadge a lift, because I can't drive like this."

"Sure."

Stephen's mother came in then, and Jack went through his story again.

"Oh, that's a shame, Jack. Still—it could be worse, I suppose. We're leaving any minute now, so you came at the right time."

Jack reached for the crutches, and got to his feet again, as Tony appeared, his mobile phone at his ear.

"I think you two should go up there without me," he said. "I'll

get there as soon as I can. I've got someone ringing me from—"
He saw Jack. "What's happened to you?"

"Turned my ankle," said Jack.

"Oh, that's too bad. Hello? Hello—yes, it's me. Hang on—I'll
just go where it's quiet." He disappeared along the corridor, and
went upstairs.

Stephen's mother pulled a face. "That means we won't be
able to use the VIP car park," she said. "All the spaces have been
allocated. But the other one shouldn't be too full, at this time in
the morning." She smiled. "Are we all ready to go, then?"

"Well, I am," said Jack.

Stephen's mother looked questioningly at him as Jack jingled
his way back up the corridor to the front door, and Stephen
shrugged, smiling.

"Don't ask me," he said. "He wants to go back up there, for
some reason." Waterman's May Day extravaganza held an attraction for Stephen that no one else knew about, but he couldn't
imagine why everyone else seemed so desperate to get there.

"I'm ready," Jack called. "What's keeping you?"

Stephen laughed, and joined him at the front door, opening it
as his mother turned and called upstairs.

"We're off, Tony! See you when you get there—don't forget
you've got that competition to judge."

Tony came out onto the landing, the phone still at his ear.
"I'm not forgetting. I'll see you later. My car will be parked at the
lake, Grace—I'll meet you there at eleven."

"And don't forget to lock up!"

"I won't."

They went out into the warm spring sunshine that had, to
everyone's surprise, greeted the bank holiday. A break in the
weather was always expected as soon as a public holiday dawned,
but not today; the sun continued to shine as it had for the last
fortnight. Stephen opened the rear passenger door of his mother's
car, and Jack leaned one hand on the car, handing Stephen the
crutches.

"My God, Jack—they weigh a ton!" Stephen took Jack's weight as he sat sideways on the backseat, then helped him swing his legs in, his bells tinkling as he arranged the crutches round him. "You can take traditional costume too far, you know."

"Very funny."

"Why haven't you got NHS crutches?"

"I have. I don't like them. Flimsy things, if you ask me."

With a final wave to Tony at the window, his mother got into the car, and started the engine.

"They're not flimsy," Stephen pointed out, after he had joined her, and they were at last on their way. "Just lightweight."

"Whatever. I lost my leg when I was no more than eleven years old—and that's quite hard for a kid. But there was an old man lived here who had only one leg, so he took an interest in me, stopped me moping about because I couldn't play football with the other kids. It's thanks to him that I never let it bother me again, and I never let it stop me doing anything." He gave a short sigh. "Well, except playing football," he said. "I can't run. But that's all I can't do. Virtually. And these were his crutches. He left them to me when he died, and I've used them every time I've needed crutches since. If they were good enough for him, they'll do for me."

The grassy area roped off for the public car park already had a large number of cars on it despite the early hour, thanks to the many attractions that Waterman had laid on for his big day. Good, thought Stephen, as his mother left the gravelled driveway and bumped over the uneven grass, that would keep Waterman busy. Getting Jack out of the car was more difficult than getting him into it, as Stephen had known it would be, but eventually Jack was once more propped up on his crutches, and they headed for the marquee with the homemade produce, the reason his mother had wanted to get here so early.

Stephen hoped that he would be able to ditch Jack when the time came, but right now he had no idea how he was going to do that. "Are you going to watch this talent contest?" he asked, already knowing what the answer would be.

"No fear," said Jack. "I'll have to see how the dancers get on without me, anyway," he added, much to Stephen's relief.

"Are you?" he asked his mother.

"No—Tony said he'd feel really stupid if I was sitting there and he was having to say how wonderful a load of talentless children were. No—I'll amuse myself with the stalls and sideshows, and then watch the Morris dancers with Jack, I think."

"Where are you off to at eleven?" asked Jack.

"I don't know," she said, her face growing slightly pink. "It's some sort of surprise he's got for me. He's promised we'll be back in time for lunch with Mike and Ben, so I can't imagine what it is." She looked from Jack to Stephen. "Well, I can, but don't laugh," she warned them. "Maybe life really does begin at forty— I think he might be going to ask me to marry him."

She got her wish. They didn't laugh.

"YES, WE WERE LUCKY WITH THE WEATHER," SAID MICHAEL, FOR the hundredth time that morning, as another group of people congratulated him on it as though he had ordered it specially.

They had indeed been lucky; he had had visions of everything taking place in teeming rain, but so far, it had been blue skies and sunshine for the May Queen and the Morris dancers, who were now minus Jack. The man whose usual job was to bang on a drum, with, as far as Michael could tell, no regard to the rhythm of the music being played, had been pressed into service as a stand-in. It was a considerable improvement all round, Michael thought.

He went back inside, and decided that it was perhaps time to make sure that Ben was up. He hadn't wanted to get him up any earlier, in view of his long train journey last night. To his surprise, Ben's bed was empty, and he could hear the shower going in his bathroom. University must have made him self-reliant in the matter of rising. When he had lived at home, it had taken a series of ever-more-urgent demands before he surfaced.

"Ben?" he called. When he got no reply, he wondered, for a moment, if he had fallen for a very old trick, but when he called again, the shower stopped.

"Is that you, Dad?"

"Just making sure you're up," said Michael, and turned to go, catching sight of some brochures on the bed. Ben must be thinking of a holiday once he'd taken his finals. But when he sat down on the bed and looked at them, he discovered that they were estate agents' brochures from several towns, some in Scotland, some in the north of England. He stared at them, his face growing dark with anger. So much for the extracurricular talks that Ben had had to attend—he had been house-hunting in anticipation of his imminent coming of age, and there was only one reason he would be doing that.

There was no way he was setting up home with Stephen Halliday, and the sooner they both realized that, the better. In fact, he thought, leaving the room as quietly as he had entered it, he would just take a trip down to the Tulliver Inn and pass that on to Halliday in person.

TONY REACHED UP TO PULL DOWN THE HATCHBACK, AND HAD JUST got back into the pub when he realized that he could hear his mobile phone ringing somewhere. Where had he left it? He mentally retraced his steps, and remembered that he had gone upstairs as Grace and Stephen were leaving.

He had missed the call, but it was from his production office in London, so he thought he'd better see what they wanted, since whoever it was had come in on a bank holiday to deal with it. He then found himself involved in a long conversation, just when his time was precious, and eventually came back downstairs to find Michael Waterman standing in the corridor, his face grim.

"The back door was open," he said. "I thought I'd better wait here until you came down."

"I was distracted," said Tony. "Thanks for standing guard." He looked at his watch. "I'm not late, am I?"

"No—no, I'm here to see Halliday. Is he around?"

Halliday? That didn't sound over-friendly. Tony was reluctant to tell him that Stephen was at the Grange. "No," he said, taking his jacket from the peg. "Did you want him?"

"I want to set him straight about something. Do you know where he is?"

"He went off somewhere about half an hour ago. If he comes back before I leave, I'll tell him you were looking for him."

"Do that."

And he was gone. A moment later, Tony heard Mike's car drive off, sounding almost as angry as its owner had looked. He frowned, not sure what to do. He dialled Stephen's mobile to warn him that it might be a good idea to stay out of Waterman's way, but it just rang out, so he couldn't even leave a message. He just had to hope that they didn't bump into each other. He didn't know how Stephen had upset Waterman, but he didn't want any petty squabbles they might have spoiling what he had planned for the day.

He shrugged on his jacket, made a quick check of the doors and windows, and left, this time locking the back door firmly behind him.

TOM HAD HAD NO LUCK TRYING TO INTERVIEW KEITH SCOPES, WHO had gone away for the weekend with his girlfriend, but he arrived at work on Monday morning to be told by Alan Marshall that they had finally traced the blind man, thanks to Gary Sims.

Sims had gone up and down Mafeking Road for three days, asking about him, until at last he found a pub where the barmaid remembered a blind man asking for directions to the Oxford

Hotel, which was on one of the side streets off Mafeking Road. The hotel had furnished him with the man's name and business address, and despite the inconvenience of the bank holiday, Gary hoped to run him to earth at his home in Leicester today, and was on his way there already. No one was sure how useful his evidence would be, but he might have some information that would help them find Headless.

Alan returned to his task of sorting through the questionnaires to produce a short list for Judy and Lloyd to peruse, and Hitchin came into the office, looking triumphant.

"I've finally managed to check out Scopes. And he was working in Stansfield the night Lewis died, and in the Lucky Seven the night Davy died."

"Was he now?"

"There's more," said Hitchin. "He was working in the casino from eight o'clock at night until well after two in the morning. He was there the whole time except for about fifteen minutes from half past ten—and the doormen at the casino wear evening dress. We didn't know that before."

"So he could be Headless?" Tom frowned. "But I agree with the acting Super. I can't see Scopes having suddenly turned into a serial killer."

"Serial killers have to start doing it at some point," said Hitchin. "And according to Tony Baker's book, they're quite often habitual petty offenders."

Tom smiled. "You've been doing your homework, have you, Hitch?"

"Well, I didn't really know about the South Coast murders thing—I thought I ought to see what it was he did. And then I read his book about all the serial killers he's interviewed. It's interesting stuff."

"I'm sure Baker knows what he's talking about," said Tom. "And they probably are often regular offenders. But Keith's whole life revolves around money. The only reason he's a suspect is that we thought he might have mugged Wilma for her winnings—and what was he doing instead? Buying drugs to sell. Money. That's what motivates Scopes. What would make him suddenly start killing for no reason at all?"

"I don't know," said Hitchin. "But he must be mixed up in it, surely."

This whole business seemed to be the wrong way round to Tom. Baker had taken up with Grace Halliday, which could certainly mean that Stephen's life had been disrupted by him, and Stephen's mind could be a little disturbed as a result, but Stephen couldn't be Headless. Keith could be Headless, but he really didn't have much of a mind to disturb. "A disturbed mind, Hitch, that's what the psychologist said. Do you think Keith Scopes has a disturbed mind? And is he obsessed with Tony Baker? Does he even know him?"

"I don't know. But it's a small village—he must know him to some extent. And no—I don't think he's got a disturbed mind. But I think he's capable of pretending he has if there's something in it for him."

Scopes would only have killed these people if someone had paid him to do it, thought Tom. And that seemed a tad unlikely, but he definitely needed to talk to him. "I expect he's still away," he said.

"No—Waterman Entertainment said he was working today. He's at Waterman's place in Stoke Weston."

"Right." Tom got up. "You'll know where I am if anyone wants me."

JUDY HAD NOW COMMANDEERED A COMPUTER FOR THE OFFICE SHE and Lloyd shared, and he was working his way through the employment histories of every employee, in or out of uniform, who was old enough to have worked on the South Coast murders, a task made no easier by the fact that four police forces had been involved.

She was trying to reword the statement the press office had

given her to read so that it sounded rather more like her and less like Raymond Yardley, uncomfortably aware that she and Lloyd would be getting on much more efficiently if they were doing each other's jobs.

"Come in," she called, when someone tapped at the door.

"I've got the filleted list of dinner jackets, ma'am," said Alan Marshall, holding a still-bulky file of questionnaires. "All men who could have been Headless, with varying degrees of interest in fishing and dogs."

Judy groaned. "How many are still on it?"

"Twenty possibles, starting with the most likely down to the least likely." He glanced at Lloyd. "Sir, you might be pleased to hear that Tony Baker isn't on it any longer, because he didn't leave the casino until ten to eleven, so he couldn't have been Headless."

"Thank God for that," said Lloyd. "Maybe the ACC won't keep looking at me more in sorrow than in anger for having consulted him." He smiled. "Of course, the man who kept Waterman's brother-in-law in charge of the inquiry until the press started asking questions doesn't have much room to talk." He held out a hand for Marshall's file. "Do you want me to take a look at it?" he asked Judy.

It was the first indication he'd given that she was technically in charge, and she wondered how much thought had gone into it, and indeed if that meant that he really wanted to look at it, was just being obliging, or was simply using the situation to establish their relative ranks.

She was cross with herself immediately for allowing these thoughts to cross her mind. She mustn't start trying to second-guess him; for one thing, she would never get it right, and for another, it was a very silly way to go on. If Tom or any of the others had asked her that question, she would simply have given him her answer, so that was what she was going to do.

"No," she said. "You're busy. Just leave it with me, Alan. I'll check through it now."

Glad of the excuse to leave her press statement-writing chore, she opened the file, pulling out the top questionnaire. And she found that the man the small executive team, in the person of Alan Marshall, regarded as the most likely to have been Headless, was John Shaw, of Drum Cottage, Stoke Weston. That surely had to be Jack Shaw, the man who confirmed Jerry Wheelan's sighting of Stephen, she thought, her eyes widening as she read the replies to the questions.

He was right-handed. His hobbies were shooting and fishing and producing a village newspaper. On the night of the Stansfield murder he was at home, alone, so had no checkable alibi. She reached for her notebook, turning to her note of Dr. Castle's snapshot.

Someone—perhaps, but not necessarily, a Waterman employee or customer—who works or engages in recreation in the evenings, in all three towns, who is literate, with a knowledge of killing, possibly as a participant in field sports, and with what amounts to an obsession with Tony Baker.

He didn't work in the evenings, and she had no idea if he had any relationship with Tony Baker, never mind being obsessed with him, but apart from that he fit the snapshot perfectly.

"Lloyd," she said, getting up and handing him the question-naire. "I think we should have a word with Jack Shaw."

KEITH PATROLLED THE GROUNDS AS INSTRUCTED, MAKING HIS WAY to where he was really going without looking as though he had a particular goal in mind.

The stalls were strung out on the grass along the side of the house, and Keith walked slowly past them, being stopped now and then for directions to various things: reuniting a small child with his mother, picking up and returning someone's dropped wallet. There had been a time when that wallet would have been relieved of its contents before anyone could blink, but Mr. Water-man trusted him to do this job, and he was going to do it properly.

He wandered through the oddly quiet fairground. The side-shows were doing good business, with people hooking ducks, rolling pennies, going on the ghost train, but the real funfair at-tractions, the rides, were having to wait until the talent contest was over, so the noise didn't drown out the singers. As Keith got nearer to the marquee where the contest was being held, he felt that a bit of drowning out wouldn't hurt. In fact, simply drowning this particular contestant might be seen as a mercy killing. The relieved applause was followed by someone speaking—Baker pre-sumably. The contest must be over.

That was when he saw DI Finch coming toward him, and re-sisted the temptation to turn and walk the other way.

"There you are," said Finch. "I've been looking for you. I didn't know a uniform came with the job—I nearly didn't recog-nize you."

Keith wished he hadn't. And he didn't really have time for a chat.

"I'm told that you went walkabout from the casino the night Davy Guthrie was killed," said Finch. "Why?"

"It was hot. I wanted to cool down and have a smoke."

"What about the night Robert Lewis died?"

"What about it?"

He and Finch stood aside as Baker walked between them, nodding to Finch as he passed.

"You were in Stansfield that night," said Finch, when Baker had gone.

Keith moved off purposefully. "You don't mind if I carry on doing my job while we talk, do you?"

Finch walked with him. "Were you seized with the desire to smoke just when he was killed, too?"

"I always go out for a smoke at about half past ten. When was he killed?"

"Some time around half past ten." Finch smiled coldly. "Odd, that, isn't it?"

*   *   *

LLOYD AND JUDY WERE ON THEIR WAY TO THE GRANGE, WHERE THE young woman opening up the pub had told them they would find Jack Shaw. Practically the whole village was up there, she said, including the Hallidays and Tony Baker.

"Shaw's a Morris dancer," said Judy. "I should have guessed he would be doing that on May Day."

"Yes," Lloyd agreed. "You should. Call yourself a detective?"

He had wondered, on Saturday, what Judy's strategy about this temporary promotion was going to be. When she had left the meeting, she had allocated tasks instantly, and he hadn't been sure if she'd been working on that throughout the meeting, or if they had been the suggestions she would have made anyway, turning into instructions. Either way, he had rather admired the way she had done it. It established her as the boss, and from then on, everything had been pretty much the way it was before.

"Do you know he's only got one leg?" she asked.

"Who?"

"Jack Shaw! Who are we talking about?"

Lloyd frowned. "Isn't Morris dancing a bit on the physical side for someone with one leg?"

"They adapted it, Scopes said." She smiled. "But have you ever heard of a Morris dancer being a serial killer? I'm sure I haven't."

"I can't say I have." He sighed. "And I'm remembering Dr. Castle's caveat. But apart from fitting the snapshot, Mr. Shaw is also very at home with a word processor. At least, I presume he is, if he publishes the village newspaper."

"Maybe he uses a printing set."

Lloyd looked at the village through which Judy was driving, a trifle too quickly, in his opinion, and could believe that he did use a printing set. Time didn't seem to have affected Stoke Weston at all. He half expected to see farmers in smocks, chewing straw, leading horse-drawn plows. There was a smithy, he noticed, though its owner had taken the day off from producing horseshoes in a concession to modernity. Or perhaps the village smithy had been closed on May Day since time immemorial, rather than since the juvenile bank holiday. And, as Judy rounded a bend in the road, as if to complete the picture, two young women on horseback trotted sedately side by side ahead of them. Judy slowed down and passed them. "Would you like to live in a place like this?" she asked.

"Not on your life." The old village of Stansfield was as close to village life as he wanted to be. He liked having urban amenities close at hand.

"Thank goodness for that."

They drove through the new wrought-iron gates to Waterman's opulent estate—another product of the smith's art, presumably—and followed the signs to the temporary car park. The May Day celebrations were in full swing, and the Morris dancers looked . . . well . . . like Morris dancers, indistinguishable from one another, but Judy insisted that none of them was Jack Shaw, and they went to find Michael Waterman, the music from the fairground growing louder as they walked toward the house.

Waterman was standing at the top of the imposing flight of steps up to the front door. "Chief Inspector Hill," he said, coming down to meet them. "It's nice to see you again. Is this a day off?"

"I'm afraid not. This is my colleague, DCI Lloyd," Judy said. "We're trying to find a man called Jack Shaw? I believe he works for you?"

"He does."

"We were told he was here, Morris dancing," Lloyd said, and frowned. "Can he really do that?"

Waterman smiled. "After a fashion."

"But he isn't one of the dancers," said Judy.

"No, he turned his good ankle during rehearsal this morning. But he was watching the dancing with Grace Halliday a moment ago." He looked across to where the comically stately Morris dancing was going on. "But he doesn't seem to be there now." He shrugged. "Sorry—I don't know where he's likely to be. You'll probably run into him. He's difficult to miss—he's still wearing the full Morris dancer's gear, and he's got old wooden crutches that came out of the ark. Anything else I can help you with? It's just that I'm a bit busy, with one thing and another."

Lloyd nodded. "You wouldn't know if Mr. Shaw has had any dealings with Tony Baker, would you?"

Waterman shrugged. "I don't know if you'd call them dealings," he said.

"But he does know him?"

"Oh, yes. Jack's a fixture at the Tulliver Inn."

"Are he and Baker friendly?"

"Well . . ." Waterman shrugged again. "Not really, I don't think. They're not unfriendly, if you see what I mean, but I think Jack's nose has been put a little out of joint by Tony's arrival."

"Oh? Why's that?"

Waterman frowned. "Is it important?"

"It could be," said Judy.

"Well, poor old Jack's carried a bit of a torch for Grace Halliday ever since she arrived in the village, and now . . ."

"And now she and Tony Baker are an item?" said Judy.

"Oh, you know about that, do you? Yes, they are. He's going to propose to her today, but I think it's a secret, so don't tell anyone, will you?"

"Do you know where Baker is?" asked Lloyd.

"He was judging a talent contest." Waterman pointed. "Over in that big marquee on the other side of the grounds. It's finished now, so I don't know if he'll still be there, but you might catch him."

GARY WAS SHOWN INTO A SMALL SITTING ROOM, ITS BLINDS DRAWN against the sun. It took him a moment to make out what he was looking at.

In an armchair sat an elderly man in dark glasses, still slimly handsome despite his years. He rose to meet Gary, holding out his hand.

"Arthur Lampton," he said. "Do take a seat, DC Sims. Forgive the shade, but light hurts my eyes, and it seems to be unseasonably and unreasonably sunny for a bank holiday."

Mr. Lampton owned his own business, and still ran it, despite his eightieth birthday having passed. He was fiercely independent, and rarely had anyone accompanying him when he went about on business, which he still did on a regular basis. On the night Davy Guthrie was murdered, he had had a meeting in Barton that was going to go on beyond the time of his last train, and had booked into the Oxford Hotel.

"I must apologize for not contacting the police," he said. "I was aware of your request for witnesses, but I really didn't see how I could be of any assistance to you."

"We never know what's likely to help us," Gary said. "That's why we ask everyone who was in the area of an incident to get in touch with us."

"But I imagine you generally assume that they will be sighted people."

"Well, yes, I suppose we do," said Gary. "But it isn't always what people see that matters."

"No." He looked thoughtful. "No, I should have realized that. But I left very early next morning—the cab driver said that there had been a bit of excitement with the police, and that he thought this serial killer might have murdered someone, but I didn't get any details, not then. Then, when I heard about it on the radio, I assumed that it had happened after I had finally found the hotel, and that I would know nothing that could be of any interest to you."

Gary frowned. "What made you think that?"

"I understood that it was the man who slept in Ladysmith Avenue who was killed." He shook his head. "Such a wanton act. But you know a great deal more about him than I do, so I don't see how I can be of much help." He smiled a little. "Unless, of course, you think that I killed him."

"No, nothing like that," said Gary. "I'm afraid he was already dead when you encountered him."

"Not if we're talking about the same man," said Mr. Lampton.

Gary stared at him, then realized that Mr. Lampton had no way of knowing the effect his statement had had. Davy Guthrie was *alive?* He asked Mr. Lampton to go through exactly what he had done that night. He had to be sure that they *were* both talking about the same man.

"I had been taken to my meeting by one of the other people attending, but I had made a mental note of how we got there, and I chose to walk back on my own. I made it quite happily to Mafeking Road, but then I have to confess that I did get a little confused with all the side streets, and I had to ask directions in a pub. I followed the directions I thought I had been given, but when I turned right off Mafeking Road, it became obvious that I was on the wrong street."

"How did you know?"

"Well, the Oxford Hotel is on a corner, and there are railings for a short distance between the entrance and Mafeking Road. This street had railings too, and I was guiding myself by tapping them with my cane. But I became aware that I had been doing that for too long. I wasn't going to find the entrance, because I must be in the wrong street."

Gary nodded, then realized that Mr. Lampton couldn't see him nodding. "Right," he said.

"And then my cane touched something soft. When he asked me for money, I realized it was someone lying in the road, and I thought to myself, well, if this man lives on the streets, he'll know where the hotel is, providing he's sober enough to tell me. So I asked him the way, and he gave me perfect directions, despite the smell of alcohol being enough to make me drunk myself. I had missed the turn, that was all."

"What directions did he give you?"

"He told me to go back down the way I had come, and turn left back onto Mafeking Road. That the hotel was on the next street on the left, on the opposite corner to the casino." He shook his head again. "A bit slurred, but quite clear and lucid."

And quite definitely directions from Ladysmith Avenue to the Oxford Hotel, thought Gary.

"I gave him a handful of change, and that was all there was to it. He was pleasant, and helpful, and I felt very angry when I heard what had happened to him. But I didn't think I could possibly be of any help. I'm really sorry if I was wrong—I had no idea that I had any information that would be of use to you."

GRACE HAD LEFT JACK WATCHING THE MORRIS DANCING, AND HE had waited until she had disappeared from view before limping off into the wooded area. There, he had removed the telltale bells, putting them in his pocket, and had taken from his belt the big handkerchief that formed part of the Morris dance, stuffing it in after them, to deaden the sound. Then he'd hoisted the crutches on to his shoulder, and made his way toward the lake, under cover of the bushes, keeping Grace in sight all the time. She had no idea he was there, as she stood where the path forked, her body language indecisive.

Years of practice had made Jack able to move as quietly and as sure-footedly as any woodland animal. Speed wasn't required for the task; an ability to stalk one's prey without being seen or heard, to keep the quarry in one's sights, and to know exactly when to stand stock-still—these, and timing to perfection the moment to make the decisive move, were the attributes he had picked up.

And he was using them all now.

CHAPTER TEN

J ACK WAS SPRAWLED FULL-LENGTH ON THE GROUND, AND NOW
he had to work out how to get up again. He tried to raise himself into a sitting position, from which he might be able to
stand eventually, but even that was anything but easy, and he
couldn't do it without some sort of support. He squinted round to
see where the crutches had gone. One was lying just within reach,
and he stretched his arm out, his fingertips just touching it. Another go, this time throwing his arm, using as much of his body
weight as he could in order to give himself that little bit of extra
reach. Making a long arm, his father used to call it. And it
worked. His fingers closed round the wood, and he pulled the
crutch closer to him.

Now, if he could just lift his body enough to get into a sitting position, he could pull himself to his feet using the crutch. It
hadn't occurred to him that he might really need the crutches,
and he had cursed having to carry them with him on his mission,
being unwilling to leave them lying around where anything might
happen to them, but he was glad now that he had them.

He lifted his upper body, press-up style, his weight on his
arms, and twisted round slightly, putting all his weight on his left
arm, and grabbed the crutch. He tried to plant it firmly in the
ground—the last thing he wanted was for it to skid away when he
put his weight on it. If he could work his hand up and grasp it
where it forked, he could lean on it and drag his good leg up to get
his foot on the ground. The crutch, he hoped, would stop him
from falling forward, and he would be able to stand up.

He had just achieved a measure of control when the crutch was kicked away from under him. He pitched forward, facedown on the ground once more. And that was when his head was struck a vicious blow that his brain just had time to register before he lost consciousness.

TOM AND KEITH WERE WALKING PAST THE HOUSE, TOWARD THE CAR park and the more traditional May Day activities, leaving behind the raucous funfair.

"Where did you go when you left the casino that night?"

"Just out. I walked round, that's all."

"Did you see anyone else?"

Keith shrugged. "Some people were leaving. I didn't notice anyone in particular."

Tom stopped and looked at the little boys and girls who danced round the maypole, and smiled when he saw the Queen of the May, aged about eight, with her white dress and crown of spring flowers, having her photograph taken by a proud mother as she danced. She looked a little like Chloe, his own eight-year-old. It might be nice, he thought, to live in a village, with village traditions and village community spirit. The twins could go to a village school, and grow up knowing their neighbors.

"My dad said that some conservation committee got up by incomers started up all the May Day business in the seventies," said Keith. "They got the maypole put up on the village green. Before that the villagers never bothered with this sort of stuff."

Oh, well. So much for his romantic notions of English villages.

"But Mr. Waterman thinks it goes back centuries," Keith went on. "That he's saving our way of life, or something. I haven't had the heart to tell him any different."

"When you were out of the casino having your break," said Tom, "did you notice Tony Baker?"

"Tony Baker? The guy that's getting these letters? The one who came out of the talent contest and walked between us, ignorant sod?"

"That's him," said DI Finch. "Have you met him?"

"No. I know what he looks like because he's never off the telly. And he's been at the casino a couple of times, but I've never actually met him."

"He was at the casino the night Davy Guthrie died," said Finch.

"Yeah—he was at the top table with Mr. Waterman."

"I'm told that he left not long after you came back in—did you notice that?"

"Yeah. He was talking to Mrs. Turner about the talent contest. Sooner him than me. He escaped from her at about ten to eleven. Is that it, Mr. Finch? I'm supposed to be working—making sure no one gets their pockets picked, and that sort of thing."

"Yes," said Tom, "that's it. Thanks, Keith."

Maybe he really was a poacher turned gamekeeper, thought Tom. He watched the maypole dancers for a moment longer, then checked his watch. It was five to eleven, and time he went back to work. He turned to go to the car park, only to find himself looking at Judy and Lloyd.

"What are you doing here?" asked Judy.

"I could ask you the same question."

"We came looking for Jack Shaw—remember him?"

"The witness that was at the casino the night Wilma Fenton was killed?"

"Yes. He gets top rating on Alan Marshall's Headless.list. But he seems to have vanished." She scrutinized the small crowd round the Morris dancers. "He still isn't here."

"I'm here because Keith Scopes is working here—as chief security officer, would you believe?" He looked round, but Scopes was no longer in evidence. "He's another candidate for Headless. I can't be certain, but I don't think he's ever had anything to do with Baker. No one I've spoken to says he has, and what he told me checks out. Besides, Baker passed us, and he nodded to me, but I don't think he knew Scopes from a hole in the road."

"Where did he go?" asked Lloyd, his voice urgent.

"Scopes? I've no idea—he was here a minute ago."

"No, Baker. Did you see where he went?"

"He went down a path into the woods," said Tom. "Back down at the fairground end."

"This is it," Lloyd said. "This is the showdown, I'm sure of it. We've got to find Baker or Shaw—one or the other."

"Then let's get after Baker," said Judy. "At least we know where he was ten minutes ago."

Lloyd needed no second invitation, and Tom and Judy practically had to run to catch up as he strode off back the way Tom had come.

"I believe Shaw's the letter writer," he said, as he walked. "Those letters were a lure, like fly-fishing. Would that be one of Mr. Shaw's hobbies, by any chance?"

"Yes," said Judy, looking puzzled.

"He knew Baker would take the challenge, would try to find out who he was before the police did. And I don't think we've been seeing the real letters at all—that's why the newspapers always heard the day after Baker did. Baker wrote to the paper himself, once he knew where and when the murders were going to take place."

"Why would he do that?" asked Judy, now actually having to run to keep up with Tom and Lloyd.

"He wanted to be sure of maximum publicity when he pulled off his coup. What was the first thing you said to him when he brought you the first letter? Don't tell anyone—right? He knew we'd try to keep the letters quiet, and that wasn't what he wanted at all. He wrote to the paper in the guise of the letter writer, so we had no chance of keeping them quiet."

"I meant, why would he show us fake letters?"

"Because the real ones said much more about when and

where the murders would take place than the ones we saw. And Baker contrived to be there in the hope that he could stop them, like he stopped Challenger killing his last victim."

Judy looked doubtful, but she nodded. "Go on," she said.

"Each of the other murders happened close to a Waterman-owned establishment, Judy. In each case, Scopes and Halliday had been working in the area, but they were red herrings, because Scopes has no connection with Baker, and Halliday couldn't have murdered Davy Guthrie."

"All right," said Judy. "But I don't see—"

"It had to be Shaw, using Scopes and Halliday as a smoke-screen by picking the nights when they were both working in the same town to carry out the murders. The rota's up on the wall in every one of these places." Lloyd was having to raise his voice now, the music from the fairground growing louder as they approached it. "And in each case, Tony Baker was there too, lured there by the letters. It's beyond coincidence. And today, Stephen and Scopes are both here, Tony Baker's here and Shaw's here."

The stage did seem to be set, thought Tom. And right now, they didn't know where any of them were. He understood Lloyd's foreboding, and his urgency.

"I think Baker's the real target," Lloyd said, as the three of them made their way along to the dust-track through the trees and bushes. "I think Shaw's lured him here to kill him."

Tom waited for Judy to point out a flaw in his argument. But if she was going to, she never got the chance, because running out of the woods came Grace Halliday.

"Oh, thank God!" she said. "Please, please go and see what's happened to Jack! He's fallen over, and he can't get up on his own—please! He might have been hurt!"

Judy put her arm round the distraught woman. "All right," she said, slightly breathless herself from her jog trot. "We'll find him, don't worry. What happened?"

"Someone shot at me! Jack saved my life. I don't know how— I don't know where he came from, but he threw himself on top of me, and then told me to get up, and run into the wood. Run toward the music, he said. Get help."

"Someone shot at you?" said Lloyd. "Are you certain about that?"

"Yes! Oh, please, you must find Jack!"

"Ring Hitch and tell him to get backup here, Tom," Judy said, in a low voice. "In numbers. We need to keep people out of the woods, in case there is someone in there with a gun." She paused. "And tell them we might need the ARV."

Tom's heart sank. In his opinion, calling out the armed response vehicle meant that instead of one man with a gun, you had four men with guns. "Yes, ma'am," he said, taking out his mobile phone.

"Mrs. Halliday, you stay here with Inspector Finch, and tell him exactly what happened." She looked at Lloyd, then back at Mrs. Halliday. "We'll find Mr. Shaw," she assured her. "Don't worry."

STEPHEN ARRIVED AT THE SUMMERHOUSE, HIS EYES WIDENING when he saw it. When Ben had told him about it, he had been imagining the sort of thing you could buy at a garden center and erect yourself. But as he opened the door and saw a large room, with a desk, a sofa bed, armchairs, a dining table, curtains, rugs—well, it seemed to him that if they bought a little camping stove, he and Ben could just move in here without Waterman ever knowing. It wasn't exactly a serious thought, but it did have its attractions.

Then he saw the rifle, just lying there, on the windowsill. He frowned, and went over to it. He had heard a shot on his way here—he'd imagined it was some neighboring farmer shooting a magpie or something. But . . . he moved closer, almost afraid to look. It was *his* rifle. No. No, how could it be his rifle?

It couldn't. Mr. Waterman must have had a pair—he gave him one, and kept one, presumably. But that didn't explain what it was doing here in the summerhouse. It had a moderator on it, so someone must have been using it. Had it fired the shot he'd heard? He went to the window, and picked it up, sniffing it. It smelt as though it had. And that was when he saw the little scratch on the stock. An accident he'd had with it . . . it *was* his rifle. He tried to eject the cartridges, but the mechanism was jammed.

He looked out of the window, as if he would see something that could explain the presence of his rifle, recently used, and jammed, in the Watermans' summerhouse. There must be an explanation. Maybe . . . maybe Ben was playing some sort of joke, though what kind of joke it could possibly be he couldn't imagine. Still, there wasn't much point in worrying about it. He'd ask Ben if he knew anything about it, and if he didn't . . . well, at least there would be two of them to puzzle over it.

The grass in front of him sloped away down toward the lake, and on the other side, he could see Baker on the tennis court, standing by his car, his jacket over his shoulder, waiting for his mother. He raised the rifle to his shoulder, getting Baker in its sights. Never point a loaded gun unless you intend to use it—he could hear Jack's voice as clearly as if he was in the room with him, and felt guilty, but not guilty enough to stop doing it. Anyway—it might be loaded, but he couldn't use it, even if he wanted to. He saw Baker glance at his watch, and automatically checked the time himself; it was just after eleven o'clock, and Ben would be here any minute.

He watched Baker through the scope, amusing himself by following him with the rifle as he paced up and down impatiently. He was being kept waiting—something Stephen was sure would irritate him greatly. Finally, at five past eleven, he started walking back up the path, and disappeared into the woods.

The door opened, and Stephen turned from the window, expecting Ben. Instead, he found himself looking at Keith Scopes in a security officer's uniform. For an instant, he was very scared, until he saw Scopes's rigid expression, and realized he still had the rifle at his shoulder, his finger on the trigger. He smiled. "Did you want something?" he asked.

"No. No—forget it."

Scopes backed away, and Stephen took great pleasure in kicking the door shut in his face.

KEITH RAN, ONCE THE DOOR HAD BEEN SLAMMED, DIVING INTO THE woods as soon as he could, running along the shortcut to the path that would take him toward the fairground.

Everything had gone wrong. Everything. He had never been so shocked in his life as he had been when he'd found Stephen Halliday standing there, pointing that rifle at him. And he wasn't about to argue with a man with a gun.

TONY WAS ON HIS KNEES BESIDE THE PRONE FIGURE, AND TOOK OUT his mobile phone, dialling 999.

"Emergency, which service do you require?"

"An ambulance." He covered Shaw with the jacket he'd been carrying, taking care not to disturb the two banknotes that lay on his chest, weighed down by the bell-pad.

"Could I have your name, caller?"

"My name is Tony Baker, and I'm calling from a house called the Grange in Stoke Weston, near Stansfield in Bartonshire. There's an injured man in the grounds—it's a head injury, and he's unconscious. If you can dispatch an ambulance, I'll make sure there's someone to meet it at the gate and direct it to the scene."

"What are the nature of the injuries?"

Tony raised his eyes to heaven. "It's a head injury," he repeated. "I've just found him—I don't know what happened to him."

"An ambulance is on its way, Mr. Baker. Please don't attempt to move the casualty. If I could just have a few more details . . ."

*   *   *

LLOYD COULD SEE TONY BAKER KNEELING BESIDE SOMEONE DRESSED in a Morris dancer's costume, lying on the ground, blood from his head soaking into the jacket that covered him, and hurried over to them. Grace Halliday had been right: Shaw had indeed been hurt. The pathway forked into a rough Y shape, and Baker and the victim were a few yards along the left-hand fork.

"What happened?" he asked, kneeling down beside Shaw.

"I've no idea—I was waiting for Grace at the car. It's parked by the lake—down that way." He pointed. "She was late, so I walked back up to meet her, and I just found him like this. It's Jack Shaw—he's a close friend of the Hallidays. I've phoned for an ambulance—they said not to move him. And I've tried to get hold of Mike Waterman, to tell him to put someone on the gate to guide the ambulance when it gets here, but he's not answering his landline or his mobile."

"It's all right," said Judy. "Mrs. Halliday can tell the ambulance where to come. I'll tell DI Finch what's happened."

Lloyd heard footsteps, and twisted round to see a security officer emerge from where the path forked off the other way. Another player in this drama who he had never met, but from the uniform and the general description, it had to be Keith Scopes. He was breathless, and agitated. He stopped when he came upon the tableau.

"Keith—have you any idea what's been going on here?" Judy asked.

"No. But Stephen Halliday just threatened me with a rifle. I think he's gone mad."

"I thought I heard a shot," said Baker.

Lloyd groaned silently. Halliday was shooting at his own mother? This just got messier and messier.

"I paid no attention to it—you hear shots all the time round here." Baker looked at Shaw's head wound. "I can't tell if that's a bullet wound or not."

"When did you hear the shot?" asked Judy.

"About ten minutes ago," said Baker. "Didn't you hear it?"

"No, but we were at the other side of the grounds ten minutes ago." She turned back to Scopes. "Did you hear a shot?"

"No. That would be when I was talking to DI Finch up where the Morris dancing is."

"So where's Halliday now?"

"In the summerhouse. That path's a shortcut to it from here." Scopes looked at the injured man. "Is that Jack Shaw? Has he been shot?"

"Did Halliday actually threaten you?" Judy asked.

"Not in so many words. But when I opened the door, he pointed the gun right at me, and asked if I wanted something— you know. Like he'd shoot me if I said yes."

That was a threat, thought Lloyd. It was technically an assault.

"Is there anyone in there with him?"

"No."

No hostage, then, thank God. But a man threatening people with a loaded rifle, who had already shot someone, meant that Judy had no option but to bring in the ARV. Poor Judy. If Lloyd were a cliché man, he would think that this was a baptism by fire.

"Did you see anyone when you were here before?"

Scopes frowned. "I wasn't here before."

"When you were on your way to the summerhouse," said Judy.

"Oh—no. I used the other path. The one from the house— near where I was talking to Mr. Finch. It goes directly to the summerhouse."

Lloyd was worried about Shaw. Baker had done as much as anyone could do to help him; all they could do now was monitor his pulse and his breathing and wait for the ambulance. He lifted up the jacket covering the man to see if he had any other injuries, and frowned. "What's that?" he asked.

"The bells that are part of the costume. But if you look more closely . . ."

Lloyd bent his head closer, and could see the two five-pound notes underneath. He could also see the other set of bells just poking out of Shaw's pocket, which was odd.

"But he's still alive," said Baker. "Maybe our man's slipped up this time."

He was indeed alive, and breathing—laboriously and evidently breathing. Which was even odder, in Lloyd's opinion, than the business with the bells. He replaced the jacket.

"Is Grace all right?" asked Baker. "Was she involved in this?"

"Yes," said Lloyd. "To both questions." Baker's concern seemed a little belated to him. "Were you worried about her, that you came looking for her?"

"No—I just thought I'd walk up and see if she was on her way. Time was very tight, because we were due back here at one o'clock."

"Did you see anyone on your way down to the lake?" asked Judy.

"No—no one at all."

Judy pointed to a ragged scar on a tree behind where Shaw lay. "Look, Lloyd—what's that?"

Lloyd stood up and moved cautiously closer to it, not wanting to disturb any possible evidence. It was level with his eyes, and he was as certain as he could be that the SOCOs would find a bullet lodged in there. Ballistics would know the angle of trajectory. They would find out exactly where the bullet had come from, where the gunman had been when he fired. "You heard only one shot?" he asked Baker.

"Yes, just one."

The bullet must have grazed Shaw's head as he threw himself onto Grace Halliday, then lodged in the tree, Lloyd thought. He'd remained conscious long enough to tell Grace Halliday what to do, then passed out.

"Where were you when you heard it?" he asked.

"I was waiting in the VIP car park—well, that's what we're calling it. It's a couple of tennis courts down by the lake. It would

have been about five to eleven when I heard it, I think. But I
didn't think anything of it—you often hear shots round here.
When Grace hadn't arrived by five past, I started walking back up
to meet her, and I found him a moment before you got here."

"How far away is the summerhouse?" Lloyd asked Scopes.

"It takes about a minute to get there along that path—it goes
straight through the woods. You can see it from the lake, but you
can't get to it from there unless you've got a boat. Do you want me
to show you?"

"No, I do not. If we can see the summerhouse, then Halliday
can see us. And he's the one with the rifle."

"Oh, yeah."

My God, Lloyd thought, if they had brains, they'd be frightening.

"Do you know if there's a phone in there?" asked Judy.

"There never used to be," said Scopes.

"Stephen's got a mobile phone," said Baker. "But I didn't get
an answer when I tried it earlier." He gave her the number.

"Did you see Stephen entering the summerhouse?"

"No, but I wasn't looking at it—I was watching the pathway
for Grace."

"Well—thank you for your help, Mr. Baker," said Judy. "We'll
take it from here. Mr. Scopes, could you escort Mr. Baker back to
the fairground, please? You'll find DI Finch there." While Lloyd
checked Shaw's pulse again, she rang Tom and told him to expect
Baker and Scopes, then dialed another number, waited for a few
moments, and gave up with a sigh. "I thought if I could contact
Stephen, we might avoid what's going to happen," she said. "But
he's got it switched off, or its battery's dead." She rang Tom again,
and reluctantly told him that they needed the ARV. "How's Shaw
doing?" she asked, when she finished her call.

"Not too well," said Lloyd.

"The ambulance is here—it's on its way down now."

"Thank God for that."

"Tom's going to let Waterman know what's going on before

the place is crawling with police. And by the time Shaw's on his way to hospital, the ARV should be here." She sighed. "Marks out of ten?"

"Ten, of course." Lloyd smiled.

"Seriously. Am I doing what you would have done?"

"Seriously?" Lloyd thought for a moment. "No, not really."

"Why?" she asked, her face falling. "What would you have done differently?"

"I would have nipped along to the summerhouse, disarmed him myself, got loads of commendations and saved the taxpayers a lot of money, but . . ." He paused, shrugged, and smiled indulgently. "You're just a woman, and you're doing your best."

THERE HAD BEEN NO POSSIBILITY OF CONFUSION, BUT GARY HAD had to be certain. And now it was beyond doubt. Davy was still alive at eleven o'clock. That meant that Headless had nothing to do with anything; it was just some well-behaved citizen putting his rubbish in the bin, not someone dumping the knife. Gary was painfully aware that this meant rubbing out everything they thought they knew and starting again.

He rang DI Finch's mobile, and told him that Headless was a red herring, and that Davy Guthrie could have been killed any time up until he was found. "I'm sorry, sir," he said. "But I thought Davy must have been dead by quarter to eleven, because I was so sure Gertie had seen the murderer dump the knife."

"You weren't alone," said Finch. "We all thought that."

Gary sighed. "I suppose that's what you get when your star witnesses are a bag lady, a drag queen and a blind eighty-year-old."

"Well, maybe it is, but it might have got us on the right track by accident—get back to Barton as soon as you can. I've a feeling we're going to need all hands on deck."

"Yes, sir."

Gary put down the phone, started the engine, and pulled out

of the lay-by. He hadn't told DI Finch that he was halfway back to Barton already. That was how long it had taken him to pluck up the courage to ring him.

MICHAEL AND BEN HAD HAD A LONG TALK ABOUT THE MONEY. IT was a considerable sum, and Ben had discussed various things he might like to do with it. Michael would have enjoyed it more if he hadn't seen those brochures, but perhaps they hadn't had anything to do with Halliday, because Ben hadn't shown any sign of wanting to slip away, and now Halliday would be safely at the Tulliver, because Grace was definitely here at opening time, watching the Morris dancing with Jack Shaw.

Ben was upstairs getting dressed. He wanted to enjoy the fair, he said—it wasn't everyone who got to have a fairground in their own backyard. And Michael brightened a little, as he thought what the brochures might mean. Maybe Ben had finally met a girl—maybe he was home to tell him that. Maybe that was why he was house-hunting. Could he have misunderstood that conversation he'd heard him having with Halliday in February? He thought about what he'd heard, and reluctantly concluded that he couldn't have misunderstood. But perhaps that had been a final fling—getting all that nonsense out of his system. At any rate, they didn't seem to be too interested in each other now, so things were definitely looking up.

"I'll get it!" Ben called, rattling downstairs, when the doorbell rang.

Michael came out into the hall, to see him open the door to Detective Inspector Finch. "Good morning, Inspector," he said. "I don't think you've met my son Ben. Ben, this is Detective Inspector Finch."

"Pleased to meet you," said Finch, then looked at Michael, his face troubled. "I'm afraid there's been a serious incident here this morning, Mr. Waterman."

Michael frowned. "What sort of incident?"

"Someone's discharged a firearm in your woods, and we have a casualty, I'm afraid. We're having to cordon off the approaches to the summerhouse and the lake."

"But a friend of mine's waiting for me in the summerhouse," said Ben. "I was just on my way to meet him there."

Michael stared at him. "What did you say?"

Ben ignored him. "His name's Stephen Halliday. Have you seen him? Is he all right? Who's been hurt?"

Finch looked slightly thrown. "Well—that whole area's been cleared of everyone but police personnel, sir, so . . . I shouldn't worry about him. He isn't the casualty." He turned back to Michael as Ben was trying, unsuccessfully, to make a call on his mobile phone. "And I'm afraid we're having to clear the grounds, Mr. Waterman. We'll be making an announcement over the loud-speakers, asking people to make their way to their cars, and leave."

Michael couldn't take all this in. "But—but some of the people here have their cars parked at the lake," he said.

"I'm sorry, but they can't collect them at the moment. Don't worry about it—we'll sort something out."

That boy was waiting for him in the summerhouse? He had been right in the first place. Ben's sudden desire to be home had had nothing to do with May Day, or filial concern, or even advice about his legacy. All he was interested in was seeing that boy so they could . . . he couldn't even think the words.

"And, I'm sorry, but we must ask you and your staff to stay in the house until further notice, for your own safety. We'll keep you informed, sir—and I apologize for the disruption."

Finch left, and Michael slammed the door, turning to face Ben. "So that was your game, was it?"

Ben looked at him in disbelief. "He's just told you that there's a gunman loose in the grounds," he said. "He's shot someone. They're evacuating all these people. Is that all you can think about, at a time like this? My sex life?"

"I want to know what game you think you're playing."

"It isn't a game. Stephen and I have been together for almost three years."

Michael stared at him. It had been going on for three years? "Oh, I know it isn't a game," he said. "I saw the estate agents' literature! I know what you and that Halliday boy are planning— well, you can forget it! Do you hear me? Forget it!"

"What right had you to go through my things?" demanded Ben.

"They were lying on your bed! That's not going through your things, for God's sake!"

"You're interfering in my private affairs!"

"Affairs is the word! Well, let me tell you something. You are my son, and no son of mine is a poof. Is that clear enough?"

Ben shook his head, his eyes still blazing. "You can't tell me how to live my life," he said. "I'm gay, and you're stuck with it. I'm not going to get married and give you grandchildren, so just get that fantasy out of your head."

Michael closed his eyes. "You're not gay," he said. "You're just confused, that's all. You're not gay! I should never have sent you to that bloody school."

"Oh, for—" Ben hit the side of his fist against the wall in frustration. "The school had nothing to do with it. I didn't know myself until after I'd left school."

"See? You didn't know. You've not given girls a chance, Ben."

"I have. And they do nothing for me."

"And that boy does?"

"Yes. We love each other."

"Don't make me sick."

"How did you find out about us, anyway?"

"Never mind how. The fact is that I did, and I always will."

"You really do respect my privacy, don't you?"

"I would if I wasn't so worried about you all the time! You could get AIDS or anything!"

Ben sighed impatiently. "I could get run over by a bus—you

don't try to stop me crossing the road! And if you knew, why didn't you say anything?"

"Actions speak louder than words. I told you what I'd do to anyone else you took up with, and I meant it."

"And I make you sick?" Ben shook his head.

Yes. The whole idea made him sick to his stomach. "Halliday's card's marked," Michael said. "The minute the opportunity presents itself, he'll be given a beating he won't forget."

"And you think that will put him off?"

"It put that other one off, didn't it? And are you prepared to let that happen to him?" Michael wanted to reason with him, and he didn't know how. But he knew how to bargain. "If you tell me now that you won't have any more to do with him, I'll call it off."

Again, Ben shook his head, his face set and angry. "He knows what you had done to Charles. I told him I was bad news, and to forget about me, because if you found out, it would happen to him too. And he said he'd risk it."

"Oh, and why do you think he's prepared to risk it? What do you think he's interested in, eh? You? Don't kid yourself! It's the money he's got his eye on."

"Stephen knows nothing about the money."

"Oh, I see! You love him so much that you haven't even told him about your legacy. Why not?"

Ben took a step closer to him. "Because I wanted to be able to look you in the eye and tell you that he is not after my money, because I knew that was what you would think. As far as he's concerned, I'm a penniless student whose father is probably going to disown him once he realizes he can't bully everyone into submission."

No. No, it had to stop. It had to stop now. If bargaining didn't work, the next step was to issue threats, so that's what he would do. Whatever it took. "I've only got to say the word, and he would be dead. That would get rid of him once and for all. Is that what it's going to take?"

Ben stepped back again, looking almost afraid. "Listen to

yourself! You're mad. You're *mad*—do you know that? What's the big deal about me being gay? I love Stephen and he loves me."

"Don't be ridiculous! What do you know about love, anyway? You're too young to know what you want!"

"I'm older than you were when you met Mum. And I would have thought that you of all people would understand how I feel about Stephen."

Michael felt himself go pale with anger. "Don't you dare compare that little sod with your mother!"

"Why not? He's good, and kind, and he makes me feel better than I've ever felt with anyone. And he makes me better than I am—I *am* your son, whether you like it or not. I've got the same instincts. Stephen keeps me from getting into trouble, which is more than your precious Keith ever did."

"He's not fit to be mentioned in the same breath as your mother!"

"Isn't he? She kept you from getting into trouble—you've told me that yourself! And you took Stephen on as soon as he left school because you thought such a lot of him—you told me that, too. You had plans for him. You thought one day he could end up managing the business for you—just like Mum did when you got married. So you compared him to her yourself. You even gave him Mum's Winchester! But as soon as you find out that he's involved with me, you're arranging for him to be given a beating. Now you're talking about killing him, for God's sake!" He shook his head. "You should get help."

"I won't have you talking to me—"

But Ben was taking the stairs two at a time, and moments later, Michael heard his bedroom door slam.

THE AMBULANCE PERFORMED A TRICKY TURN BY BACKING INTO and out of the shortcut to the summerhouse, and at last, it was pointing in the right direction to take Jack Shaw to hospital, and proper medical treatment. John Hitchin was going to go with him, in the doubtless forlorn hope that he would soon recover consciousness, and might be able to tell them what had happened. The latest dispatch from Tom about Gary's interview with the blind man meant that Stephen Halliday no longer had an alibi for Davy Guthrie's murder, so what with one thing and another, things weren't looking good for him. And it seemed that he had intended meeting Michael Waterman's son at the summerhouse—Judy had no idea if that had any significance or not.

And she might have had worse days in her life, but it was very hard to think of any offhand. If her heart could have sunk any lower, it would have, as the ARV sergeant made his way toward them, appearing from the dense trees, having walked up from the lake through cover until he was out of sight of the summerhouse. "Superintendent Hill?" he asked, approaching Lloyd.

"That's me," said Judy.

"Oh, sorry, ma'am. The situation is that my crew has him under surveillance from the roadway at the rear of the property—he seems quite agitated, pacing up and down, picking up the rifle, putting it down again. Well—it was his mother he shot at, wasn't it? And it was a close friend that he hit, from what I gather."

Judy nodded confirmation of that.

"So he's going to be in a highly emotional state, isn't he? My men can't cover all the angles—literally. There are two windows, a door, and a skylight in that building. Once out of the building, there are three ways he could get out of this area and into the public area."

Judy, having looked it up as Lloyd had suggested, found herself thinking that the man had used a dangling participle. She was letting her mind dwell on anything other than what she was facing, and she couldn't do that. This was her responsibility. She nodded, and waited to hear what all this added up to.

"He's already shot someone, and threatened the only person who's tried to approach him. I've called out the Firearms Unit, and they're clearing the grounds."

Oh, my God. Twenty armed officers at least.

The sergeant saw her reaction to that, and smiled. "Don't worry, ma'am. You can't imagine the paperwork if anyone actually fires a weapon. And shooting someone doesn't bear thinking about."

She wasn't really in the mood for being patronized, though she did think that this man probably patronized everyone who wasn't a firearms officer, rather than just women. "You don't think there's any chance it can be resolved without bringing in even more armed police?"

"Well, there's always a chance, ma'am, but I don't deal in chance."

Oh, a put-down. That was just what she needed. She was already beginning to acquire a hearty dislike for this man, but there wasn't much point in having experts if you didn't take their advice.

"We have to be prepared for any eventuality. He could hide anywhere in these woods and pick people off at will, if he got out."

As he said that, Judy found out that her heart could, and did, sink lower, and all because of a word that hadn't even been spoken.

He meant if he got out alive.

CHAPTER ELEVEN

STEPHEN PACED UP AND DOWN THE ROOM. HE DIDN'T UNDER-stand what had gone wrong. Where was Ben? It was almost midday. Why was his rifle in here? And why had Keith Scopes been here? His first thought on seeing him had been that Mr. Waterman had found out about him and Ben, and had sent Keith to beat him up. But while that could explain why Ben wasn't here and why Keith was, it didn't explain the rifle. Any-way, the more he thought about it, the more he believed he had been wrong about that. He was sure Keith Scopes hadn't expected to find him here.

He went over to the windowsill and picked up the rifle, trying yet again to free the mechanism so that he could empty it and get it back safely where it belonged. But he couldn't. He sat down, the rifle resting on his lap. He'd tried to ring Ben, but his phone was dead, and that meant that Ben couldn't contact him. He didn't want to leave, not until he knew for certain that Ben wasn't going to be here. Ben had said he would have to be back at the house for half past twelve, but lunch wasn't until one, so he would give it till then. He didn't want to go without even speak-ing to him.

He stood up again, and carried on pacing, then stopped at the window, and frowned. That was strange, as well—Tony Baker hadn't come back to his car, which was still sitting there, and his mum hadn't appeared at all. So their plans had also fallen through, apparently. But why? His mum was only going to watch the Morris dancing—she couldn't have got held up.

Maybe something had happened to Mr. Waterman—or Ben. He felt alarmed, then. If something had happened to Ben, then his mum and Tony would naturally stay with Mr. Waterman rather than go wherever they were going, and it would explain why he hadn't arrived. No, he told himself. Calm down. It didn't explain the rifle, and it didn't explain Keith. It was all very strange, but there would be an explanation to account for all of it.

"Stephen?"

The voice, coming out of nowhere, echoing over the lake, disturbing the ducks, made Stephen jump. What the hell was that? It was like God, or something, calling him. He couldn't see anyone.

"Stephen. This is DI Tom Finch. There are armed police officers surrounding the building, so please don't do anything silly. Just open the door, and throw your weapon out."

What? Stephen shook his head. What the hell was going on? Who was that? Was this some sort of joke? Of course it was. It must be. Outside, the ducks settled back on the lake, and the sun shone on the water, glinting off the expensive cars on the tennis courts. It was a calm, sunny spring day. Of course there weren't armed police surrounding the building. Was he dreaming?

"Stephen? Open the door, and throw out the rifle. Then we can discuss everything quietly. Do it now."

Stephen looked at the rifle, then looked back out at the peaceful scene in front of him, smiling, shaking his head. It was a joke. It must be.

"Throw out the rifle, Stephen."

It *must* be a joke. He went to the window at the back, and looked out at the grass, and the wood beyond. Blossom fluttered to the ground, birds sang. It was a dream, or he was imagining things, or someone was playing a very complicated practical joke. It couldn't be anything else.

"Throw out the rifle. Now."

It didn't sound like a joke. But it was ridiculous. Why would Finch be talking to him like that? You would think that he was holed up in here, hiding from them, the way Finch was talking to him. Slowly, his head was getting round the fact that they did think that. They really, really did think that. Finch—if that really was Finch—had told him to throw the rifle out, but if he threw the rifle out like someone surrendering to them, that would just make them think it all the more, and they'd got it all wrong. He couldn't do that.

"Stephen. Open the door, and throw out the rifle."

He shook his head—no. No, he had to explain, make them understand. If he could just talk to them—oh, why had his phone had to run out of juice now? If he could call someone, tell them that it wasn't the way they thought, that would sort it out. He turned away from the window. If he could just explain to them what had happened, they would know that none of this was necessary. But how could he? He didn't *know* what had happened. And he couldn't contact anyone anyway.

"Stephen. It might not be as bad as you think. No one's dead. Just throw the rifle out, and we can talk about it."

Stephen sat down on the arm of the sofa with a bump, as his legs gave way beneath him. No one's dead? What did he mean? That someone had been shot? And they thought he'd shot whoever it was? He closed his eyes. He'd heard a shot. And this rifle had been fired recently. Oh, my God. My God—they didn't understand. He had to make them understand.

"We can't talk while you're in there with a loaded rifle, Stephen. Just throw it out—things aren't as bad as all that. Believe me."

He had no option. He got up slowly, and went to the door, standing behind it, afraid to open it. What if they shot at him? No—no, they wouldn't, not if he was doing what they said. He licked dry lips, took as deep a breath as he could manage with his heart pounding the way it was, grasped the door handle, and turned it slowly, pulling the door open just wide enough to throw out the rifle, then shut it again before they started shooting at him.

There was silence for a few moments, and Stephen waited, leaning his back against the door, breathing heavily, feeling tears prick the back of his eyes. It was all right, he told himself. It was all right. Finch would come and talk to him now, and he could explain.

"Stephen? This is Sergeant Digby. I'm a firearms officer. I want you to come out slowly, with your hands on your head."

Oh, no. No—this wasn't happening. No. No, he didn't want to do that. He slid into a sitting position behind the door. Please, he didn't want to do that. Where had Finch gone? Just come and talk, he pleaded silently with Finch, tears streaming down his face. Just come and talk, like you said you would. Don't make me do that.

"Stephen? Can you hear me? Come out slowly, with your hands on your head."

He had to do it. He stood up, his mouth dry, his legs shaking, sweat pouring down his back, and opened the door again, a little wider. With his hands on his head, moving as slowly as he could, he stepped out onto the grass.

"Step away from the weapon. Take three long steps to your right."

Stephen did as he was told.

"Now get down on your knees, and lie facedown on the ground."

Stephen dropped to his knees, almost glad that he didn't have to trust his legs to keep him standing any longer. He still couldn't see anyone.

"Lie down on the ground, facedown."

He dropped his hands in order to get into the position requested.

"Keep your hands on your head!"

Stephen's hands shot back up on his head. Don't shoot me. Please, don't shoot me. He clasped his fingers, so he wouldn't forget again.

"Lie facedown on the ground."

He bent forward until his head was almost touching the ground, then, supporting himself on his elbows, slid his knees backward until he could lie flat, his hands still tightly clasped on his head.

"Don't move," said a voice.

Out of the corner of his eye, he saw someone scoop up the rifle and put it in a bag. Then suddenly, his hands were pulled from his head, and someone was handcuffing him. It hurt, and his hands automatically pulled away from the pain, but that hurt even more.

"Keep still!"

He was searched then, and pulled to his feet by two policemen as a woman came up to him. She had a warrant card in her hand, but he couldn't focus on it.

"Acting Superintendent Hill," she said. "Stephen Halliday, I'm arresting you for the attempted murder of John Shaw. You do not have to say anything, but it may harm your defense if you fail to mention when questioned anything that you later rely on in court."

Stephen stared at her, and tried to speak, but his voice was just a croak. He swallowed, and tried again. "This is all a mistake," he said. "I found the rifle in there." Then he realized what she had said. "John Shaw? Is that Jack? What's happened to him? Has he been shot? I heard a shot."

"All in good time, Stephen," she said. "DI Finch is going to take you to the station, and we can talk about this."

The policemen who had handcuffed him, just ordinary policemen, led him to a car. One of them put him in the back, and got in with him. After a few moments, Finch got in the front, and Stephen stared at the scene as the car drove off, twisting round in his seat, disbelieving, his eyes wide as he saw policemen with body armor, helmets, and guns come out from behind the building, behind trees, behind cars. They really had been surrounding the building.

And it was all a mistake.

* * *

JUDY HAD FELT LIKE CRYING HERSELF WHEN STEPHEN HAD BEEN standing there handcuffed, his face white and tear-stained, grass streaks on the knees of his fashionable, expensive jeans, his close-fitting, well-cut shirt soaked in sweat. He had got dressed up for a date, if you asked her, not for a murder. She had only seen him once before, and very briefly, and yet she felt, as surely as Tom Finch did, that he was no killer.

She turned to the firearms sergeant as he came up to her, handing her the bagged-up rifle. "Thank you," she said. "That was very efficient." It had been. She still felt that it had probably also been unnecessary, but she couldn't have taken the risk of dispensing with the firearms unit's services. And she'd upset Tom. He had wanted to go and talk to Stephen as soon as he'd thrown out the rifle, but the sergeant had pointed out that Tom didn't know what other weapons he might have on him, and she had had to let the sergeant take over, much to Tom's annoyance.

"I had visions of a shoot-out," Lloyd confessed, as they got back to where the path forked, and walked down to the lakeside, where the ARV was parked.

"I've never been in a shoot-out," said the sergeant. "It's not very often like it is on the telly. It's not always that easy to winkle them out, but his rifle had jammed, and he obviously couldn't get it unjammed."

Judy wondered about that. "What makes a rifle's action jam?" she asked.

"Mostly, bolt-action rifles are very reliable," said the sergeant. "It could be mechanical failure, but if the operator is under stress, he can jam the action himself by fumbling the maneuver."

"Could it happen to someone who wasn't used to the gun?"

"Well—no, it's unlikely to happen just because of that. Someone not used to firing any sort of gun might fumble it, obviously. But that bullet in the tree was dead on target to hit the head of an adult standing in front of it, so it was no novice who fired it. It's more likely to be something unexpected happening, panicking the operator and putting him off his stroke."

Like Shaw throwing himself on top of Grace Halliday, thought Judy. Dr. Castle said that their man wouldn't react too well to a contingency he hadn't planned for. But that didn't help Stephen much.

"And it's got a moderator on it," added the sergeant.

"What's a moderator?"

"A sort of silencer. He's got a license for it."

Lloyd frowned. "Why would he need something like that?"

"It's to cut down nuisance to neighbors and to make it easier to shoot foxes and suchlike without alerting all their mates." Sergeant Digby smiled grimly. "But what with the moderator and the funfair—he could be pretty sure the shot wouldn't attract much attention. It doesn't muffle the sound like a silencer does, but it would sound more like an air rifle to anyone who heard it." Back at his car, he removed his body armor with a sigh of relief. "That's better. Well, we'll be off now. Sir," he said, nodding a farewell to Lloyd. "Ma'am."

Judy and Lloyd watched as the ARV drove out of the lakeside car park, to join the other police vehicles that lined the back road, all, thankfully, going back to where they belonged without a shot fired.

"I think we can let these people come and get their cars now," said Judy. "They'll need to take the long way round, but there's no need to cordon off the car park any longer." She looked at Lloyd. "We'll have to seal the summerhouse. And seal off both the pathways."

"Baker didn't ask if Grace Halliday was all right until we'd been there for about ten minutes," Lloyd said.

"Does that surprise you?" She reached into her pocket and took out her mobile.

"Well—they're supposed to be practically engaged."

"Waterman might believe that, but I doubt it. The romance blossomed as soon as he realized that he was going to be here for the long haul and not the month or so he thought in the first place. If you ask me, he was missing his creature comforts, and Grace was easy prey."

Lloyd smiled. "You're so romantic. How do you know she isn't the love of his life?"

"Because the love of Tony Baker's life is Tony Baker." She glanced at the phone. "I've got a text message from Hitch," she said, and read it aloud. " 'Shaw not shot. Severe blow. Something approx inch and a half in diameter. Fractured skull, in coma. Emergency op in progress.' " She looked up. "So he didn't just get in the way of the bullet," she said. "He was deliberately attacked. I wonder what was used? It would be best if the SOCOs knew what to look for."

She made the calls arranging for the VIPs to be told that they could collect their cars, for the crime scene to be protected, and for the SOCOs to come, putting her phone away with a tired blowing out of the cheeks that turned to a smile.

"Lloyd, look," she whispered, pointing along the bank of the lake to where a duck was leading her fluffy brood to the water.

The mother duck slipped down the bank into the water, and two of the ducklings more or less fell in after her. Two others stayed on the bank, and she quacked to encourage them to follow suit. The fifth and smallest one had fallen behind, unable to negotiate whatever it was over which the others had hopped.

"Is it ecologically incorrect to give it a helping hand, do you think?" asked Lloyd. "Are we supposed to let nature take its course?"

Judy laughed. "Go on," she said. "Go and help it."

Lloyd walked over to where the duckling was, close to the pathway back through the woods. "It's one of Shaw's crutches," he called back to Judy.

Oh, of course, she thought, cross with herself. Waterman had told them Shaw was on crutches. "I had completely forgotten about them," she said, going over.

"So had I. But I suppose we can be forgiven, what with one

thing and another." Lloyd squatted down, removed the duckling, sending it to join its brothers and sisters, and pointed. "Look," he said. "I think the duckling's found the weapon for us."

Judy bent down to see that the rubber cup at the foot of the crutch had worn away over the years until it was just a useless ragged ring round the shaft, and the exposed wood beneath it was covered in what was almost certainly Shaw's blood. She straightened up. "The attacker must have held it with both hands like a spear," she said. "If Shaw was lying on the ground, and he drove down with it . . ." She shook her head, not wanting to visualize the scene anymore, and looked back up the path. They had found Shaw just beyond where it twisted back through the woods, and a good throw from there would have caused it to land where it now lay. A better one would have sent it into the lake, and perhaps destroyed some evidence, but Shaw's attacker must have used all his strength hitting Shaw. At last, they had been given a break.

Lloyd stood up. "It's a puzzle, though."

"Is it?"

"Think about it—the gunman tries to kill Grace Halliday, but Shaw throws himself on top of her, and he misses, hits the tree. He thinks he's been seen, and that panics him, makes him jam the rifle. Grace gets away, but Shaw can't get up, and though he's a sitting duck—" He grinned. "If you'll pardon the expression, madam," he said to the duck, who was trying to persuade the last duckling to take the plunge, "—he can't shoot him. If you were going to hit him on the head with something, what would you choose?"

Judy was still holding the rifle, and the answer was staring at her. "The butt of the rifle."

"But he didn't. Why not?"

Judy thought for a few moments. "Because he'd planned to do something else with the rifle, and he carries out his plans to the letter," she said. "If Dr. Castle's right about him."

"I think he must be right—using the rifle butt would be the

first thing that occurred to anyone. So perhaps he wanted to leave the rifle in the summerhouse. Maybe Stephen really did find it there."

Judy frowned. "But why not use it on Shaw, and *then* leave it in the summerhouse? That wouldn't interfere with his plan."

"Perhaps because it had to be there before Stephen was, and he was running to a tight schedule. He would be able to see that Shaw was like a beached whale—he could afford to take the two minutes to run along the shortcut, deliver the rifle, and come back. Shaw wasn't going anywhere, and no one else was likely to come down the path to the lake."

Judy nodded slowly. That made sense. And she agreed with Lloyd that someone was deliberately implicating Stephen in these murders. Neither of them was saying so, but they were both talking about the same someone. Tony Baker was at the bottom of all of this. But why? If they could answer that, they might get somewhere.

"Did you experience a moment's déjà vu when Baker told us his story?"

Judy nodded. Yes, she had. He had been here, waiting in the car park, and had decided to walk back the way he had come. The last time he did that, he found Wilma Fenton's body. This time he found the badly injured Jack Shaw.

"We need to find out who knew Stephen was meeting Ben at the summerhouse," she said briskly. "And who else could have got hold of Stephen's gun. And if Tony Baker knows how to handle a rifle."

Lloyd looked a little surprised. "You're going with my theory? After the last one?"

"I'm not discounting your last one—you were right about this being the showdown, I'm sure. And I suspect you were right about a lot of other things, too, as usual."

"I'm always right."

She smiled. "Can I leave you to deal with the SOCOs and

any inquiries you think should be made in the village? I'll send Gary Sims over here for you, so you won't be stranded. But I want to be in on Stephen's interview."

"Sure."

She took out her mobile phone again, and had a small argument with herself. Yardley had today off like normal people, now that he wasn't on the inquiry. Waterman would almost certainly be talking to him, and it really wouldn't be very pleasant for Yardley to know nothing at all about it. She wouldn't tell him any more than he would have known in his capacity as head of CID. No details. If she confined herself to what would appear in the newspapers, and the name of the man arrested, she wouldn't be breaking any rules.

"I'm going to ring Yardley," she said. "He has a right to know what's happening."

"Good," said Lloyd.

MICHAEL LOOKED OUT OF HIS STUDY WINDOW AT THE RUINS OF HIS great May Day celebration. The police had told everyone to leave, to go home. The place was silent, the grounds littered with abandoned stalls. The fairground people had been told to stay in their caravans, and the solution the police had come up with for the drivers who couldn't simply walk home, and whose cars were parked at the lake, was to make them wait in one of the marquees until the all-clear. They would be less than pleased about that. His grand gesture had been a catastrophic failure.

Ben had remained in his room, but now the door opened, and he was there.

"Can we leave yet?"

"They haven't said so."

"The armed police have gone—I saw their vehicles drive away. The others are still here, though. I want to talk to them. I'm worried about Stephen."

Michael stiffened. He didn't want even to hear his name spoken, but now he was a little confused as to why. Partly anger. Partly guilt.

"I can't raise him on his mobile, and Rosie says he's not at the pub. And she doesn't know where his mother is."

"Neither do I," said Michael. "She's supposed to be here for lunch, but I expect the police have told her and Tony that they can't come into the grounds."

"But where's Stephen? I told Finch he was in the summerhouse—he didn't seem to be too bothered, did he? Surely they should have checked to see if—" He broke off as Michael's phone rang.

Michael glanced at the display. He'd ignored the one from Tony Baker, but this one was from Ray, so he answered.

"Mike? You asked me to keep you posted about Stephen Halliday—well . . . it's not good news, I'm afraid. He's just been arrested for attempted murder. But you probably know that already, since it happened at your place."

"Was he involved in this firearms incident?"

"He *was* the firearms incident. I don't know any details, not being on the inquiry anymore, but I thought you'd want to know."

"Thanks, Ray." Michael put down the phone again, and looked at Ben. "Well, you can stop worrying about your little friend," he said. "And you won't be setting up home with him after all. Not unless you want to move into Parkhurst with him. Or Broadmoor. Or wherever it is that he belongs."

Ben frowned. "What are you talking about?"

"He's just been arrested for trying to murder someone. He was the cause of all the armed police being here—that's why they weren't too bothered about his safety."

"You're making that up! I don't believe you."

"You don't have to take my word for it. I'm sure it'll be on the news sooner or later. They think he's the one who's been killing all these people round here."

"They think *what?*"

"You heard me."

"But that—that's ludicrous! What on earth has Stephen got to do with it?"

"He's been taken in for questioning after every one of them—didn't he tell you?"

Ben shook his head, his mouth slightly open.

"You don't tell each other much, do you?"

"But—hang on," said Ben. "What about the first one? The one Tony Baker witnessed—the one in Malworth? It happened the last time I was home, and it happened at nine o'clock. Stephen was with *me* at nine o'clock."

"I know. But he wouldn't tell the police where he was."

"That's because he knew it would get back to you!" Ben jumped up. "He was frightened to tell them where he was! I have to tell them."

Michael shook his head, and went to the study door, standing in front of it. "No," he said. "You're not going to the police."

"Of course I am! He was with me when that woman was killed!"

"You are not going to the police and telling them that you and that boy were—" Michael couldn't bring himself to say the words. "In one of my own flats? You can't do that to me!"

"Why not? Because Uncle Ray will get to know? Because he'll find out that your son isn't the macho man you wanted him to be? You'd rather they suspected Stephen of murder? Well, tough. I'm going to the police, and that's final. What in God's name would make them think that Stephen's killing people? And what on earth was going on here today?"

Ben—bigger, taller, stronger, younger—pushed Michael out the way, and opened the door to find the housekeeper right outside, trying to look as though she had heard nothing. She glanced at Ben, then stood on tiptoe to address Michael over his shoulder.

"Excuse me, Mr. Waterman, but there's a police officer downstairs."

"Good," said Ben, pushing past her.

Michael went after him, following him downstairs to where a uniformed inspector was standing in the hallway.

"I want to come and make a statement," Ben said.

"And you are . . . ?"

"My name's Ben Waterman. I'm Stephen Halliday's partner."

Michael had known that he couldn't stop him, but hearing him say those words made his whole body go limp.

"And this statement would be about what, Mr. Waterman?"

"These murders. The first one in particular. I was here that weekend, and I know where Stephen was when that happened. And today—Stephen was here to see me. I don't know what's been going on, but you've arrested the wrong man, and I want to talk to someone."

"Well, Mr. Waterman, I'm sure the inquiry team will want to take your statement. They're operating from Barton HQ. Do you know where that is?"

"Yes, but I don't have a car."

"Then we can take you, if you'd like."

"Yes. Now, please."

"Shortly, sir." The inspector turned to Michael. "Mr. Waterman, I just came to tell you that the incident has been resolved, and that your guests have been told that they can collect their cars from the lakeside whenever they like. Parts of your grounds are still cordoned off, I'm afraid, though. The scene-of-crime officers will be working there for some time."

"What happened?" asked Michael.

"I'm afraid all I can tell you is that someone was seriously injured in your woods, sir."

"Not by Stephen!" shouted Ben.

"All right, sir—don't worry, we will take your statement in due course. Please just calm down." He turned to Michael. "Well, thank you for your cooperation, Mr. Waterman, and our sincere apologies to your guests and yourself for the disruption to your May Day celebrations. Right, sir," he said to Ben. "Shall we go?"

Ben looked back over his shoulder at Michael as he went out

with the inspector. "For your information," he said, his voice calm and measured, "I won't be back. Not tonight—not ever again."

He meant it. That wasn't being said in the heat of the moment—he *meant* it. Michael stared after him, unable to say anything, unable to move, then gathered his wits, and ran to the door.

"Ben? Ben! Ben—please! Ben!"

But Ben wouldn't even turn round again, and Michael watched helplessly as he went off with the police. Today couldn't have gone any more wrong if the sun had risen in the west.

TONY UNLOCKED THE BACK DOOR, AND PULLED THE BOLT BACK. IF he was going to be alone in the pub, he was going to make certain the door was locked at all times, after today's bit of absentminded-ness.

He opened the door to Lloyd and a young man who was intro-duced as Trainee DC Gary Sims.

"Grace is at the hospital with Jack Shaw," he said. "I thought you would know that."

"Yes, we do," said Lloyd. "It's you I'd like to speak to, Mr. Baker."

"I was at your headquarters all morning. I gave someone my statement, such as it was. I told you everything I knew earlier."

"Just some additional queries," said Lloyd.

"And I'd like to look at Stephen's gun cabinet," Sims said. "I've got a search warrant here."

"Certainly." Tony didn't bother looking at the warrant. He fished the keys out of his pocket again. "It's in this room here," he said, opening the door. "The keys are kept in that desk—the right-hand drawer. And the key to the drawer is on this ring. It's that one," he said, selecting one of the small keys.

"Thanks," said Sims, taking the keys from him.

Tony left Sims to it, and showed Lloyd into the sitting room. "So how can I help you?"

"Could you tell me exactly what arrangements you had made with Mrs. Halliday for this morning?"

"I've already told you. I had arranged to meet her in the car park at the lake at eleven o'clock."

"With a view to doing what?"

"Oh, I see. Sorry. I'd booked a trip in a hot-air balloon. Just up and down again. There's a place near here that does that. I arranged it three weeks ago—I couldn't believe my luck when I saw the weather this morning. And then this awful thing had to happen."

Lloyd smiled sympathetically. "Like the man said—life is what happens when you've made other plans."

"Quite." He still didn't know what *had* happened to his plans. Why was Jack Shaw there at all? Was Grace bringing him along on their date? He didn't understand, and she had been too worried about Jack to talk to him properly.

"Did anyone else know of your arrangement to meet at the car park?"

"I didn't mention it to anyone, but Grace might have done, obviously. It looks as though she must have told Jack—she said he saved her life."

"And when did you tell her about it?"

"I didn't—that is, the balloon trip was going to be a surprise. I told her I was taking her somewhere, but I didn't say where."

"No—I meant about meeting you at the car park."

"Oh, of course. This morning, I think."

Sims came back in, and handed him the keys. "Do you know when Stephen last used his rifle?"

"He went out shooting with Jack Shaw last night."

"You didn't happen to see him put the guns away, did you?"

"No—Grace and I had gone to bed before he came home." Tony looked over at Lloyd, who was perusing the bookshelf, taking out his glasses. "I shouldn't bother," he said. "Grace isn't what you'd call a great reader. It's all travel guides."

"Did you all leave for the Grange together this morning?" asked Sims.

"No—we were going to, but I got held up with business. Jack came, and he and Stephen and Grace all went up in Grace's car. I followed about half an hour later."

"So you were on your own for that half hour?"

Lloyd seemed excessively interested in the travel guides, for some reason. Tony was finding it difficult to concentrate on what Sims was saying. "Yes," he said, then remembered that he wasn't. "Except for when Mike Waterman was here," he said.

That got Lloyd's attention. He snapped shut the book he'd been looking at. "What time did Mr. Waterman come here?" he asked.

Oh, dear. He was going to have to admit to his lack of security-consciousness. "I can't tell you, exactly," he said. "Some time between ten and twenty past nine. I was upstairs, and came down to find him standing in the corridor—it seemed I had inadvertently left the back door open."

"So anyone could have come in?" Lloyd put the book back on the shelf.

Tony hadn't thought about that. "Well . . . yes," he said. "I suppose they could. But if you're thinking that someone could have taken Stephen's rifle—I had the keys in my trouser pocket. They'd have had to force the drawer. And they didn't, as you saw."

But even so, Lloyd was looking just as grimly disapproving as Mike Waterman had, Tony thought, as he showed his visitors out, and locked and bolted the door once again. For God's sake, it was a simple moment of forgetfulness—not the crime of the century.

KEITH WAS ON HIS WAY BACK TO STOKE WESTON, WISHING HE'D left the summerhouse the way he had gone to it. His only thought at the time had been to get back to civilization as quickly as possible, and that meant using the shortcut through the woods to the other path. If he hadn't done that, they would never have known he'd been anywhere near the summerhouse. But they'd been there, and he had been given a considerable fright, so he had broken the habit of a lifetime and volunteered information to the police.

They had wanted him to give them a formal statement about it, and he'd had to wait forever before someone could see him, all so that he could tell them exactly what he had already told them.

Keith had thought that his last moment had come when he saw Halliday with that gun. He'd never liked guns himself. They were too complicated for him. He'd read a gun magazine once, and hadn't understood a word. It was all calibers and cartridges and weird names. People in Stoke Weston loved them—some of them had got up some sort of pressure group when the laws were being tightened up. But as far as Keith was concerned, they could ban them altogether.

Give him a good old blunt instrument any day.

TOM LOOKED AT THE YOUNG MAN WHO SAT OPPOSITE HIM AND Judy, and tried to see him as a psychotic killer who would take his resentment of Tony Baker's arrival in his life to the lengths of attempting to murder his own mother, and he couldn't. He had waived his right to legal representation, as he had on each occasion that he had been questioned, something Tom felt was a bad mistake, but he could always change his mind.

He had wanted his mother informed of his arrest, and she had charged over from the hospital, creating enough of a scene at the desk that Judy had decided that it was best all round if she acceded to her repeated and very loud requests to see Stephen, in the interests of moving the inquiry along. Now she was back at Jack Shaw's bedside, thank goodness.

Tom had spoken to her when Lloyd and Judy had gone looking for Shaw. She had told him that she had given Jack Shaw a lift up to the Grange, and had left him watching the Morris dancing when she went to meet Baker at the lake. She had seen no one on her way down to the lake, and had had no idea that Jack was there. The first she knew of his presence was when he pushed her to the ground. She saw nothing of who was shooting at her, because she was too busy staying alive to care who was trying to kill her. It was enough to know that someone was. When she'd been told of Stephen's arrest, she had dismissed out of hand the possibility of it being him, of course, but she had told Judy that Stephen was having what she had called "a bit of trouble" adjusting to the idea of her and Baker. And that, of course, brought Dr. Castle's snapshot into perfect focus.

Stephen had explained why he was in the summerhouse, and had explained, convincingly, Tom thought, what his thoughts had been on finding the rifle there, and why he hadn't complied immediately with the disembodied orders.

"You hold the license in order to shoot pest animals on a neighboring farm," Judy said. "What sort of animals?"

"Foxes, rabbits. Gray squirrels. That sort of thing."

"Do you like shooting animals?"

"Not particularly. Jack taught me to shoot, and he did it, so I did it. But they cause a lot of damage, and shooting's better than poison or traps or gas. And much better than foxhunting. So it doesn't bother me."

"And your rifle is usually kept in the gun cabinet in the storeroom of the Tulliver Inn?"

"It's always kept there."

"Who else has access to the gun cabinet?"

"Jack. He keeps his rifle in it." Stephen looked anxious. "What happened to him? Is he all right?"

"He wasn't shot, but he was seriously injured. He's had an emergency operation to relieve the pressure on his brain, but he's still in a coma."

Stephen's concern seemed genuine enough, thought Tom. "Why does he keep his rifle in your gun cabinet?" he asked.

"Because a couple of years ago they tightened up on security, and Jack's cottage wasn't burglar-proof enough for them. It would have cost a lot of money to make the changes they wanted, so they agreed that he could keep his rifle at the pub. That's when Mr. Waterman gave me the gun cabinet—it complied with the new regulations, and mine didn't."

"Does Jack Shaw have a key to the cabinet?"

"Yes."

"When did he use it last?"

"Last night—we were out shooting, and he put the guns away while I made us some coffee."

But Shaw couldn't confirm that, not at the moment, thought Tom. "Was anyone else there?"

"No—they'd gone to bed."

"So you could be lying, couldn't you?"

Stephen frowned. "What about?"

"Putting your rifle away. Maybe you left it in the summer-house at the Grange, ready to use this morning."

"Of course I didn't!"

"So how did it get there? Does anyone else have access to it?"

"Not officially, but well—my mum, I suppose. And Tony, now. I mean—they live there, so they know where the keys are kept."

"Does Tony Baker shoot?" asked Judy.

"Yes. I think he goes deerstalking."

"You said earlier that you heard a shot when you were on your way to the summerhouse. Were you worried, when you heard it?"

"No. You hear shots all the time at this time of year. People shoot birds with air rifles. It's all properly organized and legal."

"What time was it?"

"I was about halfway along the path to the summerhouse, so I suppose it was about five to eleven or so."

"Which path did you use?"

Stephen looked puzzled. "I didn't know there was more than one," he said. "Ben just said to take the path nearest to the public car park, and it would bring me out at the summerhouse."

"But if you had run," said Tom, deliberately making his voice hard, "you could have gone to the summerhouse, picked up the rifle, taken the shortcut through the woods to the other path, and you'd be there well before five to eleven, wouldn't you? You would have had plenty of time to get into position and wait for your mother to come along. Is that what you did, Stephen?"

"No! Why in the world would I want to do that? I love my mum!"

Tom was finding this difficult. It was his usual style of interviewing: accusatory, disbelieving. He did it simply to see if he could shake the interviewee or not. And he hadn't shaken Stephen; his reaction had been simply that he had no desire to shoot his mother, rather than saying again that he didn't know of the existence of the other path. That suggested, in Tom's experience, that both statements were true. As an interview style, it had worked for him in the past, and it was working for him now, but his heart wasn't in it.

Stephen still reminded him of Bobby. It was something about the care he took with his hair and clothes, and his skin, and his teeth. Everything had to be in perfect condition. Bobby might only be eleven, but he was a follower of fashion too, and spent hours grooming himself. Tom just kept seeing Bobby in Stephen, and he simply didn't believe he had killed anyone, never mind tried to kill his own mother. But to conduct the interview in his usual style, he had to behave as though he did, and he didn't like doing that.

"Well—that's the problem, isn't it? You love your mother. Your father left her, and you had to become the man of the house when you were thirteen years old. For seven years, it was only you and your mother. And then along comes a man who your mother falls in love with—you didn't like that, did you, Stephen?"

"I—I just don't like him very much."

"But it was your mother who let you down, wasn't it?" Tom insisted. "By falling for this man you don't like very much. You were angry, weren't you? Angry with her?"

Stephen's face grew red. "No! I—I just . . . I wouldn't—" He shook his head, and stared down at the table. "I just hoped she wouldn't get involved with him, that's all. I wasn't *angry* with her. I was just a bit fed up." ·

Every time Tom had spoken to Stephen, he had been pleasant and polite, and open about everything except where he'd been the night Mrs. Fenton died. But Judy believed that Keith Scopes had been telling the truth when she saw him that morning, and that he had been badly frightened when he encountered Stephen at the summerhouse, because Stephen had threatened him with the rifle. Why would he do that? Tom thought about that one area in which Stephen was less than forthcoming. Had he been with Ben on the night of Mrs. Fenton's murder? And if so, why didn't he tell them? Because Ben was a secret lover? Scopes could be going in for a spot of blackmail—that wouldn't surprise Tom at all. Keith Scopes would do anything that he thought might make him a few quid. Blackmail would be par for the course. So perhaps Stephen was keeping his sexual orientation a secret from his mother.

"Does your mother know you're gay?"

"Yes."

So much for that. Well, maybe he was keeping Ben a secret from her, for some reason. "Does she know about Ben?"

"Yes."

He wasn't really winning here.

"Did she know you were going to meet him in the summer-house today?" asked Judy.

"No—no one knew."

In that case, thought Tom, why did Keith Scopes go there? And what had made Stephen threaten him?

"Does Michael Waterman know about you and Ben?"

· Stephen flushed.

At last, thought Tom. "Was Keith Scopes blackmailing you and Ben?" he asked.

Stephen shook his head. "No," he said. "Nothing like that."

"Why did you point the rifle at him?"

"I didn't."

"He says you did. He says you had it at your shoulder, ready to fire."

"I just forgot I had it. I turned away from the window toward the door when it opened. I was just holding it like that."

Just holding it like that? Tom visualized what Stephen was telling him. He had been holding the rifle, in the firing position, while looking out of the window. Seconds before Scopes got there. And that was when Tony Baker was in the car park, waiting for Mrs. Halliday. He didn't like the way this was shaping up, but he had to carry on.

"Is that the way you usually hold a gun that you aren't actively firing?"

"No."

"Then *why* were you holding it like that?"

"No reason."

"No reason," Tom repeated. "Never point a gun at anyone unless you intend to shoot them—isn't that what you're told? You pointed your rifle at Keith Scopes. Did you intend to shoot him?"

"No. It was jammed. It wouldn't fire."

"Then why did you point it at him?"

"I didn't mean to point it at him! And I wouldn't have been pointing it at anyone if it hadn't been jammed."

He had slipped up, as Tom had hoped he would, when he started the rapid questioning. "So who *were* you pointing it at?"

"No one."

"Someone you could see through the window?"

"No." Stephen looked uncomfortable.

"Someone waiting in the car park, maybe?"

He didn't answer.

"Waiting for your mother?"

Stephen went red.

"You were pointing it at Tony Baker, weren't you, Stephen?"

Stephen looked resigned. "Yes," he muttered. "But it isn't

how it sounds. It was—it was just . . ." He sighed. "Like when someone's annoying you, and you pretend to shoot them—point your fingers at them, pretending you've got a gun."

"But you did have a gun."

"It was jammed! It might just as well have been my fingers! It was stupid—I just wasn't thinking what I was doing."

"What *were* you thinking about?" asked Judy.

Stephen turned to her, his face relieved, now that she had interrupted Tom's constant flow of questions. With another interviewee, that might have irritated Tom, but he felt almost as relieved as Stephen, because he didn't like doing this to him.

"I was looking forward to seeing Ben. I was worried because I didn't understand why my rifle was there, and who'd been shooting with it. I was annoyed by Baker pacing up and down because he didn't think my mother should be keeping him waiting. I was wondering if two people could actually live in the summerhouse— I was thinking about a dozen different things."

"And when Keith Scopes came to the door?"

"I thought it was Ben—I just turned from the window, that's all."

Judy shook her head. "No," she said. "That wasn't all, Stephen. I accept what you say about pretending to shoot Baker, and that you forgot you were holding the rifle when you turned to the door. But if it had been Ben, you would have lowered the rifle as soon as you realized what you were doing. And you didn't lower the rifle, did you?"

Stephen shook his head.

"What you said was intended to make Scopes leave, wasn't it? You did threaten him, in effect, didn't you?"

"Yes." Stephen's face burned a painful red, and he looked down at the table.

"Why?"

"Because I was scared."

"Why? What were you scared of?"

He looked up. "Keith Scopes isn't just a security man. Mr. Waterman uses him to beat people up."

"How would you know that?" asked Tom.

"He was in the pub one night about eighteen months ago, getting drunk and buying drinks for all his mates. He doesn't very often drink, and when I asked him what he was celebrating, he said he'd had a win on the horses. But when everyone else had gone he told me Mr. Waterman paid him to sort people out for him. He's got a cosh—a real one. It's old. He showed me it. It's a leather thing with a plaited handle, and a heavy lead ball inside it."

Judy glanced at Tom, frowning slightly.

Tom knew what she was thinking, because that sounded remarkably like whatever had caused Mrs. Fenton's injury, but Keith Scopes couldn't have killed her—he was miles away when it happened.

"It's the truth!" Stephen said, misconstruing the look. "I didn't want to be on the wrong end of that. So yes, once I realized I could, I got rid of him."

"What made you think he was going to beat *you* up?" asked Judy.

He looked down again, and spoke in a low voice. "Because Mr. Waterman had one of Ben's boyfriends beaten up really badly, and told Ben he'd do that to all of them until he stopped having boyfriends. That's why I couldn't tell you where I was the night Wilma died. Because I was with Ben, but if I told you, his dad would find out from Ben's uncle."

It took Tom a minute, but then he realized that Ben's uncle was DCS Yardley. He decided to leave the details of the belated alibi for the moment. For now, he was more interested in what Stephen was saying about Waterman senior.

"Did Ben tell you that his dad had had his boyfriend beaten up?"

"Yes. I thought it must just have been a coincidence that his friend got beaten up after his dad had threatened to do that, but then when Keith told me what he did on the side . . ." He shrugged. "I realized Ben was probably right. His dad must have got Keith to do it."

Were Ben and Stephen out to get revenge on Keith? Had Stephen simply got mixed up in something Ben had arranged? Had Grace Halliday been shot at by accident? Was Keith the intended target? Tom didn't know which question to ask first, so he asked the obvious one.

"Did you tell Ben that it was Keith who beat up his boyfriend?"

"No. Because Ben and Keith used to be best friends when they were kids—I couldn't see how it would help to tell him. It would just upset him. I knew who to avoid, and that was all that mattered. And I did avoid him until recently."

Tom leaned forward. "How do you mean?"

"He wouldn't dare do anything to me in the village, and he was only in Malworth on Sundays, so it was easy to keep an eye out for him. But now . . . well—we're *always* working in the same towns. I'm getting moved about all the time, and it's always to where he's working. So I began to wonder if Mr. Waterman knew about me and Ben after all. And when he came to the summer-house, I thought he'd—" He sighed. "But I was probably imagining it. Because I think he was surprised to see me there."

No, thought Tom, I don't think you were imagining it. I think he was there to beat you up, and he was surprised to see the rifle.

"Is Scopes often in the pub?" he asked.

"Quite often. Lunchtimes, and on his evenings off. There's nowhere else to go in Stoke Weston."

Tom's next question clearly surprised Stephen a little, but Tom really wanted to know the answer.

"Does he smoke?"

"STEPHEN WAS WITH ME IN THE FLAT UNTIL HALF PAST NINE. THAT was when I left to get my train. I called a cab, and Stephen took it with me as far as the bingo club, then went home on his bike."

Which was why Jerry Wheelan hadn't seen Stephen coming back, thought Lloyd, sitting back. In as much as it could be checked, the story checked out.

"Which cab company did you use?"

"I don't know. I just hailed one on Waring Road."

Damn. They could have proved it one way or the other if he'd known the company. Was that just bad luck, or careful lying? Ben Waterman impressed him; he had made his statement about the night of Mrs. Fenton's murder clearly, calmly, and without a hint of evasion. But if Ben was quite happy to discuss it now, why not before? That smacked of a newly wrought alibi. Lloyd sat back, and regarded him, his head slightly to one side. "Why has it taken you two and a half months to come forward with this information?" he asked.

"Because I knew nothing about it!"

"It's been all over the national press," Lloyd said, shaking his head. "Even if the Scottish papers didn't cover it, the TV news did. And presumably you do occasionally contact someone here."

"I knew about the murders, of course I did. But I had no idea Stephen was a suspect. The first I heard of it was when my father told me he'd been arrested. It's ridiculous."

"Why wouldn't Stephen have told you?"

"He wouldn't want to worry me in the run-up to the exams. That's what he's like."

"But if he had an alibi for the first murder, why didn't he tell us?"

"I imagine it's because he knows that it would get straight back to my father through my Uncle Ray."

Lloyd raised his eyebrows. "Your uncle being Detective Chief Superintendent Raymond Yardley?"

"Yes—and before you tell me how the police don't pass on information to unauthorized persons, forget it. Ray tells my father all sorts of things. I wasn't surprised to hear that he'd been taken off this inquiry if you thought someone at Waterman Entertainment was involved. I just never imagined it was because you suspected Stephen."

"That's quite a serious complaint you're making."

"I'm not making a complaint. I'm simply stating facts."

Lloyd thought about that. And played over in his head Ben Waterman's answer to why he hadn't come forward before. That the first he'd heard of it was when his father told him that Stephen had been arrested. And Ben *did* know that Stephen had been arrested when the duty inspector called there to give them the all-clear. But how did Michael Waterman know? The only people who knew at that point were those present and Yardley, once Judy had phoned him. Even the duty inspector hadn't known. It wasn't conclusive, but it did suggest that Stephen might have been right to worry about Waterman finding out, and presumably he disapproved of the relationship.

"All right," he said. "I won't argue with you. But even if your father did find out—why would that matter to Stephen, compared to being suspected of murder?"

"Because he *hadn't* murdered her. He hasn't murdered anyone. Why should he put himself in danger by giving you an alibi that will almost certainly get him beaten senseless, when he knows that he has nothing to do with these murders?"

Lloyd frowned. "How would it get him beaten senseless?"

"That's what my father would do to scare him off, and Stephen knew that, because I told him. It happened to a previous boyfriend of mine, four years ago. Someone put him in hospital for ten days on my father's orders, and he said then that anyone I took up with would get the same treatment. Stephen's the only other person I have taken up with, so fortunately it's only happened once."

"That's another serious complaint."

"It's another fact. I knew he meant it—even though the last time was years ago. I knew he would have Stephen beaten up if he found out about us. And today I discovered that it would have made no difference if Stephen had told you where he was that night, because my father already knew."

"But Stephen's still all in one piece."

"It just hasn't happened yet. He told me that he's got someone waiting for the opportunity to present itself. So when Stephen ends up in hospital, you'll know where to look."

Lloyd didn't speak for some time as he tried to evaluate what he was being told. Michael Waterman's background wasn't criminal, but it was the nearest thing to it, and he did operate in a world where violence wasn't unknown. That criminal connection was doubtless what Tony Baker's documentary would be about. Gambling debts were sometimes discouraged in this way, so ordering violence to be done to someone might well be something Waterman practiced from time to time. But Waterman senior's violent objection to Stephen didn't seem to make sense, given the situation.

"If your father is so unhappy with Stephen, why does he continue to employ him?"

"Because he has no choice. Stephen is a very good employee— he's popular, and capable. He's punctual. Reliable. Honest. What reason could he have for sacking him? If he did, Stephen might take him to a tribunal and tell everyone he was sacked because he was having a relationship with me. My father would sooner die than have that happen. Anyway—he isn't unhappy with Stephen as a person—just the opposite, until he found out about us. He just wants to discourage his relationship with me, any way he can." He looked a little embarrassed. "He even suggested that he could have him killed if he wanted to. He wouldn't—I'm sure he wouldn't. But that's how crazy it makes him."

"How long have you known Stephen?"

"He moved to Stoke Weston seven years ago. I met him once or twice when I was home from school. I liked him, but it didn't go any further than that, not then. My father took him on when he left school, and after I'd started at university I was home during the summer and I happened to be with my father when he called in to one of the bingo clubs to see about something. I met Stephen again, and we talked. We found out our birthdays were close together, and that we had a lot in common, and . . . well, I think we both knew then that . . . that we were right for each other."

The last statement had been delivered with a hint of defiance, but Lloyd had no problem with other people's life choices. And he was quite happy to believe that Ben and Stephen were ideal for each other. All that he was trying to work out was whether it was a match made in heaven or hell. Had they cooked up this alibi between them? Was Waterman really out to get Stephen, or were Stephen and Ben some sort of deadly duo out to get him by committing murders in close proximity to his establishments? He was inclined to believe the young man, but he needed evidence one way or the other.

"Stephen was still seventeen, and I was eighteen. To be honest, we weren't altogether sure where we stood with the law, so we were being careful anyway. But I told him what my father had done, and what he'd threatened to do to anyone else I took up with. At first, he didn't believe me—he thought I was overdramatizing. He only knew my father as the man he is most of the time—generous, kind, easy to please—a good man to work for."

"In general, then, you get on well with your father?"

"If it wasn't for this. That's why Stephen couldn't understand—he's really fond of him. But eventually, I made him understand that my father was totally irrational about my sexuality, and that he was running a real risk." He smiled a little sadly. "I expected him to go and find a less complicated relationship, but he just said that in that case, he'd be very careful. And we've kept it hidden until now."

Lloyd was puzzled. "But you couldn't live like that forever," he said. "You're both adults now. How is it going to resolve itself?"

"I thought perhaps Stephen could get a job in St. Andrews, come and live there. But he didn't want to leave his mother alone in the pub. She depends on him quite a bit for moral support—

Stephen's father running out on her was difficult for her to cope with. He was hoping she would eventually marry again, and he wouldn't feel so responsible for her."

That was even more puzzling. "But now that she has found someone else, he isn't very happy about it, according to his mother."

"No. He really doesn't like Tony Baker. It's unusual for Stephen—he usually just takes people as he finds them. And to be fair, it might not be Baker's fault—I think Stephen always hoped his mother and Jack Shaw would get it together. But now that he knows she's open to the idea of a new man in her life, he feels he can leave her, so the situation *is* resolved, more or less. That's why I'm here today, really."

"Oh?"

The young man took a breath. "This is going to sound odd, but next week, I come into a lot of money left to me by my mother, and Stephen doesn't know about it yet. There were reasons I didn't tell him, which had nothing to do with Stephen himself."

Lloyd pushed his chair back onto its back legs, and swayed gently as Ben spoke. Today was what he wanted to know about. Today was what mattered. So he looked as if he wasn't remotely interested, and said nothing.

"I wanted to give him a surprise, cheer him up a bit, because I knew he'd been a bit down lately—I thought it was his mother taking up with Baker that was getting to him, but no wonder he was down, being suspected of all this."

The two things might not be unconnected, thought Lloyd, as he listened impassively.

"Anyway, I went house-hunting over the weekend, and I was going to make a flying visit here, tell him about the money, show him the houses I'd found, see if any of them appealed to him. We were going to go off somewhere together for the afternoon. But, as things turned out, we were only going to have about an hour and a half free, so we arranged to meet in the summerhouse to make the most of it."

That was interesting. Lloyd let his chair fall forward with a bang, making the young man jump. "What happened to change your plans?"

"Two things. Stephen couldn't get the afternoon off, and my father wanted me to meet Tony Baker—he invited him and Grace Halliday to lunch, and I was the guest of honor, more or less, so I couldn't get out of it."

"Did anyone else know of your arrangement to meet in the summerhouse?"

"No. Unfortunately, my father found out because I had to tell DI Finch where Stephen was when he said that they were cordoning that area off. That's when everything came out. We had a furious row, and then I found out you'd arrested Stephen."

Lloyd nodded slowly. He had a lot to digest from this interview. "Thank you," he said. "Thank you for being so frank. I take it you will be available, should we want to talk to you again?"

"Yes—but I won't be at the Grange."

"Oh?" Lloyd raised his eyebrows.

"He's gone too far this time—he knew Stephen was too scared to tell you where he was that night, and he would have let him be suspected of murder sooner than say anything. He tried to stop me talking to you."

"Even so," said Lloyd, "is that what you really want? To cut yourself off from your father altogether?"

"No. But he's left me no choice. I'll be staying at the Tulliver until this nonsense about Stephen is sorted out."

Lloyd was sorry that the young man's relationship with his father had been damaged to that extent, but he would sleep a little more soundly tonight knowing that Ben Waterman was at the Tulliver.

The young man leaned forward, his elbows on the table, and looked Lloyd straight in the eye as he spoke, quietly and firmly. "Stephen is quite simply the most levelheaded, straightforward, caring person that I've ever known. The idea that he's going around killing people for any reason at all is ludicrous."

* * *

GARY WAS IN THE OFFICE WITH ALAN MARSHALL, DI FINCH AND Acting Superintendent Hill, discussing Halliday's interview, when DCI Lloyd came back and told them what Ben Waterman had said about his father.

"That's what Stephen said, too," said Finch. "Doesn't mean it's the truth, though, does it? They could have cooked it up between them."

"I thought you were on his side."

"I am. But just because I want to believe him doesn't mean that I should. I'm playing . . . what is it you call it?"

Lloyd smiled. "Devil's advocate," he said. "But he was probably right that it would get back to Waterman if he gave us his alibi. So if we assume, for the moment, that Ben and Stephen are telling the truth, and the consensus seems to be that we should, then where does that leave us?"

"Someone's framing Stephen," said Finch. "And my money's on Michael Waterman. He knew that Stephen had an alibi for the first murder that he was afraid to give us, he can have him working wherever he wants, he can arrange for Scopes to hurt people, and now he's saying he can just as easily have them killed. And I know Scopes—he wouldn't think twice, if the price was right."

Lloyd looked doubtful. "Ben says his father knew nothing about the assignation in the summerhouse until after the incident. I think whoever it is knew Stephen was going to be there."

"And why would he go to all that trouble?" asked Marshall. "If he can arrange murders, why not arrange for Stephen to be killed?"

"Because Ben would know that he'd done that, and would never forgive him," said Lloyd. "He does what he does because he loves Ben—however cockeyed that seems."

Finch looked thoughtful. "Waterman gave Stephen the gun cabinet," he said. "He could still have a key to it, couldn't he?"

Gary's eyes widened when he heard that. "He was in the pub this morning, sir, on his own. If he has got a key, he could have got hold of the rifle and given it to Scopes."

"As your acting superintendent, I would caution against rushing out and arresting them."

Everyone looked at their acting superintendent.

"I would remind you that neither of them could have killed Davy Guthrie," she said. "They were both in the casino from when we know he was alive until well after he was found dead. The firearms officer says whoever fired that gun was an experienced shot, and Scopes seems to have no interest in guns whatsoever. Circumstantial evidence is what's landed Stephen where he is, so let's not jump to conclusions about anyone else."

Gary smiled. The DI had said that she could demolish what seemed like a perfectly good theory in two seconds, and she just had.

That was when Hitchin came back from the hospital. "You're not going to believe this, ma'am," he said.

"Try me."

"I was just leaving the hospital when a nurse comes running after me. She said that in the rush to get Shaw to the theater, they had forgotten to tell me that when they undressed Shaw, they rolled down his white stockings and took off the crêpe bandage to see how bad the sprain was, and what they found was a load of cotton-wool padding to make his ankle appear to be swollen. There was nothing wrong with it at all."

"You're right, Hitch," she said. "I don't believe it."

Gary loved working on this team—it wasn't like anything else he'd done at all. After the first few days, they hardly even bothered with ranks, or anything. You could say what you wanted to anyone, and if they thought it was rubbish, they'd tell you. But if they didn't, they would listen. It was like being at home with your family, and it was the best job he'd had, in or out of the police. From having longed to get back to normal CID duties, he now found himself wishing he never had to go back to them, and half hoping that the inquiry into the Anonymous Assassin would go on forever.

"And then there's the bells," said Lloyd. "Which have just become even more of a puzzle."

"The bells?" said Superintendent Hill.

"Jack Shaw's would-be murderer used one set of bells to weigh down the money. But the other set wasn't still round his leg—it was in his pocket. Now, I can't see his assailant bothering to remove both sets and put one of them in Shaw's pocket, so I think Shaw must have removed them himself beforehand."

She frowned. "What's odd about that? Would you go round with bells on your legs if you didn't have to?"

"No, but Shaw did, didn't he? He must have had to take them off in order to prepare his fake sprained ankle, then put them back on again, just to take them off again later. Why?"

The idea of removing bells was reminding Gary of something. When he realized what it was, he thought he might have solved that little puzzle. "We've got a cat," he said. "When he was a kitten, my mum got him one of those flea collars, and put it on him. And he sat there pulling at it with his teeth, and we thought he didn't like the feeling of it round his neck. But my mum said to leave him for a while, and he'd get used to it. He was pulling at it for about half an hour, and when he stopped, the bell was lying on the floor. He couldn't have cared less about the collar—he just didn't want his prey to hear him coming."

Lloyd beamed at him. "The boy's a genius—of course that's why! And it's why Grace Halliday didn't know he was there. He was stalking her, and in order to do that, he had to get out of the Morris dancing, so he faked a sprained ankle."

"And he made sure that he was with Grace Halliday from the moment she got there, by going home and getting a lift back up there with her," said Marshall, slowly, then frowned. "But if he wanted to stalk her, why wear the costume at all? If I wanted to merge into the background, a Morris dancing costume wouldn't be my first choice of camouflage."

Sergeant Hitchin smiled. "I think camouflage is more or less exactly what it was. I mean, let's face it—Morris dancers look a bit silly, don't they? So Stephen and his mother wouldn't spend too long wondering why he hadn't stayed at the Grange, if that was where he wanted to be—they would just indulge him. He turns up in his silly costume, jingling wherever he goes, hobbling about on crutches, wanting to go back to the May Day festivities. It obviously means a lot to him, so they just humor him." He shrugged. "No questions asked."

Lloyd went into a sort of reverie then, and everyone looked at him, waiting for an inspired theory.

"No," he said, after a moment or two. "I have tried very hard to produce a scenario in which Jack Shaw somehow managed to shoot at Grace Halliday at the same time as apparently saving her life."

Finch laughed. "Not even you, guv."

"Oh, don't be too sure. If it had ended there, I might have suggested that he and Stephen had devised it between them to make Shaw seem more glamorous in Grace's eyes, but it didn't end there, did it? Because someone then hit him so hard with his own crutch that he's in a coma."

"Shaw must have known that Grace Halliday was in danger," Finch said. "But knew that she wouldn't listen to him if he warned her. That means that she was in danger from either Stephen or Tony Baker. She would surely have listened to him about anyone else."

"I think so," said Lloyd. "And I think you're right—he was following her to be on hand if she needed him. And she did need him. He saved her life."

"And almost got killed himself in the process," said Marshall.

"Yes," said Lloyd. "He almost got killed. And that's the real puzzle. Why isn't Jack Shaw dead?"

CHAPTER TWELVE

THE NEXT MORNING, STEPHEN, LOOKING SLIGHTLY CRUM-pled, was waiting in the interview room when Gary and DI Finch got there. Things weren't looking good for him, thought Gary, as they confronted him with the evidence gathered by the scene-of-crime officers.

His prints had been found on the rifle, of course, and the bullet in the tree had been fired from that rifle. Ballistics had done their homework on the bullet's trajectory, and had marked on a photograph where they thought the gunman had been when it was fired. Stephen could easily have been there in the time at his disposal, and then run along the path to the summerhouse. The crutch found by the lake had inflicted Jack Shaw's head wound, and the other had been lying in the undergrowth near where Shaw had been found. Stephen Halliday's prints had been found on both of them. The only other fingerprints were Jack Shaw's own.

Add to that the facts that he had admitted threatening Keith Scopes with the rifle and had at first refused to surrender to the police, and that seemed to Gary to add up to evidence of attempted murder.

On the plus side, as far as Stephen was concerned, the test done on his hands was inconclusive; there were traces on the skin of the residue left when someone fired a gun, but he had been shooting the night before, and it could have remained there even after he'd washed, so that would probably be thrown out. Gary tried in vain to find something else in his favor that was less damning than that.

Halliday explained that he had handled Shaw's crutches that morning when he and his mother had taken Shaw up to the Grange, and Gary was sure that his mother would confirm that, but Shaw's confirmation would be needed to make it entirely believable, and Shaw was in a coma.

But if Halliday was their man, they had to get him for more than just attempted murder. DI Finch opened the file in front of him and took out six photographs, two from each murder scene, placing them silently in front of Stephen one at a time.

Stephen looked down at them, and frowned. "I didn't know he did that with the money," he said. "What's that all about?"

"We thought you might tell us."

Stephen sighed.

"Did you kill these people, Stephen?"

"No." He frowned. "I thought you said Ben had confirmed that I was with him when Wilma was killed. Why are you showing me her photograph? Do you still think I did it?"

"Well—you and Ben could have made all that up about being in his father's flat, couldn't you?"

Stephen nodded. "I suppose we could," he said. "I can't win, can I? If I do have an alibi, you don't believe it."

He looked at all the photographs, and reacted in exactly the way everyone who looked at them did. They weren't horrific; Gary had seen much worse even in his short time in the police. But it was never nice to look at photographs of dead bodies, and Stephen wasn't looking at them any more closely than he had to. But if they had been hoping that he would somehow give himself away, then they had been wrong.

Finch nodded, and Gary picked the photographs up again to put them back in the file.

"Hang on," Stephen said. "Can I see that one of Wilma again?"

Gary handed him the photograph.

"No—the other one. The one showing how the money was all spread out like that." Gary found it, and Stephen took it, this time looking at it carefully. He shook his head. "That isn't the money I paid out to Wilma," he said. "I gave Wilma three tens and eight fifties, because I thought she'd probably prefer to have smaller denominations. That photograph shows four twenties and seven fifties." He sat back, looking as puzzled as Gary felt. "But that's what I paid out to Tony Baker, not to Wilma."

Finch stared at him. "Are you sure?"

"Quite sure, but you don't have to take my word for it. We log the numbers of the fifties, so you can check—the numbers go on the computer against the name of the winner. Mr. Waterman's got a thing about it."

MICHAEL'S HEART ENDED UP SOMEWHERE NEAR HIS BOOTS WHEN his secretary told him DI Finch was on the line.

All night, Josephine had haunted him—not in the guise of an actual ghost, but as good as. Ben had walked out on him, she had told him, walked out of his house, walked out of his life, because of his refusal to accept him the way he was, and the vicious, brainless way he had reacted. Ben had forgiven him once for that brutal behavior, but he couldn't forgive him again. Michael had learned nothing in the four years since that previous incident, she had said. He had accepted Ben's forgiveness as his due, and hadn't thought twice about ordering the same treatment for Stephen, had been glad when Stephen had come under suspicion of murder because he was too afraid to give the police his alibi. And now Michael felt foolish, sad, and indescribably guilty.

As a result, he really couldn't follow what Finch was saying, because it seemed to have nothing to do with anything. Finally, he understood that he wanted to know about the cash payouts for some reason. "Yes, we do keep a record of the numbers," he said. "I once got taken for a lot of money by someone who had a big win and asked us to change the fifties for twenties, and when I paid the money into the bank, I discovered that I had been landed with five hundred quids' worth of counterfeit money. So now I make sure that won't happen again."

"Could you ask your office to confirm the numbers of the fifties paid out to Wilma Fenton and Tony Baker?"

"I can confirm it now—it's all on the computer. What's all this about?"

"I'm afraid I can't discuss that, Mr. Waterman."

"Is it going to help Stephen?"

"I really couldn't say." Finch's voice was cold.

Of course, he thought. Ben had been telling them everything, and why not? Who could blame him? Finch would think he was a monster. And Finch would be right, he could hear Josephine saying. His behavior had been utterly despicable, and he deserved the contempt.

He took a deep breath. "Well, I don't know if this will help or not, but on the night Mrs. Fenton died, I came home in the early evening and overheard Ben arranging to meet Stephen in one of the flats at half past eight. He told Stephen he'd be quicker going through the alley on foot than taking his bike round the one-way system, and that's why Stephen was going through the alley rather than just going to get his bike. When I told Chief Inspector Hill that I'd seen him following Mrs. Fenton, I . . . I may have given her the wrong impression."

There was a silence before Finch spoke. "Oh, right. Well— thank you for telling me." He sounded a little surprised, as well he might.

He couldn't tell the police everything, though, not without landing Keith in trouble, and that wouldn't be right. Keith had never let him down, and he wasn't going to let Keith down. But at least that would strengthen Stephen's alibi. It was all his fault that the boy hadn't just given them it in the first place.

He called up the information on the payout, and gave it to Finch, who thanked him for being so helpful. And that just made him feel worse than ever.

· * ⁕ ₄ *

"BUT WHY WOULD BAKER SWITCH THE PRIZE MONEY?" SAID LLOYD.

"Search me, guv. But he did." Tom sat down. "I knew all along that his story about Wilma was iffy."

He had indeed, thought Judy, making a note of this latest little puzzle, adding it to the list. At least this one told them something concrete: Baker hadn't simply witnessed a murder. At the very least, he had interfered with the scene of a crime, but she would much rather know why he did before she had him arrested.

"All right," she said. "Let's use logic, and we will assume that Baker is our man. Dr. Castle says that he does nothing without a reason, so what reason could he have had for switching the prize money?"

"No reason," said Tom. "It makes no sense."

"Logic dictates that if there was no reason to switch the money, then he didn't switch it."

"But he did," said Tom.

"No," said Lloyd. "We only know that he left his own money on Wilma's body. That doesn't mean he took Wilma's money in exchange."

"But then Wilma would have had both lots of money."

"And she *didn't* have both lots," said Lloyd. "Therefore someone other than Baker *did* take it. And Baker replaced it with his own money."

Tom's eyes widened. "You mean it really was just a mugging that went wrong? Someone did steal Wilma's prize money? But why would he want to make it look as though it hadn't been stolen?"

"Who knows?" Judy shrugged. "To make it look less like an opportunist mugging, and more interesting to his news editor? To make our job practically impossible because he wanted the police to fail? To give himself a head start in the hope that he could catch the killer before we did? Possibly all three." She tried to think logically about what happened next. "He brought us a letter that was supposed to be from Wilma's killer," she said. "And the next day, the newspaper got one, too." She looked at Lloyd. "I'm sure you're right," she said. "I'm sure he did get a letter, but not the one he gave us."

"So do you think he *was* trying to carry out his own investigation?" asked Lloyd.

"Possibly, but for the moment, I'm making the assumption that he is the serial killer."

Lloyd looked a little doubtful. "But if Castle's right that the killer does everything for a reason, that kind of lets Baker out, doesn't it? What reason could he have for committing random murders in some pointless duel with himself? As Castle pointed out—he might be enjoying the publicity, but he certainly didn't need it, not that badly."

Judy's eyebrows rose. Castle had said that if they could work out the reason for the duel, they could find their man. She looked down at her notebook, and at last she could see that this final puzzle of the prize money revealed a cause that had produced an effect. She worked through the puzzles, crossing them off as she accounted for them. If she was right, then everything that had happened was all *because* Baker had replaced the stolen money. It went round in a circle, and it worked out. She sat back. "The duel wasn't pointless," she said. "And it wasn't with himself."

Lloyd smiled. "I spy a gundog."

"Maybe—but I can't prove any of it." She leafed through her notebook. "Dr. Castle's snapshot," she said. "He described the perpetrator as 'someone—perhaps, but not necessarily, a Waterman employee or customer—who works or engages in recreation in the evenings, in all three towns, who is literate, with a knowledge of killing, possibly as a participant in field sports, and with what amounts to an obsession with Tony Baker.' I think that's a picture of two people, not one."

Lloyd nodded slowly. "One is someone who spends time in the evening in all three towns, and has the local knowledge that

Castle rightly pointed out that an outsider wouldn't have had time to acquire . . ."

". . . and the other is Tony Baker himself," said Judy, finishing the sentence for him. "Who is literate, with an interest in field sports, and is obsessed with Tony Baker. I think he was being blackmailed about interfering with the scene." She turned to Tom. "You said that the knife in the Jiffy bag looked like a blackmail drop. I think that's exactly what it was meant to look like. We weren't supposed to find it—the blackmailer was. Baker was trying to frame the blackmailer for Davy's murder by dressing up the murder weapon to look like the payoff."

Lloyd frowned. "Being blackmailed by whom?"

"I think there's only one person who could have blackmailed him. Wilma's murder was all over the paper the next morning, and the report said that her winnings had been left intact. Only one person besides Baker knew that they *hadn't* been left intact, because he knew he had stolen them."

"Wilma's killer?" said Tom. "But how could he tell anyone what Baker had done without confessing what he'd done?"

"At the time, it would have been relatively easy," Lloyd said. "If someone had come to us and said that he'd witnessed the whole thing, but had been frightened to come forward straight away—it would have been his word against Baker's, and the tables would have been turned, because Baker couldn't expose *him* without incriminating himself."

Tom looked disbelieving. "But are you saying that Baker murdered people to frame the blackmailer rather than pay up?"

"Yes," said Judy. "As Dr. Castle said—we're dealing with a disturbed mind. And an ego the size of a house. Someone who had already murdered was threatening to expose him as a cheat and a fraud—his reputation would go down the drain. He would go to prison. He's the one who saw it as a duel, and he upped the stakes. A murder would be committed when the blackmailer could have no alibi, because he would be all on his own, and would be in the vicinity, looking for his payoff."

"But how would that help?" asked Tom.

"Baker wrote the letter that he brought to us, establishing a would-be serial killer, so that when it happened, we would connect it immediately with Wilma's murder. We would even half-expect Baker to be in the vicinity, because the letter said that he'd killed Wilma right under his nose, and we would think the killer was simply doing that again. I imagine Baker thought that turn of events would be too rich for the blackmailer's blood, and that would be the last he'd hear of him, but it clearly wasn't, because he got another letter, and now he was being blackmailed about Robert Lewis's murder."

"The duel had begun in earnest," said Lloyd, still swaying gently as he thought. "So next time, Baker went a step further, leaving the murder weapon where the blackmailer would be looking for his money. The blackmailer would open the envelope, pull out what was inside, and would find himself holding a knife with blood on it. He'd have to decide what to do with it. Drop it back in the bin? Keep it? Either way, he'd be running a risk."

"But because Tony Baker was held up as he was leaving the casino, the blackmailer had been and gone before he ever put the knife in the bin." Tom smiled grimly. "Headless wasn't some concerned citizen putting his rubbish away—for one thing, he was wearing gloves on a very warm night, and you don't wear gloves to put something into a rubbish bin. But you wear gloves if you want to take something *out* of one. Gertie said he was rummaging, and she was right."

Lloyd was still swaying. "The blackmailer didn't find the knife, so once again he wasn't put off. Another murder had been committed, and he doubtless upped his demand once more." He let his chair fall forward. "And I'm willing to bet that this letter said that the money had to be left in the summerhouse at the Grange, which is why Baker left the rifle there, knowing the blackmailer would be there in the hope that this time he was going to collect."

"But it was Stephen's rifle," said Tom. "Does that mean he thought it was Stephen who was blackmailing him?"

"Well, Stephen was the last person to be seen with Wilma, and he wouldn't tell anyone where he was when she was killed," said Judy. "And Baker didn't know that we had witnesses who saw Stephen leaving the alleyway twenty-five minutes before the murder took place, so as far as he was concerned, Stephen could have been in Wilma's flat all along. And Stephen was working in the appropriate towns on the appropriate nights . . . yes, I'd say he could easily have come to the conclusion that it was Stephen."

"Of course you know who else was working in the appropriate towns on the appropriate nights, and turned up for no apparent reason at the summerhouse, don't you?" said Tom. "And Stephen couldn't have been Headless, because he was still in the bingo club when Headless was doing his rummaging. But Keith Scopes was out having a so-called smoke. If he isn't Headless, I'm a monkey's cousin." He scratched his head. "But Scopes didn't kill Wilma, so it makes no—" He broke off, and tapped his head. "But Wilma *wasn't* killed at nine o'clock, was she? Baker lied about that too."

Of course, thought Judy. The missing half hour. That was another bit of window dressing—another way to confuse the investigation.

"It happened the moment Stephen left her, before she had time to go into her flat," Tom said. "Scopes hit her, and stole her money. And Baker saw it happen as he went into the alley from the bingo club, so when Scopes ran away from him, he would run toward Waring Road, not Murchison Place. Baker had us looking for witnesses in the wrong place at the wrong time. No wonder we came up empty."

Judy nodded, and crossed off the second to last puzzle. "And as far as Baker was concerned," she said, "he had seen Stephen go into the alleyway with Wilma, and when he got there two minutes later, he saw the person with her attack her. No wonder he thought it was Stephen."

"Why would he want to give Stephen an alibi?" asked Tom.

"Because he could." Lloyd let his chair fall forward. "That's all the reason he'd need to do that. But this is all conjecture, of course."

"I know." Judy looked at the ticks she had made against the puzzles in her notebook. "There's no proof. But it answers all the little puzzles, except why Jack Shaw wasn't killed."

"Ah—you're fallible after all. You've got that one wrong. I asked why Jack Shaw wasn't *dead*, not why he wasn't killed."

She looked up. "Is there a difference?"

"Oh, yes. Because Baker must have thought Shaw had seen him, or why would he hit him at all? But the blow hadn't killed him, and he couldn't have believed that it had. No one could have thought he was dead. He was very evidently breathing."

"He couldn't keep on hitting him," Judy pointed out. "He'd be bound to get blood on his own clothes if he did that."

Lloyd got a faraway look in his eyes. "Yes," he said. "He would, wouldn't he?" He sighed. "In fact, he almost certainly did. That's why he so considerately covered Shaw up with his own jacket."

Of course, thought Judy, Baker knew exactly how to play this deadly game, and right now, he was winning it, because as Lloyd said, it was pure conjecture. They had no proof at all.

"Maybe he just tried to hit him hard enough to affect his memory, guv," said Tom. "Or at any rate make people believe it might be a bit suspect."

"Yes," said Judy. "And he probably succeeded."

"But then why do the thing with the money?" Lloyd shook his head. "He puts money on his murder victims, and according to Castle, he wouldn't deviate from that, because that was part of his plan. So he thought he *had* killed him, and yet he *couldn't* have thought that. I repeat: Why isn't Jack Shaw dead?"

"Well," said Judy. "Let's not tempt providence. He's still in a coma, remember."

"So he is," said Lloyd, the faraway look back. "Oh, yes." He closed his eyes. "He is, isn't he?" He opened his eyes again, and they were sad. "And I'm very much afraid I know why he isn't dead." He sighed. "But if I'm right—and I believe I am—then he's as good as dead, and there's nothing we can do about it, because we can't prove a thing."

Judy was about to ask him to explain when Hitchin knocked, and came in. "It's good news, ma'am. Jack Shaw's coming out of the coma."

Lloyd stared at him. "He's doing what?"

"Recovering," said Hitchin.

"But that makes no sense! The only thing that makes any sense is if Jack Shaw is *dying*."

"Well, sorry, sir." Hitchin looked a little helpless. "He isn't. He's getting better."

STEPHEN WAS BACK IN THE CELL, SITTING ON THE BENCH, HIS knees drawn up to his chin, waiting to see what was going to happen next. He didn't understand about that money. How could Wilma have ended up with Tony Baker's prize money? He didn't understand why he was here. He had an alibi for the night Wilma died—wasn't that supposed to mean they let you go? But they thought he and Ben had made it up between them.

At least he could understand why he was a suspect in Wilma's murder—he didn't understand the others at all. They had no reason at all to suspect him of them, except that he couldn't prove where he was when they took place. They had both happened when he was on his way home from work, on his own, with no witnesses. But that could be true of dozens of people—why did they think he'd had anything to do with murdering these people?

He knew why. It was because the bike had broken down when he was on his way home from Barton that night. It had taken a quarter of an hour to get it started, but they didn't believe that it had broken down at all. If those women hadn't held him up for so long, he would have been home before eleven o'clock, and they said that the Barton victim was still alive then. So he would have had an alibi for that one too. But then, he thought, his alibis didn't seem to carry very much weight, so did it really matter? They would probably have said that everyone was making that one up, too.

And now they thought he'd shot at his own mother, and tried to kill Jack, of all people, and it was hard to see what else they could think, in view of the way they'd found him.

From the moment he'd heard that voice coming out of nowhere, telling him to throw out his rifle, what had been a wor- rying situation had turned into a nightmare, and he had no idea how he had got caught up in it.

He just wished with all his heart that he could see Ben.

THE REVELATION THAT JACK SHAW WAS RECOVERING HAD THROWN Lloyd, until, after ten minutes of wondering if the solution they had worked out could possibly be entirely wrong, he realized why Jack Shaw wasn't dead or dying. He had spoken to Jack Shaw, and sweet-talked Freddie into doing him a favor, and now at least they had proof of a kind.

Grace Halliday had been at the hospital, and though Lloyd hadn't been allowed to speak to Shaw at any length, what Grace had told him had prompted him to apply for a search warrant, and now the files, photographs, papers and computer disks found in Tony Baker's room in the Tulliver Inn were being packed into boxes and taken away.

Lloyd drove out of Stoke Weston, bound for Barton. The af- ternoon sun shone down, and thanks to Jack Shaw, the village wasn't in mourning as it would have been if Baker had had his way. Grace Halliday was working in the pub right now, with Ben Waterman helping out, both trying to take their minds off Stephen's predicament. Lloyd wasn't sure how Stephen was going to come out of this, not yet.

Baker himself was under arrest for attempting to pervert the course of justice, being the crime for which they had straightforward, conventional evidence, but Lloyd's Acting Superintendent was grimly determined that he would be charged with considerably more than that before the day was out.

TONY HAD BEEN PUZZLED WHEN HE'D HEARD THE KNOCK ON HIS door—Grace didn't knock, and Stephen was in a police cell, where he belonged. It had all gone wrong, but it had turned out reasonably well, he'd thought.

It had turned out to be Ben Waterman, whom he had forgotten was staying there. He'd arrived late yesterday afternoon, and Grace had introduced him. She said he'd had some sort of bust-up with his father.

"There are two police officers downstairs," Ben had said. "They said they'd like to see you."

Tony had smiled. "This is getting to be a habit," he'd said. "When they're stumped, they come to me."

But it wasn't anyone he'd thought it might be. Not the devious Lloyd, or the decorative Hill, or even the deceptive Finch. It was two uniformed constables, who said they were arresting him for attempting to pervert the course of justice, and several detectives who waved a search warrant at him and began to remove all his documents.

He was taken to Barton, to Highgrove Street Station, and now he was in an interview room with Detective Chief Inspector Lloyd and Acting Detective Superintendent Hill, at something of a disadvantage, as the tape wound round slowly and silently, and he was cautioned. There was little point in talking to a solicitor; he *had* attempted to pervert the course of justice, and he wasn't going to deny it. But he couldn't work out how they knew what he had done.

"Can you explain how the money found on Wilma Fenton's body was the money paid out to you, and not the money paid out to her?" asked Acting Superintendent Hill.

That was the last thing he'd thought would catch him out. How did they know? And before he told them it was a fair cop, he would make certain that they weren't just taking a flyer. "I take it you can prove that?"

"We can. We have the numbers of the notes paid out in each case."

Well, wouldn't you just know, thought Tony. But what had seemed so important once was no longer important. Things had moved on.

"Then, yes," he said. "I can explain it. Her money was stolen. I replaced it with my own."

"And would we be right in assuming that you also removed any possible fingerprints from Mrs. Fenton's bag, and altered the time of the murder from a few minutes after half past eight to nine o'clock?"

"You would."

"Why did you do that?"

Because he had been irritated that he should have witnessed a murder that was nothing more than a sordid little mugging. Because he had wanted to make it just a little more interesting than that. But that wasn't the reason he was going to give them. "To give Stephen Halliday an alibi."

"Did you recognize Halliday as Mrs. Fenton's attacker?" Lloyd asked.

"No!" Tony was shocked by the suggestion. The glimpse he'd got of Mrs. Fenton's attacker could have been anyone—he had seen only a shadowy figure. "Of course I didn't—I saw no more than I said. But Waterman and I saw Stephen running after Wilma Fenton and going into the alley with her. I was about two minutes behind them, and when I got to the mouth of the alley, I saw what I described in some detail to you, Superintendent, except that the mugger merely made off with the victim's bag."

He saw Lloyd and Hill glance at each other, then she looked back at him. "Go on," she said.

"I went after him," he said. "But he was running way too fast for me to catch up. In the car park, I found Wilma's bag, and I found the discarded envelope. I've no doubt he was hiding in the car park somewhere, but I couldn't see anyone at all. And I knew how bad it would look for Stephen—though I didn't know him particularly well, I honestly believed that he wouldn't have done such a thing."

She shook her head slightly. "You committed a serious offense in order to stop Stephen Halliday coming under suspicion?"

"Yes. Because I know how police minds work. There can be no other explanation than the one that immediately presents it-self. Waterman had seen Stephen with Wilma, and if I called the police . . ." He shrugged. "I thought that another innocent man would be gobbled up by the system. My first instinct was simply to carry on to my car, and let someone else find her body. But as I looked at the envelope, I realized that I could make it look less like a mugging. I could replace the money—I could wipe the bag and her purse and everything else, and put them back beside her."

"And spreading the notes out on her body?" said Lloyd. "What was that all about?"

Tony smiled a little. "A theatrical touch. I wanted it to look as though the motive was something other than theft. Envy, per-haps. Or disapproval."

He had wanted it to look interesting. He had wanted to have witnessed something that baffled the police. He had wanted the murder that he had witnessed to be one that caused a bit of a stir. He'd wanted it to be a murder of substance.

"And when I'd set the scene, I waited for as long as I could be-fore I rang the police, because I thought that Stephen would be wherever he was going by then, and would have an alibi. I said I'd been working in my car, and had been going back to the club when I saw it, so I had to say it happened the opposite way round from the way it had."

He was getting nothing back from Lloyd as he spoke; he was just sitting, his eyes cold, listening without reaction. From Judy Hill, he was getting waves of disbelief, but that didn't matter. His motive was his own business—it made no difference. It wouldn't lessen the offense. But an altruistic motive might just lessen the disapproval of the press and public. And that did matter.

"What can I say? It was a very stupid and very inappropriate thing to do, but I did it."

It would have been very stupid and very inappropriate if he really had been trying to save Stephen's neck, he thought, but it had been purely to make a mundane murder less humdrum. It wasn't until long afterward that he began to realize that Stephen really had killed Wilma Fenton. And by then his spicing up of that unintentional murder had started something almost unstoppable.

"He did kill Mrs. Fenton," he said. "I know that now. And then he went on to kill again, as a sort of challenge to me. Grace must have told him what I said about the money being spread out, though naturally she denies that. I feel so stupid about telling her, but as I told you, I genuinely believed that Stephen was innocent at that point, and that theatrical detail was one that I thought might stop her worrying so much. It was much later that I began to realize how wrong I'd been." He shook his head. "I, of all people, should have realized that murderers come in all varieties. I tried, I swear to you, I tried to make up for what I'd done. I thought, if I could only work out what was in his mind, I might be able to stop him killing the next person, but—"

Lloyd held up a hand. "I know you were a journalist," he said. "And a writer. And now you're a columnist and broadcaster. You're a very versatile man, Mr. Baker. Were you an actor, too?"

Tony frowned. "I'm sorry?"   .

"The distress is very good," said Lloyd. "Very good. And, I have to admit that you had me fooled. My superintendent here was never just as beguiled as I was, I have to admit that, too. And her predecessor was even less taken in by you. But then I have this tendency to be a little bit starstruck. Not unlike Mrs. Halliday."

"I have no idea what you mean."

"Of course you have!" Lloyd stood up, and walked over to the old-fashioned frosted-glass sash window, open slightly to admit fresh air on this warm day, but barred, presumably to prevent escape from this ground-floor interview room. He leaned on the windowsill, and looked out. "Stephen Halliday may or may not have killed Wilma Fenton," he said. "But he didn't kill Lewis, or Guthrie, or try to kill his mother or Jack Shaw. You did that."

Tony looked at Judy Hill, whose brown eyes regarded him with curiosity. He smiled. "I think," he said, "that you're making the same mistake as Grace. You've found my research, and jumped to conclusions."

"No, Mr. Baker," she said. "What we found in your room merely confirmed what we already believed."

He didn't launch into the explanation that he'd offered Grace—somehow he felt that it would be unlikely to have the same effect on the cool, composed woman who sat opposite him. But the photographs and plans weren't enough to convict him— not even to charge him. He could prove that was how he had hunted down Challenger's potential victim, that it was how he worked. He had kept them for the book he was going to write for publication after his death, telling the world how he had led the police in a murderous dance while apparently working with them. When Grace Halliday had found them, he had thought of destroying them, but then he had realized that such an action would suggest his guilt, so he had kept them quite openly. What guilty man would do that?

He looked over at Lloyd, but he seemed to be engrossed in whatever it was he could see through that window.

"The psychological profiler that we brought in said that the writer of the letters had what amounted to an obsession with you," said Superintendent Hill.

"It does seem that way," said Tony.

"And the only person I've met during this investigation who is obsessed with you *is* you," she said.

Tony dismissed that with a smile and a shake of his head. "I realized when I got the very first letter that you might consider the possibility that I'd written it to myself, but really—that does seem a very flimsy basis for an accusation of serial murder."

"Oh, it is. Very flimsy," said Lloyd. "But you see, real murder has a motive. It doesn't matter whether it's God telling someone to kill, or someone trying to get his hands on Wilma Fenton's prize money—there is always a motive, and that gives the investigators something, however nebulous, to get hold of."

In the street outside, Tony could hear traffic rumbling past, and Lloyd was still staring out at it as he spoke.

"But there was no motive for these murders. The victims were chosen for ease of dispatch. And, to be perfectly frank, all that the police can do in a situation like that is wait for the murderer to make a mistake. And you finally did make a mistake."

Lloyd turned as he spoke the last sentence, and Tony wondered if he had seen the moment's irritation that he had felt at the suggestion that he had made a mistake. He mustn't give himself away, because they were on a fishing expedition, and nothing more. He had left them no evidence, and he didn't make mistakes.

"May Day was your downfall, Mr. Baker," he went on. "Grace Halliday was your intended victim, but Jack Shaw saved her life. You knew that he must have seen something, so he had to go. But the rifle had jammed, and you found out as soon as you hit him that Shaw couldn't be beaten to death without spattering his murderer with blood, so he had to be got rid of some other way." Lloyd left the window, and sat down opposite him once more. "That puzzled me," he said. "Because Jack Shaw wasn't dead, and no one could have thought that he was. And yet you had chosen to leave your signature as if he were dead. Why? This morning, I realized why. And two hours ago, I had my suspicions confirmed—a massive dose of insulin had been administered as Jack Shaw lay unconscious."

Tony was amused. "Really? I always understood that insulin was absorbed into the body too quickly for there to be a reliable test for its presence. Besides, it's impossible to distinguish from the body's own insulin." He looked at Judy Hill. "I'm disappointed in you, Superintendent. I would have thought you would know better than to let your subordinates get up to tricks like that."

"I can assure you that the test was thoroughly reliable," she said, her voice as crisp and frosty as a January midnight.

Oh, dear—she really was disappointing him now. It was all on tape, and telling fibs wasn't allowed. He had always been quite impressed by her, but she would never get to be a real superintendent at this rate. He smiled. "In that case, I obviously need to update my medical knowledge."

"Of course," said Lloyd, "Jack Shaw can never tell us who fired that shot at Grace Halliday and therefore who administered that injection, but I don't think we need his testimony."

Tony regarded Lloyd with amusement. Perhaps they did have some sort of test these days. But even if they had, what sort of proof did they think that was?

"Are you seriously suggesting that because insulin was used on Jack Shaw I must be the one who used it? Anyone who was at the Grange yesterday could have got hold of it—it's kept in the fridge, for God's sake! Stephen could have got it. Grace. Mike Waterman. Even that security guard—Scopes, or whatever his name is. He drinks in the Tulliver—he could have got into the kitchen when no one was looking."

"But each of them would have had to know that he or she was going to need it," said Lloyd. "The assailant had planned a shooting—why would he be carrying insulin with him? Unless, of course, he was diabetic, on a clinical trial that necessitated a lunchtime injection, and had been invited to lunch."

"Oh, please." Tony laughed, shook his head. "Do you imagine that would stand up in court?"

"I think it would carry some weight," said Lloyd.

"Not enough, unfortunately. I suggest that Stephen took it for his next victim, but had to use it on Jack instead. I further suggest that I was going to be his next victim, and that he had it with him for that purpose. He used a different method for each victim, remember—I expect he thought it an appropriate way for me to die. And I think that but for the intervention of Jack Shaw, I would have been the person lying in an irreversible coma. It's Shaw who's in the coma, however, and without his eyewitness testimony, you're stuck with the fact that anyone who was in the vicinity could have injected him with insulin."

"No, Mr. Baker. I'm not. You see, none of the other people who were there—Stephen, Grace Halliday, Keith Scopes, or Mike Waterman—could have intended murdering Jack Shaw that way."

"And how do you arrive at that conclusion?"

"Because if any of these people had wanted to kill Jack Shaw," said Lloyd, "they wouldn't have injected the insulin into his artificial leg."

Tony blinked at him, not speaking.

"I know," said Lloyd. "You'd never guess, would you? He's even a Morris dancer. It's wonderful, isn't it, how some people can overcome adversity like that? Grace Halliday was telling me that it's a very expensive leg—Jack got a good deal of compensation for the accident, and it was invested well for him. He's always had top-of-the-range, state-of-the-art legs. That's why he can dance. And why you'd never know he had an artificial leg at all. There are very few things he can't do with ease. But getting up when he's fallen is one of them."

Tony still just stared at him, motionless, speechless.

"So that's how we know insulin was used. The pathology lab at the hospital carried out a test and it was found in his artificial leg, which I think you will agree produces none of its own to confuse the issue."

Tony was trying to come to terms with what he was being told, but his head was spinning.

"The coma that you hoped would be put down to the head injury was indeed caused by that, and was fortunately by no means irreversible. Jack's alive, Mr. Baker. Alive and awake. He began regaining consciousness in the early hours of the morning, and I was able to speak to him very briefly just before I came here. He was fortunate—no brain damage, and his memory of the incident is intact."

Game over. Tony steepled his fingers and pressed them to his lips, closing his eyes. This wasn't how it had been supposed to end, but that was how it was with games of chance. Someone won, someone lost.

He opened his eyes, and looked at Judy Hill. "I expect you would like to know why I did it."

"I know why you did it," she said. "You were being black-mailed."

"Has Stephen confessed?"

She shook her head. "We used our powers of deduction," she said. "We do have some."

They were much sharper than he'd imagined they would be. He smiled. "I was indeed being blackmailed," he said. "I'm afraid I've destroyed all the letters." He hadn't been too worried when the detectives came with their search warrant, because the letters were the only thing that could have helped them, or so he had thought. "I got the first one after Mrs. Fenton's murder."

He could still remember how he had felt when he had opened that letter, and realized that it had to be from Wilma Fenton's murderer. He could remember all the blackmail letters, word for word, because he had examined them minutely in the hope of finding a clue to who was writing them.

I know what you did in that alleyway on Sunday. You made that woman's murder look different. Her bingo prize was stolen, but you left yours there instead and changed the time it happened. Leave £1000 in a padded envelope in the yellow wastebin behind the Civic Center in Stansfield by half past ten at night on Friday March 24 or your newspaper will get the story.

Lloyd turned from the window again. "What I don't under-stand is why murder seemed to you to be the solution to the situation."

Tony smiled. "It was the trigger, Chief Inspector. I told you se-rial killers are born, not made. I played fair—I told you the money might be meaningless. I explained that the ultimate in murder was the motiveless, random killing. I think I've always known that eventually I would murder someone myself. The mind of the murderer is so fascinating, and I knew I had the mind of a murderer."

And he fancied that Lloyd was looking at him with a kind of horrified fascination.

"I thought if I ever did murder someone, it would be simply as an experiment, an experience. But as you say, most murders are motivated, and I needed more motive than mere curiosity. That letter provided it. Only Mrs. Fenton's murderer could have written it, because only Mrs. Fenton's murderer and I knew that her money had been stolen. Her murderer—at that point I still didn't believe it could be Stephen—was writing to me, and threatening me with exposure that would ruin my reputation, my career, my life. Paying him his paltry thousand pounds wouldn't alter the fact that he had this power over me. He had given me the motive that I needed. That's when I conceived my plan."

"Your plan being what?"

"Plan A was to establish the blackmailer as a serial killer, and once his existence was undeniable and his identity was suspected, to kill him—in self-defense, of course." He smiled a little ruefully. "It didn't work out that way, but I thought plan B was working, until today."

Lloyd frowned. "I don't quite understand."

"Why should you? You don't have the devious mind of a serial killer."

Lloyd acknowledged his shortcomings in that regard with a nod of his head.

Tony glanced at Judy Hill. "I wrote the letter that I brought to you, Superintendent. I made it look exactly like the letter I had received, and I put it in the genuine envelope. Then I wrote to the newspaper."

"Why did you do that?" she asked. "Just so that you would be back on the front pages?"

Tony shook his head. Of course, they were bound to think that it was for the publicity it had generated, pushing him right back into the public consciousness, but that had been the effect of it, not the reason for it.

"I know that I'm seen as having little regard for the way the police go about their business, but I don't have that low an opinion of your capabilities, and I was embarking on a very risky venture. I wanted to be certain that you and your colleagues were working under as much pressure as I could possibly produce. I knew I would leave you virtually no evidence to go on, and by giving the impression that you were being fed with information by the murderer and still getting nowhere, I could rely on the British press dogging your every move, criticizing your lack of results, and making your job difficult to the point of impossibility."

"That part of your plan succeeded admirably," said Lloyd.

Tony looked over at him. "Thank you. I was particularly gratified when Detective Chief Superintendent Yardley stepped down from the inquiry on Saturday. Turmoil at the top—that's always a distraction for the investigation team."

"And once you had set that in motion?" asked Judy Hill. "What then?"

"The blackmailer had chosen the site, the date, and the time, so all that remained then was to plan the murder. The victim was chosen, as you so rightly said, for ease of dispatch. I used to see him when I was working late in my office in Stansfield. Every night, regular as the town hall clock, he would pay in his no doubt meager takings. I reconnoitered the area, working out which part of this man's routine rendered him most vulnerable to murder and me least vulnerable to detection. As you've seen, I did my homework very carefully."

Lloyd looked troubled. "Does it bother you at all that two children were left fatherless?"

No, it didn't. Tony saw no reason to display any remorse that he didn't feel. "The victim was of no importance. Death is random, Chief Inspector. He might have been involved in a motorway pileup the very next day. The important part was that he was habitually abroad at half past ten at night, not far from the spot where Mrs. Fenton's murderer would be going to collect his blackmail money. When suspicion fell on him, as it eventually would, he would have no alibi."

He sat back. This little room with its barred windows was not unlike a prison cell. But the Tulliver Inn, his home for almost the last four months, had begun to seem like a prison cell itself, especially once he had engaged the affections of Grace Halliday. Even having sex with her—his usual method of changing whatever subject she was wearying him with—had begun to pall. But now, he would find out what a real prison cell was like, quite possibly for the rest of his life. He could write his book, perhaps. They might allow him to do that, if the proceeds went to charity, or something.

"That murder could have scared the blackmailer off altogether," he went on, "in which case, I might have stopped there, but probably not. The experience was . . ." He searched for the right word. "Exhilarating. I think I would have felt compelled to repeat it, whatever happened."

"And it didn't scare him off," said Judy Hill.

"No. He wrote to me again with another turn of the screw, as blackmailers will."

You killed that man instead of leaving my money, so the price just went up. I want £10,000 now. Leave it in the bin on the corner of Ladysmith Avenue and Kimberley Court at the same time as before, on Monday April 17. Don't try anything funny this time.

"I did the same as I had before. Gave you a rather different letter."

"And you left the murder weapon in the bin instead."

Yes. He had tried something funny, despite the blackmailer's advice. "That didn't quite pan out the way I'd hoped. When I saw how easy it would be to kill the man who chose to sleep on Ladysmith Avenue itself, I thought I might net my real prey that night, because this time the murder would take place within yards of where the blackmailer was going to be. That I might catch him in the act of retrieving his envelope, and finding, not ten thousand pounds, but a bloody knife. That I could reveal to the world that I had once again worked out where a murderer would strike next, but that this time, sadly, I had been too late to prevent him murdering again, and had had to kill him with his own knife when he came at me."

But he had been held up on his way out of the casino, and then again by a blind man who had engaged the derelict in conversation for some reason, and a drag artist from the Queen Bee, who had been standing in the doorway of that establishment for what seemed like an eternity.

"As it turned out, it was too late by the time I had killed the tramp to leave the knife for the reasons I had intended. But I thought it might be fun to let you puzzle over it."

Lloyd strolled back to the table once more. "So now we come to yesterday," he said, sitting down.

"Almost—almost. You see, I got a nasty shock when I did get home that night. Grace Halliday had been in my room, and she'd found the documents that you removed this afternoon. She was all for calling the police then and there. I toyed with the idea of telling her that if she did, her precious Stephen would go to prison too, because there was now no doubt whatever that he was sending me these letters. That was the thanks I got for trying to save his skin."

"But you didn't tell her about Stephen," said Lloyd. "Instead, you used the fact that she was attracted to you to persuade her that she had got it all wrong."

"Indeed. She hadn't had a man for seven years, and she hadn't had much of a one then. She had never met anyone like me—she had thrown herself at me ever since I'd got here. I was a catch, as I told you. It took little effort to persuade her that she had overreacted to what was simply my way of trying to catch this nameless terror that stalked the streets of Bartonshire. I offered her my undying devotion in return for her unqualified trust."

"And once you had her unqualified trust," said Judy Hill, "you began to plan her murder?"

"Yes." Tony smiled at her. "She was just as dangerous as her son now. And by Wednesday morning, I had the next letter. He wanted fifty thousand pounds now. I had to leave it in the summerhouse of the Grange at 11 a.m. on May Day. It came as no surprise to me to find that Stephen had developed a sudden desire to attend the May Day festivities. It was a duel to the death. So I devised a way of ridding myself of both of them, but in the end I rid myself of neither. I've no doubt it would have continued, had you not stumbled on the solution. I wonder which of us would have cracked first?"

"Plan A was to kill him, you said. How were you going to do that?" asked Lloyd.

"I made an excuse not to accompany them to the Grange, took Stephen's rifle, wrapped it in plastic sheeting and put it in my car. I was interrupted by Waterman's arrival—it was very stupid of me to leave the back door open, but he saw nothing. He seemed to be very angry with Stephen about something, and I had no desire for him to interfere with Stephen's or Grace's plans by having some argument, so I didn't tell him that Stephen was at the Grange. I tried to ring Stephen to tell him to keep out of Waterman's way, but—as I told you, I got no reply." He shook his head. "I thought that might make my plans go awry, but in the end, that wasn't what went wrong."

They were both looking at him with slightly bemused expressions, mixed with deep disapproval.

"Sorry—did you want remorse? I don't do remorse. I drove to the so-called VIP car park, and left the rifle in the bushes on my way up to the fairground. I judged my competition, left, walked back toward the car park, and waited for Grace, my intention being to kill her shortly before the time I presumed Stephen would be at the summerhouse, looking for his money. I would then take the rifle to the summerhouse and wait for a few minutes. If he turned up, I would shoot him too, and explain that I, on my way to meet Grace, had witnessed her murder, seen him run away, chased him, fought with him, and the gun had gone off in the struggle."

"Do you seriously believe you would have got away with that?" asked Judy Hill.

"Yes. You already suspected Stephen—you've questioned him after every incident, just as I planned you should. I knew how to make the evidence fit my story of a struggle. I had sown the seeds of animosity between him and his mother. He went out shooting almost every day, so any tests you did for residue on his skin would almost certainly be positive. Yes, I believe I would have got away with it."

There was a silence before Lloyd spoke. "And this plan B you spoke of?"

"Timing is always a variable. I could only stay in the summerhouse for a few minutes. Stephen might not get there before I had to leave, in which case I would leave the gun, and he would find it, and almost certainly pick it up. I would go back along the shortcut and down to the lake, where I would be waiting for Grace by eleven o'clock, and Stephen himself would see me from the summerhouse, and thus give me *my* alibi. That seemed to me to be poetic justice."

"But Jack Shaw ruined your plans," said Superintendent Hill.

"He did. I had no idea about his leg—I thought it was because of his sprained ankle that he clearly couldn't get up. And I couldn't unjam the rifle. So I ran to the summerhouse, left it there—and when I got back to Shaw, he was very nearly on his feet, pulling himself up on one of the crutches. I kicked it away, picked up the other one, and tried to kill him with it. But I got blood on my jacket, so I stopped. I left him, and went down to the lake, carrying my jacket. I left the crutch there where you'd find it—I knew it would have Stephen's fingerprints on it, because I saw him helping Jack into Grace's car."

"But you were agitated," she said. "Stephen Halliday watched you pacing up and down."

Tony smiled. "I don't mind admitting that I was more than agitated. I was panicking. I had no idea what to do—I couldn't rely on Shaw not being able to remember anything, and I was obviously right to be worried about that. Then I realized that I had the means of his destruction in my jacket pocket."

"So you walked back up, injected him with insulin, laid the money he was carrying on top of him, covered him with your already bloodstained jacket, and called an ambulance."

"Correct in every detail. But I could never have hoped for what happened after that—the place crawling with armed police officers, the clearing of the grounds, a siege . . . it was wonderful. And all for one very confused would-be blackmailer with an obstinately jammed rifle. I do congratulate you on your sense of the absurd, Superintendent."

If that annoyed her, she showed no sign of it.

"In plan B you knew that Stephen wouldn't be dead," said Lloyd. "How could you stop him talking?"

"*Has* he talked? No. Because his choice is to explain that he is a murderer, a thief and a blackmailer, or simply to deny everything. I assumed, correctly, that he would choose the latter course. As I told you—plan B was working, despite things going wrong. But I was tripped up by a variable that I had not bargained for."

"Jack Shaw's artificial leg," said Lloyd.

"Tripped up by Jack Shaw's artificial leg." Tony smiled. "I could have injected him anywhere—I chose the calf because I thought the time it took the insulin to take effect from that area was best for my purposes. My mistake was to choose the wrong calf." He shook his head. "Jack Shaw," he said, shaking his head. "Who never did or said anything of consequence in his entire life. It's almost too much to bear that he should be my downfall. Significant, though, that it was his prosthetic—clearly considerably more remarkable than the man himself—that led you to the truth."

"Well, I'm sorry if the rest of us poor mortals don't come up to your exacting standards," said Lloyd. "But despite that, we've somehow muddled through and are about to charge you with murder."

It was much easier to get under Lloyd's skin than it was to irritate the composed, serene Acting Superintendent Hill. Tony thought it would be fun to irritate him even more.

"Well, if Jack's alive and talking, then you already knew that I tried to kill Grace Halliday and him, so that wasn't such a great feat of detection. And I've freely admitted that I stabbed the tramp in Barton and strangled the burger bar owner in Stansfield. But I want it very clearly on record that I didn't kill Wilma Fenton. Stephen Halliday did that. I merely and misguidedly gave him an alibi."

Lloyd stood up. "Well, thank you, Mr. Baker, for being so frank. But, as I told you, Jack Shaw will never be able to tell us who fired that shot. Because though his memory of the incident is indeed intact, all he saw was the barrel of the rifle."

Tony closed his eyes again. Had he been tricked into that confession? Undoubtedly, the answer was yes, he had. But it was equally true that Lloyd had told him that Jack couldn't identify him, so he doubted that he could have his confession ruled inadmissible on those grounds. Perhaps he should have had legal representation.

"That was your real mistake, Mr. Baker. You didn't need to use the insulin at all."

TOM WAS IN THE BRIEFING ROOM, LISTENING TO JUDY THANKING everyone for their hard work. She wasn't in a celebratory mood, because Stephen Halliday had to be regarded as the prime suspect for Wilma Fenton's murder now that his alibi was no longer any good, but the serial killer had been caught, and celebrations were in order.

Mrs. Fenton's murder was technically Malworth's pigeon again, but it was by no means straightforward, because whatever Tony Baker thought, they all believed that Stephen was innocent, and that Keith Scopes had murdered Mrs. Fenton and blackmailed Baker.

Tom and Judy went for the almost obligatory celebration drink, leaving as soon as they could without giving offense. They had a ticking clock: Stephen had to be charged or released by 2 a.m., and they had witness statements placing him at the scene and running away from it, plus Baker's statement that he had tried to give him an alibi.

Lloyd, no longer officially involved, was still at the pub, hoping to have a quiet word with Yardley about the advisability, or lack of it, of talking so freely to his brother-in-law. Despite the difference in ranks, he felt that the younger man would listen without taking offense, and Tom thought he probably would. But he also thought that he would listen without taking the advice.

Now Tom and Judy were back in the office, arguing the toss about Halliday, with Gary Sims as a spectator, looking from one to the other as if he were at a tennis match.

"It's obvious," Tom said. "Waterman told me himself that he overheard Ben arranging to meet Stephen, and we know what he did that evening, guv. He went to Malworth bingo club—everyone I spoke to said that they were surprised to see him there. He was there to let Scopes know when Stephen left, so he could be waiting for him in the alleyway with his cosh."

"We don't *know* that's why he went there."

"We know he hadn't intended going anywhere before he overheard that phone call, because he'd been drinking, and he won't drink and drive. But suddenly, he's so keen to go somewhere that he never goes—on a Sunday, when he never works—that he pays Jack Shaw to chauffeur him? I think we do know."

"All right, we know. But we can't prove it. And we have to approach it from an angle that doesn't involve Waterman, because what he told you about overhearing that conversation is as close as he's going to get to admitting that he set Keith Scopes on Stephen."

Tom felt his spirits sag. Stephen's best defense was that

Scopes had been in the alleyway, too and could have carried out the assault, but no jury would believe that Baker had interfered with the scene in order to give an alibi to some man he'd never even met. If only Baker had kept the blackmail letters, they might have had something to go on, something that implicated Scopes. But he hadn't. "If we could get a search warrant, we could find the cosh and prove that it was the murder weapon," he said.

"We need some evidence to get a search warrant."

"Headless was the blackmailer, looking for his envelope. And we know that couldn't have been Stephen. Scopes, on the other hand, left the casino at ten-thirty, and was away for a quarter of an hour, having his phantom cigarette. I think we can safely assume that he drove over to the bingo club to try and fulfill his commission for Waterman. But once again, he couldn't, this time because Stephen was still inside. And before he left for the bingo club, he checked the bin. Gertie heard him driving off."

"But it's entirely unprovable, Tom! We don't know that Headless was the blackmailer—it just seems highly likely that he was. And we certainly don't know that Scopes was Headless."

"Think about it, guv—Baker got that first letter on the twenty-first of February. The blackmailer only wanted a thousand quid, but he gave him until the twenty-fourth of March to get it—why? Because Scopes was off on holiday, that's why. With the proceeds of the drug money."

Judy smiled tiredly. "That isn't proof."

"We can't go charging Stephen with murder, guv—we know damn well it was Scopes! He would be waiting for Stephen practically opposite Wilma's door—it's the perfect place, with that great pillar to hide behind. He couldn't get Stephen without Wilma seeing, but he could get Wilma once Stephen had gone. So he used the cosh on her instead."

Judy seemed not to be listening. She was frowning slightly, looking into the middle distance.

"Maybe we *can* get him," she said, her eyes focusing on Tom at last. "Because where did he get the money for the drugs, if he didn't steal it from Wilma? He didn't have any money earlier in the evening—he borrowed a fiver from Jerry, remember. And since he didn't beat Stephen up, Waterman wouldn't have paid him."

All that was true, but it was Tom who was going to pour the cold water this time. "I hate to remind you, guv, but at the top of this conversation you said we had to find an angle that didn't involve Waterman, because he won't admit to us that Keith was waiting for Stephen."

"But that's because I don't believe he'll say anything that would incriminate Scopes directly," she said. "But *not* paying him money isn't the same thing, is it? He might be prepared to confirm that he *didn't* give Scopes any money that night."

He might, thought Tom, his spirits rising once more. And then he would have something he could use when he talked to Scopes. Yes, he thought. Oh, yes. They were nearly there now. He could feel it in his bones.

JACK'S HEAD FELT AS THOUGH IT HAD BEEN RUN OVER BY A STEAM-roller, and he had been told that he had a stay in hospital ahead of him until he recovered fully, but none of that mattered. He had been there for Grace, just as he had intended.

The turnaround in Baker's attitude to Grace had bothered him. At first, he hadn't been able to see past his own jealousy, but then, standing behind the bar in the Tulliver, pulling someone's pint, when he had been asking himself why Tony Baker would be pretending to have fallen in love with her when he so clearly despised her, he had finally realized.

It had happened the night she found his research. Jack had been quite happy to accept his explanation, but Grace hadn't—she had remained so suspicious of Baker that Jack had thought that he'd better not leave her alone with him, because she was genuinely frightened. And she had been right to be frightened. That was why Baker had turned on the charm, because he had had to get Grace on his side, get her confidence.

And that was when Jack had realized that Baker's next step would be to kill her, because if he left her he could never feel safe, and he certainly wasn't going to saddle himself with her for the rest of his life. But Jack couldn't do anything about it—there was no point in going to the police. What could they do? Baker would just tell them the same story, and they would probably have believed him, too. Grace knew him better than anyone else round here. She must have felt in her heart that he was capable of it. But the police would have believed Baker.

And when Baker had been so anxious for her to go to Mike Waterman's May Day celebrations, Jack had realized that he was going to do it there, where there would be any number of suspects, especially poor Stephen, who had been questioned over and over again, and who felt aggrieved at Baker's presence in the first place. Baker had even started needling him, deliberately trying to make him unhappy, make him blame his mother for his life being made uncomfortable.

So Jack had taken a leaf out of Baker's own book. If he couldn't do anything about Baker himself, he could do something about his intended victim. He could make sure that he was with her every single minute of the day. He'd faked the twisted ankle to get out of the Morris dancing, and had gone to the pub before they left, to make certain that Baker wasn't alone with her. Then he'd found out about this mystery outing, and he had known when it was going to happen. Baker had arranged it so that she would be deep in the wood, and alone.

He had followed her when she went to meet Baker, watching all the time for anything that might threaten her. He had no idea how Baker intended doing it, but whatever it was, he had been determined to stop it. And just as she came to the fork in the road, and stood indecisively, wondering which way to go, he saw the rifle being pointed at her from the bushes. He still wasn't sure how he'd managed the leap—maybe he could do real Morris dancing if he put his mind to it.

He couldn't tell Chief Inspector Lloyd the whole story when

he came to see him that morning, because the doctor had allowed the man one question, saying that Jack shouldn't really be talking to anyone at all. Lloyd, however, had asked two questions. The first had been to ask him if he could take his leg away for forensic examination. Puzzled, Jack had said that he could. He still didn't know what that was all about. The second had been if he'd seen who shot Grace, and Jack had said no, he hadn't, he had seen the barrel of a rifle, and the doctor had bundled Lloyd out.

He wasn't sure that telling the police his story would prove anything, though of course he would, but the odd thing was that despite the answer he got to his second question, Lloyd had seemed pleased. No—more than pleased. He had looked positively smug.

KEITH PULLED ON HIS JEANS AND LUMBERED DOWNSTAIRS IN RE-sponse to the persistent knocking. He'd have let them get tired of it and go away, but Michelle had said it seemed important, and made him go and answer it. What with him working half the night and Michelle leaving for work at half past five in the morning, the hour between five and six in the evening was the only time they got together, and if it was someone wanting to know where he got his gas and electricity, he'd—

"Good evening, Keith," said DI Finch. "Did I get you out of bed?"

Keith pushed his hair out of his eyes. "What do you want?"

"Can I come in?"

"Do I have a choice?" Keith stepped aside and followed Finch into the sitting room. He didn't know why he was getting a visit from the police, but they were never good news. "I gave my statement yesterday," he said.

"That's not why I'm here."

"Well, I need some coffee." By the time Finch had gone, he'd have to get ready for work anyway. And even if Finch left right now, Michelle would give him the third degree about why he had been here, so he could forget resuming his former activity. He went into the kitchen and filled the kettle. "Do you want some?"

"No thanks."

Keith waited for the small amount of water to boil, and made his coffee while Finch waited in the sitting room.

"Right," he said, rejoining Finch. "What do you want?"

"We've been hearing some very bad things about your boss," said Finch.

Finch hadn't sat down, so Keith stood, too. He didn't want to be at a disadvantage. "Oh?"

"Yes. We've heard that he sometimes wants people sorted out. Would you know anything about that, Keith?"

Keith sipped his coffee. "Me?" he said. "Why would I know anything about it?"

Finch smiled. "Well, you're displaying the reason right now. That is a magnificent torso you've got there, Keith—how often do you work out?"

"Every day." Keith looked at Finch with a critical eye. He wasn't overweight—he had a good build. He was just a bit out of condition. "You should try it," he said.

"Too lazy," said Finch. "But if I wanted someone sorted out, I think I'd come to someone with finely honed muscles like you. Does Mr. Waterman come to you when he wants someone sorted out?"

"Don't know what you're talking about, Mr. Finch."

"I think you do. And I think Mr. Waterman wants Stephen Halliday sorted out."

Keith drank some more coffee, and looked back at Finch, his face expressionless.

"It isn't against the law to be *told* to beat someone up," Finch said. "It would be against the law if you did it, but you haven't done it. So where's the harm in being straight with me? He did tell you to get Stephen Halliday, didn't he?"

"I've no idea what you're on about."

"Well—here's a coincidence. You told me yesterday that

when you're working you go out for a smoke at about half past ten."

Keith nodded.

"And Stephen Halliday finishes at the bingo club at half past ten. And here's another coincidence. Since March, you've always been working in the same town as Stephen."

"Amazing. You should write to the papers about that, Mr. Finch. It's spooky."

"Stephen always parks his motorbike at the rear of whatever club he's in," said Finch. "Ideal for a spot of grievous bodily harm, I would think. A bit dark, a bit lonely. Not too many passersby. Of course, you have to time it just right. And he has to be alone. You made the mistake of telling him about your sideline, so he's been watching out for you, which makes it trickier still. So it could take a while to get the circumstances exactly how you want them. But if you keep going out for a smoke, I expect you'll find him alone and vulnerable in the end."

"Not me," said Keith.

"And another odd thing," Finch went on. "I had a word with one or two of your colleagues last night. And they said they didn't understand why you suddenly needed to go out for a smoke every night—they always thought you were a nonsmoker."

"Did they?"

"And . . . if I look round this room—no ashtrays."

"She doesn't let me smoke in the house."

"And don't they let you smoke in the Tulliver Inn? That doesn't seem very fair. Everyone else can smoke if they want to. But no one ever seems to have seen you light up. Anywhere. And with all that working out that you do, I wouldn't have thought that smoking would be your thing."

"I don't smoke much."

"You don't smoke at all. So what were you doing in the alleyway the night Mrs. Fenton was murdered? I'll tell you what you were doing. You were waiting for Stephen Halliday. You were going to beat him up for Michael Waterman, but he was with

Wilma Fenton, so you couldn't. You heard about her prize money, and you coshed her and stole it."

"Not me," said Keith.

"Then when you read about the murder in the paper, it said the money had been left intact, so you blackmailed the only man who could have replaced it at such short notice—the man who shared the prize with her. The man Stephen and Wilma had been talking about. The man who found her body."

Keith hadn't meant to kill the old girl—when Finch had come to the nightclub that night and told him it was a murder inquiry, it had been all he could do not to say that he hadn't hit her that hard. He'd got scared, and then he'd realized that Finch wanted to know where he was at nine o'clock, and that had confused him. And even though he seemed somehow to have an alibi, he couldn't tell them where he'd been. But they found out anyway. He frowned. So why was Finch here?

"I was in Barton at nine o'clock," he said. "You've got me on video."

Finch smiled. "We know the murder happened half an hour earlier than that, Keith. At about the time you say you were in the alleyway, having a smoke."

Shit. He'd never have said he was in the alleyway at all, except for Jack Shaw—he couldn't be sure Shaw hadn't seen him.

"I spoke to Michael Waterman tonight," Finch said. "After all, you told me you'd been doing a job for someone, and if it wasn't beating up Stephen, then it must have been the drug deal."

Keith smiled. Finch must have got an earful if he'd suggested that to Mr. Waterman. "I wasn't doing a drug deal," he said.

"Mr. Waterman seemed to agree with me that you were," said Finch. "But he was very upset when I suggested that he gave you the money to buy those drugs—very upset indeed. He's very anti-drugs."

"I know."

"And he said that you didn't buy those drugs with his money—that he didn't give you any money that night." Finch stepped closer to him. "And you were broke—you had to borrow a fiver earlier in the day. So where did you get the money for those drugs, Keith?"

"I wasn't buying drugs, Mr. Finch. I was paying back money I owed."

"Whatever you were doing—where did you get the money?"

"I had the money all along. But that was all I had, and I needed petrol to get to Barton, so I borrowed the fiver from Jerry."

Finch went slightly pink with frustration. "You coshed Wilma Fenton, you stole her money, and then true to form, you saw another moneymaking opportunity when you read the paper, and you blackmailed Baker."

Keith had been annoyed that he hadn't been able to give Halliday a going-over—every time he'd gone to the bingo club, he'd be with someone, or still working. He had forgotten that he'd told him what he did that night he'd been celebrating in the pub; of course Halliday would be watching out for him if he'd crossed Mr. Waterman in some way. That was why Keith didn't drink as a rule—you did stupid things when you were drunk, and talking to Halliday had been really stupid. He didn't know what Halliday had done to Mr. Waterman, but he felt bad about not sorting him out for him. Now, he realized that he could do something that was even better than beating him up, and would get him out of Mr. Waterman's hair for a long time.

"Look, Mr. Finch—I didn't want to grass the guy up, but if you're going to come here accusing me of murder and blackmail and I don't know what else, I've no option. I saw Stephen Halliday take a baseball bat out from under his jacket, hit that old girl over the head and snatch her handbag. He dropped it at the mouth of the alley, and ran across Waring Road toward the old police houses. And I'll give you a formal statement any time you want."

CHAPTER THIRTEEN

TONY LAY DOWN ON THE BENCH, THERE BEING NOTHING else to do. He might as well try to sleep. Now, he really was in a cell, and he didn't suppose any of these people would ever understand. He had had to commit murder eventually. Talking to murderers, writing about them, watching them die in gas chambers and in electric chairs—what good was that if you had never experienced the taking of another human being's life first-hand?

When he had had to get inside Challenger's mind, when he had had to *become* Challenger, he had experienced some of the power that Challenger must have felt as he homed in on his victims. He had known then, though he hadn't fully acknowledged it at that time, that he was a serial killer. He was just one who hadn't murdered anyone yet.

He had told Lloyd that murder for murder's sake was the purest form of murder there was. He hadn't achieved that, because he had to have a reason to do something, and because there seemed to him to be little point in murdering total strangers with no motive—where was the sport in that? It was like Halliday shooting foxes. But motives were so mundane. Murder for gain was crass, and murder for emotional reasons was nothing more than a lack of self-discipline. Removing some perceived ill from society had its merits, but it was a little too evangelical for Tony.

He felt he had achieved a nice balance, all in all. He had murdered people whose deaths he had no active desire to bring about, and had therefore been able to murder to order, leaving no clues for the investigators. But it had all been building up to the death that he did want to bring about, and he was entirely convinced that if he had been able to see his carefully laid plans through to fruition, he would have succeeded in doing that without the crime ever being brought home to him.

He couldn't have foreseen Jack Shaw's intervention, and it was only then, when he deviated from those plans, that it had all gone wrong. In effect, then, he had achieved what he set out to achieve. But now he would go to prison, and he hadn't wanted that at all. He was not one of those who subconsciously wanted to be caught. He had wanted to get away with it.

But he had the satisfaction of knowing that Stephen Halliday wouldn't get away with it either. Halliday's murder had been a sordid affair, not worthy of anyone's attention. That was why Tony had arranged things to make it seem a little more intriguing. But in the eyes of justice, who had no taste in these matters, murder was murder, and even for that undistinguished little crime, Stephen Halliday too would be receiving a life sentence.

"Tom, WE HAVE TO CHARGE HIM. WE HAVE FIVE WITNESS STATEMENTS." She counted them off on her fingers. "We've got Waterman, who saw Stephen enter the alley with Wilma Fenton. We've got Baker, who interfered with the scene of the crime in order, he says, to give Stephen Halliday an alibi. We've got Jerry Wheelan and Jack Shaw, who saw Stephen running from the scene. And now we've got Keith Scopes, who says he saw Stephen do it."

Tom was shaking his head, his face flushed. "What do they amount to?" he asked. "There are only two normal people in that lot, and they both saw the same thing. The others are a man who wanted Stephen beaten up, the man who was going to do the beating up, and a man who was trying to frame him for murders he himself committed." He was pacing backward and forward as he spoke. "Who's going to believe a word they say?"

"Sit down, please, Tom, you're making me dizzy."

He threw himself down on a chair, like Charlotte did occasionally when she wasn't allowed her own way.

Judy sighed. "We've got no proof that Waterman wanted Stephen beaten up," she said. "So he is simply a respected businessman, Scopes and Wheelan are two of his security officers, and Shaw is another long-standing employee of his. And with the sole exception of Scopes, they are telling the truth. Even Baker isn't lying, because he does genuinely believe that Stephen killed Wilma Fenton."

"But we know he didn't."

"It isn't up to us. And for the very reasons you've just given, the waters are muddy enough for the CPS to decide not to prosecute. Even if they do, Stephen won't necessarily be found guilty. If the defense can make a case that it could just as easily have been Scopes, it might well succeed. We'd be prosecution witnesses, and we're not going to argue with that, are we?"

That wasn't the right thing to say, obviously. Tom jumped to his feet again. "What good will that do Halliday? He might not be in prison, but he'll have to spend the rest of his life with people wondering if he really did it or not. If we can get a search warrant—"

"But we can't. Anyway—if he's got the sense he was born with, Scopes will have got rid of the cosh by now. He probably got rid of it as soon as he found out Wilma had died."

Judy knew exactly how Tom felt, but she could hardly release Stephen without charge with five witness statements like that. And she had to do something very soon, so charging him seemed the only course open to her.

IN THE BIG OFFICE, GARY COULD HEAR EVERY WORD THAT WAS being said, as he read and reread the files, racking his brains to think of anything that anyone had said that would prove that Stephen couldn't have killed Mrs. Fenton, but there was nothing.

It was ridiculous that everyone but Scopes could be telling the truth and still leave Halliday as the fall guy.

He thought of what DCI Hill had said about Scopes buying drugs with Mrs. Fenton's money, and of Scopes's performance when Sergeant Kelly had been interviewing him, sitting there smugly aware that they had nothing on which to hold him, because he hadn't any of the stuff in his possession anymore. He had unloaded three hundred and fifty pounds' worth of drugs to street dealers in less than an hour—Gary hated to think of the damage that had done, and to how many kids. And because he had done that, the police had found nothing to incriminate him. A good night's work all round. And then he had sat there almost laughing in their faces, saying that he'd been given the package to post, that he'd owed Cox the money that he was so evidently handing—

Gary's head shot up, and he went over to the closed door, hesitating a moment before knocking, waiting for a lull in the heated conversation.

"COME IN!" CALLED JUDY.

Tom was relieved that someone had interrupted this frank exchange of views, because he knew he was being unfair. There was nothing Judy could do. Before, when it had been circumstantial, she might have been able to let Stephen Halliday go, but thanks to his bright idea of going to see Scopes again, now she had someone who was prepared to stand up in court and say that he had witnessed Stephen murdering Wilma Fenton.

It was all his fault, and he felt terrible about it. He had thought he'd been so clever, maneuvering Waterman into declaring hotly that he hadn't given Scopes any money that night, but the whole thing had backfired, and he was looking for someone to blame.

Gary Sims came in, looking excited. "I'm sorry, ma'am," he said. "I couldn't help overhearing."

"I shouldn't think you could," said Judy, smiling. "The silly thing is that we actually agree. What can I do for you, Gary?"

"I think we do have evidence."

Tom and Judy exchanged glances, and Tom knew that he looked like she did, almost afraid to hope that Gary was right.

"What evidence?" she asked.

"The money. Scopes bought drugs with it. Only two other people went there that night, and they were being tailed, so we know they were nowhere near Malworth."

Tom frowned, wondering where this was heading. Gary seemed to think it was heading somewhere good, but then he'd thought that more than once during this inquiry.

"We've got film of Scopes handing money over to the dealer, and he was quite happy to admit that he did give him money—he just denied that it was for drugs." He smiled. "But it doesn't matter what it was for, because that flat was raided, and the equipment, the drugs and the money were all taken as evidence. We've still got it, pending trial. And we know the numbers of the fifty-pound notes taken from Wilma. If those notes are among the haul from the drug dealer, then there's only one way they could have got there."

"Gary Sims," Tom said, "I could kiss you."

"I'd much rather you didn't, sir."

"MIKE? RAY HERE. HOLD ON TO YOUR HAT."

Michael frowned. "Why? What's happened now?"

"What hasn't happened? Tony Baker has confessed to two murders and two attempted murders. He was killing these people himself, would you believe? I expect he'll go for diminished responsibility. I wondered about him once or twice, but never really seriously. But he killed those people without a second thought, just because it suited him to do it."

Michael had been listening, his mouth slightly open, glad

that Ray was chattering on, because he couldn't speak. At last, he found his voice, but he could only think of one word to say.

"Why?"

"Oh—sorry, Mike, I can't really go into it. I shouldn't really have told you that, but most of it will be public knowledge quite soon, and I thought you ought to know, because you were quite friendly with him, weren't you?"

"Well . . . yes, I suppose I was. It's a shock."

"And I'm afraid I've got another shock for you. Keith Scopes works for you, doesn't he?"

"Yes."

"He's being charged right now with the murder of Wilma Fenton, plus some other stuff. That isn't classified—it's going on a press release as we speak. But it's not all bad news, because it means that Stephen Halliday is completely in the clear, and will be released any time now. I wondered why you asked me to keep you informed about him—I didn't know about him and Ben. You must have been really worried. Anyway, it's all over now, so you can all get back to normal."

Michael thanked him, and hung up. Normal? What was normal? Suddenly, all his certainties had been blown away. Baker, who he had thought was everything a man should be, was a cold, calculating, callous murderer. The man he had wanted Ben to meet, to talk to, the man he had wanted Ben to *emulate,* was a murderer. A murderer who killed innocent people without a second thought.

And Ray—Ray had just accepted that Ben and Stephen were a couple, and thought that he had too. He had just assumed that Michael knew and approved. What's the big deal about me being gay? That's what Ben had said. No big deal, compared to being a multiple murderer who even tried to make it look as though Stephen had attempted to kill his own mother. No big deal, anyway, as far as Ray was concerned. No big deal, period.

And Stephen. What was it Ben had said? That he was good,

and kind, and kept him out of trouble. Michael had known that about Stephen, once, because Ben was right; something about Stephen reminded him of Josephine. He was decent, kind, straightforward and honest, and yet he had managed to demonize him in a matter of moments, when he had pressed the redial button that night and confirmed that it was indeed Stephen Halliday on the other end of the line.

If Josephine had lived, she would have made him understand that Ben had his own life, his own mind, his own emotions. If he was attracted to other men, that was something Michael just had to accept. If he was attracted to someone like Stephen, that was something he should welcome.

But she hadn't been there to keep him out of trouble, and he had behaved like the thug he was, and had encouraged Keith to carry out his thuggery for him. He had set him on that boy Charles, used him in the way lowlifes used half-starved pit bull terriers. He had tried to set him on Stephen, who had never done anyone a bad turn in his life.

And, as he had feared all along, it was Keith who had murdered poor Wilma Fenton. Whose fault was that? Keith's? Or his? A bit of both. Unlike the pit bull terriers, Keith would have been a thug even without his encouragement, and he had certainly never encouraged him to mug anyone. But he wouldn't have been in that alleyway at all if it hadn't been for him and his insane attitude toward Ben's sexuality. Ben was right. He was mad. Had been mad. Not anymore.

Had he really wished that Keith was his son, and that Ben wasn't? Not quite. But he came very close. He had wished that Josephine was there to make Ben see sense, but that wasn't how Josephine had read the situation, so she had made him see sense instead.

Oh, he had no doubt of it. Josephine had stepped in to save him before it was too late.

*   *   *

STEPHEN WAS GIVEN BACK HIS BELONGINGS, SUCH AS THEY WERE, and the police—all of them—seemed genuinely pleased to be letting him go. He wasn't sure what had happened, but when he saw that photograph of Wilma's body, and saw that she had the wrong prize money, he knew that Baker had to be at the bottom of all his problems. At first nothing seemed to have changed, and then, suddenly, they knew he hadn't murdered anyone.

And he had always known, really, that Baker was trouble. Lately, he'd begun to blame his mother, but that wasn't fair. All she had done was fall for him, and that wasn't so surprising. He was handsome, glamorous—famous, even, in his way. And she had been lonely, Stephen knew she had. But he had always felt that there was something sinister about him, something not right. And whatever he had done with Wilma, it hadn't been right.

As he left the police station, he saw his mother and Ben waiting outside in her car. They both scrambled out when they saw him coming.

"I'm free," he said, smiling at them.

Ben threw his arms round him, and gave him a bear hug that practically lifted him off his feet. "Why didn't they let you go sooner?" he demanded. "I told them you were with me that night."

"Tony Baker did something," Stephen said. "I'm not sure what, but I think he must have replaced the money that was stolen. I don't think it happened like he said it did."

"Don't you know?" said Ben. "The police arrested him this afternoon. We think he killed those people, and he tried to kill Jack Shaw. But Keith Scopes has been arrested, too, so we're not sure what it's all about."

Stephen looked at his mother. "Are you all right?" he asked.

"I am now," she said, hugging him. "I think I must have taken leave of my senses. How I let him persuade me that all that stuff was—"

"Oh, who cares?" said Ben. "Stephen's out now. There's plenty of time to explain later."

Stephen had no idea what stuff his mother was talking about.

His mother was crying, Ben was laughing, and he didn't really know which to do. "How's Jack?" he asked his mother.

"He's conscious, and being allowed visitors now. I'm going to see him tonight—do you want to come?"

Ben, behind her, shook his head, grinning, winking. Stephen didn't know what that was all about, but he took the advice. "Er—no, tell him I'll see him tomorrow. Is he going to be all right?"

"Yes, they think it'll take a little while, but he'll be fine."

As the three of them made to get into the car, another drew up behind it, and Michael Waterman got out. Stephen felt Ben tense up as he came over to them.

"Don't worry," said Mr. Waterman. "I know I'm probably not welcome at the coming-out party. I . . . er . . . I just wanted to tell you—both of you—that . . . well, that you don't need to go away and live somewhere else, not unless that's what you really want to do. I know what I've done, and I don't expect your forgiveness. But that's all over now, I promise you that. And there's always a home for you at the Grange."

Ben nodded briefly, and got into the car, closing the door. Stephen managed something approaching a smile. "I'll . . . I'll talk to him," he said.

"Thanks." Waterman got back into his own car and drove off.

Stephen looked at his mother. "What's happened to change his mind?" he asked.

"I don't know," she said. "But you'll have your work cut out for you to change Ben's, I can tell you that."

Maybe. But Stephen knew how Ben really felt about his father, and he hoped he might succeed.

KEITH SAID NOTHING IN RESPONSE TO THE CHARGES, AS ADVISED by his solicitor. It was over. The biggest gamble he had ever taken was over.

It had been crazy, carrying on after Baker killed that man in

Stansfield. He had realized then that he was up against someone who would genuinely stop at nothing, and still he had tried. He already had the go-ahead for his brief absences from work, so arranging the blackmail drops had been easy. And all he had seen when he heard about the Stansfield murder had been the chance to put the price up. How long would he have gone on letting the body count pile up? That was what Finch had asked him, and he had made no comment.

He didn't know. Finch said he was as bad as Baker, because he was letting innocent people die because of what he was doing, but Keith didn't see it that way. He wasn't making Baker murder them. Baker was trying to frame him, and he was trying to get as much money as he could out of Baker. It was a gamble. And he had lost.

But then Jerry had told him that he was a born loser.

JACK SMILED FOR THE FIRST TIME SINCE . . . HE COULDN'T REALLY remember when. Certainly for the first time since Stephen had told him about Baker and Grace. He didn't know how they'd got on to Baker, but it seemed that he had been arrested despite the fact that Jack had seen nothing useful, and still hadn't been able to tell the police his story. It had something to do with his leg, he supposed, but he couldn't begin to imagine what.

And now Grace was here with him, saying that she didn't know how she could have let herself be taken in by Baker.

"I believed him, too," he said.

"Not for long."

"Well, he thought the whole human race was beneath him, so I couldn't really accept that his feelings toward you were genuine. That was when I worked out what he was up to."

She was holding his hand, clasping it tightly, and tears weren't that far away. Maybe she was still a little in love with Baker.

"I can't believe how stupid I've been," she said.

"No, you weren't stupid. You were lonely, and he was a bit of a step up from us village yokels."

"Don't," she said. "It's you I've been stupid about."

"Me?"

"I didn't know how you felt about me." She smiled. "Every-one else did, apparently. But I didn't."

"Then I was the stupid one, not you. I never knew how to tell you."

"I think saving my life was as good a way as any."

The nurse came in. "Mr. Shaw should have some rest now," she said. "Doctor's orders."

Grace let go of his hand, and stood up. "I'll be back to see you tomorrow," she said, then bent down and kissed him.

She *kissed* him. The smile was still there, long after she had gone.

LLOYD SWITCHED OFF THE TELEVISION, FINISHED HIS NIGHTCAP, then went round doing what he called putting the cat out—checking doors and windows and gas taps, to make sure the house was safe for the night. He didn't know why he called it that—if he had a cat he certainly wouldn't put it out. And that reminded him that he'd never talked to Judy about getting a kitten.

He had capitulated, of course, in the matter of the loft con-version, and he was glad that he had, because it was much more pleasant being a proper family. He couldn't imagine Gina tucked away up at the top of the house like some madwoman in the attic any more than Judy could. Of course they sometimes got on one another's nerves—that's what families were for. He felt much less self-conscious now about his late-night video-watching activities, since discovering that Gina didn't think he was mad. She just thought he should get more sleep, and she was probably right, he thought, as he went into the bedroom and undressed in the dark. He was very sleepy.

He slipped into bed beside Judy, only to jump into alert wake-fulness when she who slept through thunderstorms and earth tremors spoke to him.

"Yardley told me something when I saw him tonight," she said.

He smiled, when his heart rate had returned to normal. "Would that be the same thing he told me?" he asked. It had to be. He could imagine that it would cause Judy to lose sleep.

"About this major crime unit?" She sat up, and switched on the bedside lamp. "What did he tell you?"

"That the small executive team idea was by way of being a pilot scheme, since the opportunity had presented itself. What did he tell you?"

"That I should apply for it."

Lloyd nodded. "So you should."

"What about you? Don't you want to apply for it?"

He smiled. "Fat chance I'd have if you were a candidate."

"He said the panel wouldn't have him or the ACC on it—I asked him. I don't want favoritism."

"Even so." He shook his head. "Sometimes I wonder about your detective skills. Why do you think they made you Acting Superintendent when Yardley had to stand down?"

She flushed slightly. "Do you think they were trying me on for size?"

"I'm sure they were. And within seventy-two hours, you wrapped up an inquiry that was heading for its thirteenth week."

She looked appalled. "But I didn't! You thought of the in-sulin, and Gary Sims realized that the money had been taken as evidence in the drug raid—what did I do, except cause the fire-arms unit to terrorize poor Stephen Halliday?"

He kissed her. "What you did was create an atmosphere in which everyone could work to their full potential."

She pulled a face.

He grinned. "And you worked out exactly what Baker had done and why, which is why we were able at last to exclude any other possible solution, and concentrate on proving it. Apart from that, you were useless." He smiled again. "You'll be halfway there, if you get it," he said.

She frowned. "Halfway where?"

"To Chief Constable."

She hit him. "I don't want to be Chief Constable."

"Once, you would have said you didn't want to be a superintendent."

"I know, but this is different. I can pick my own team. And I already have, if everyone wants to do it." Her brown eyes fixed him with a steady gaze. "The truth," she said. "If I got the job, would you want to be on the team? Yardley says the Chief is serious about encouraging married couples to work together. Apparently some survey or something has shown that it makes things work more smoothly, not less. So would you want to do it? Or would it bother you? The truth," she said again.

The truth. The truth was that Lloyd was always happiest working with Judy, and that even though he had only had seventy-two hours to get used to it, he had discovered that he didn't give a toss which of them outranked the other. The truth was that though he had finally been given command of Stansfield CID, he had discovered that he preferred having a boss to rein in his hastier conclusions rather than subordinates who acted on them, and that boss might as well be Judy as anyone else.

But the truth also was that he was very glad she had wrapped up the Baker business as quickly as she had, because the press hadn't had time to discover their relationship. If he was to become her second-in-command in the major crime unit, they certainly would, especially if the Chief Constable was seeing himself as a trailblazer, and he wasn't altogether sure how he would feel about that. How he and Judy saw their respective roles was one thing—how outsiders saw it was quite another. But she had asked only for the truth. Not the whole truth.

"Oh, yes, ma'am," he said. "I would."

"Really?"

"Really. So be sure you do apply for it. Now," he said, his voice serious. "I want to ask you something, and I also want the absolute, unvarnished truth."

Her eyes, still looking into his, grew apprehensive. "What?" she said.

"Would you like a tabby cat?"

A native of Argyll, Scotland, JILL MCGOWN has lived in Corby, England, since she was ten. She wrote her first novel, *A Perfect Match*, in 1983. Among those that have followed are *Gone to Her Death*, *Murder at the Old Vicarage*, *Murder . . . Now and Then*, *The Murders of Mrs. Austin and Mrs. Beale*, *The Other Woman*, *A Shred of Evidence*, *Verdict Unsafe*, *Picture of Innocence*, *Plots and Errors*, *Scene of Crime*, and *Death in the Family*.

Visit the author's website at
www.JillMcGown.com.

This book was set in Goudy, a typeface designed by Frederic William Goudy (1865–1947). Goudy began his career as a book-keeper, but devoted the rest of his life to the pursuit of "recognized quality" in a printing type.

Goudy was produced in 1914 and was an instant bestseller for the foundry. It has generous curves and smooth, even color. It is regarded as one of Goudy's finest achievements.